WICKED WAGERS
THE COMPLETE TRILOGY

New Zealander Bronwen Evans grew up loving books. She's always indulged her love for story-telling, and is constantly gobbling up movies, books and theatre. Her head is filled with characters and stories, particularly lovers in angst. Is it any wonder she's a proud romance writer?

She writes both historical and contemporary sexy romances for the modern woman who likes intelligent, spirited heroines, and compassionate alpha heroes. Her debut Regency romance, Invitation to Ruin won the RomCon 2012 Readers Crown Best Historical and was an RT Reviewers' Choice Nominee Best First Historical 2011. To Dare the Duke of Dangerfield is a FINALIST in the Kindle Book Review Indie Romance Book of the Year 2012. Look out for her first Entangled Publishing Indulgence release in Fall 2012, The Italian Conte's Reluctant Bride.

Bronwen loves hearing from avid romance readers at
romance@bronwenevans.com

You can keep up with Bronwen's news by visiting her
website www.bronwenevans.com

BRONWEN EVANS

Wicked Wagers

THE COMPLETE TRILOGY

Wicked Wagers: The CompleteTrilogy
Copyright © 2012 by Bronwen Evans

ISBN-13: 978-1480154438
ISBN-10: 1480154431

Book design by Maureen Cutajar
www.gopublished.com

CONTENTS

To Dare the Duke of
Dangerfield

CHAPTER ONE

Shropshire, England, May 1821

"If you're going to point that delectable rump at a man you're asking for trouble."

Caitlin cursed under her breath and ignored the cultured baritone voice goading her from behind. She remained bent, focused on her task, and determined to clear the stone from her horse's hoof. Still, irritation dribbled down her back. If she were a cat her hackles would have risen.

She knew who the voice belonged to. She'd heard the melodically ducal tones in church and the village store often enough. Harlow Telford, the Duke of Dangerfield, consummate rake and the most powerful man in the Kingdom next to the Prince Regent.

The man determined to see her father ruined.

Of all the damnable luck. Why did she have to run into the likes of Dangerfield on her very first gallop upon *Ace of Spades*?

She rarely rode her horses off the estate, and certainly not dressed in men's clothing. Why did he spot her today of all days? She'd needed to put the stallion through rigorous race-condition tests and had ridden farther than she'd envisaged.

"A woman with a *derriere* as luscious as yours should not wear trousers. It is most distracting."

He'd moved closer.

She inwardly sneered at Dangerfield's banal approach. She expected nothing less of him. The tall, arrogant duke lived for pleasure and frivolous pursuits. He was a typical rakehell who cared for nothing but himself.

She held in her sigh and would not let him distract, or unnerve her.

With the stone removed from her horse's hoof, she straightened and turned to face him. Too fast. She gripped her horse's mane for support, the sudden rush of blood from her head making her dizzy. It certainly wasn't his captivating, sensuous smile. She, of all women, was immune to the fancy ways of rakes.

Yet her breath hitched as her traitorous eyes appreciated his beauty. She looked up, and then up further. Goodness she'd forgotten how tall he was. Not too tall though. Any shorter and his massive build would have made him look decidedly out of proportion. His glossy, black curls were tousled from his ride, and her immediate reaction was to tug them straight and watch them curl around her finger. They were wasted on a man.

His eyes sparkled with amusement, the deep grey as beguiling as the man. A sensual mouth, creased in a knowing smile, had her licking her lips wondering what his would feel like against her own.

She took a step back.

It would be so much easier to hate the man if he didn't look like every woman's wicked fantasy.

And didn't he just know it.

It was definitely time to leave. "If I'm distracting, then the solution would appear simple. Don't look." And she made to move around him.

He blocked her path. "But where would be the fun in that?"

Caitlin gritted her teeth, wishing for the millionth time she'd been born a man. Then she could punch him on his too-perfect nose. A little dent might make him look more human.

"I'm not here for your amusement, sir."

He moved to stand directly in front of her with the languid grace of a large panther. Dark and dangerous.

"More's the pity."

"If you'll step back, I'd like to mount my horse."

"I know what I'd like to mount," she heard him say under his breath. A scandalous utterance that she wisely chose to ignore.

He gave a smile that she suspected melted the resistance of the majority of women and, if she were honest, had too much impact even on her. He rubbed *Ace of Spades*'s nose. It appeared her finely bred stallion wasn't impervious to the wretched man's charms either. Her horse snorted and pressed his head toward the enemy as if longing for Dangerfield's touch.

Caitlin longed for no man's touch, especially not the tempting touch of the Duke of Dangerfield.

"This is quite a piece of horseflesh for a woman to be riding. Who does he belong to?"

Ace of Spades was to be *her* ace in the fight to hold onto her home. Her father might try to gamble away everything they owned, but she would not lose Mansfield Manor. It had been her mother's. As the eldest and, as it turned out, only daughter, Caitlin would inherit the Manor upon either her marriage or her twenty-fifth birthday.

That birthday was still two years away and, with no suitor in sight, Caitlin intended to make sure there was still a house left to inherit. She refused to allow her father, trustee or not, to run it into the ground.

The three-year-old stallion would win the Two-Thousand Guineas race at Newmarket even if she had to use her father's name to enter. Once she won, the stud fees she'd earn from her champion stallion would be worth a small fortune. That's if she could keep her operation a secret from her money-hungry father.

Dangerfield gave her another superior smile before looking her over in a thoroughly indecent perusal. His eyes lingered over certain parts of her anatomy, which in her groomsman's clothes, were shown off more than she would have liked. Men's trousers were the only outfit in which she could ride comfortably to test the stallion's speed.

"*Ace of Spades* belongs to me, Your Grace."

"Is that so?" His mouth tipped up at the corners as if he'd thought of a private joke. She sucked in a breath. A man should not be allowed to own a smile such as that.

"Are you sure you can handle such a magnificent beast? You look as if a strong wind could blow you over."

He stood so close her body found it difficult to remain upright. Her legs certainly felt as if they were wobbling and wouldn't hold her weight.

Damn the man.

A gloveless finger stroked her face. "Who is your protector? He must value you very highly to have 'given' you such a horse." His eyes drank her in once more. "Given your attire, and the way it deliciously displays your abundant bounty, I can clearly see why."

"I don't have a protector." She pulled her riding crop from its slot in her saddle, feeling more in control as soon as she fisted it in her hand.

"I'm in luck then." He drew her other hand off Ace's mane and raised it to his lips. His kiss on her bare knuckles was like a brand—hot and sizzling.

She quickly pulled her hand away. "You misunderstand me, Your Grace. I don't need a protector and I certainly don't desire one." She turned her back on him and swung herself up into the saddle. "And you, Lord Dangerfield, would be the last man on earth I'd ever let in my bed."

"Ah, but you do let men into your bed?"

Her face flooded with heat at his jibe, while he simply chuckled.

He showed no surprise that she knew his identity. The arrogance of the man. He reached out and stayed Ace, gripping the bridle close to the bit.

"You do realize men love a challenge and you, my lovely, are a challenge incarnate. I would have your name."

It was her turn to smile. "I'm surprised you don't recognize me."

His brows drew together in a frown, making him look much younger than his thirty years. She knew his age. They shared the same birthday—April third—but he was seven years older than her.

He let the bridle go and stepped back to study her. "We have never met. I'd remember. A local beauty like you would not have escaped my interest."

She wanted to laugh. The last time he'd talked with her was eight years ago, and she'd been covered in mud from head to toe. Hardly surprising he did not recognize her.

She'd been fifteen. It was early on a spring morning. Fog covered the ground. She'd got stuck in the bog while trying to free a deer, and he'd stopped to help. He was still half foxed, probably from a night of drinking and whoring. He certainly stank of drink and women.

"You must be getting old," she said, sweet as honey. "Your memory is going."

Annoyance flickered over his face, sharpening his handsome features. "Well, pretty wench, don't keep me in suspense. Who are you?"

She lifted her nose in the air and whirled her stallion around so his rear was in Dangerfield's face. He took a hurried step back.

"I'm Caitlin Southall," she called over her shoulder and, filled with satisfaction at seeing his mouth drop open, she kicked *Ace of Spades* and tore off at a gallop—spraying His Grace with clods of earth.

The string of curses behind her made her laugh out loud. Bumping into the duke or, rather, leaving Dangerfield in a shower of dirt, made her day.

Bloody hell. God damn the little hellion. He'd realized the plump bounty pointing to the sky—enticing enough to tempt a saint—was female from a dozen paces away. He'd studied, worshiped, and played with too many bottoms not to recognize one ripe for plucking. Besides, the long, black tresses cascading down her back like rivers of ink from a spilt inkpot left little doubt. But he'd had no idea it was the brat from the neighboring property.

Perhaps *brat* was no longer the appropriate word to describe her. His body hummed with lust.

The last time he'd interacted with Caitlin Southall he'd also ended up covered in mud. Seeing her stuck in the bog he'd gallantly gone to her rescue. Unfortunately, having rescued the damsel in distress, he couldn't rescue himself. The memory of his fall, face-down, into the very mud he'd rescued her from still mortified him. As did the look on the little wretch's face as she'd stood there laughing at him.

He shifted in discomfort, and glanced around to see if anyone had overheard their latest exchange.

Back then, he had been a tad overbearing. Grumpy. Angry at being laughed at by a slip of a girl. Especially since he was suffering from one of the worst self-inflicted headaches he could remember.

Then, when she'd told him her name and he'd learned she was the daughter of his sworn enemy, the Earl of Bridgenorth, he'd been furious, accusing her of deliberately getting stuck in the mud to taunt him. Rubbish of course, but he had not been at his best. Frankly, he'd been less than gracious, mocking her, and frightening her off.

His last image of Cate-The-Waif was of her poking her tongue out at him as she ran off. Crying.

He ran a hand over his face. At least today he hadn't made her cry. He also wasn't hung-over. However, while his temper wanted to see him ride after her and put her over his knee for a thorough spanking, he was shocked to realize he wanted to chase her for another reason altogether.

Desire.

Little Cate, as he remembered her, had grown up or, rather, filled out. In all the right places. She was still a waif. Thin and willowy. "Delicate" described her, outwardly at any rate. Her inner core looked to be of iron. She appeared self-assured and confident. Mocking a duke, especially "Lord Danger" as he was often called, was daring and risky, considering her inappropriate attire.

Gone was the skinny child with drawn and rather plain features.

Why hadn't he noticed her eyes before? The pale green, an unusual shade, gave her face an ethereal glow, especially against that hair as black as a starless night. The combination was intoxicatingly sensuous. He'd found it impossible not to look at her.

When she'd spoken in that soft, breathy voice, his gaze reluctantly dropped to her mouth, only to be enchanted there too. Her lips were a perfect pout that made a man want to dive in for a taste.

As for the luscious curves under those breeches and jacket . . . He'd taken one look at the round globes poking up at him and known he'd find heaven when seated there. Never had his body roared to life so quickly.

He was still hard, imagining in full detail what lay beneath

9

the clothes. Her legs were long and slender, and he pictured them wrapped around him. The pleasure he'd feel when running his hands up those long lengths of silken skin would no doubt unman him. The purr of satisfaction she'd give as he kissed from her feet all the way to the hidden treasure between her thighs . . .

Christ. Stop it. He refused to lust after Caitlin Southall. It was not honorable. There was no way he'd marry the daughter of the man who'd seduced and disgraced his widowed mother.

Fourteen years ago, shortly after his father passed, his mother had been lost in grief. As a boy of sixteen, he thought the support and condolences of their neighbor, the Earl of Bridgenorth, a great kindness. He had no idea how vulnerable his mother had been to a complete and utter cad.

Over the following months, the long-widowed Bridgenorth had preyed on her fear of having to raise her son and run an estate alone, seducing her in every way possible. But when she found herself with child and the Earl learned "her" money was not only entailed on Harlow but also controlled by sharp and upright lawyers, the man showed his true colors.

Harlow's gut clenched as it always did when his anger mounted. He'd been far too young to protect her from the spiteful gossip, or the shame that followed Bridgenorth's ruination and desertion.

But he protected her now. And his younger half-brother, Jeremy.

He'd tried to speak with the Earl over the years. Why would Bridgenorth not acknowledge his son? The Earl only had Caitlin. If Bridgenorth had been a gentleman and married his mother, the estate would belong to Jeremy.

One way or another Harlow was determined to procure Jeremy his birthright, and soon he would have it. Harlow knew Bridgenorth's weakness. Cards.

Harlow would either win it from him in a game, or buy up

his vowels until Bridgenorth had no choice but to hand over the estate to his unacknowledged son.

It was only fair. It was Jeremy's birthright. It was his, Harlow's, duty to protect his brother and ensure he got what he was entitled to.

He clenched his fists, and with willpower he didn't realize he possessed he stilled the roaring desire in his blood.

After several painful minutes he was finally back in control of every part of his body. He whistled for *Champers*, his trusty steed, who grazed behind him on the grass. As he swung into the saddle he thanked God he was off to London that night. A turn at the gaming tables and a visit with his lovely mistress, Larissa, would take his mind off the annoying Southall vixen.

He swore into the breeze. Caitlin Southall could unseat his plans. She should be the last woman on this earth he desired. As he rode toward Telford Court he tried to talk his body into recognizing the danger of such a dalliance. However, since he'd grown harder by the time he'd reached home, it appeared his body had refused to listen.

CHAPTER TWO

Shropshire, Telford Court, three months later

If the Duke did not grant her an audience soon, Caitlin was going to be sick all over his expensive Persian carpet.

She knew calling on him so late at night was scandalous, but his mother and younger brother were still in London, and she did not wish anyone, especially her father, to learn why she was here. The entire village knew the duke was a night owl, rarely to bed before dawn. So, when the clock struck midnight at Mansfield Manor, she had crept out of her home and ridden across the gully to Telford Court.

Caitlin tried to sit demurely and wait for His Grace to deign an audience, but he had kept her waiting for hours and it was now almost three in the morning. She flicked her gaze to the window. She didn't have much time. She still had to sneak home before dawn. Her hope was fading with the dark night.

Her stomach churned from nerves and tiredness—and the fact she'd had nothing to eat or drink since earlier in the afternoon, too sick with apprehension to face dinner. However, the only reason she cared about losing the contents of her stomach was that His Grace wouldn't be the one cleaning it up.

Over and over she'd rehearsed what she would say to him. Now, she just wanted it finished. She was not leaving his huge, imposing residence without gaining his agreement.

The only good thing to come from the enforced wait was that her rising temper had displaced her taut nerves.

The *cheek* of the man. Even a duke should have manners.

Her pique, having reached its tipping point, had her walking to the door and opening it. The footman, placed strategically in the hall, leaned back against the wall, eyes closed, snoring softly. How inconsiderate of the duke to keep his staff up so late. And how dare he keep her waiting hours as if she, too, were a servant?

She'd had enough.

From further down the hall came the sound of raised male voices. Inebriated voices. Before she lost her courage Caitlin stepped out of the room and marched toward the ruckus. Without allowing herself time to think, she threw the door open wide and walked straight into the room.

The heat hit her first. A fire blazed in the hearth, yet the night, when she'd ridden across the gully separating the duke's estate from Bridgenorth, had been mild. She also found it difficult to breathe for the haze from three smoking cheroots.

The duke had visitors.

Her face felt as if it was on fire too, but not from the heat. She stood in the middle of a room where three very large males sprawled about in a state of undress—cravats undone, waistcoats off and shirts half open.

"Look," one of them drawled. "Additional entertainment. How thoughtful of you, Harlow. She's come dressed as a man. Should I infer anything from that?"

Only then did she notice the women. Given their sparse clothing and designation of 'entertainment' she quickly understood their profession. Mortified, she did not know where to look.

She turned to the man who'd spoken and her mouth went dry. He lounged in his chair with a half-naked woman on his knee. One of his hands held a nearly empty brandy balloon. The other appeared to be glued to the woman's breast. He looked like the Devil himself—with his dark brown hair and darker, hooded eyes, regarding her with bored amusement.

This, Caitlin thought, frantically, had been a terrible mistake. Her body had already come to that conclusion and begun its retreat.

But Dangerfield was too fast. He reached the door first and shut it. Inside the room the heat seemed to double.

"*Are* you the entertainment?" Dangerfield asked. "I'm never sure what to expect when you are in my presence, Lady Southall."

The other two men threw startled and worried looks at each other.

"*Lady* Southall?" The third man, the fair-haired man, sat up straighter and began to retie his cravat.

His Grace ignored his friend's concern. He moved until he stood quite close behind her.

"Yes, I *am* Lady Caitlin Southall." She shivered even though she could feel the heat from his broad chest through her light jacket. "And no, I most certainly am *not* part of the entertainment."

"I struggle to see what purpose, other than for our entertainment, you'd have for arriving at my home, without a chaperone, this late at night. Or should I say 'early in the morning'? And dressed in such a provocative fashion. You know how much I admire you in trousers."

Late? Provocative? She was the one decently dressed, even if she was in men's clothing. "I came for a private word with you over three hours ago. I grew tired of waiting. I must get home before dawn."

"I was not told you were here." A gentle touch on her back made her jump. "A private word?" The pressure of his touch grew. Glided slowly down her spine. "Now that sounds promising. However, my friends and I share everything. Don't we, ladies?"

Two of women giggled and crooned. The third simply sent her a frosty stare. Caitlin reached behind and swatted Dangerfield's finger away.

"Harlow," his fair-haired friend warned. "This is not a good idea,"

The duke moved to her side. "Henry is worried about my reputation, given you've walked into one of my private bachelor parties."

"*Your* reputation?" Caitlin couldn't help herself.

"Yes, mine. A lady discovered in this room at this moment would be compromised beyond repair. It would likely mean I'd have to offer her marriage—and that is something a man of my reputation fears most of all."

She almost snorted. "Then your reputation is quite safe. I have no intention of allowing myself to become wed to a man such as you."

His two friends burst out laughing, and the, as yet, unnamed man said, "Oh, my. She's priceless. Wherever did you find her?"

"Marcus doesn't know you as well as I do." His Grace continued, "Lady Southall has a terrible habit of bothering me."

She couldn't suppress her shiver of awareness as he moved to stand over her, brushing her with his body. Blocking her view of the others in the room he looked down his perfect nose at her. "Did you come for your pleasure?" he purred. "Or mine?"

It was the arrogant smile that did it. Her hand, apparently operating on its own initiative, whipped up like a snake. The sharp crack of flesh meeting flesh—together with the pain in her

15

palm—brought Caitlin to her senses. She gasped and stumbled back as the marks of her fingers began to appear on Dangerfield's cheek.

Dangerfield touched fingers to his face, and winced. "As usual, for no one's pleasure I see." He turned around to face the room. "Gentleman, may I present Lady Caitlin Southall, my neighbor."

The fair-haired man rose to his feet and gave a slight bow before retaking his chair. The brown-haired man simply stayed seated and nodded his head in her direction.

"I'm sorry for the slap." Caitlin couldn't believe she had actually done it. She felt appalled. Terrified. Furious. "It's just you have the annoying habit of making me want to punch you."

"Really?" Dangerfield's eyes narrowed. "You, my lady, make me want do many things. Hitting you isn't one of them."

She ignored his remark and glanced once more out the window. It would be getting light soon. How could she get the duke alone?

She turned back to Dangerfield. "Your Grace, I—"

At her pointed stares at the other gentleman, Dangerfield gave a little grin. "Of course. Introductions. Lady Southall, I hesitate to introduce you to such rakehells. However this"—he gestured to the man in the chair—"is Lord Marcus Danvers, the Marquis of Wolverstone. The reprobate busy straightening his clothes is the archangel of our group, Lord Henry St. Giles, the Earl of Cravenswood. Would you like me to introduce you to the other . . . ladies in the room?"

Her face warmed until she assumed it glowed as bright as the coals in the grate.

Refusing to be distracted by his deliberate intention to make her uncomfortable—*ladies indeed*—she said, "Since I am here, may I have a private word? If you have time." Sarcasm dripped from every syllable. "If you aren't too busy. I must speak with you."

He gave an overly dramatic sigh. "Ladies, please excuse us. Perhaps you would wait for us above stairs. I'm sure this won't take long."

Muttering, two of the women stood and made their way out the door. The third did not.

"I'm staying." The stunning fair-haired woman, her daringly-cut silk gown shimmering as she moved, glided to Dangerfield's side and put her hand on his arm. "The sooner she delivers her message the sooner she can leave. I'm sure we have more pleasant activities to enjoy than talking with this,"—she waved a dismissive hand—"smelly urchin."

His Grace laughed and scooped her up in his arms. "I swear, Larissa, you're good for a man's soul." He carried her back to his chair and sat with her on his lap, looking like a king who'd claimed his bounty.

"Speak, then, Lady Southall," he commanded.

Caitlin swallowed her pride. This was her chance—probably her only chance—and she would not let pride prevent her from receiving her due.

"I have come to demand my home be returned to me."

Dangerfield frowned. "Your home?"

"Mansfield Manor. My father had no right to stake a game with it. The house belonged to my mother and, according to her will, is to pass to me."

"I gather your father was the trustee."

She wanted to squirm where she stood and wring her hands. But she didn't. "A mistake my mother made." She rushed on. "She did not understand my father's weaknesses. She died before she learned of them, thank God, and saw his *penchant* for gambling destroy him. She would never have made him my trustee if she'd known. The house was to be left to the eldest daughter—as it has been for several generations."

Dangerfield's expression didn't change. "Then, as the trustee, your father had a legal right to stake the house. I'm sorry but I cannot help you. The house belongs to me. I've explained to your father I want him out by the end of the month."

What right did Dangerfield have to sound so angry? *He* wasn't the one being evicted from his own home. And why? Why did he hate her father so much? Because he did—and no one would explain the cause. Her father would not give any reason why she was never to set foot on Dangerfield land. When she tried to ask the servants they'd looked embarrassed and hurried away. No one in the village would speak of the rift—not to her, anyway.

She couldn't stem the welling tears of frustration. "What of our tenants, Your Grace? Do you propose to honor my father's obligations to them?"

"Of course. I'm a fair man. I'm not a cold-hearted bastard like your father."

Fair? She saw her chance and took it. She stepped forward. "You're a fair man? Then you'll give me a chance to win the house back."

The room became deathly silent. Dangerfield's steel grey eyes bored into her, assessing the trap he'd allowed himself to walk into. "I don't wager with women."

"Why not?" she flashed back. "Afraid you'll lose?"

Marcus snorted. "She has you there, Harlow." He appraised her, head to toe, with the inbred arrogance of the aristocracy. "I'd love to see what she's going to challenge you to do."

"Shut up, Marcus."

"A horse race." Caitlin lifted her chin. "I challenge you to a horse race to be run over a mile. If I win, I get back my house."

Dangerfield sat studying her for several minutes. "I've seen your stallion. I've also seen you ride him. Why would I be foolish enough to accept that wager?"

"I've heard it said you never refuse a dare. So,"—she drew in breath—"if you refuse this time it must be that you are afraid to lose to a woman."

Her taunt found its mark. His eyes darkened almost too black and his face closed in, all expression gone.

"I'll consider your challenge, but only if you win back your house the same way your father lost it. By playing faro."

Dangerfield knew himself to be the best faro player in all of England, and he'd be damned if this little hellion bested him again.

"That's hardly fair," she said. "I don't really know how to play."

He shrugged. "Don't play, then. I don't care. You're the one desperate to win your house back." He paused and flicked lint from his sleeve. "Besides, you haven't told me what I would win when you lose."

She frowned, and it made her pretty nose screw up into a delightful button. "You simply get to keep the house."

He wanted more than that. "I already have the house."

"I don't have anything else of value."

He looked her over and, as it had previously—and did even now, with a stunningly gorgeous, sexually experienced, woman on his lap—his body hungered for her. Only her.

"I want you."

In his lap Larissa gasped, her affected boredom gone.

Harlow watched Caitlin closely and saw the instant she understood what he was saying. Her face went pale. Then red.

Then, "No." She shook her head. "No. Definitely not. No. Never."

"You can't be serious, Harlow," Larissa cried. "Think of the scandal. Do you want to end up *married*? To *her*?"

His mistress's passionate appeal drew his attention back to her. God, she was beautiful. It was why he'd procured her services—that and the fact she knew how to pleasure a man better than any woman he'd ever known. But Caitlin, even dressed as a stable boy, tugged at every one of his senses. His body recognized her. And wanted her.

He smiled down at Larissa. "It won't come to that, my dear. Will it, Lady Southall? You have as little desire to marry me as I have to marry you." He looked his lovely neighbor over. "When you lose, I'll be discreet. No one but those present here tonight will be aware you've come to my bed. And who knows? If you're good I may give you your house anyway."

He ignored the expression of growing horror on Caitlin's face. It was probably an act. She was twenty-three years old. She ran around at all hours of the night, unaccompanied, and in men's trousers. He wondered if she was indeed still a virgin.

Women were all the same. He knew that. Most used their beauty and bodies to get what they wanted in this world. He hardly blamed them for they had little else with which to make their way. He was only surprised Caitlin hadn't offered herself in exchange for the house to begin with. Simpler and more effective. He'd have seriously considered it. She must be aware of how much he lusted after her.

As a young man, he'd believed in love. Bridgenorth's seduction of his mother had dented his faith, but it was Margaret Crompton who had filled his heart with stone and made it impossible for him to love any woman.

Since the day he'd put on long trousers, females had thrown themselves at him. But always for his dukedom, or his wealth. Or his looks. No one really wanted him . . . Harlow . . . the man behind the title. No one except Margaret.

And that had almost destroyed him.

Ten years ago he'd become a wiser man. Women were merely objects of beauty. He took what he wanted from them and was careful to only engage in mutual pleasure, passion, and desire.

When he eventually married—and he would marry to beget his heir—it would be a marriage of convenience only.

His convenience.

He looked around the room. At his friends' faces. Henry's horrified, Marcus's amused.

He clenched his fists by his side and refused to let any soft feelings for Caitlin's plight enter his heart. Jeremy deserved the estate. He would certainly be a better landowner than a slip of a girl who, if her behavior was anything to go by, was destined to remain a spinster.

She'd remained silent a long time. Apparently, he'd rendered her mute. "Well, do you accept my terms? If you win, you get your house. If I win, you come to my bed—and you might earn your house back. It would seem a fair wager. You could end up with the house either way."

Caitlin had never hated anyone more than she hated Dangerfield at this moment. He held the power to simply give her the house, yet he intended to take everything from her—including her dignity, pride and self-respect.

Struggling with both temper and despair she blinked back the tears that threatened behind her eyes. She would not cry in front of him. She knew, deep in her soul, that she had little choice. This was the only way she'd ever have a chance of taking back Mansfield Manor.

Damn the man. It might be just a house to him but to her it was—had been—her mother's pride and joy. It was her own security; an estate that meant she need not be forced into a hateful marriage but could take her time and choose her husband. Choose a man who met all the requirements on her list. A man so far removed from the Duke of Dangerfield it was laughable. She had worked all her life to preserve that security, to keep it intact to pass on to her own daughter. Now? She shivered. At least she need not worry about ending up married to Dangerfield. The man obviously had no honor.

She would not, could not, let Mansfield Manor go. God forgive her.

"Only if we race—over a mile." If he agreed to race her, she would not lose. Not on *Ace of Spades*.

"I distinctly recall that I offered to play cards for the house."

"May I suggest," Marcus interjected, "that the wager is the best of three challenges? Lady Caitlin has chosen a horse race. Harlow has chosen a game of Faro. Now there should be a third challenge in case of a tie."

"But who gets to pick the final challenge?" Caitlin knew she had no friends in that room. "I am clearly at a disadvantage. No one here wants me to win."

"*I* do." Larissa snaked an arm around Dangerfield's waist and pressed against him. "May I select the last challenge?" The look she threw at Caitlin was cold enough to kill. "I don't want you in his bed."

It wasn't precisely friendship but it was better than nothing. Dangerfield's mistress had not been at all pleased when he'd declared his terms and been bristling jealousy ever since. He was such a bastard.

"I have no objection to . . ." Caitlin didn't know what to call the woman. "I'm sorry. We have not been introduced."

"Larissa du Mar," the beauty said, baring her teeth. "His Grace's mistress."

"Then I have no objection to Miss du Mar choosing the final challenge, as long as I have right of veto."

Both Marcus and Henry sat up straighter.

"Now this," Marcus muttered, "could be very interesting."

Henry shook his head. "It's a terrible idea. And—quite frankly, Harlow—beneath you. Dishonorable. I realize you are thinking of Jeremy. What her father did to your mother was unforgivable, but Lady Southall is not to blame—oh damn."

Caitlin rounded swiftly on Henry. *What her father did to*

your mother . . . "What do you mean?"

But Henry, the tips of his ears growing pinker every second, was studying his feet with great attention and wouldn't meet her eyes. So she turned instead to Dangerfield. Who simply returned her puzzled stare with cold indifference.

"I don't understand," she said. "What did my father do?"

The room stilled, as if in the eye of a huge storm. Everyone straining, readying for the final assault.

Lord Dangerfield ignored her question. "There is no need to speak of it. Jeremy is the reason I cannot simply hand back the house."

"Your mother would not approve of this, Dangerfield," Henry muttered.

"Leave it, Henry."

There was such coldness in Dangerfield's voice that Caitlin could feel any chance to reclaim her property freezing into impossibility.

"This has nothing to do with our parents." She wasn't sure she believed that now, but it wasn't the immediate issue. "This is now between Dangerfield and me. I want the opportunity to win back my home. Please." She stepped forward, closer to where he sat, and placed her hand gently on his sleeve. "Don't deny me this chance."

At her touch, Dangerfield started and looked at her as if only really seeing her for the first time. Their gazes locked and something passed between them.

Caitlin's breath hitched and her fingers tightened on his arm. His heat, his strength burned beneath her fingertips like some primal flame.

What would it feel like, she wondered, to have to submit to this man? To lie in his bed. To lie naked and exposed, and watch and feel him prowl over her . . .

She gulped back her fears.

"Larissa." Dangerfield's voice was rough, and he didn't take his eyes off Caitlin's face. "What is to be the final challenge?"

"In a moment." Larissa stared pointedly at Caitlin's fingers where they still rested on Dangerfield's arm. Caitlin withdrew her hand, but the heat and feel of him remained, seared on her brain.

The woman slid off Dangerfield's lap, smoothed her gown and then began to stroll around Caitlin, looking her over from top to bottom. "I have to find something you're good at."

Caitlin's hopes soared. She was about to open her mouth to explain exactly what she was very good at when Marcus interrupted.

"Now, now, Larissa. You cannot ask Lady Southall questions that would give her an advantage. We must keep it fair." And he laughed, as if the idea of Caitlin winning—fairly or not—was a huge joke.

Caitlin had no intention of attempting to win by fraud. Nonetheless, she stood silently, praying Larissa would pick something like shooting or archery—things she excelled at. *Please,* she begged in her head, *not sewing. Not playing the piano.*

Meanwhile, Larissa was talking. ". . . she's the daughter of an Earl. She must be accomplished. Harlow is always telling me how tedious it is to have to sit and listen to young ladies sing or play the harp."

Caitlin agreed with Harlow about recitals. *And please! please don't pick those pursuits either.*

"Still, she is dressed in male attire, and she sought out Harlow at night, so she is most likely not like most young women of the *ton*."

Dangerfield's face signified agreement. He cleared his throat and rose to his feet. "Very true."

Yes, Larissa was clever. She'd have to be. Caitlin could not imagine a woman remaining as His Grace's mistress for very long if she did not have a brain.

"So, perhaps I'm focusing on the wrong person." Larissa

turned a seductive smile upon Dangerfield. "All I have to do is find something that you, my darling Harlow, are terrible at doing."

A flicker of unease crossed Dangerfield's handsome face and he shifted on his feet. Only a slight movement, but Caitlin caught it. He was nervous. Good.

Larissa laughed delightedly and clapped her hands. "I've got it—"

"Remember who keeps you, my girl."

"That's not fair," Caitlin cried. "You can't threaten her. I can always veto, remember?"

"He's only teasing." Larissa moved to stand in front of Dangerfield. Letting her hands slide up his chest and over his wide shoulders she pressed her ample breasts against him. "He would never get rid of me." Her fingers gripped his buttocks and pulled him tight against her.

Caitlin felt as though her eyes would pop as she watched one of Larissa's hands slide over Dangerfield's hip and down toward his groin.

"He knows the pleasure my body, my hands, and my mouth can give. I'm the best at what I do." Larissa threw her a scornful look. "You don't look as if you know the first thing about pleasuring a man. Perhaps I should help Harlow win. Once he's had you, he'll realize how much better off he is with me."

"Enough, Larissa." Dangerfield removed Larissa's hands from his body. "That's enough."

It was certainly enough. Caitlin felt sick. Larissa was right. Hands and mouth? Mouth? What did she do with her mouth—kissing perhaps? She had no idea what to expect to find in any man's bed—let alone a man like Dangerfield. And she did not wish to know.

Not much, anyway.

CHAPTER THREE

Caitlin had always believed that she would only give herself to a man she loved, her husband. She wanted to be important to him, not simply a child-bearing necessity. She wanted to be wanted for who she was. In order to find a man who would complement her, she had devised a list of attributes her future husband must have—and she would not waiver from it.

He had to be kind. Kind to all members of Society, not just the wealthy. He would acknowledge that a woman was just as capable as a man. He would encourage her to be involved in the day-to-day running of Mansfield—the estate as well as the house. He would be a true partner in life, not a dictator. He would not expect her to obey his every command. He would most definitely *not* be a gambler or a man who enjoyed any game of chance. And, last of all, he would love her above anyone else. No mistress. No other woman. He would have a true heart and forsake any other pleasure.

Caitlin wanted love—true love—and this desire was the reason she thought she'd never marry. She didn't know if true love even existed.

Would she ever find a man who would cherish her, and appreciate the fact she'd trusted and gifted him her virginity?

A shiver skittered down her back. A man like Dangerfield did not understand the word 'love'. Nor did he value a woman for anything other than his pleasure, or for begetting his heir. He would not appreciate her gift in his bed. In fact, Larissa was probably right. He'd scorn her inexperience. He'd be disappointed in her.

Oh, he would pleasure her and himself, of that she was sure. But pleasure was fleeting. He'd soon move on, and think nothing more of the woman he'd bested in a dare, taken to his bed, and discarded as soon as he had what he wanted.

Something of her thoughts must have shown on her face, for Dangerfield turned his head to the window and the approaching dawn.

"There is still time to halt all this foolishness," he said, quietly. "Go home and accept your circumstances, for if you agree to the wager I cannot stop until I have won. I give you fair warning. If you value your reputation, or if the idea of sharing my bed holds such revulsion for you, leave."

She shook her head and stood straighter. "I will have my house."

He gave her a searching look. "So be it. You've made your bed, young lady. I pray you are prepared to lie in it."

"Cake baking!"

Caitlin jumped at Larissa's sudden cry and tried to conceal her horror. She'd never cooked anything in her life. She didn't really take much notice of food. Cook always said she had the appetite of a sparrow.

Dangerfield drew himself up. "I beg your pardon?"

Marcus was laughing so hard tears appeared in the corner of his eyes.

Larissa turned to her and winked. "You will both bake a

cake, and the best cake wins."

"No," Dangerfield snapped. "Absolutely not."

He didn't want the challenge so Caitlin jumped at it. "I do not believe you have the right of veto."

"She's right. We only granted her the right of veto; it does not apply to you," Marcus chortled.

Larissa stood with hands on hips. "Well, do you agree?"

Caitlin took her time and studied Dangerfield. He tried to school his features, but she saw real annoyance—and something else—hidden there. He stared her down, trying to make her nervous. He wanted her to veto the task.

She smiled for the first time that evening. She might not be able to cook but she knew where to find an excellent teacher. "The wager is perfectly acceptable."

Dangerfield rolled his eyes. "Christ." And threw his hands in the air.

"Who is going to judge this cake off," Henry asked.

Caitlin and Dangerfield exchanged glances.

"The vicar?" Caitlin had no idea where the idea came from but she thought the vicar a fair man.

Every eye fixed on her in disbelief.

"Are you mad?" Dangerfield said. "I can't ask the *vicar* to judge this wager."

"Guilty conscience," she taunted.

"Not at all." Dangerfield ran his hand over his nape and felt like punching Marcus's amused face. He did have a guilty conscience, and that's what worried him. "But, while I may be lecherous I put my foot down at involving the church in the affair."

Marcus coughed. "The vicar doesn't need to know why he's judging the cakes. You could say you'd like to appoint a new cook and you'd be honored if he would pick the best cake. We'll think of something." Marcus stood, walked to the sideboard, and then rummaged in a drawer before turning around to face them, a fresh pack of cards in his hand. "In the meantime, I've thought of a way to decide which challenge is completed first."

Harlow eyed the cards and prayed for faro. "How?"

"Whoever draws the highest card gets to pick the first challenge, and so on." Marcus spread the cards on the small side table, and indicated to Caitlin. "Ladies first."

She picked one and Harlow noted her lips turn up slightly. He could read her like a book.

At his turn he drew a card and, without looking, turned it face-up on the table. From the expression on Caitlin's face, and Larissa's sigh, he knew he'd drawn the higher card.

"I should have warned you, Lady Southall," Larissa purred. "He always wins. It's one of his most annoying traits."

He let a hint of smugness enter his tone. "The game of faro will be the first challenge."

He watched Caitlin's back straighten and her mouth firm into a grim line. "Then I demand a sennight to learn how to play." She stared at him, animosity glittering in her eyes. "And I expect *you* to teach me. You boasted that you're the best player. If that is true then I want to learn from the best. What's more,"— she lifted her chin—"St. Giles can be there to ensure you are teaching me properly."

Henry nodded his head in acquiescence.

Harlow gritted his teeth. A week in her company was likely to drive him insane. "Where do you propose we meet in order for me to teach you? You cannot come here. My mother returns tomorrow—"

"Well, you can't come to the Manor. My father would likely shoot you on sight. We don't have to vacate the property for another four weeks."

"My hunting lodge," Henry said. "It's no more than three miles from here at the base of Clee Hills. I could stay there until this dreadful wager is complete, and you could conduct the lessons under my watchful eye." He raised his eyebrow at Caitlin. "Would that be agreeable?"

She nodded.

"Good," Marcus said, sounding far too cheerful. "The first challenge has been accepted. A sennight from today we'll adjourn to Henry's hunting lodge for the Faro challenge." He spread the cards across the table once more. "Perhaps you'll be luckier this time, Lady Southall."

Caitlin selected a second card and her smile fled. Harlow chose a card from the top of the pile. The King of Hearts. He laid it face-up and thought he heard a very unladylike curse from Lady Southall's direction. Once again he'd won.

"The cake baking."

Marcus raised his eyebrows. "Not the horse race?"

"No." Harlow wanted to win before the race. Her horse was good. He'd seen her ride *Ace of Spades*. Not only was she highly competent, her weight gave her an advantage. Over the longer course he might lose. He needed to know before the race what was at stake. If he had to win the last challenge then he'd risk his finest three-year-old stallion. He'd pick a course that suited *Hero*. He'd been keeping the horse a secret, training him up for the Two Thousand Guinea's race at Newmarket. The odds would be in his favor if no one realized just how good he was. But to win this confounded wager he'd let his secret out.

If he had to. For Jeremy's sake.

He turned to Caitlin. "I'm granting you a week to learn faro, so I'm asking for a week to learn how to bake a cake."

Caitlin could hardly refuse. She'd need time to practice as well. She would get Mrs. Darcy to teach her. Mrs. Darcy had won the cake-baking contest at the village fete for the past five years.

All the same, there was no way she wanted Dangerfield to know she couldn't cook either, so she took her time before she answered as though she were assessing his request. Slowly, she nodded. "I suppose that's fair."

Marcus collected the cards. "Which leaves the mile long horse race for the following weekend. Perfect. Caitlin will know before the end of the month whether she and her father must vacate their home." He put the cards back in the desk. "I shall organize the horse race." He bowed in Caitlin's direction. "Over a mile as requested. I shall pick the course, the starting point, and the end point."

She frowned, doubting his motivation. "I'm not sure I trust you. It must be run locally."

"I think it's a trifle late to start negotiating terms. You agreed to race Harlow over a mile. You didn't specify where the race was to take place."

She sent Henry an appealing look, but he simply shook his head and held up his palms. Marcus Danvers was right. She had forgotten to specify terms. She swallowed down her plea.

The handsome Marquis was enjoying her discomfiture. "I'm open to persuasion," he murmured, a sensuous smile on his lips as he moved to stand before her. Taking her hand, he raised it to his lips and pressed a long kiss to her knuckles. "I find it difficult to deny a beautiful woman anything."

Before she could respond, Dangerfield was at her side prying her fingers from Danvers hold. "That's enough, Marcus. She is not a toy to play with."

"But perhaps a woman to fight over, eh?" Marcus replied with a light laugh. "My, we seem rather possessive for a man who, in the last ten years, has shown no interest in a lady of quality."

While the men argued, Caitlin took the opportunity to move toward the door. There was nothing more to be gained here. She'd accomplished what she'd set out to do—obtain a chance to win Mansfield Manor back, and right the wrong her father had perpetrated against her.

Once at the door she cleared her throat. "Good evening, gentlemen."

Lords Danvers and Dangerfield stopped their low-toned discussion and Henry stood.

"I'll see you out," he said. "Shall we say mid-afternoon at my lodge to begin the lessons?"

Dangerfield looked at Larissa, and then back to Caitlin. His eyes bored into hers and she felt her heart squeeze in her chest as he gave a dazzling smile. "I should be *compos mentis* by then."

She hated the spear of jealousy that lodged in her chest. Why should she care that the heartless rake would no doubt spend the rest of the night with Larissa in his bed? She had to stop this ridiculous hold he had on her senses. There was no way she could win if she couldn't think straight.

"I shall look forward to teaching you—many things—over the course of the week." His voice, filled with a husky promise of all things decadent, plucked its way down her spine.

Caitlin sent up a silent prayer for forbearance. What an impossible man! It was difficult to concentrate when he stood there looking so rumpled, and unrepentant, and utterly gorgeous. Her eyes kept sliding toward the sliver of tanned neck and chest exposed by his open shirt. The absence of a civilizing cravat or a waistcoat lent him a reckless air of danger.

She'd best remember that when one played with fire the burns hurt. Her stomach pitched; her hands trembled. Her heart seemed to have slipped its moorings and anchored in her throat.

Lord help her. She tried to resist but she couldn't stop herself from taking one last lingering look at his chest.

"Lady Southall?" The amusement in his voice told her he knew exactly what she was thinking, and the effect he had on her.

Her face flooded with heat. She straightened and held her head up high. "I look forward to teaching you how to lose—and I don't care if it's gracefully—just so long as you lose."

With that she swept from the room as majestically as she could, given her attire.

Little did she know that three pairs of eyes followed her departure with a great deal of male appreciation.

Henry flashed a smile at the other two men before following Caitlin from the room and closing the door.

"Larissa." Dangerfield held Marcus's amused gaze. "Go to bed. It's late and I have some things to discuss with Marcus and Henry."

She pouted but did not contradict him, no doubt sensing his mood. That's what he liked about her. She knew when to leave him be.

"Will you join me later?" she asked.

He looked at her for a long time before replying. "Probably not," he said at last. "It's late. And you and the ladies must leave first thing in the morning before my mother and brother arrive home." To pacify her jealousy he swept her into his arms and gave her a deep and thorough kiss. "I'll see you at the end of the month in London. Off you go." And he all but pushed her out the door.

He was shaken by how little desire he felt for such a beauty. His body wanted someone else. Someone he should not want. Lady Caitlin Southall.

Marcus sighed. "Another mistress soon to be discarded, I wager. Giving up the lovely Larissa? Tut tut. You badly want Caitlin Southall in your bed. There is no way you'd risk losing Mansfield Manor if you didn't. To procure it for Jeremy has been your driving ambition for over fourteen years. Now to risk losing it and ending up leg-shackled speaks volumes. And you are—risking marriage, that is. A part of me wonders if that is actually your plan?"

Dangerfield's eyes narrowed as he lit a cheroot. "I risk nothing."

Marcus continued. "You always said that, despising love—as we all do, except perhaps for Henry—you'd marry for your convenience. What is more convenient than marrying Caitlin Southall? I know you, Harlow. You're appalled that you've allowed her father to gamble away a house in trust for her." Marcus also lit a cheroot. "One wonders why you simply don't offer her marriage. A perfect solution. She seems desperate to gain the house back. Perhaps desperate enough to marry 'a man like you' if I remember her words correctly."

Dangerfield wasn't surprised at his friend's insight. As soon as Caitlin appeared in his house, late, unescorted and dressed so inappropriately, he knew his fate was sealed. But he couldn't stop from playing with her. Her damned pride and her blatant lack of respect for him had him wanting to bring her down a peg or two.

The fact Mansfield Manor was supposedly in trust for her made him feel better about the leg-shackle in which he was now caught. For his mother would learn of her visit, and once she knew what Lord Bridgenorth had done to Caitlin—stealing and gambling away her inheritance—Harlow would never hear the end of it. His mother would insist on his doing right by her.

Besides, Marcus knew him too well. He *did* want Caitlin in his bed, and with a consuming passion that terrified him. He could not allow that to happen without marriage.

Before he could reply, Henry arrived back in the room bristling like a wounded bear.

"Dangerfield," he snapped. "If you go through with this appalling wager and force her into your bed you, my man, are going to marry that girl. I'll not stand by and see her dishonored. She came here out of desperation, and you've taken advantage of her."

Dangerfield tightened his lips around the cheroot and drew in a deep breath before deliberately removing the cigarillo and blowing smoke directly toward Henry's saintly glower. "You're assuming I'll win the contest. With a woman like Caitlin Southall, one can never be sure of victory. Each time I've tangled with her I've come out the wounded party."

Henry waved the smoke away and dropped into a chair. "Well, I'll not stand by and see her ruined. She's already had to suffer a despicable father."

"Oh, do be quiet. I have every intention of marrying the chit."

"Yes." Marcus thumped the arm of his chair. "I knew it."

Henry blew out a breath. "You are? Good. I'd hate to have to call you out. I realize you haven't spent much time around ladies of the *ton*, but I did hope you'd not forgotten how to behave like a gentleman."

"To the future bride." Marcus raised his glass in a toast. "I'm not surprised you want her. She's all fire and brimstone wrapped in a curvaceous package of soft skin and silken hair. Imagine unleashing all that passion in your bed."

Harlow fought down the urge to strangle him. "I'll have you imagining no such thing. She's to be my wife."

And he was serious. When he'd seen Marcus raise Caitlin's hand to his lips he'd wanted to slice his friend in two. Never had he had such a primal and possessive response to a woman. There was no doubt Caitlin Southall had wormed her way under his skin. He was more than sure that once he'd married and bedded her, the itch would be scratched. Then he could get on with his life, knowing he would satisfy his mother's desire for an heir.

With Caitlin as his bride he could still give Mansfield Manor to Jeremy. He'd buy her any other estate she wanted as a wedding gift, but Jeremy got Mansfield Manor. He deserved it.

Other than that, there was no reason why Caitlin Southall need change his life in any way.

"May I ask what you hope to gain from this silly wager then?

Why not simply offer her marriage?" Henry's interest appeared genuine.

"She won't marry me if I merely ask. She has too much pride."

Marcus's eyes widened. "Once she's compromised she'll have no choice, is that it? Drastic, I must say. What happened to the Dangerfield charm? Why can't you simply seduce her? I've never met a woman who did not desire to marry a duke."

"Caitlin is not like most woman," Harlow muttered dryly.

Henry's eyes bored into his, "Are you sure this is the right course to take. If you feel nothing for her . . ."

He felt something for her all right. "When she originally walked in, I couldn't think of anything worse than marrying the hellion, male dressing daughter of bloody Bridgenorth. However, on reflection, I believe she'd make me a perfect Duchess."

"How so?"

"There is no denying she's enchanting. Getting an heir will prove to be very enjoyable. She's local. The villagers love her. And she prefers the country to town." He took a large gulp of brandy. "Which will leave me free to spend the majority of my time in London away from her, knowing my interests in Shropshire are in good hands. A marriage for my convenience."

Marcus gave a gruff bark. "What of your mother? Will she mind having Bridgenorth's daughter—and, of course, Jeremy's half-sister—living here?"

Dangerfield merely quirked an eyebrow. "Mother is fond of the girl and bears her no ill will. I suspect she'll be pleased with my choice. She'll assume my marrying a local girl means I intend to settle down at the estate. She couldn't be more wrong." He stretched his legs out and sighed. "As for Jeremy, he already knows she's his half-sister. Besides, once he has Mansfield he'll be too busy on his estate to care who I've married."

"But," Marcus said, slowly, "it would appear Caitlin doesn't know of her father's disgraceful conduct, or of her resulting sibling. How do you think she'll react?"

Henry answered Marcus's question. "I suspect she'll be pleased to have a brother. It's tiresome being an only child." Henry undid the cravat he'd hurriedly straightened when Caitlin had arrived. "The one person who loses the most in this is Caitlin. She loses her freedom and her house. A tad unfair if you ask me."

Dangerfield sighed. "Henry, you are far too noble to be friends with the likes of Wolverstone and me. No one forced her to accept the wager. In fact, she offered the first challenge. And one can hardly call ending up married to a duke 'unfair'. She'll have everything she desires. Riches. Clothes. A home. Once she understands the benefits this marriage brings her she'll forget all about Mansfield Manor."

Henry pursed his lips "I'm not so sure. There is more to her than other simpering ladies of the *ton*. She cares about her home and her tenants. I don't believe the trappings of a grand life drive her."

Marcus merely drank more brandy, apparently bored now the parameters of the wager had been decided.

Harlow sipped his drink in contemplation. Henry was right. Caitlin had never had a Season. He wondered if lack of funds was the reason. She would have taken the *ton* by storm and probably have received many proposals of marriage. He ran his hand over the back of his neck. Why did that idea bother him?

His plan was the only correct option open to him. He might be a womanizer and a consummate rake, but he drew the line at taking advantage of a young woman whose home her disreputable father had gambled away. She'd come to him in desperation. He would not take advantage of that.

The most uncomfortable aspect of the situation was that he was not displeased at the outcome. He kept asking himself, had he known the house was held in trust for Caitlin, would he still have accepted Bridgenorth's wager?

Probably not. Which meant he could never have contemplated taking Caitlin into his bed. And he wanted her in his bed. Wanted it a great deal.

His blood heated at the thought of her soft curves in his hands . . . her tender, creamy skin beneath his lips . . . her body moving against his in the throes of passion . . .

Larissa. Thank God she and the other ladies were leaving tomorrow because he'd lost all and any desire for her. Not really unusual given she'd been with him for over twelve months—the longest he'd kept any woman. But the fact he wanted *only* Caitlin was telling.

With the number of women he'd bedded, with the many more he could easily seduce, he should not hunger for one woman to this degree. He thought he'd taught himself that one woman was much like another. But his body recognized what his mind refused to believe.

Caitlin Southall was different.

And therein lay the danger.

CHAPTER FOUR

Caitlin arrived in plenty of time for her first Faro lesson. She was early on purpose, hoping for time alone with Henry and the opportunity to play on his chivalrous nature and learn all of Dangerfield's secrets.

She'd slept little during what had remained of the previous night. Tossing. Turning. Worrying.

What on earth could the Duke of Dangerfield gain by forcing her into his bed? He certainly was not short of bed partners. Why would he want the likes of her for his bed sports? Was it his ultimate revenge against her father, to see his daughter ruined?

If only she could learn why the pair hated each other so. Perhaps she could put an end to the bitter quarrel and appeal for time to reimburse her father's debt. If she could delay the settlement until after the race at Newmarket, then she might be able to afford to buy the Manor back.

Henry would likely know the answer. And that was another thing. This wager didn't sit easy with Henry St. Giles, Earl of Cravenswood. How strange. He appeared genuinely appalled at Harlow's behavior, yet he too was a renowned rake. Perhaps some rakes were more honorable than others. Well, she would soon find out.

She halted her gig outside Ashley House, the Earl's grey stone, impressive hunting lodge. It was a large house—much larger than she remembered.

A stable lad arrived to help her down and take care of her horse and equipage. She'd come dressed as the very proper Lady Southall this afternoon, hoping to remind Dangerfield of her status—a virginal, well-bred lady, and not some fallen woman he could seduce.

She'd barely had time to straighten her dress when she heard the sound of thundering hooves. She turned in time to watch Dangerfield gallop up the drive on *Champers*, streaking past the trees lining the driveway. They seemed to bend in his wake.

She tried not to, but she couldn't help but drink in the sight of his board shoulders braced against the wind, his muscular thighs hugging the horse's barrel. The daredevil billow and furl of his greatcoat as it fluttered behind him completed the picture of perfect masculinity.

He reined in and skidded to a halt not far from where she stood, mesmerized. The large stallion pranced in place, as magnificent as its rider. The duke gave her a ridiculously arousing smile before dismounting in a graceful slide.

So much for getting time alone with St. Giles.

He swept off his hat and bowed. "How lovely you look this afternoon, Lady Southall. I thought I'd catch you arriving early for our lesson. No doubt ready to prey on Henry's good nature."

Their gazes clashed, and annoyance coursed through her veins—mixed with something that edged the annoyance higher. Excitement. His dark-lashed, grey eyes twinkled. The man knew precisely the impact his arrival was having on her.

Caitlin's lips parted. Her heart pounded against her corset, which was obviously tied far too tightly. She had to remind herself to breathe. In. Out. *Ignore him.*

Harlow's smile widened, and he brought her limp hand to his lips for a butterfly-light brush of a kiss. Heavens, but his eyes seemed to be burning right through her, reading her thoughts as a blind man reads the darkness. He was all male, preening before a female.

Her lungs burned. But still she kept looking . . . looking . . . powerless before him . . . powerless to wrench her hand, or her gaze, away.

"I still prefer you in trousers."

His husky declaration broke the spell that held her captive. "Then I shall ensure never to wear trousers again," she said, warmth flaring in her cheeks.

He straightened. "Quite right. My apologies." His little bow mocked her. "I don't prefer you in trousers. I'd prefer you in nothing at all."

She should have been angry, but the notion of being naked before this man's gaze made her pulse quicken. What was the matter with her? "That will never happen."

"When I win this wager it will. I'm looking forward to it. In fact, it is all I could think about last night. You—naked—in my bed."

She suppressed a shiver. He made it sound as though it were a foregone conclusion. "*If* you win, don't you mean?"

He smirked. "Not even getting Henry on your side will change the outcome. I will win. I always win."

Before she could think of a retort, he offered her his arm—and, in that instant, the rake disappeared and a focused, determined competitor took his place.

"Now, Lady Southall," he said, with a flash of white teeth that reminded her of predators and danger. "Shall we step inside and begin your Faro lessons?"

Her tiny hand fluttered uncertainly on his arm, and he could sense her reluctance to touch him.

He wanted to touch her . . . everywhere

She looked beautiful this afternoon. His groin reacted to the vision before him when he drew up beside her on Champers. When Henry saw her dressed like this, dressed like an angel, he'd try to call the wager off. Her innocence shone like a beacon, enough to lighten any dark soul.

Even his.

For a brief moment he wondered what he was about.

Yet beneath her innocent cloak of respectability a vibrant, lush, and sensual woman curled and stretched, wakening to life. He could almost see it happening. The delicious flush that bloomed across her cheeks. The pale green of her eyes as they darkened and flashed almost as deep as emeralds. Emeralds. He wanted to see her lying naked on his bed with only emeralds draped at her neck and wrists.

He had not lied when he told her he'd dreamed of her. He'd dreamed of nothing *but* her.

Nonetheless, in the early hours of that morning he'd decided his seduction of Lady Caitlin Southall would serve several purposes.

First, it would unsettle her and make it easy to win the wager. Second, he hoped it would make the idea of marriage to him less repugnant to her. And third, the most primal reason of all, he wanted her.

Henry's arrival—and his expression of utter consternation at the demur and virginal looking Caitlin on his friend's arm—confirmed every one of Dangerfield's fears. Henry's lips formed into a straight line and he turned his disapproving gaze Harlow's way.

Oh, yes. The man wanted to put a stop to the wager—would probably do his best to do so.

But Dangerfield could not allow gentlemanly scruples to ruin his plans. In order to keep Mansfield Manor for Jeremy, yet still protect Caitlin from the poorhouse or worse, he had to marry her. She was beautiful enough to garner many an offer even without a dowry, but he refused to consider the notion that he could arrange an acceptable match, and see her married off elsewhere.

He also denied it was guilt that drove him. Guilt at seeing her lose something that by rights should be hers. Given her stubborn pride—which he admired—and her dislike of him—which he didn't admire at all—Harlow doubted she'd accept a straight marriage proposal. A wager, even a scandalous wager, was far more acceptable to her.

Panic gripped as he realized what lay behind his reluctance. Possessiveness. She was his. No other man could have her. He would not allow it.

"Lady Southall," Henry said into what had become a difficult silence, "how lovely you look today."

She inclined her head in a regal nod and Henry reddened like a schoolboy before clearing his throat and continuing. "My lady, I must ask you again; are you quite certain you wish to continue this wager? As a gentleman, His Grace would not hold you to it. I'm sure he will allow you to withdraw."

No, he bloody won't! He wanted to shout it at Henry—at them both—but he remained silent, wondering what her response would be.

She took a deep breath. "I do not wish to withdraw." She removed her hand from Dangerfield's sleeve and placed it instead on Henry's arm. It took all his composure not to snatch it back. "Thank you, for your concern. But"—she flashed a defiant look his way—"I'm more than positive I can beat His Grace. If I do not then at least I know I have tried."

Not until that moment did he realize he'd been holding his breath.

A few hours later, Harlow had to admit to himself that she

was rather good—for a woman. She'd already known Faro to be a game of chance where the odds were enhanced with mathematical skill. She'd also known the players had to keep track of the cards that had been played in order to ascertain the odds of what was still to be played.

She'd also picked up the nuances of the game very quickly and, unfortunately for him, had a good head for numbers.

Most men had to use a case-keeper to keep track of the cards that had been played, but Harlow could keep them in his head. It would appear Caitlin, to a certain extent, could too. It was most annoying. He'd hoped to have that advantage at least.

However, while she had won the last few turns, she had yet to understand that one needed a strategy when playing faro.

"This is not as difficult as I imagined." Her beaming smile took his breath away, and for once he remained silent.

Henry, however, did not. "I would be remiss if I didn't suggest that, for this wager, it is not how many turns you win, Lady Southall, but how much money you earn off each turn. It is the total money won over the course of the game that counts. Whoever wins the most money in this game of faro will be the victor in this challenge."

Her frown squinched that cute nose of hers up, and Henry demonstrated.

"Let's think about this turn. Given you're near the end of the fifty-one cards, and you know the cards that have been played, you can place higher bets knowing the odds are more in your favor."

She fiddled with the bracelet at her wrist and studied the layout. "I see. I know there are still a king and two queens left, and there are more low value cards left than higher. Therefore, as we get closer to the end of the deck I should place more money on the lower cards. Is that right?"

"Yes, this is what Harlow has been doing. He increases the

amount of money he bets as he calculates the odds of the cards that are left falling due."

"But it's still a gamble," she insisted. "You could lose more."

Harlow let his gaze wander over her. "That is why it's a hazardous game. There is always an element of luck. Are you feeling lucky? Luckier than your father?"

The mention of her father cooled Caitlin's satisfaction in picking up the game so quickly.

"How can you sit there and boast of the way you ruined my father?" she snapped. "I assure you, I won't be as easy to ruin."

He didn't look away or appear embarrassed. Instead, he reached out and cupped her face in his hand. "If I made it known you were here on your own, alone with two rakehells, you'd already be ruined. No, it is not your ruin I want."

In spite of her resolve not to let him rattle her, Caitlin's breathing quickened. Her heart missed a beat, then jumped into her throat. After a quick swallow, she managed to curl her lip. "No, it is a house that does not belong to you."

He had the audacity to laugh. "But it *does* belong to me. That is why you are here. Let's not forget that point."

Caitlin fought to focus her mind back on the task at hand: to learn faro and to win the first challenge. She did not wish to have to win the cake baking. That challenge could go either way given her lack of cooking skills.

The glittering regard in Dangerfield's darkening eyes made her feel hot and uncomfortable—and more than a little unsettled. She itched to cross her arms over her breast, even though she had little in the way of a bosom to ogle. She was half convinced he could see through her layers of clothing to her naked form beneath and she was worried that what he saw wouldn't entice him. Her mind pictured Larissa's voluptuous figure, and envy streaked over her heated skin.

What was wrong with her?

She glanced at the clock on the mantle and then back down at cards in front of her. "It's time I left. My father may miss me if I'm out too long."

"I shall see you home."

She had been placing her coppers back on the table, but Dangerfield's cool effrontery had her chin jerk up. "No. That won't be necessary. If my father saw me with you . . ."

"I shall escort Lady Southall home."

Henry's voice brooked no nonsense. Her shoulders relaxed in relief. The journey would give her a chance to question him.

"No." Dangerfield's response came out as a growl. "I don't trust her with you, Henry. She'll beguile you into revealing secrets best kept. Won't you, vixen?"

Provoking man. "Of course I will," she snapped. "Or I'd try." She turned to Henry and gave him a smile that was both apology and thanks. "Please stay, my lord. I'm quite capable of seeing myself home. I've been seeing myself home for quite a few years now."

"Nevertheless," Dangerfield said as Henry bowed and reddened once more. "I shall ride with you until you reach the boundary of Bridgenorth."

His tone told her it would be useless to argue, so she didn't. "Suit yourself." She pulled on her gloves, determined not to speak another word to him, and to drive home as though he were merely a shadow in her wake.

If the woman thought she was going to treat him as though he didn't exist she was going to have to think again. More than once.

Dangerfield waited until she tried to sweep out past him before catching her elbow.

The delicate bones under his hand did not match her Amazon personality. The softness and heat of her body through the cloth sent messages racing to the part of his anatomy he should keep under control around her. The last thing he needed, if he were to win this challenge, was a woman who understood the power she had over him.

She immediately wrenched her arm free. "Let go. There is no need for you to touch me."

He stared down into eyes stormy with anger . . . and something else. Desire? Yes. She was affected by him—and the reality of what that could mean almost unmanned him. The impulse to make those stunning, ethereal, green eyes deepen in sensual delight, nearly overcame his good sense.

But no. He would not deviate from his plan. While he had no qualms about seducing her it would be on his terms and according to his timetable. Winning the wager came first. Her seduction second. Her agreement to marry third. In that order.

He stepped away from her. "All that fire," he murmured. "Save it for when you come to my bed. It will enhance the pleasure." He noted the flare in her gaze, the ripple in her throat as she gave a hard swallow, and smiled. "After you, my lady." And gestured for her to precede him from the room.

Stepping around him, she dragged in a breath that held a distinct—and satisfying—tremor. "I can't see what women see in you. You're such a bore."

"Ah," he said to her departing back. "But then you've not had the pleasure of seeing all of me."

Henry sighed. The only response from Caitlin was the tightening of her shoulders and a small misstep.

She had driven no more than a mile from the lodge, with her unwanted escort on *Champers* trotting along beside her, when they rounded a bend and almost collided with a large carriage. A carriage bearing the Dangerfield crest.

Luckily, neither vehicle was moving very fast and Caitlin

had time to pull the reins hard to the left and run off onto the grass verge.

Dangerfield, cursing, rode ahead to chastise the coachman. But before he could reach it, the carriage came to a halt, the door was flung open, and a young lad sporting a very black and swollen eye jumped down.

"I say," he called. "That was close. Are you all right, miss?"

Caitlin had no time to answer him. He'd already seen the horseman heading his way.

"Harlow." The boy raced toward Dangerfield's horse. "You *are* still at Telford. I was concerned you'd leave before I arrived home from school."

This must be Dangerfield's younger brother, Caitlin decided, still humming with shock at the close call. At least he appeared to be unaffected by the incident.

Dangerfield did not dismount as the boy ran up. "I promised in my letter I would be here." He glanced across to where she sat, and there was the oddest look upon his face. But only for a moment. Then he returned his attention to the boy. "Jeremy, why don't you jump back in the carriage and calm mother? I'll see you back at Telford Court. Then," his tone turned dry, "you can tell me all about the black eye."

Before the boy could respond a woman stepped down from the carriage. "No need, Harlow. Your mother could do with a stretch."

Walking toward Caitlin's gig she smiled wryly. "I'm Lydia Telford. I'm sorry, my dear, I hope we did not give you a fright."

Caitlin had never met Dangerfield's mother. She'd seen her from afar but never been invited to approach. Harlow looked so much like her.

The Duchess was still an attractive woman. Only a glimmer of grey showed in the fair tresses. However, while Harlow's face resembled his mother's fine aristocratic features, he must have received his dark curls from his father. Caitlin didn't remember the previous Duke at all.

"Likewise, Duchess," she responded, politely. "I hope you were not hurt."

"Not at all. Harlow you must introduce me to your companion, although I can guess who this delightful young woman is. You must be Lady Caitlin Southall."

As she spoke the young boy—Jeremy—moved to his mother's side, staring at Caitlin as though she were some evil monster he'd discovered under his bed. The ferocious expression on his face made him far less attractive than she'd originally thought.

"Lady Southall." The Duchess spoke hesitantly. "May I present my younger son, Jeremy. Jeremy, make your bow to our neighbor, Lady Southall."

But the boy didn't move—except to look her over. Then a sneer formed on his lips. "I refuse to acknowledge a Bridgenorth," he said. And with that he turned on his heel and stalked back to wait by the carriage.

The Duchess's face paled to the color of milk and her fingers tightened.

"Mother." Harlow urged his horse closer. "It's late. Lady Southall must get home."

Caitlin understood neither the hatred spewing like sulphur from Jeremy's mouth nor the urgency in Harlow's tone.

His mother ignored him. "Caitlin—I may call you Caitlin?"

Still completely taken aback, Caitlin could only nod agreement.

"Thank you. Please, Caitlin. Forgive my son. He is young and does not think before he speaks."

It was more than that, Caitlin knew, but as she had no idea as to the origin of the bad blood between the Dangerfields and her father there was little she could say except, "Think nothing of it, Your Grace." After all, it wasn't the duchess's fault that her son—both her sons—seemed unable to be civil to their neighbors. Why should Caitlin care? All she required was the opportunity to win her house back.

"Since Jeremy has chosen to be rude," the duchess continued, "I do hope my eldest son is not bothering you."

"Not at all. He has been helping me with a project dear to my heart." That, at least, was true.

"How interesting." The duchess sent Dangerfield a beaming smile. "I do hope Harlow remembers that he is a gentleman."

Dangerfield looked even more uncomfortable and his mother laughed. "I heard some interesting gossip in London, Harlow. I shall discuss it with you when you get home."

Caitlin watched, fascinated, as the dreaded Duke of Dangerfield's cheeks flushed a very unmanly shade of pink.

"Mother, is there any need for this?"

"Absolutely. We shall discuss the significance of your social schedule later this evening. Don't be late I shall be waiting up. It has been lovely to meet you, Lady Southall." And, with another smile, the duchess turned back toward the carriage. "Come along, Jeremy."

"Can't I ride back with you, Harlow?" Jeremy asked.

"Not today," Dangerfield said. "I have to see Lady Southall home first. You go with mother. We can go out riding tomorrow morning."

Once again the boy shot a furious glare at Caitlin. She, in turn, studied him, making sure to keep her face as expressionless as she could. What on earth was wrong with the boy? She couldn't understand why he'd taken such an aversion to her.

He didn't look much like Harlow. They both had dark hair, but Jeremy's face was longer, not as square. He had the same nose, like their mother's, straight and in proportion to the rest of his face, but his eyes were nothing like Harlow's. Harlow had his mother's beautiful, wide gray eyes, accentuated by long black lashes. Jeremy's eyes were more hooded and she couldn't quite make out the color. But he looked somewhat familiar. And he certainly looked a mess with his black and swollen eye. He'd been in a fight. There were scratches on his cheek and his knuckles were scabbed.

She tried not to listen to the pair's private conversation, but Jeremy was so loud.

"How did you get the black eye?" Dangerfield looked grim.

Jeremy flushed and bit his lip. "It was nothing of importance. A few of us were practicing our boxing. My face accidentally got in the way."

Harlow couldn't see Jeremy's expression, but Caitlin could. The boy was lying. Why?

Harlow must have guessed this because he said, "Do you need me to come to the school?"

"No." Jeremy's chin lifted and his fists clenched tight. "I can fight my own battles, thank you. I don't need you to treat me as if I'm still a child. I can manage on my own. But what are you doing with *her*?" He stabbed a finger accusingly at Caitlin. "I don't need my older brother, the Duke, to marry a Bridgenorth just so I . . ."

"Be quiet." The ice in Dangerfield's tone was enough to freeze his brother into silence, but it was too late to retrieve the words.

Need him to marry a Bridgenorth? What on earth did Jeremy mean by that? Was this why Dangerfield was trying to ruin her? To try and force her into marriage?

Caitlin almost laughed aloud. The Duke of Dangerfield was the last man on earth she'd consider marrying. The Duke loved women. All women. Numerous women. More women then she could imagine. And that was the problem.

She wanted her husband to love only her.

Besides, if they married they would undoubtedly come to

51

blows. The man was so arrogant, so overbearing, so . . . so . . . so male! And her response to him frightened her.

She glanced at him out of the corner of her eye. There was no doubt he was handsome. Too handsome. How could she compete with the rest of the female population? They all longed to be in his bed. Even her own body responded to his beauty. But somehow his spectacular dark looks made the prospect of . . . of sharing his bed—

Her panic built, threatening to choke her.

Now it was more imperative than ever to win their wager. She couldn't find herself betrothed to the Duke of Dangerfield. Not after what he'd done to her father. To her.

She gave herself a little shake. It was getting late. She must hurry home. The last thing she needed was for her father to ask difficult questions. She hated lying.

"Thank you for your escort, Your Grace," she said with all the calm and *hauteur* she could manage. "I can see myself home from here—"

Jeremy snorted. "See, there is no need to fuss over a Bridgenorth."

"Jeremy, that is enough." Harlow's voice fairly shook with anger. "Apologize to Lady Southall. Immediately."

Jeremy bowed exaggeratedly low. "I do *apologize*. Give my regards to your father." And he marched back to the carriage without a further glance at either his brother or Caitlin.

Really, Caitlin thought as she maneuvered the gig back onto the road, the boy seemed a trifle unhinged. There was real animosity in those cold eyes. Why? What had her father done to deserve this hatred? She wasn't sure she wanted to know.

By the time she—still escorted by Dangerfield—reached the gates of Mansfield Manor she was fuming.

Nor did Dangerfield give her any time to ask him questions. He merely inclined his head, said, "Until tomorrow," and galloped back off toward Telford Court.

"How extraordinary." Caitlin said out loud.

She wished she had someone she could talk to about the Duke and her father. What had happened in the past to cause such a rift? Why did he want the Bridgenorth estate so badly? Why should he consider marrying to get it when he'd already won it? And why, if the house meant so much to him, risk losing it again in a wager? Unless he was sure of victory.

She rubbed her nape. Nothing about this made sense.

Cheat. Would a man like the duke cheat? No. The idea was laughable. It was beneath him. *Yet he would force you into his bed.* That was not honorable.

Caitlin didn't know what to think. She'd have to watch him closely. She didn't mind losing in a fair wager, but if he tried to anything underhanded, she'd . . . What would she do?

Well, she certainly wasn't going to offer herself up to a *cheat.*

She'd draw the line at that.

CHAPTER FIVE

His mother's inspection might have been as disinterested as that of a stranger, but Dangerfield had to fight to resist the urge to tug at his cravat. She knew him too well. Dammit, he could even feel embarrassment warm his cheeks.

He made his face form a relaxed smile. "I hope you had a pleasant stay in town."

His mother shrugged, clearly enjoying his discomfiture. "It was lovely to catch up with friends. Listen to the gossip doing the rounds. However, it was rather unnerving to hear my son was the topic of conversation. I learned you'd managed to win Mansfield Manor. All they could talk about was how skillful, you'd been when playing Bridgenorth. And how ruthless."

"I did not force the man to play, or to wager his estate."

"You understood his weakness and played on it."

Harlow's voice turned cold. "As he played on your weakness fourteen years ago. I thought you'd be pleased. I managed to hurt him in the only place he feels anything—his purse."

"It is his loss, my dear. In every way." She smiled, but her eyes glittered with unshed tears. "But it is hard for me to stay angry at the man who gave me Jeremy. I'll never think of my boy as a mistake or a sin."

Harlow's anger lessened at his mother's smile. "I did this for Jeremy. I promised him." She was right. It was Bridgenorth's loss. Jeremy was a fine boy. "Jeremy's a corker. That's why he deserves Mansfield Manor."

"Come." His mother patted the settee beside her. "Don't look at me like that. You're not too old to sit with your mother. I'm lucky to have Jeremy, with you so grown up and busy with your own life. I hope winning Mansfield Manor will help you let go of the past. Are you satisfied now?"

"Perfectly." He sat and she took his hand in hers.

He would not be made the villain here. Not after he'd had to pick up the pieces of his mother's shattered heart when not much older than his brother. "Jeremy will get what rightfully belongs to him." He let none of his simmering resentment show on his face.

Such a pity his mother smelt blood.

"So interesting, then, that the first person I see you with on my return is Caitlin Southall. She is as innocent as Jeremy in this mess."

He felt his cravat tighten around his neck. "She is upset, obviously, to lose her home."

"Of course. And?"

It took work to keep his features blank, but the last thing he needed was his mother interfering in his plans. "She asked for the chance to win the house back." When his mother's eyebrow lifted, he continued, "And I gave it to her."

"Oh?" Lydia laughed, a ripple of amusement. "I wonder why? Everyone in London knows how long you've waited to get your hands on Mansfield. And yet all his daughter had to do was ask and you're ready to give it up?"

Caitlin's face and succulent body shimmered into Harlow's

mind's eye. He shifted restlessly and cursed his mother's interference. "I felt honor-bound to do so. The house was her mother's and held in trust for her. Bridgenorth didn't really have the right to stake it."

"Then why not simply give it back to her? If it was to be Caitlin's it never really could have been Jeremy's. Maybe that is why Bridgenorth wouldn't acknowledge him. He was embarrassed to admit there was nothing to give him. The title couldn't go to Jeremy as he is illegitimate, and the estate was not Bridgenorth's to dispose of."

"Perhaps." His mother's question left him unsettled. "But I can't simply give it to her. People would assume the worst and talk."

"Is that because she's a beautiful, unmarried young woman?" He nodded. "I see. So will you let her win?"

"That depends on Jeremy—and I can't see him releasing me from my promise. He hates Bridgenorth. I can't say I blame him." He met his mother's disconcertingly sharp gaze. "Therefore I've instigated a plan where *when* I win I both keep the house and protect Caitlin's reputation."

His mother's hand fluttered outward. "I don't see how you can achieve that unless you marry—" Her mouth dropped open for a second before she composed herself. "Marriage? You'll offer her marriage? That seems somewhat extreme. You hardly know her."

He shrugged. "She has everything I require in a wife. Breeding, beauty, intelligence—what more do I need? First, I have to win the wager, and second, Caitlin has to accept."

Her eyes narrowed and her stare sharpened even more. "You like her, even admire her. That's why you have no objections. Good. It's a fine start to a marriage." She kissed his cheek. "Why not simply ask for her hand? You think she won't accept?" At his nod she laughed. "I believe this girl might be perfect for you. You need a woman who sees past that smile of yours." Her own smile died and she looked dismayed. "But Jeremy won't like it."

Harlow rubbed his jaw. "I can't think of what else to do. This way everyone wins. Jeremy can still have Mansfield Manor, Caitlin is protected by marriage to me and you, mother, get your much sought-after grandchild, while I get my heir."

"Your solution sounds logical, but I have a feeling this will become far more complicated. What happens if you don't win the wager?"

"Then I am honor-bound to give her back Mansfield Manor."

His mother shook her head. "Then you best ensure you win. Jeremy would never forgive you for gaining him his dream and then gambling it away. I don't want him hurt. He has been hurt enough. Did you see his face? School is not easy but he refuses to give in and leave."

"Don't worry. I have no intention of losing. There is no way I will lose the first challenge and Marcus is overseeing the final challenge. A horse race over a mile. I believe he is picking a course more suited to *Hero*. Caitlin thinks she has the fastest horse. She has no idea I own a horse like *Hero*."

"*The best laid schemes o' mice an' men . . .* Take care, Harlow. Nothing is certain where people's lives and feelings are concerned."

Outside the door to his mother's sitting room Jeremy let the fury Harlow's words released flow through his veins like a river in flood.

His brother was about to betray him.

Harlow had promised Mansfield and the estate would be his by right, and that Harlow would procure it for him. It was Jeremy's boast of ownership that earned him his latest fight at school. But he hadn't cared about the pain of the beating because he'd done it. He had Mansfield and he no longer cared that his father, his sire, abandoned him and left him to wallow in illegitimacy.

So, how could his brother go back on his promise after everything Jeremy had endured? Now he risked losing it—and to Caitlin Southall.

He crept back to his room, his mind in turmoil. Beautiful women were Harlow's weakness, and Caitlin was very pretty. But to wager Jeremy's birthright when his brother had sworn he'd get it for him? No. Many women lay down and opened their legs for his brother. Why did Harlow have to lust after Caitlin Southall when he could have any woman he chose?

Jeremy's stomach roiled and churned. Had Harlow sold him out for a pretty smile and a woman to bed? He could not let that happen. Mansfield Manor was his by rights. The Earl of Bridgenorth had denied him his birthright when he made him a bastard. He would not let the man's daughter destroy his rightful future a second time.

He needed to think. He needed to plan. He needed to ensure Caitlin Southall did not win.

Whatever it took, he would become the owner of Mansfield Manor.

CHAPTER SIX

Caitlin presented herself at Ashley House a little before seven in the evening. The Faro match would begin at seven-thirty. Thankfully, her father had gone to London the previous day.

Her body hurt with each step, her muscles drawn tight as a bowstring about to be released. Nerves jangled and her stomach churned. She wondered if the duke was regretting his behavior. Could she, perhaps, play on his conscience and get him to withdraw.

Either way, she wanted it over. She'd learned all she was going to learn of Faro in the past few days. Her nerve would either hold or it wouldn't. She had just as much chance of winning as Harlow did.

However, just in case, she'd taken great care with her appearance tonight in order to give her an advantage. Her dress was cut indecently low. Very daring. Extremely daring, for her. She tried to ignore the chill settling on her chest. A good portion of her *décolletage* was prominently on display.

She needed the duke as distracted as possible if she was to have any hope of out-maneuvering his skilful wagers. She would create a diversion and hope his mind was on the bedding rather than the betting. If she won the first challenge, then the odds of winning the wager increased dramatically. Her baking skills could not be relied upon, but she had *Ace of Spades*. The horse race was hers for the taking.

Her cloak hid her "diversions" from view, but when Henry's butler signaled for the footman to take it from her shoulders her instinct was to tug the garment tighter around her shoulders. It took everything she had in her to let it go.

She felt naked and exposed.

The butler led her along to the library where she'd been practicing all week. She hadn't beaten Harlow once in their previous encounters. Surely tonight must be her night to win.

She asked the butler not to announce her and quietly slipped into the room. Marcus was laying out the Faro table. Henry was nowhere to be seen. Harlow stood facing the fire, a brandy balloon in his hand. It appeared as though he was trying to read the flames and, deep in thought, he did not hear her enter.

She stood watching him in that unguarded and somehow more human moment, the slightly stubborn jut of his chin pronounced. Despite her anger at being put in the position of having to barter herself in order to win back that which was rightfully hers, Caitlin couldn't fault the man in any other way.

He looked exceedingly handsome tonight and she was pleased that she'd made an effort to match him with her latest attire.

Her fascinated gaze traced the strong lines of his throat as they disappeared into a stark white cravat. His evening coat of midnight blue gave a bluish tint to his black curls. The cloth fit him like a tight glove molding a hand, stretching over his broad shoulders, tapering down to accentuate his muscled chest and lean waist, before curving over his *derrière* like a caress.

She scrunched her itching fingers into a fist. She mustn't touch. The urge to move closer and somehow absorb his masculinity almost overpowered her. Look away.

She ran an assessing gaze down the length of her body. Would he be as captivated by *her* charms? At the very least Caitlin hoped her looks would unsettle him as much as he unsettled her. She took a few deep breaths and moved silently into the room, heading toward the rows of books on the opposite wall.

She needed time to compose herself. He was too good at reading people. Like any predator, he'd circle her fear and dart in for easy pickings.

She sensed the moment when Harlow first noticed her arrival. The fine hairs at her nape bristled.

"I'm pleased to see you know how to keep time. You're early." He was standing too close behind her, the low *timbre* of his voice coaxing her to turn round.

She did so. Slowly. Wanting the full impact of her dress to overcome him. When she finally faced him, she looked up into his eyes, her composure complete.

He gave a choked cough. "Good God, how's a man to concentrate with those staring at him all night? And I thought I preferred you in trousers." His eyes narrowed. "Well played, Lady Southall."

"Thank you." She felt a hint of smile crease her lips.

It soon disappeared—shattered—when he reached out and trailed his fingers over the creamy swells of her breasts. She batted his hand away. His fingers returned, sweeping over the skin.

"What do you think you are doing?" she asked breathlessly. "Stop it."

"I'm evening the score," he almost growled.

He moved closer and she stepped backed until she hit the bookshelf behind her. He kept moving forward until the hardness of his chest crushed her breasts. She felt her nipples harden against the lace that was holding them discreetly hidden, just, from view.

"Can you imagine how good it will feel when my lips replace

my fingers? When I lick every inch of your delectable, milky skin until you're purring with pleasure? When I finally take your taut nipple into my mouth and suckle, you'll scream my name."

The husky words saw her wits scatter.

Her corset was too tight. She couldn't breathe—and when she did, the scent of him invaded her senses, clouding her thinking. She felt her stomach flip, and heat pool between her thighs.

She was going to lose.

"When you come to my bed," he whispered. "I'll introduce you to such passion your head will spin."

It was already spinning. The passion already burned. It was hot and needy, just like the tension pooling in her belly. She had never been so aware of her breasts, or of the way a man could worship her body with just his eyes. Her small breasts, for once, felt trapped behind her clothing, begging to be freed.

Begging for his bare hands to glide across—

She looked into his eyes and saw triumph. He knew he could make her body crave for, burn for, combust with want of his touch. And he knew—*knew*—she would be thinking of nothing else all evening.

"Harlow." Henry's stern voice broke the spell.

With shame filling her body, and any advantage now in tatters—like her pride—Caitlin slipped out from between his hardness and the bookcase, away from the disturbing essence of him.

She walked toward the faro table taking big gulps of air. She could hear Henry's murmured chastisement . . . something about behaving like a gentleman. *Gentleman?* Harlow didn't know the meaning of the word.

The game commenced on time and Caitlin couldn't help the fleeting image of her house passing before her eyes. If she could only win this game. There was no way *Ace of Spades* would lose to Dangerfield's stallion *Champers*. She'd done her research. *Champers* was the fastest horse in his stable—in fact, the fastest horse he owned. *Champers* had also been entered into the Two-Thousand Guineas at Newmarket.

Her own light weight and small size gave her added speed. A win tonight would take the pressure off the baking challenge.

She gathered her wits and, as the first turn played, remembered her strategy.

She started conservatively, watched Harlow, and matched his bets. However, as they got nearer to the middle of the pack, she knew she'd have to change strategy if she were to win. She needed more coppers than he before they got down to the last few cards. If she were well ahead, Harlow would have to risk more on the last few turns.

To her frustration, the rest of the turns progressed evenly. When she won big, the next hand she lost big as well. Harlow won consistently. Not large amounts, but enough to see him inch into the lead. She was not losing, but neither was she gaining enough ground on his winnings. He watched every bet she made and countered it accordingly.

Finally they arrived at the moment of truth. The next turn would decide the game. They were down to the last three cards. She knew they were the Ten of Hearts, the Three of Spades and the King of Diamonds.

"I've taught you well," he said affably. He stared at the pile of coppers in front of her and then at his pile of the same relative size. "But are you willing to risk it all at the end? Women are not known for their bravado."

"I believe I've aptly demonstrated bravado by accepting this wager." With that statement she looked at his current bet. Harlow had wagered his entire pile of coppers on the King of Diamonds.

Caitlin closed her eyes to block out the glittering dare in Harlow's sinful eyes. He was goading her into making a mistake. If she simply matched his bet, then he would win as he had

63

slightly more coppers than her. If she simply bet everything on the chance a higher card was dealt—a two in three chance—she'd win if the losing card turned up happened to be the Three of Spades.

There was only one way to beat Harlow if the King of Diamonds was the player's card. She couldn't simply match his bet. That would only prolong the game. She opened her eyes and steeled herself for what was to come. Ignoring his raised eyebrow Caitlin said, "I call the last turn."

To call the last turn was to name the order in which the last three cards would play. Very risky, but this would see her trounce Harlow. It was the only way to win. All or nothing.

Harlow's mouth curved up. "Risky. Don't want to bet with me, sweeting?"

"It hasn't worked at any of our practices. This way, if the King is turned, I will still have a chance to beat you." She gave a mocking smile, "How's that for bravado?"

Henry sighed. "Caitlin, don't let him force you into taking risks."

Caitlin hesitated for a moment before impatiently saying, "This wager is a risk and no one forced me into it." She simply wanted it over. Her nerves were frayed and for once she felt the cards were on her side.

"So, what order do you call the last three cards?" Marcus asked, as the banker.

"Ten of Hearts, King of Diamonds, and Three of Spades."

Harlow shifted his feet slightly. She gave an inward whoop of triumph. He was nervous. If the King was the player's card, and she got her order right, then she'd win four times the amount he'd win and, more importantly, she'd win the game.

Win the first wager.

Marcus asked if they were ready, and when they both nodded he drew the loser's card. It was the Ten of Hearts, and Caitlin couldn't stop a squeal of delight. Henry clapped—before getting a cold look from Harlow.

The tension in the room was nearly audible as Marcus drew out the player's card. He hesitated before turning it over and Caitlin's heart rose to lodge in her throat. When she looked down the Three of Spades greeted her.

She'd lost.

But so had Harlow. Her shoulders slumped and she resigned herself to having to play another game.

"I win the first wager." Harlow's voice was filled with satisfaction.

Her head jerked up. "How so? You lost too, if I recall. You bet everything on the King."

He raised his hand and twirled a copper across his knuckles. "I bet everything but this one copper. I believe that makes me the winner."

Her mouth dried. She looked to Henry and saw her defeat in his eyes.

"I knew you'd be all in, it was the only move that would see you win. So I held one copper back. If I didn't win with the King, neither would you." Dangerfield leaned forward until his face was inches from hers. "But it wasn't who won the last turn. It was who won the most money overall. You kept nothing back. I did." He withdrew to his side of the table and held up the copper. "I win by one copper to none."

Caitlin looked as though a mule had kicked her in the stomach and, when she rose to her feet, she swayed, her face pale.

Henry rushed to her side to offer support.

She straightened and turned to him, her head held high. "Well played, Your Grace. If you'll excuse me gentlemen, it's been a long night and I wish to go home."

"I'll escort you." There was no way Harlow was letting her

drive home alone at night, especially in this state. She was hiding her disappointment well, but he saw through her stoic countenance to the devastation underneath.

"That won't be necessary," she said with steel in her tone.

He moved around to stand before her. "I insist. It's late at night and I'm responsible for you being here."

He watched her fight for composure. Her breaths were short and sharp and her fists clenched at her side.

Henry urged her to agree. "Don't let your pride drive your decisions. It would be safer to let Harlow see you home."

She eyed him as if he were a fire-breathing dragon. "Safer than what, I ask myself," she said, dryly.

"I assure you I will conduct myself as an utter gentleman."

"Do you know how?"

Her witty reply made Marcus laugh, and something akin to annoyance heat Harlow's blood. He *was* a gentleman. Only the hoyden standing in front of him ever made him forget that. Why was it so easy for her to bait him? He never usually cared what women—or for that matter, anyone—thought of him.

By the time she'd donned her cloak, Henry's butler announced her gig was ready.

"I'm sure you'll have better luck with the cake baking, Lady Southall," Henry said as he helped her into the driver's seat.

Caitlin patted Henry's hand and nodded goodbye to Marcus. Harlow secured *Champers* to the back of the gig before joining her.

The night was dry and warm, with a full moon above—the perfect setting for seduction and a romantic carriage ride with a beautiful woman. Except, of course, the woman was feeling anything but romantic.

The first mile flew past in stony silence with Caitlin sitting as far away from him as possible. He moved his leg sideways until it brushed hers, and felt her shiver at the contact. Whether in pleasure or dislike he wasn't sure.

"Do you have to take up so much room?" she snapped at last.

Dislike. "Tsk. I'd never have thought you a sore loser."

"Just because I do not wish to rub against your person does not make me a sore loser. Besides, I'm not stupid. You touched me on purpose."

"Why do you have to make everything a battle, Caitlin? I did not challenge you to this wager. You approached me. I also did not have to accept your challenge. I won Mansfield Manor fairly."

"Why?" The word seemed to sigh from her. "I do not understand why you hate my father. You don't need Mansfield Manor. You deliberately went after it. Why? That's all I wish to know."

Harlow's jaw clenched. What did he tell her? He'd promised Jeremy that he would never reveal the truth of Jeremy's parentage to her. The boy was adamant. "You need to ask your father that question."

"My father?" Caitlin gave an unladylike snort. "He won't tell me either. Besides, my father rarely speaks to me unless it is to berate me. I'm a disappointment. He wanted a son."

Harlow tried to keep the anger out of his voice. "If he wanted a son why did he not remarry? Your mother died when he was still in his prime."

She finally faced him. "I don't know. I've often asked myself that question. He was always looking for a wealthy heiress, or someone with a large dowry. Perhaps they saw that all my father was really after was money. A woman with means is unlikely to waste herself on a man who sees her as nothing but a way to procure a fortune."

"You don't like your father much."

"How can I like him when I don't respect him? He's done nothing with his life. And now he's taken from me the one thing that was supposed to be mine."

The pain in her voice was a living thing. "Why is the house so important to you? You are young and beautiful. You could marry and leave your past behind you."

She laughed, and the desperation in the sound sent shivers down his back.

"How, Your Grace? How would I meet these men who may wish to marry me? Me, with nothing. My father forbade me a Season, because it was a waste of money. I'm sure he is already planning to auction me off to the highest bidder. His decrepit friend, Viscount Bassinger, has been sniffing around my petticoats almost since I left the schoolroom. Father is simply trying to wear me down into accepting him. He thinks that now Mansfield is gone, and I have nothing, I'll surrender. If I had my home, if I had a way . . ."

He stiffened. Horror cloaked his skin in a slick sweat. *This* was why she wanted the house so desperately. Knowing Viscount Bassinger he could well understand it. The man was a pervert of the highest order and riddled with the pox.

His mouth firmed into a grim line. Bassinger would offer indecent amounts for an untouched beauty like Caitlin in his bed, and neither Bridgenorth nor Bassinger were beneath kidnap and coercion.

Now, more than ever, he needed to persuade her to marry him. "You've met me. Why not forget this silly wager? You can marry me."

She gasped beside him, her head almost spinning in her haste to look at him. "But . . . But . . . Why? You have won the first wager, and are well on the way to winning the whole bet. Then I'd be forced into your bed. Why offer marriage for something that looks more like a sure thing? You can't want me that much." She shook her head, her eyes open wide. "I'll never understand men."

He'd expected a refusal. Even so, it hurt. "Why are you opposed to marrying me? I believe you're the first female ever to decline a duke's proposal. In fact, you're the first woman I've ever proposed to."

"You wouldn't understand. You're a man. Men view marriage differently."

"Tell me," he urged.

She was silent so long he began to believe she wouldn't answer. Then—

"I want to marry." It was a bitter whisper. "I want children and a family. But I want love too. My parents, believe it or not, had a love match. My mother loved my father, faults and all. He was a penniless Earl and she the daughter of a wealthy Baron. He didn't marry her for Mansfield Manor. In his youth he could have had any wealthy heiress, but he picked my mother. He was very handsome, my mother told me. Cook says he really only started gambling when mother got sick. It took her two years to die—such a painful death—and watching her fade away broke his heart, Cook said. He could not cope with his grief, and used drinking and gambling as an escape."

She stopped speaking and he let the sounds of the night soothe her until she spoke again.

"Her death changed him. He became bitter. Mean." She turned to look at him in the moonlight and shadows. "The thought of spending the rest of my life with a man who does not love me, saddens me. It would be very lonely."

"But you'd have children and a house to run. Your life would have purpose."

In a quiet voice she said, "What happens when the children are grown, and my son marries, and I no longer have a house to run, or a family to take care of?"

He didn't know what to say to that.

She continued. "I guess a man like you would still have other women to spend time with. You might no longer be the handsome catch you are now, and you may find it more difficult to attract the most sought-after courtesans when you're middle aged, but there will still be those who, needing money, would be happy to spend time with you. If I cannot compete with courtesans while in my youth, if my husband valued his relationship with them more highly than he regarded me, how could I compete with them when I'm old? Only a man who loved me—and only me—would see that growing old at my side would give him far more joy than meaningless romps with women who see him as simply a purse to pluck."

Dangerfield swallowed back a lump in his throat. He had to admit he'd not thought about growing old. Didn't like to think about it. He assumed he'd have a family. Estates to run. He'd arrogantly assumed that would be enough. But her words jarred something deep in his soul.

He remembered his father, and the way he'd looked at his mother. It was as though, for him, the light left the room whenever she did. Harlow couldn't remember a time when his father stayed away from home unless his wife and son were with him.

His father loved his mother and she'd loved him.

That sort of love—the all-consuming love—scared him. He saw what it did to his mother when his father died. But what was the alternative? A life of duty and empty pleasure? He was already growing tired of the empty, meaningless beddings with women whose names he could scarcely recall.

For the first time in his life he wanted more. Caitlin made him want more.

She spoke, and it was as if she'd read his thoughts. "Sometimes you can be surrounded by people and still be alone. I wish for something more from my life. I want companionship, shared joys and love. Is that wrong?"

He took her tiny hand in his and squeezed. "No." He shook his head. "No, it's not wrong. Mayhap hard to find, but not wrong." He let her hand go and immediately missed its warmth.

70

"I'm sorry. For what it's worth I'm sorry your father lost your home."

"Don't be. If it hadn't been to you it would have been to someone else. At least you have allowed me a chance to win it back."

She'd barely finished speaking when Harlow guided the gig in through the gates of Mansfield Manor and drew it to a halt.

Then, to her astonishment, he turned to her and took her face in his hands. "You," he said, softly, "are an amazing woman, Lady Southall. Any man would be lucky to have you as his wife." And before she could gather her wits, he kissed her.

It was a kiss that sent latent heat to her every extremity. His lips on hers were pure bliss. His tongue swept into her mouth, stoking her pleasure, and melting her from the inside.

She moaned. He answered her moan with a deep groan of his own and pulled her onto his lap. His throaty sounds of pleasure roused a burst of eager sensations within her. She had never experienced anything like it. It was terrifying. Exciting. Terrifying. Excit—

A whimper escaped her as his hand, burning in its gentleness, stroked her neck, her throat, her shoulders in searing caresses.

She pushed into his hardness and he deepened the kiss. The slow, deliberate licks of his tongue sent joy arrowing down her spine until her toes curled. She felt as if she was being consumed by him, being pulled into his world of pleasure and lust, and she finally understood its allure. She liked it.

She wanted more.

Perhaps coming to his bed would not be difficult at all.

Harlow, too, had fallen under pleasure's spell; she could feel it in him, hear it in his needy moan, soft and low. He groaned her name and tilted his head the other way, kissing again with a sweet, drowning depth.

His hands crept under the edge of her dress, and warmth seared along her weakened limbs as his fingers trailed up her legs. Her womanly centre pulsed with need. She knew it was wicked, but she longed for his touch.

As though he had heard her Harlow suddenly stopped, his breathing rough. He stayed close, his forehead resting on hers. His fingers continued stroking her leg. "Your skin is like silk beneath my touch."

She squirmed in his lap and felt his arousal beneath her bottom. He groaned.

"Christ, I want you."

She froze.

His hand rose to the top of her thighs. He hesitated, but only for a moment. "Let me give you a taste of the pleasure you'll find in my bed." Before she could respond, his finger stroked through her curls . . . and any thought she might have had of stopping him, fled.

"God," he whispered in her ear, "you're so wet for me."

She didn't know if that was a good thing or bad, but at that moment she did not care. She clung to him, not wanting him to stop.

His thumb brushed over her nub as his finger slid deep within her. Her breathing faltered, and then returned in little gasps. She couldn't stop her hips from lifting in time to the penetration and withdrawal.

Soon one finger became two, his thumb continued to circle, and when he took her mouth again and plunged his tongue deep within, her world erupted behind her closed eyelids. Stars burst and music echoed in her head as she shattered in his arms.

She came down to earth slowly. His hand was still stroking her bare thigh above her stocking. She finally opened her eyes and saw him watching her with concern etched into his features. She gave a shaky smile.

His mouth broke into a relieved grin but his eyes were still full of molten fire and his arousal pulsed beneath her . . . and she knew it was time to leave before she did something foolish. Even more foolish.

She moved off his lap, straightened her clothing, and gathered up her horse's reins. "Thank you, Your Grace." She couldn't look at him. "That was . . . quite enjoyable. But now I must get home."

For a heartbeat nothing happened. Then Dangerfield threw his head back and laughed. Still laughing, he jumped to the ground and moved behind the gig to untie his stallion. "When I have you in my bed, I hope the words you use to describe our joining will be more honest than 'quite enjoyable'."

She still didn't look at him. "Just because I have lost the first challenge does not mean I will lose the wager."

"Perhaps." She recognized the movement beside her as a bow of farewell. "But think how enjoyable the losing will be."

Her face heated and she couldn't think of a reply, so she simply coaxed her horse to move. Dangerfield's delighted chuckle followed her as she rolled up the drive. Worse, she could think of nothing but the pleasure he'd given her. For one fleeting moment the desire to lose almost outweighed her need to win. Then she rounded the bend and saw Mansfield Manor before her. Remembered what it stood for—freedom to live the life she wanted.

And yet, everything had changed.

What *did* she want?

Dangerfield had offered her marriage. He must think he was going to lose. So he'd dangled in front of her what he thought was the greater prize—his name.

Mansfield Manor was her safety net, the object that would ensure she did not end up marrying a man like Harlow Telford, Duke of Dangerfield. He was a man who saw a woman as a pleasurable pursuit rather than a true partner. Harlow was a man who did not know the meaning of the words 'love' or 'commit-ment'. She would be safe, cared for, but not loved.

His own needs came first.

But they hadn't tonight. Tonight the only one who had received true pleasure was her.

And she enjoyed it.

And she wanted more.

CHAPTER SEVEN

The long ride home gave Harlow time to cool the agony of his arousal. While he always ensured his partners received mind-blowing pleasure, never before had he denied his own. It was a painful jolt of reality.

Tonight, all he'd wanted was Caitlin's pleasure. The thought disturbed him.

He knew, whichever way the wager ended, she would have little choice but to marry him. However, he'd rather she accepted his proposal of her own free will. Although she hadn't been repulsed by the idea, she hadn't swooned with joy, either. He respected her need for more from a marriage. However, she wanted something he didn't think he could give. She wanted his heart.

Why did the thought of opening up to her and letting her share his life—all of his life—scare him? Was he worried she would find him lacking?

When he really considered how he lived his life he was embarrassed by how little he actually did.

He rarely bothered with his parliamentary duty. What did

he know of running a country? He employed the best managers so his estates ran perfectly well without him. His investments flourished due to Marcus's skills, and his home ran perfectly thanks to his mother.

But what did *he* do? What did *he* contribute?

He moved uneasily in the saddle, uncomfortable with the man Caitlin was forcing him to meet.

He'd accepted this wager as a means to relieve his boredom. It didn't matter if Caitlin won her house back. It only mattered that he got what he wanted—Caitlin in his bed, a wife he could leave to run his household and provide heirs, and the chance to make good on his promise to Jeremy.

He hadn't considered that Caitlin wouldn't be in raptures over the idea of marrying a duke. In fact, he hadn't considered Caitlin's wishes at all.

He was an arrogant son-of-a-bitch.

He handed *Champers*'s reins to his groom and walked into his house, sober and chastened.

Tonight had been a revelation. Caitlin stirred more than his lust. He wanted her respect. He wanted to be . . . more. More for her. He suddenly found himself in the unenviable position of wanting a woman to be proud of him. He wanted her to look at him with pride, rather than simply seeing him as a title and a means to a life of wealth and ease.

However, from where he stood, winning the wager would be easier. Caitlin had stripped him bare and she was not enamored of the man underneath his title and trappings. What could he do? He had to think of something.

There was one way certain to earn her respect, and perhaps soften her toward him: give her back Mansfield Manor.

But therein lay the problem. He'd promised Jeremy—the innocent party is all this—that he would procure Mansfield Manor for him, and he would not go back on his word. Not without Jeremy's approval. Caitlin would understand that his honor dictated he fulfill his promise to his brother.

Especially since Jeremy was her brother too.

Which led to another problem. Caitlin still considered herself an only child. She did not know she had a brother . . . a half-brother. Would she be pleased? He was sure she'd be thrilled to find she had more family, but Jeremy refused to let him tell her.

Yes, he decided. It was time the past was dealt with. It would help everyone—his mother, brother, and Caitlin—if they could all move on.

He'd talk to Jeremy in the morning. Perhaps the boy would not hold him to his promise. He could buy Jeremy any estate he wanted, and give Mansfield Manor to Caitlin with a clear conscience.

He would not use it to force her to marry him. He needed her to marry him because it was what she wanted. Because the fulfilling life she had dangled in front of his eyes he *also* wanted—and he wanted her to choose to have it with him.

As he walked up the stairs to his bedchamber he marveled at how suddenly the word "wedding" brought only a satisfied smile to his lips.

Caitlin spent the next morning racing across the Bridgenorth fields trying to erase Harlow's lovemaking from her mind. She was only partially successful.

He'd offered her marriage. *Marriage.*

She kept reciting her list, and pointing out to herself that Dangerfield did not meet her stringent requirements. He did not love her and—other than keeping her from winning back Mansfield Manor—he had no interest in her.

Yet, for all that, the offer was tempting. Her body sang at the thought of him and suddenly she felt like tearing up her silly list.

She was, therefore, very pleased to have a week before she'd have to face him in the bake-off. Perhaps by then her body would accept what her mind already knew—the Duke of Dangerfield was not husband material.

The afternoon found Caitlin in the village ensconced in Mrs. Darcy's over-heated parlor while the old lady fussed about, making tea and tempting her with freshly baked scones. As she smothered her scone with jam and cream, Caitlin managed to slip in her request that Mrs. Darcy teach her how to bake a cake.

"A cake?" A sly smile twitched on Mrs. Darcy's lips. "You wish me to give you cooking lessons? How interesting. Why have you not asked your Cook to teach you?"

"I wish to learn from the best." It was no lie, but she would use flattery to get Mrs. Darcy's agreement if she had to. "You have won the village bake-off for the past five years."

"Well, well." Mrs. Darcy leaned back in her chair. "It appears I'm in demand today."

Caitlin willed her face to hold her beguiling smile. "I'm sure you're baking is always in demand, but I'm here for lessons."

"So you said." Mrs. Darcy beamed knowingly. "But how strange. His Grace was here only this morning requesting the same thing."

Damn the man! "Really?" Caitlin bit viciously into her scone. "That *is* odd."

"Yes, indeed. He wishes to surprise a lady love I assume, for he would not divulge who he was making the cake for."

The scone stuck in Caitlin's suddenly very dry throat. Coughing, she scrabbled for her cup and a hasty gulp tea. How on earth could Dangerfield know about Mrs. Darcy? He'd never once attended the church fete.

Once her coughing fit ended, she took the napkin Mrs. Darcy offered and wiped her eyes.

"Quite the coup for me to teach the Duke of Dangerfield," the old lady said, happily. "I'll be the envy of every baker from here to London, I should think."

"Quite. Very advantageous for you. I know it's a lot to ask, but would you have time to teach both of us—separately?"

But Mrs. Darcy shook her cap-covered head. "I would have time if I could teach both of you together."

Caitlin's head lifted and her face went hot. "Oh, I'm sure the Duke won't wish to share your services."

"Why ever not?" She poured Caitlin more tea. "He's due any minute. Stay and finish your tea. I'll ask him. He's a lovely man. When he was young he used to come several times a week to my bakery. He loved my apple pie. He'd buy several slices, and then take them outside and share them with the other children. Such a polite and generous boy. He never lorded it over the other children. He always thought of others before himself."

The man had certainly changed then. Now the only person he thought of was himself. But before she could refuse Mrs. Darcy's offer there was a resounding knock at the door.

"That will be him now." And Mrs. Darcy bustled off to open the door. "Oh, Your Grace," Caitlin heard her say in delighted tones, "are those for me?"

"From my garden," replied Dangerfield. "I picked them myself."

As she heard Harlow step inside, Caitlin's misery swamped her, and sweat trickled down her back. She couldn't face him. Not after last night. Her nerves were too raw, her body too on edge. Her emotions still in a whirl. She'd caught the 'Dangerfield' disease and she was sure there was no cure. Her body craved both Mrs. Darcy's cream-covered scones and the Duke of Dangerfield, and neither was good for her—even in moderation. Abstinence seemed the only safe precaution.

To make matters worse, Caitlin couldn't forget that he'd proposed marriage last night, as calmly as if discussing the weather on a fine day. A man should be consumed with poetry, or at least demonstrate devotion, when offering marriage. A proposal without a declaration of undying love was nothing more than a business proposition.

Did he think that if she married him she'd simply forget about claiming Mansfield Manor? If she married him, he'd still own it. The house should be in trust for her and any of her female descendants.

Her eyes narrowed and she shot dagger looks in his direction as he sauntered into Mrs. Darcy's drawing room. Oh yes, he was up to something.

He was so tall—so large—in the confines of the room that it seemed as if all the space and air had been sucked out, making her light headed. When he saw her there, he halted, and a flicker of surprise crossed his face. Then he smiled, a slow, inviting smile.

A hot blade of excitement stabbed deep in her belly.

Eyes twinkling he bowed. "Beautiful as ever, Lady Southall. I hope I did not keep you out too late last night." He moved to take her hand and press a long, lingering, and totally inappropriate kiss on her knuckles. "I have not been able to think of anyone or anything but you, sweet lady."

Mrs. Darcy clapped her hands. "Oh, how nice. I did not realize you were so well acquainted. I have a favor to ask, Your Grace. Lady Southall would also like to learn how to bake a cake. Apparently she wishes to surprise her father."

His smile did not dim at the mention of her father. "I could not think of anything I'd like more than to share any experience with Lady Southall. I have wanted—no, *prayed*—for an excuse to spend more time with Caitlin."

Caitlin watched Mrs. Darcy's mouth drop open at Dangerfield's use of her first name. In essence, he had all but announced to the village that he was courting her. Now the news would spread faster than the bolt of lightning that had run down the bell tower last summer. The destruction would be just as severe.

If her father got wind of this . . .

A rush of emotion made Caitlin's face heat and her throat constrict. If he wished to see her ruined he had just planted the seed. The expectation of marriage would germinate in the villagers' heads and she would be forced to accept him.

He'd trapped her. Expertly.

She tried not to show any reaction to his ploy. "Your Grace, how kind. But I couldn't possibly intrude—"

And the stupidity of her words hit her like a hard slap. She was about to throw away her chance to win the wager, keep her home, and be free to make her own choices. What a fool! No. Dangerfield would not drive her away from her best chance to win the next challenge. Mansfield Manor was worth the discomfort of his closeness. She would stay. She would learn. And, what's more, she would *win*.

The silence in the room drew her attention to the fact both Mrs. Darcy and Harlow were watching her closely; Mrs. Darcy with suppressed excitement, and Harlow with mocking amusement.

"What time would be convenient for you to teach us, Mrs. Darcy," she asked, as sweetly as she could through clenched teeth, and pretending not to notice the triumph on Dangerfield's face.

Mrs. Darcy's face was wreathed in smiles. "No time like the present, is there, Your Grace? Come now, into the kitchen with you both. I have the prettiest apron for His Grace to wear."

Despite Caitlin's misgivings, the lesson was fun. She even saw a different side to Dangerfield. He was witty, amusing, and not above poking fun at himself. In fact, he'd been utterly charming. If she hadn't known that underneath his smile lay a ruthless wastrel and womanizer, she too might have succumbed.

It was almost four in the afternoon before Caitlin managed to slip away. The old lady still had Dangerfield trapped in conversation as she tried to cajole him into judging the bake-off for that year's village fete.

The sun was still sweltering hot. So was Caitlin, after hours in the heat of the kitchen—hot, sweaty, and covered in flour. Lily Pond, her swimming hole at the edge of Bridgenorth land, seemed to call to her.

And why not? None of the villagers used it. It wasn't stocked with fish, and the eels were easier to catch upstream. It was relatively private. High rushes bordered all sides, and the fact it was boggy in places and one could get stuck, kept most away.

Caitlin knew where to enter and leave the water, and the single time she had ever gotten stuck—eight years ago—she'd been rescued by the most handsome, and rudest, man she'd ever met.

She grumbled about that man now as she moved into the reeds and began to disrobe. She couldn't stop thinking about him and the wicked things he'd done last night. She'd never experienced anything like it. Passion. No wonder men and women frequently partook of pleasure.

After the afternoon's cooking lesson she finally had the courage to admit it to herself; she was attracted to the rake. It was impossible not to be.

Unfortunately, although the water lapping against her skin cooled her skin it didn't cool her memories. Dangerfield's touch, his lips, his fingers—her body remembered it all. And wanted more.

Wading in until she stood waist deep, Caitlin collapsed onto her back with a splash and a sigh, her arms outstretched, and let herself float. That was better. Soon all her silly thoughts of Harlow's animal magnetism would be washed and cleared by the silky coolness. *But losing the wager might not be so bad . . . and marrying Harlow . . . could be heaven . . .*

Dangerfield knew he should have resisted, but in all truth, he didn't want to. Hadn't intended to from the moment he'd seen her stepping like a naked goddess onto Lily Pond's lapping edge. Strange that they should both have the same idea—a cooling dip.

She'd reached waist high water by the time he'd flung off his clothes, eased into the pond, and dived. Now she was within reach . . . And he was out of breath—

He kicked up hard, cannoning out of the water beside her, tossing his hair so drops of water sprayed her shocked face.

Her squeal ripped the air apart, terror suddenly choked off as her mouth filled with water and she sank beneath the pond's surface.

She wouldn't drown—she swam too well for that—but it was fortunate for Harlow that the water was only waist deep. Fortunate in many ways. When Caitlin finally floundered to the surface and scrambled upright she was too shocked to realize how much of her was exposed. Yes, it was most fortunate indeed.

Urgent and driving lust arrowed to his groin.

"What a vision," he said, soft as a sigh. "A mermaid sent to tempt me into sinning." He took her unresisting hand and dragged her closer. Sighed at the feel of her small, pert breasts pressed against his chest. "Fancy the proper Lady Southall following me to my favorite pond."

"*My* pond," she corrected, still breathless. "You should let me go."

"You don't want me to, do you?"

He lifted his gaze from the delicate hand still pressed to the centre of his chest to the fine porcelain features of Caitlin's face. Her beauty held him spellbound. Desire hit like a lightning bolt, heat igniting in his veins until he was on fire. He could not resist her like this; her black hair plastered to her head, her eyes flared wide as if she'd discovered a present yet to be unwrapped, and her lips plump and glistening in the sun. He swooped down for a taste.

Her mouth was hot and welcoming. He plundered his bounty sweeping her hesitation aside.

When he released her for breath, and she looked up at him from her exotically tipped eyes—so potent a stare—he swore he felt her gaze caress his soul. Tightness travelled down his body in hot waves, settling low in his belly.

Mouth drying, pulse quickening, he stared back, his hand fisting beneath the water. Her lips parted.

He wondered how much of him she could actually see. She could certainly *feel* all of him. Had she ever encountered a naked man before? Was he her first? The thought thrilled him, increasing the tempo of his pulse considerably.

Caitlin continued to study him, her pale-green eyes reflecting everything she was experiencing. She liked what she saw and was affected by his nakedness. He knew she could feel his arousal, yet she did not step out of his embrace. Interestingly, she did not appear afraid of him.

"Do you like what you see?"

He waited for her to push away and avert her gaze in embarrassment, but to his chagrin she stayed within his arms and continued her perusal—a straightforward, clinical stare, as though she were assessing a statue. Her hand on his chest moved slowly over his skin, leaving a trail of heat beneath her touch.

Then a dragonfly buzzed past, and the spell was broken.

"Stay away." She pushed against his chest. "Stay away from me."

Immediately he dropped his arms from around her. "I can't. You're expecting more strength than I possess if you think I can stay away. You're so perfect . . . Your beauty leaves me speechless."

She bit her bottom lip but didn't swim to safety.

That was a mistake—an innocent's mistake—but a mistake, nonetheless.

He could take her now, and then there would be no turning back. Wager or no wager she would be his. But something held him back. Did he want to win her like this? Force her to become his wife? Force her to his bed? How would she ever respect him if he did? How would he respect himself?

Honor was damnably inconvenient where a virginal lady was concerned.

He splashed water at her with his open palm. "Go. You know the outcome if you stay. There are many things I wish you to feel, but anger and regret is not one of them."

Caitlin could not believe it. He was letting her go?

The cool water did nothing to diminish the fire burning under her skin. Droplets of water clung to him like a jealous lover. His curls glistened in the sunlight, their ringlets lending the consummate rake an air of innocence. He looked delicious.

His jaw tightened and a hint of color tinged his cheeks. "I've released you, Caitlin. Go. Now. You're playing with fire if you stay."

Was he blushing? Dear heaven, he was! He was also warning her. Telling her she should jump at the chance to escape him. That he was giving her the choice spoke volumes about the real man behind the rakish persona. Perhaps he wasn't such a rogue after all.

That afternoon she'd found his self-teasing delectable. The way he'd poked fun at himself, how he made Mrs. Darcy feel relaxed in his presence as he allowed her to scold and tease him. Caitlin warmed to that side of him and could now understand why so many women fell under his spell.

"Did you hear me?" he asked, his voice ragged. "I can't vouch for how much longer I can stand here without reaching for you. I'm not a saint, Caitlin. I'm a man. A man who wants you very much."

She could see that he wanted her. Although she didn't wish to feel anything other than revulsion for Harlow Telford, nothing she could *see*—and she could see quite clearly through the water—revolted her. And he certainly had a sizeable "nothing".

She should run a mile.

But at that moment the idea of ruination was no longer frightening. In fact, the idea of marriage to him looked incredibly appealing.

Muscle rippled and flexed in his arm, and down the trim taper of his waist as he wiped the water from his eyes.

The words left her mouth on a soft sigh. "What if I don't wish to leave?"

Dangerfield couldn't believe what he'd heard. Wasn't sure he had heard it. The deafening roar in his ears, *take her*, blocked out any other sound.

She was offering herself to him? He had wanted to seduce her in order to make his proposal more appealing, but God's truth, did she understand the consequence of her actions?

Was he strong enough to resist even if she didn't.

He scooped her up in his arms and waded to shore. The feel of her naked fragility against his chest flooded him with such a wave of protectiveness he barely knew what to do with himself.

When she looked up at him, uncertainty in her eyes. He gathered her closer, the tightness around his heart unexpected.

He found the flat, dry, and very private place where she'd shed her clothes, and lay her reverently down upon them—her beauty, which had long haunted his dreams, displayed for him to see and worship.

"Harlow." She trembled a little as she breathed his name. She stared into his eyes—her own, liquid pools of emotion, their glowing greenish hue dark with want. And she rose up and feathered little kisses on his chest.

He quivered, breathless with wonder as her silken lips caressed his skin. Caresses so innocently given. He knew with absolute certainty he'd remember this moment for the rest of his life.

He ran a shaky hand down one of her long limbs, her firm, damp flesh luscious to the touch. To his surprise she lay back and smiled encouragingly.

Her faith in his ability to give her pleasure awed him. He knelt at her feet, suddenly unsure.

His fascination with her took him by surprise.

He knew the secrets of a woman's body—none better. But this wasn't "a woman". This was Caitlin. This was different. This was important. This was real.

Yes, he wanted her. He wanted to sheath himself deep within her and find heaven. But he also wanted her. Her. He wanted her to . . . Christ . . . not just to respect him. He wanted more. He wanted her to admire, to adore . . . He wanted her to love him.

Her finger had been gliding down his torso. Now it halted, shyly, near his rampant arousal, which stood straight and hard against his stomach. Her touch was driving him insane, calling to his blood like a bewitching song.

He could think of nothing else. He had to take her. Claim her. Make her his. Forever.

With real reverence he stroked one hand down her body, tracing the curves of her breast, the indent of waist, the flat plane of her stomach, before sinking his fingers in the soft, black curls at the apex of her thighs. Her legs parted, allowing him access to the treasure within.

He hesitated. Gave her one last chance.

"Caitlin, sweetheart, I've never wanted anyone more in my life, but if we do this, there is no turning back. Understand? You will marry me. Agreed?"

"Harlow."

The way she moaned his name was the only permission he needed. He did what he'd dreamed of doing the moment he'd first seen her in trousers. Lifting one tiny foot, he began kissing up her leg. The heady scent of her arousal urged him to rush. But he took his time; she deserved at least that.

Caitlin's last few nights had been filled with restless dreams. Dreams about Harlow and what it would be like to give herself to him. Reality was so much . . . more.

He looked like a conquering warrior. The living, breathing definition of irresistible.

His massive arousal throbbed against her thigh and her hips twisted, wanting to answer its call. Passion drummed a beat in her brain. She could think of nothing else—no one else—but the man, tenderly pressing kisses up her thigh.

She was lost and drowning in a sea of desire. It was beyond anything she could have imagined. And it was wonderful.

From the moment she'd thought up this hare-brained wager, she'd been determined to resist him. Now she asked herself why? Now there was only the honeyed sweetness of his gaze, the fiery need of his touch, and the fierce primal wanting he had awakened in her.

All her fear about the price she'd pay for this one sweet moment fled as his lips trailed higher up her thigh.

Her breath rasped as he moved to kneel between her parted legs, and when he lifted his head and gazed up her body to meet her eyes, his face was gravely worshipful.

"You are an exquisite woman," he whispered hoarsely. "You will make a fine duchess. I'm honored that you have chosen me as your first, and I promise to make it memorable."

Her position afforded her a breath-taking view as her warrior leaned down to set her skin ablaze once more. At the touch of his lips, she lay back and half closed her eyes, and put her resistance aside once and for all. Becoming a duchess was no punishment, especially as Mansfield Manor could still be passed to her daughter.

His lips were hot against her damp skin. Anticipation sent a series of tremors ricocheting through her, but it did not prepare her for what he did with his tongue. Gently, he parted her folds and his lips tasted the very heart of her womanhood. His tongue slid through her curls and licked the most intimate part of her, until she could no longer think.

She could not believe that he was kissing her there, let alone that she was *letting* him. It was mortifying, yet at the same time she knew she'd beg him to continue if he tried to stop.

The sensations his clever tongue roused in her made her eyes roll back, her hips lift, and a desperate moan escape her lips.

When he draped one of her legs over his shoulder, opening her wider to his ministrations, her body exploded with need, and want, and desire.

Caitlin's fingers threaded through his curls, tangling in their damp softness as she clutched his head, urging him closer.

She hovered on an airy precipice, her soul teetering on the edge of nothingness. The sensations overwhelmed her and she heard herself cry out his name. "Oh, Harlow. Oh, God."

Her limbs went taut, her body shook, and she felt as if she were losing her mind to the pleasure. Then his wicked tongue entered her and she spasmed, and plunged over the edge, writhing against his mouth, her fingers clutching his hair in the sweet, amazing tide of her release.

She was still humming with the joy of it when he began to move up her body.

"Beautiful. You are so beautiful," he whispered, as he reached her mouth.

She reached for him, and slid her palms slowly up his muscled biceps to his shoulders. Then she wrapped her arms around his neck and held him close. "That was incredible."

He smiled and brushed her lips with a kiss so tender she wanted to weep. "There is more. So much more."

"Is there?" How could there be more than perfection?

"Yes." He nuzzled her nose with his own. "Don't be nervous, darling. You won't regret this, I promise."

She didn't.

His hand glided over her body until she was a quivering mess. His mouth followed, first to her throat, where her pulse hammered. He claimed her neck in deep, open-mouthed kisses, nipping her delicate skin until goose-bumps rose on her arms. His mouth trailed lower, leaving not an inch of her breasts unexplored. They were not very big, but he seemed to enjoy suckling them.

She certainly enjoyed it. When a deep moan escaped her she felt him smile against her skin. She gasped as his finger found the hardened nub of her womanly centre, still pulsing from his previous loving.

"So wet for me," he whispered, sliding his fingers inside her, stretching her, preparing her for his entry.

He eased down onto her, settling heavy between her thighs, all hard muscle and leashed passion. Almost drunk with desire, and with the roughness of his sculptured chest abrading her aching breasts, she trembled, yearning as she clung to him, moaning a little at the depth and rising urgency of his kisses. Her hips rose with shocking wantonness, caressing his hardness trapped between their bodies. He groaned into her mouth and drove his pelvis hungrily against hers as their tongues mated.

"I have to have you now." He quivered like a lusty stallion.

She pulled back a little and looked into his storm-colored eyes, their grey a darkening tempest against the brilliant sunshine above.

She knew her acquiescence was a gamble. Her heart was in play, and the damage if it were lost far surpassed that of her house. But when he smiled down at her, his body thrumming in the same way as hers, she knew she did this without regret. She'd never been more ready for anything in her life.

"Make love to me, Harlow."

It was all the encouragement he needed.

He took her face between his hands and slid his tongue deep within her mouth, stroking until her body trembled with rapture, begging to have him inside her.

He guided his erection to her entrance and touched her pleasure centre with his fingertip as he edged slowly and tenderly into her tightness. She could see the control it took for him to go slow, to press into her, to claim her, inch by careful inch.

"Tell me if it's too much," he rasped through gritted teeth. "I can stop."

Her only answer was to bend her knees so he could sink deeper within her and run her hands down his body, enthralled by each flowing ridge of powerful muscle.

He halted, breathing hard. "Relax, Caitlin," he said. Then he smothered her in fevered kisses and surged deep within her, tearing the only barrier left between them.

She gasped through the pain. It hurt. And he felt so large within her.

He stilled. "I'm sorry, love," he said, and caressed her cheek with the back of his fingers. "Are you all right?"

She pressed a kiss to his chest where it glistened in the sunshine with a fine sheen of sweat, and nodded. She lay swamped in sensations; the feel of the lean, hard length of him was intoxicating. She closed her eyes while he nuzzled her cheek and stroked her breasts, arousing her to a new fever pitch.

Then he moved. Rising above her on muscled arms he slowly withdrew from her body, and then slid back in.

The pleasure was exquisite. Her head fell back and her moans mingled with the breeze and the bird song.

He began to move with more purpose; deep, slow strokes full of leashed male power and tenderness.

Her hips rose to meet his, desperate for the reward she knew he would give her. He took her mouth in a searing kiss, riding urgently between her thighs, their bodies in complete contact, one in every way. Her hands glided down and gripped his buttocks, willing him closer, deeper, more . . .

She dug her nails into his flesh, and he groaned into her mouth. "God, Caitlin, I can't last much longer. You're so tight, so hot, so perfect . . ."

He bowed back, slipping his hand between their joined bodies, seeking her centre. At his expert caress she screamed out her mindless pleasure as she, once again dived from the precipice into the brilliant lights of release. His thrusts grew in pressure and the cords of his neck tightened. He stroked deep within her and continued to pleasure her hardened nub with his thumb.

"Come again for me, with me, Caitlin. Look into my eyes. I want to feel it with you, be with you in the moment."

She didn't think she could take any more pleasure but he spasmed above her, gave an almighty groan, and thrust into her again and again, his own violent climax prolonging the exquisite shudders racking her body. She tumbled from bliss into ecstasy, calling out his name as he shouted hers.

He collapsed on her, gasping hard, ragged breaths beside her ear.

Caitlin had no strength to hold him. She was still floating amid a million stars. She came back down to earth slowly, loving the weighty feel of him pressing her into the flattened reeds. Lifting her hand, she drew sweeping circles on his back, contentment like none she'd ever known wrapping around her.

"That was beautiful," she whispered.

Harlow turned his head and gave her a tousled, heart-skipping smile. "I had no idea it could be like that."

She laughed. "I have nothing to compare it to but I know it was wonderful. Magical."

"I swear it was magical." He lifted her hand and pressed a kiss into her palm.

They lay content, looking into each other's eyes. Neither one wanting to leave.

Finally Caitlin said, "I suppose being married to a man who can worship me like this every day won't be too unbearable."

He winked. "If you're lucky, mayhap I'll worship you like this twice or several times a day."

CHAPTER EIGHT

Several times? A *day*? Surely he was joking.

"In fact, if this wasn't your first time, I'd likely ravish you all over again—as soon as I'd caught my breath." He rolled to his side, pulling her with him and hugging her to his chest.

Under her cheek his heart thudded like the hooves of a galloping horse. It made her think of *Ace of Spades* as he flew past his competition . . . There would be no need for that race now. Marriage to Dangerfield had more than one reward.

"You know," she rubbed her cheek against the heavy muscle of his chest. "When this silly wager started, I never considered for one moment that I'd keep Mansfield Manor for my daughter by marrying you."

The sudden tension in him was like a fire bell rung in the night. Her contentment fled. She pushed out of his embrace and up onto her elbow.

He would not meet her eyes.

Behind her breastbone something jabbed and ached. "I will be able to pass Mansfield Manor onto our first daughter? Won't I?"

Dangerfield could have cursed the grass blue. This wasn't

the conversation he'd anticipated having with his betrothed after such a cataclysmic bout of lovemaking. It certainly was not one he intended to have naked. Or while being eaten by midges and guilt. Especially the guilt. He couldn't even look at her, fearing what she would see in his face—or what he would see in hers.

Gently, he set her aside and sat up. *Damn, no clothes.* He'd entered the pond from the other side.

He ran a hand through his tangled curls as panic and frustration rose within him. "I don't want to have this conversation here. Let's get dressed and I'll take you home—to Telford Court."

Her face paled. "What is there to talk about? I'm assuming you'll honor my mother's legacy now we are to be married. You could give me Mansfield Manor as a wedding gift."

For God's sake. Mansfield Manor? Was that all she cared about? His frustration overflowed. "Is that why you slept with me? Offered up your virginity to ensure Mansfield Manor was yours?"

The instant the words left his mouth he'd have given anything to haul them back. But it was too late.

Her beautiful eyes narrowed and she scrambled to her feet. "If I were a man I'd call you out for that insult. I can't believe you've just suggested that I'd prostitute myself to gain back my home. You've been around women like Larissa too long. If I'd wanted to do that I would have done so at the beginning. I could have offered myself in exchange for the house and you would have accepted."

His cheeks burned as though she had slapped them. She was right. Jeremy's situation would have ensured his refusal, but he would have been sorely tempted to accept. His words were uncalled for. He'd followed her to the pond knowing exactly what he was doing. If anyone was setting a trap it was him.

"Is this to do with the feud with my father?" She pulled clothes on as she spoke, in sharp, vicious tugs. "Don't you think that since we are about to marry—if, indeed, we are—I should understand what happened all those years ago. Surely we can put any feud behind us."

He felt ridiculous standing naked before her, about to crush her dreams into dust. "It's complicated and, really, I think it would be better if we discussed this once we are clothed and in more civilized surroundings."

He couldn't concentrate with her curves still on display. Her small breasts rose and fell rapidly and he couldn't help his body's response to her nakedness. He tried to focus on something—anything—except the vision before him, but all he could think about was the driving need to taste her again.

Her tiny hands fisted at her sides. "Just tell me one thing. Will I be able to pass Mansfield Manor to our daughter?"

He hesitated. "Not exactly."

"You bastard." The shoulder of her dress slipped down her arm and she hauled it back up with a jerk. "You did this on purpose. You followed me here, seduced me, and made me think marrying you would be a good idea, purely to steal what is rightfully mine." She gave a little hiccup and swiped at her eyes with the heel of her hand. "I knew this was a mistake. How could I have thought I would be happy with the likes of you?"

"That's not how it is." But the words were a lie. He'd originally thought it a fine solution and he was sure, once Caitlin learned of her half-brother, everything would play out as he planned.

She'd managed to straighten her dress at the front but it gaped open at the back. She didn't seem to notice. "Well, you can forget about marriage. I wouldn't marry you if you were the last man on earth. We *will* continue with this wager. I *will* have my house—and no underhanded, manipulating rakehell is going to stop me."

"Don't be ridiculous." He felt like an imbecile standing in

the open air, naked, arguing over something that was already set in stone. "I've ruined you. Of course you will marry me."

She'd drawn up one stocking and was pulling up the other one. It fell back down her leg, her eyes narrowed to spitting green pinpoints and, before he could react, she rushed forward and shoved him hard. Taken completely off guard he staggered backwards, tripped, and went sprawling into the pond.

He came up spluttering and coughing, and ready to throttle her, but by the time he'd cleared the water from his eyes she'd gone. She'd bloody well *gone*. He could hear her scrambling into her carriage, which had been hidden from sight by the reeds.

He'd have to go after her.

Harlow swam back across the pond, a heavy weight in his chest. The pain and desolation in Caitlin's eyes . . . he'd caused that. Suddenly, he wanted to tell her everything. He wanted to help both Jeremy and Caitlin but he wasn't sure how. His solution of offering her marriage appeared to be the best he could come up with. This solution was win-win for all concerned.

But more than that, he wanted to tell Caitlin how getting to know her had changed him. Made him look at his life. At himself. He didn't like what he saw.

He'd sworn many years ago to never again engage in the risky game of love. A true gambler understood the odds in any game, and where the game of love was concerned the stakes were astronomical and the odds were always against you. Love was a lie that carved out the heart and left a man hollow inside, with nothing left worth wagering. At least, that's what he'd thought until recently.

Until Caitlin.

Was this ache in his chest, this driving need to erase the pain from her eyes, and this primal craze to possess her, love?

He'd thought himself in love once before and that had been disastrously painful. His pride, his purse, and his heart had been left in tatters.

But he'd been so enamored of Margaret Crompton that he'd been blind to her duplicity. The second daughter of an impoverished Baron and beautiful beyond measure, Margaret possessed hair the color of a brilliant, burnt sunset, a body made of curves that fitted and overflowed in a man's hands, and a face that mesmerized anyone who saw her.

She'd certainly mesmerized him. He'd been captivated the moment he'd met her. She'd also taught him that outward beauty could hide a cankerous soul—something so ugly even demons would turn and flee in terror.

Unfortunately it had taken time for him to see her for what she was. Time when he'd been the biggest fool in England.

He'd turned twenty-four—a cynical twenty-four—and was used to women who fell into his arms and his bed. But Margaret was different. She was the first woman who didn't chase him, the first one he'd had to work hard to catch. He'd been such a fool, working toward his own destruction.

He'd had copious competition. Half the men of the *ton*, wealthy important men, wanted her. He'd been so proud that she'd selected him above the more important men of the realm. And when he'd caught her, when he'd offered marriage, she said she was flattered but that she would think on it.

Think on it. His admiration for her soared. Any other woman would have jumped at the proposal, greedy to grab the wealth and status he offered. Margaret explained that she did not feel they knew one another enough. That she wanted to get to know him . . . the man underneath the title.

They were the words he'd always wanted to hear. A woman who wanted to know him—Harlow. Not the duke. The man. He couldn't believe his luck in finding such a beauty.

For months she kept him at arm's length. No kisses, no touches, nothing sexual at all. It made him want her even more. His need for her raged like a fever. He'd stayed true to her, forgoing his mistress, and any other female entertainment. He almost went out of his mind with suppressed desire.

Finally, after months of him begging, pandering, buying her gifts, she consented to be his wife. He'd been the happiest man in the world.

Until he'd caught her fucking her father's groom.

And her father's gardener.

And her father's hounds man.

At the same time.

It had all been a lie. She'd used him, despised him as a love-sick fool, like all the rest of her admirers. She preferred real men, men who took what they wanted, who liked it rough and dirty.

What was worse, half the *ton*—the older, wiser, male half—knew what she was like. It was the reason she'd been so popular. They all wanted to bed her. Most had succeeded.

He'd been so proud. He'd been such a fool.

And all for love . . . or what passed for it.

Harlow tugged his shirt over his torso, ignoring the ripping sound as the fine lawn stuck to his wet skin.

It was ironic that he had finally found a woman who truly did not want him for what he could provide. Who wasn't impressed by his title or wealth. But wasn't Caitlin still like all the others? She didn't really know him. She only saw the title and wealth. But, unlike the other scheming females, she despised him for it. She'd rather marry a commoner as long as he gave her his heart.

Harlow was wealthy beyond measure, but he wasn't sure he could give Caitlin his heart. It probably wasn't worth anything anyway.

He also couldn't give Caitlin her second desire—Mansfield Manor. Jeremy refused to release him from his promise. In addition, Jeremy had called on Harlow's honor to ensure he tried his hardest to win the wager.

Now decently clothed, Dangerfield whistled for *Champers*. He didn't know what to do. He'd been dealt a rubbish hand, and no matter what he did a person he loved—yes, *loved*—would be hurt by having their dreams shattered.

He had no choice but to continue with the wager and let fate chose the victim. But, either way, Caitlin was his. She would be his wife. He only hoped that over the coming days he could prove to her that he really was a man worthy of her. One worth the risk of happiness, life, and heart.

Caitlin egged her horse toward home as if the devil were chasing her. The gig rattled dangerously over every little stone, but she pushed on hoping the wind whistling past her would blow away her stupidity and anger. She rubbed her chest to ease the pain, furious at her wanton feelings. Even now, all she could taste and scent was Harlow.

How could she have been so stupid as to fall for his seduction? Reason was only now returning. She'd been played. He had fooled her by dangling marriage, and like a rat greedy for a taste of the cheese, she'd let her guard down. Now she'd lost more than a house. She'd lost in every way a woman could lose—her dignity, her pride and—a sob escaped from deep within her throat—her heart.

Her heart. That was the loss that hurt the most.

Harlow had blinded her with passion. She'd let him seduce her as easily as he would a common milkmaid. And she'd enjoyed it. Reveled in it. And would love to do it again, with him.

Damn him to Hades! She'd just given Harlow her virginity, her very being, and he'd use it to trap her. But if he thought marriage would make her give up her claim to her house, he was sorely mistaken.

Her anger arrowed directly to her stomach and she burned with humiliation. No, she could hardly blame Harlow. Twice he'd given her an opportunity to say no. Twice she'd not taken it. This was all her own foolishness.

He might have her trapped, but Mansfield Manor would still be hers if she won the wager. Correction; *when* she won. The house would be safe because, according to the terms of the deed, it would be in her name upon her marriage.

She swiped a hand across her face and flicked away tears. Perhaps she should have stayed and talked to him, but it was easy to see that, for some reason, he did not intend to simply give her Mansfield Manor. Why? She didn't think the man she'd come to know was that spiteful. But did she really know him?

Another sob escaped into the wind. She might have lost her heart, but Caitlin would be damned if she lost anything else of importance to Harlow Telford, the Duke of Dangerfield.

CHAPTER NINE

It was six days before Caitlin returned to Mrs. Darcy's house, and it felt as though every eye in the village was upon her as, her cloak clutched tightly around her shoulders, she made her way to the front door and knocked,

All of Bedstone already assumed she would be Harlow's Duchess. Two days ago, her father's Cook had informed her—during one of their cooking lessons—that the villagers were taking bets on when the betrothal would be announced. Apparently, they thought Mrs. Darcy had been commissioned to make the wedding cake.

Caitlin drew in a deep breath. She knew when any announcement would be made. It would be the day the final wager was finished . . . if she lost.

However, over the past few days she'd decided that if she won the house she would not marry Harlow. If she had control of the estate and finances she could live her own life. A man who loved her—who truly loved her—would not judge her for one indiscretion.

Harlow could rant all he liked, but he did not love her. If he did he'd give up the wager. Holding onto the house for revenge against her father was petty, and any man who put a feud ahead of his future wife's happiness didn't love her. No. He obviously did not love her.

With heavy heart she knocked on the door and heard footsteps inside the cottage.

The thought of coming face to face with Harlow made her body hum with a potent mixture of eagerness and dread. How could she face him? What would she say?

She hadn't seen him since the day at the pond and the lovemaking that had made her body shiver with unbridled yearnings. She closed her eyes to block out the erotic images playing in vivid detail, but the darkness behind her lids only made the memories of that day more potent.

The door was flung wide. Caitlin opened her eyes.

And there he stood.

Handsome Harlow. Gorgeous Harlow. The Harlow of her dreams.

Desire dissolved in her blood and spread through her veins like molten lava. She wanted him. She wanted him as badly now as she had on the fateful day at the pond. More so, now that she understood about pleasure . . . the pleasure his hands, mouth, and body could give.

He looked magnificent standing in the shadowed doorway, his eyes searching her face, his chiseled features etched with concern. Perhaps he did care for her, but it wasn't love. If he loved her he'd give her her heart's desire.

Caitlin realized they were drawing a crowd as they stood staring at each other in the doorway. She didn't care, but he obviously did. He took her hand and pulled her inside. She stumbled against him and clutched his lapels for support.

He closed the door and pulled her into his arms. "Mrs. Darcy's in the kitchen, but I have to know. Are you all right? The day at the pond—did I hurt you?"

She wasn't going to let him off easily. "Not physically-no."

In the kitchen a pot clanged.

Harlow's hands tightened on her arms as he set her away from him. "Look, there is a lot I'm not at liberty to explain, but I want you to know that, if I could, I'd give you the house."

She wanted so much to believe him. But . . . "Is this another ploy to unsettle me?"

He shook his head. "No," he whispered. "I mean it."

"Why the sudden change of heart?" she hissed back, and jabbed his rock hard chest with her finger. "Assuming you still have one in there somewhere. I haven't heard from you all week."

"That is hardly my fault. You didn't come for any more cooking lessons."

"I decided my father's cook could teach me. You didn't seem to miss me. You didn't even send me a note to ask—"

"I thought it best—"

"Not a lover's spat I hope."

At Mrs. Darcy's coy question they jumped like guilty children caught stealing apples.

"Come along." The old lady waved them both toward the kitchen. "There will be time for holding hands once we have finished the lesson. His Grace informs me this is to be the last one, but I'm happy to continue with more for you, Lady Southall, to make up for those you missed."

"Thank you, Mrs. Darcy," Caitlin gave her a grateful smile. "But that will not be necessary."

It wouldn't be necessary because that afternoon she, Harlow, Henry, and Marcus would be visiting Reverend Foley for his verdict on who baked the best cake. This lesson was the bake-off.

Caitlin brushed past Harlow and made her way to the kitchen. Her stomach seemed filled with lead and it was an effort to get her feet to move. She had to win the bake-off, or Harlow won the wager.

Four long hours later she sat in the kitchen at Mansfield Manor with Cook, eating the remainder of her winning cake, and celebrating with a few glasses of her father's best wine. His hidden stuff. He'd be furious when he found out, but Caitlin didn't care.

She'd won the second wager.

There had been no doubt as to the winner as soon as the cakes came out of the oven. Harlow's cake had a sunken middle and, when tapped, it was rock hard.

They hadn't even needed the vicar to judge them. Harlow'd had the grace to concede.

She'd raced home from Mrs. Darcy's in order to savor her triumph. It wasn't only the wine making her senses reel—the wager was now drawn. She could taste victory. She had the better horse so the race was hers for the taking. *Ace of Spades* ran like the wind and would beat *Champers* by a country mile. Mansfield Manor would be hers.

So why did she feel so hollow inside? Her win should be making her happy. But her chest ached. Once the race was over she would say goodbye to Harlow . . . and at the thought, bleakness engulfed her.

She'd miss him.

These past two weeks, for the first time in her life she had not been lonely. Whatever Harlow was, he was a man who challenged her and treated her as an equal. She'd thought about it long and hard. Not many men would have allowed her to confront him in this way. Certainly not at cards or in a horse race!

She'd had more fun, more experiences, and more happiness in the last two weeks then during most of her life. She'd never felt more alive. Every nerve broke into song when she saw him. Her heart fluttered in her chest and her pulse raced. He made her want things she'd never wanted before—especially passion. Ever since the day at the pond she could not get the image of his powerful, naked body out of her head. Riding her, caressing her to blissful ecstasy

She took another swallow from her wine glass. The idea of marrying him was suddenly highly intoxicating. Perhaps she should not be so hasty in her plan to decline his proposal. Mayhap, over time, she could make him fall in love with her. He certainly desired her. That was the perfect start to any relationship.

But desire diminished. She frowned into her glass. And a man like Harlow didn't take long to tire of a woman. He went through mistresses like a blacksmith went through nails.

She relaxed back in her chair and mentally went over her marriage list. The main qualifications she'd missed off were passion and desire. She now knew they, too, were important ingredients in a marriage, and . . . No. She couldn't imagine feeling a smidgen of either for any other man.

In more ways than she cared to reveal, Harlow had ruined her for anyone else.

A fat drop of water plopped onto the back of her hand, and she jumped and almost dropped her glass in surprise. She hadn't even known she was crying.

Lips suddenly quivering, Caitlin downed the rest of the wine in her glass, and poured another. Maybe she'd imitate her father and learn how to drown her sorrows. Perhaps then the pain in her chest would turn to a bearable ache instead of this violent, searing flame that was burning out her heart.

Dangerfield returned to Telford Court after his baking *debacle* in a surprisingly good mood for a man who'd lost the second wager.

It had been worth it to see the sparkle back in Caitlin's eyes when he'd conceded defeat. The damned cake had been as hard as stone. He didn't need a vicar to tell him it was inedible—

especially when Caitlin's was perfection, its aroma alone making his mouth water.

He'd yearned to talk to her, but she'd kept him at arm's length, the very stiffness of her body telling him he was not welcome. Not wanted. Soon, once the silly wager was over, he would make her understand why he'd made the decisions he had. Maybe then she'd forgive him.

The idea that she might hate him sent chills to his core. What would he do if she didn't understand why he had to go through with the wager? But he'd marry her and prove his worth. Once they married he could confess everything. He would not keep secrets from his wife. Jeremy could not expect that of him. Then he'd spend the rest of his days making up for his shortcomings.

"Did you lose on purpose?"

Harlow had barely stepped through the front door. He drew up short at Jeremy's stony question, struggling to hold onto his patience. "How could you even ask that of me? I gave you my word I'd do everything in my power to win. It was baking a cake, for God's sake."

Jeremy's mouth firmed into a thin line and he shook his head. "I still can't believe you endangered Mansfield Manor after you won it for me. A *horse race* will decide my future? If you lose I'll never forgive you. You promised."

"Yes. Yes, I did." And he'd never regretted anything more. If he hadn't promised such a foolish thing then perhaps Jeremy would have learned to move on, and Caitlin would still have her home. *But would she still want you if that were true?* He didn't want to face the answer.

"*Hero* can't be beaten." Jeremy suddenly smiled. "You'll win, brother."

He thought of the Caitlin he'd seen that first day, almost part of the horse herself. "Don't underestimate Caitlin's stallion.

Ace of Spades is fast, and will be carrying less weight."

"But she's a girl. She's tiny. She won't be able to ride as hard as you. Her strength will wane well before yours."

How could he make his young brother comprehend a woman like Caitlin? She had an iron will and believed passionately in her right to the house. That belief, in itself, was a powerful motivator.

"I wish you'd meet her," he said. "I'm sure if we explained the situation—"

"No." Jeremy cried. "She'll look down her nose at me like everyone else. I couldn't bear it if she rejected me, too. What would I do then?"

Harlow's heart almost broke as his younger brother fought back tears. "Caitlin won't reject you. In fact, I think she'd love to learn she has a brother. She's lonely too."

Jeremy wiped a hand over his eyes. "Please, Harlow. Just get me Mansfield Manor like you promised." He drew in shuddering breaths. "That's all I need. All I want. It's different for you. How can you understand? You weren't born a bastard."

Harlow pulled the boy into his arms. "Don't *ever* say that word to me. You're my beloved brother and I don't care what anyone says. You are a Telford."

The boy was growing tall. Harlow could rest his chin on Jeremy's head. Soon he'd be too big—and too old—to hold. "I understand perfectly why you're obsessed with Mansfield Manor."

"But you don't agree with me." Jeremy pulled away. "You think I should let Caitlin keep it."

Harlow sighed. "I think that maybe once you have Mansfield Manor you'll realize it's only a house. A house with bad memories. A house doesn't make a home. It's the people in it. You'll hold onto your hate, and that will only hurt you."

Jeremy folded his arms across his chest and looked mulish. "One of the reasons I want Mansfield Manor—besides the fact it should be mine—is because it's close to Telford Court. If the Earl had married our mother I would always be near my family. You gave me your word." Jeremy started to walk away. "You are honorable. You're not like my father. I know you won't lose Mansfield."

With a heavy heart Harlow watched his brother disappear up the stairs. He, too, knew he would win. He only hoped that, by doing so, he did not lose Caitlin forever.

CHAPTER TEN

The day of the race saw the sun break through the cloud, but, saturated by two days of relentless rain, the ground was heavy underfoot. Mud flew up behind Caitlin as she rode toward the meeting point.

Marcus had delivered the planned route for the race to her at Mansfield Manor two days ago. It would be held on Henry's land, at the base of Clee Hills. Reluctantly, Caitlin agreed he'd been fair. The course did not give *Champers* any advantages and, although it was not as flat as she'd hoped, neither was it too hilly. The heavy ground would slow both horses down. Caitlin still had the advantage. She was much lighter than Dangerfield.

The ride to Henry's hunting lodge allowed Caitlin time to give Ace a good warm up before the start.

Her stallion had been decidedly manic that morning. Due to the wild weather she'd not been able to give him a solid workout the last two days, and he was champing at the bit to stretch out and run like the wind. It took all her strength to rein him in. She didn't want him to use up all his energy before the race. The safety of her heart and home relied upon the outcome.

Even though her body was a mass of nerves, she wasn't panicked. She knew her stallion's capabilities. *Champers* was no contest for *Ace of Spades*, especially carrying a man of Harlow's size and weight.

But her heart leaped up and lodged in her throat as she drew closer to the official starting line and saw, not the sturdy, golden-brown *Champers*, but a black, menacing-looking beast. The sleek thoroughbred stallion pranced around as if he owned the world while Harlow sat astride the fierce creature trying to keep him in check.

Harlow was minus jacket and waistcoat. His fine linen shirt was undone at the neck and she could see a glimpse of his tanned and muscular chest. He looked as wild and virile as his stallion. His hair flew about his face emphasizing the primalness of man versus beast. Pure masculinity. Pure danger.

And he was danger personified in more ways than one. She was in danger of not caring about the race. All she could remember was what it had felt like when he'd made love to her, and how she longed for him to do it again.

Panic rose swiftly—followed by bone-chilling fear, and blood-red fury.

She drew *Ace of Spades* to a halt a safe distance from Harlow's mystery stallion, not prepared to risk her horse to a kick or bite. She could see the whites of its eyes. Ace would have to run the race of his life to beat this creature.

"Who is this?" she asked coldly.

"Don't come too close," Dangerfield said. "*Hero* is likely to challenge another stallion." The stallion reared as he spoke. "I've had my trainer training him for the Two-Thousand Guineas race at Newmarket. He's been down at my estate in Devon. I was trying to keep him a secret."

She arched an eyebrow. "Really? You haven't suddenly purchased a horse just to beat me? I'm not sure that would be fair."

"Ask Henry," he replied, obviously affronted at her suggesting he would cheat.

She looked over to where Henry sat upon his horse. He nodded. "Harlow's owned *Hero* since he was a colt."

The sting of misplaced pride soured her mouth, making swallowing difficult. She'd assumed she'd be racing against *Champers*. This giant, black beast was something altogether different.

Harlow sent her a look that would freeze a warm bath. "Let's get the race over with. Then we can get on with our lives."

"I should have known you'd pull something like this." Anger scored through her words like vicious claws.

He swung the stallion back around to face her, his angry gaze making his eyes almost as dark as his horse's glossy coat. "I have done nothing underhand. I can't help it if you dared me without specifying which horse I was to race. Stop behaving like a spoilt brat. You wanted this race, not me, and by God, you'll have it. Then we shall end this stupidity and do what we should have been done the night you barged into my house. Marry."

His harsh words, spoken in front of his friends, hurt. He was like a stranger. Any hint of feelings for her hidden under a blanket of formality. Well, if that's what he wanted . . .

She swung her horse away and trotted to the starting line.

At the line, Dangerfield could barely hold *Hero* still. The stallion was at least two hands taller than *Ace of Spades*. He'd have a longer stride. However, *Hero* carried more weight. Caitlin's gaze swept over Dangerfield's massive frame. They would be very evenly matched. As, she admitted, were she and Harlow—damn him. Both stubborn, full of pride, and determined to be the victor. She could hardly blame him for being exactly like her. A queer shiver swept over her tensed muscles.

Marcus stood at the line. "On my count of one you will race." He paused, and then proceeded to count down. "Three, two, *one* . . ."

As the word "one" left Marcus's mouth, she urged Ace forward. He leapt to her touch, his head out-stretched, eager to run.

And run he did. Caitlin felt as though she rode a storm, the scenery a blur about her. She prayed Ace would handle the soft ground. She'd not really tested him in the wet. She gave him free rein, but out of the corner of her eye she could see *Hero* keeping pace beside her. Only time would tell which horse would tire first.

They were only moments from rounding Barr Beacon, a small cluster of waist-high stones. The horse closest to the stones when he took the turn would have the advantage. Caitlin intended it to be Ace. At what she judged to be the perfect moment she gathered the reins for the turn, and rose up slightly in her stirrups to help her stallion get more speed.

Then it happened. On one breath they were approaching the turn on a lean. On the next breath she felt a jerk, like something breaking, and she was flying, slipping sideways, her feet still in her stirrups, the reins tearing from her hands.

She heard herself scream, saw the ground coming at her with dizzying speed, felt an explosion of pai—

Powerless to do anything, Dangerfield could only watch as the nightmare played out in front of him. Watch her slide sideways, her saddle with her. Hear her scream. See her hit the ground with a sickening thump.

He'd begun to rein *Hero* in the instant he saw Caitlin was in trouble—not an easy task when the stallion was in full flight. But terror for her gave him the strength he needed to bring the horse to a rearing stop no more than six paces from where his heart lay entangled in her saddle.

He leapt from *Hero*'s back and ran to where she lay, her face white, and with blood seeping from a wound on her temple. Was her chest moving? He let out the breath he didn't know he was holding when he saw it lift, and then fall only to lift again.

Choking with guilt he dropped to his knees and gently eased her upright into the cradle of his arms. He'd done this to her—his damned pride and so-called honor—and it should never have happened. He should have forced Jeremy to meet with her. Forced them to sort it out. But he hadn't. He'd been having too much fun battling his wits against hers. And now she was paying the price.

Henry and Marcus thundered up and reined in beside him. Henry dismounted, crossed to where Dangerfield sat, and put a careful hand on Caitlin's neck. "She's still alive, thank God. And her pulse is steady. Let's get her home."

"I'll go for Doctor Spencer and meet you at Telford." Marcus didn't wait for confirmation; he turned his horse and galloped off.

Dangerfield hardly heard him. "God, Henry. If she dies—" Anguish gripped his insides like a claw-trap.

"She's not going to die." Henry took Caitlin's chin in one hand and carefully turned her head. "Look, she's had a nasty knock on her temple, but she's a fighter. She took you on."

But even fighters lose. "She feels so tiny, so fragile. I've made such a mess of this."

Henry nodded. "You have. But now you're going to put it right." He moved away from Dangerfield and began to untangle Caitlin's legs from the stirrups and saddle. "We'll get her patched up, and when she's feeling better, you'll sit her down with Jeremy and sort this situation out. Then you'll announce your engagement."

Dangerfield cradled her tighter against his chest and loosened his hold with an oath when Caitlin gave a groan. "Just help me get her back to Telford. I'll have to ride your horse. I won't be able to control *Hero* while holding her. Can you ride him back instead?"

Henry didn't answer immediately. He was frowning down at the saddle. "This doesn't make sense. The girth's been cut."

An odd sensation speared deep in Dangerfield's gut. "What?"

"The girth's been cut." Henry shook his head as though he was dislodging an annoying fly. "Look, let's worry about this later. Let's just get her home. Give her to me. I'll hand her up once you've mounted."

"Someone cut her girth?" Dangerfield felt each word stab him to the heart as he thought of the ramifications of such sabotage. "Are you sure?"

"You can look for yourself later. I'll bring the saddle with me." Henry took Caitlin from his arms and waited while Dangerfield stood up and then mounted the Earl's docile gelding. "Someone has frayed the girth with a knife so it would break during the race. This isn't a case of her not tightening the saddle properly. Her saddle has been deliberately sabotaged. Who would do such a—? *Jeremy.*"

Henry's eyes narrowed and disgust dripped from every syllable. "It was Jeremy, wasn't it? I know that's who you suspect. Christ. He could have killed her."

"I know that," Harlow snapped as he settled himself in the saddle and reached down for Caitlin. "Don't blame the boy. I dangled his dream in front of him. I delivered him Mansfield Manor only to put it in jeopardy by wagering it again."

Henry lifted Caitlin into Harlow's waiting arms. "That doesn't excuse this and you know it. She could have been killed."

"A fact I shall make Jeremy well aware of. But I carry the majority of blame. I should have never agreed to the wager but,"—and he bent to place a tender kiss on Caitlin's forehead—"I couldn't resist her. I wanted her and as she despised me, the wager was the only way I could think of to spend time with her." He stroked the hair back from her beautiful face with an unsteady hand and whispered, "I just never expected to fall in love with her."

"I know." Henry's smile was both understanding and grim. "Go. Don't wait for me. It may take me a while to tame *Hero*, and then I'll send someone out to find *Ace of Spades* and bring him to Telford. Don't worry about anything else for now. Just get her home."

Dangerfield's hands were still unsteady as, alone in his library at Telford, he poured his second glass of brandy.

The doctor had examined Caitlin and confirmed that she had been unbelievably lucky. Nothing was broken. The head wound, and copious bruises were her only injuries. Although she was still unconscious, she murmured occasionally—a good sign, according to the doctor.

Lydia was sitting with her.

Dangerfield had just finished dealing with Jeremy.

The boy had confessed and was awash with guilt. His tears of remorse fell freely. He pleaded for Dangerfield to believe that he hadn't meant to hurt Caitlin. Dangerfield *did* believe it. All the same, they'd had a man-to-man talk about honor, punishment, and responsibility for one's actions, and the boy had left the study an hour later a wiser and deeply ashamed young man.

However, in spite of it all, Dangerfield was proud of him. Without any coaxing or need for threats Jeremy freely gave up his right to Caitlin's house, and told Harlow to forfeit the race. He said he didn't deserve Mansfield Manor after what he'd done. Harlow tended to agree.

He knew Jeremy was sincerely and genuinely remorseful. He just prayed Caitlin lived to forgive his brother. Her brother. A lifetime of guilt on top of Jeremy's already tenuous position in Society would be a heavy burden to carry. But Jeremy, like his elder brother, had to face up to his mistakes.

He tossed back the brandy and prepared to face his greatest mistake. Caitlin Southall. He should have carried her off to Gretna Green that day at the pond. Surely, if he had abducted and married her she would not be lying unconscious upstairs. She couldn't have hated him forever. He would have won her over, eventually.

He trod slowly up the grand staircase toward Caitlin's room with an ache in his chest. He planned to stay by her side until she woke. Then he'd get down on his knees, offer her both Mansfield Manor, and his heart. He hoped they would be enough for her to forgive him.

He froze outside her door when he heard voices inside the room. When he entered and saw Caitlin sitting up in bed and talking, relief greater than anything he'd ever experienced shot through his veins.

He strode to her bedside and, with a growl, pulled her into his arms and kissed her.

She didn't respond as he had hoped. Instead, she pushed against his chest and, when he drew back, her hands moved from his chest to his face. "I'm assuming you're Harlow?"

A sob beside him made him glance away to where his mother sat. Tears rolled down her cheeks.

"Who else would I—?" And the truth dawned, awakening horror and desperation. Turning back to Caitlin he looked into her exotic, pale-green eyes. They were empty. Blank. "Caitlin? Caitlin, I—"

"It's all right, Harlow. Your mother has explained everything to me. How ironic. I now have my beloved house but"—a sob escaped from her lips and she clutched his shirt tightly as though she'd never let go—"now I can't see it."

And she broke down in his arms, in a flood of tears.

CHAPTER ELEVEN

It had been two days since the accident that had taken her sight, and Caitlin was determined to get out of bed this morning. She might be blind but she wasn't sick.

Harlow fussed over her as if she were on her deathbed. She knew guilt was eating him, but this—her blindness—was not his fault.

She could understand his dilemma. He'd made Jeremy a promise and been sworn to secrecy. What else could he have done? He had to honor his word to his brother. To *her* brother. A smile settled on her lips. She had a brother! She was not alone any more.

The door to her bedchamber opened and a beloved voice said, "It's nice to see a smile on those pretty lips."

But she hadn't needed to hear his voice to know it was Harlow. She could sense the moment he was near. His masculine scent filled her head and clung to her other senses.

She felt the bed dip as he sat down, felt his gentle touch on her face. And had her mouth taken in a thoroughly arousing kiss. It was lovely, but since her accident he had never taken it any further. Never tried to do more than kiss her. Perhaps, now that she was damaged, he no longer desired her.

He ended the kiss, stroked her hair back gently, and sighed. The bed dipped again as he stood up, and the chair next to the bed scraped a foot on the floor as he drew it closer to the bed.

"I'd like to get up today," she said as he sat down. "It's time I went home. Your mother and your staff have been wonderful but I don't want to continue to be a burden on them." *Or you.*

Silence greeted her words. Then he said, quietly, "You are not a burden. And I won't hear of you leaving until you are well."

"There is nothing wrong with me."

"The bruise on the side of your head tells me differently. Besides, I enjoy your company. I don't want you to leave."

She sighed. He was going to make this difficult. Why did he have to fight her at every turn? *Because it's thrilling and you enjoy it as much as he does.* "I have to go home sometime. I can't stay here forever."

"Yes, you can," he said softly. "Marry me."

Was this offer out of guilt, or pity, or something more? How she wished she could see his face. She couldn't bear it if he offered out of pity. Or guilt. He would come to resent her. Besides, what use would she be to him as a blind duchess?

"Don't," she said quietly. "I don't want pity and you are not responsible for my condition. It was an accident—"

"It wasn't an accident. And if my stupid pride—"

"Your pride played no part in it. You were trying to right a wrong perpetrated on your—*our* brother. I should have known when you offered marriage that there was more to this than a simple wager. I admire you immensely for trying to do the right thing for all concerned. I also understand why you couldn't tell me. Jeremy guarded his secret well, and having seen how Society treats those of his birth, I can understand why."

119

His chair creaked as he shifted. "Christ. You are too forgiving. I don't know if I'll ever forgive him. He robbed you of your sight."

She reached out her hand, and felt the warmth of his fingers as they clasped it. "He didn't mean to. He was young and angry at the world. He truly thought Mansfield Manor would change things for him. Poor darling. A house would have made no difference. He has to live with that."

They sat holding hands in silence.

Finally Harlow spoke. "Aren't you angry? I'd be furious. How can you not hate me?"

"Is that why you want to marry me?" She tried to keep the stiffness and hurt out of her voice but didn't manage it. "Because you think I hate you, and that you owe me this? Well, I don't. And you don't." She attempted to withdraw her hand but Harlow clutched it tightly. She heard the chair creak again, and then his knees hit the floor beside her bed.

"No." His lips pressed a warm and fervent kiss into her palm. "I want to marry you because I love you."

Breath seemed to clog in her lungs.

But he wasn't finished. "I think a part of me has loved you since the day at the pond—"

"When we made love?"

"No." There was a smile in his voice that tugged at her heart. "When you were fifteen, and you laughed at me as I lay wallowing in the mud. You knew who I was and didn't care. You put me in my place. And when you poked your tongue out at me I was angry and pleased at the same time."

How could this be true? "You were mean to me that day."

"Because you unsettled me like no other woman had, and yet I knew you were still a girl. I didn't know how to behave. I wanted to thrash you one minute, and then kiss you the next."

She laughed at the picture in her head. "Well, I thought you were a bully, and a wastrel. And I thought it was fitting punishment for your bad temper that you fell in to the bog."

He squeezed her hand. "No woman had ever laughed at me before. You saw *me*. The real me. The good and bad. And I knew that—when I loved—I wanted a woman who saw *me* not just my title and wealth."

He stood to his feet, and the bed dipped again as he sat down beside her on the mattress. Leaned back against the headboard. "I looked for that quality in every woman I met. I thought I'd found it in a woman once, but she was false. I'd given up hope of ever finding what I wanted. Then, when I saw you with *Ace of Spades* that day, dressed like a man but every inch a woman, and you almost shoved your horse's arse in my face . . . I knew I'd found what I'd been looking for. I'd found you."

His words left her breathless and sent her pulse racing. She swallowed down her hope. "But I can't see you now."

"You see me better than any woman ever has," was his heart-felt reply.

She might be blind, but she could still weep. "Thank you. That's beautiful."

"You're beautiful." He pulled her into an embrace. "I know you have a lot to adjust to, but will you consider my proposal?"

She nodded. She'd consider it, but her answer would still be "no". Even more so now. The irony burned like pure malt whiskey in her throat. Harlow wanted a partner in life. She'd been looking for a partner too. It was top of her "Requirements for a Husband" list. How could she be a true partner for him now that she was blind?

He deserved more in a wife. He needed someone as active as he was. Someone to be by his side. Someone to hunt with, ride with, travel with. A true partner, in every sense of the word.

She wanted time to think. "I'm tired, Harlow. I need to rest, but would you come and fetch me this afternoon. I'd like to get some fresh air."

He kissed her soundly, and rose from the bed. "I'll be back at three. That gives me time to see to my correspondence."

He crossed the room and the door to her chamber opened, but on the threshold she sensed him hesitate. "I am sorry, you know," he said. "More sorry than you'll ever know." And before she could reply he'd closed the door. His footsteps echoed down the hall.

They echoed in her heart, too. She curled up in bed, conflicting emotions fighting inside her. She wanted to marry Harlow. But she loved him. And it was her love for him that refused to let him tie himself to a blind woman. A blind woman. She was a blind woman.

The truth of it hit her in an explosion of tears, and she wept. Wept for herself. For Harlow. For the hopelessness of her situation. She had her Mansfield Manor but it meant nothing. She felt nothing for it. It wasn't Harlow. It was Harlow she wanted—and Harlow was the one thing she could never have.

She must have drifted into sleep because she came awake with a start when her bedroom door opened and hesitant footsteps approached her bed.

"Yes?" She hated how vulnerable she felt. "Who's there?"

"It's me."

Jeremy.

"I'm so very sorry, Lady Southall," he choked out. "I didn't want to hurt you, I just . . ."

"Come." She patted the bed beside her. "Sit."

His steps dragged toward her and she felt him sit.

"First of all," she said, "I want you to know that I forgive you. It was a foolish and dangerous thing to do, but I understand. Look how foolishly *I* behaved over a house. I should never have wagered against Harlow."

He gulped in a breath. "If I could take back what I did, I would, in a heartbeat. I just wanted you to *lose*. I didn't want you to get *hurt*." Shame whispered in that last word. True shame. True repentance. "I've let my cowardice ruin everything. I should have met with you as Harlow urged, and none of this would have happened."

She patted his hand. "We've both been stupid. If I'd known I had a half-brother, and what my father did, I would have gladly given you Mansfield Manor. Do you know,"—she kept hold of his hand—"I've learned that it is not the house that is important, but the family in it? I may have grown up at Mansfield Manor, but you had the riches. After my mother died, I had no one—no one who cared for, or loved me. It was a very lonely upbringing. So it's hardly surprising I focused all my love on a house." She swallowed back pain at the memory of those empty years. "You, on the other hand, had more riches than I could have imagined. You have a mother and a brother who love you, and would do anything to see you happy. That is worth more than any house."

"Not anymore." There was a muffled sob beside her. "Harlow hates me."

"He doesn't hate you. He's disappointed in you. You will have to earn back his trust and respect, but I know you can do that. Just give him time."

Jeremy swallowed. "What about you? Can you learn to forgive me and love me after what I have done?"

She nodded. "I believe so. Especially if you do something for me."

"Anything!"

"Then I want you to promise that you'll be the best owner Mansfield Manor and the estate has ever had. My father—our father—gambled everything away, and cared nothing for the estate. I want you to promise to take pride in it, and restore it to its former glory."

She'd heard his gasp. "But I can't take Mansfield Manor after what I did."

She sighed. "Jeremy, I thought you and I were realists. Harlow has lived with privilege all his life. Everyone does as he wishes. He doesn't understand what it is like in the real world. We both know I'll never be able to manage Mansfield Manor on my own—not now. Not blind. And I wouldn't want to. I want someone who has the estate in his blood, someone like you, who will restore it and show the world how prosperous and beautiful it can be. Will you let me live with you at Mansfield Manor? That's all I ask."

"But when you marry Harlow," the boy said, slowly, "he can look after Mansfield Manor for you."

Caitlin laughed. "Marry Harlow? Jeremy, what did I just say about being realists?" She turned her head least he see her unshed tears. "Whoever heard of a blind duchess? Harlow needs a wife who can stand by him in Society and help him manage his households. He does not need a woman who will be nothing but a burden to him."

"I need a woman who completes me. Who fills my soul with song, and who can bring me to my knees in adoration with one simple smile."

Caitlin started. She'd been so busy talking to Jeremy she had not heard Harlow enter the room, but suddenly his scent invaded her darkness and cloaked her in yearning.

She felt Jeremy stand and heard him quickly walk to the door and leave the room.

"I will not hold you to marriage out of guilt and pity." She kept her voice steady. "This accident is not your fault."

"Of course it is my fault. I should never have let you race."

"*Let* me? As if you could have *stopped* me."

He did not reply and silence invaded her space. How she longed to see his handsome face and read his thoughts. She almost doubled over with the pain when she realized she never would see him again. Never see that sensual smile, the fire in his

124

eyes, or the curls that lent him a boyish air. How could she marry him knowing that? He deserved a wife who could share in all his life.

Two strong arms suddenly wrapped around her and lifted her off the bed. In the next instant she was seated in Harlow's lap, hugged tightly to his massive chest.

"I don't want to marry you out of guilt or pity," he said. "Don't you understand? I *need* you. I'm a selfish bastard; I know I'm asking a lot of you to love a man who, through his own vanity and pride, did this to you. But I swear that if you do me the honor of becoming my wife, I shall worship you until the day I die."

"But I can't see you," she cried on a wracking sob.

Harlow breathed in deeply. "But you can smell me. I know, because I can smell you. Your scent is unique and it drives me wild. And you can hear me." He whispered something scandalous in her ear and her body tightened with lust. "And you can taste me." He moved his mouth to hers and kissed her deeply. While he continued to kiss her he placed her hand on his groin. Breaking the kiss, he whispered hoarsely, "And you can feel me. Feel how much I want you? And only you."

Caitlin ran her fingers over the hard length of his straining arousal, reveling in the feel of him. She slid her palm down from tip to scrotum and felt him pulse in his trousers, seeking her touch. A shiver rippled through her body.

"Does that feel like a man who desires you out of guilt or pity?" he asked, placing her hand on his chest, over his heart. "Feel how it beats powerfully for you. Without you by my side I know it will shrivel up and die. I love you, Caitlin Southall. Don't make me live without you just to punish me."

She couldn't see truth in his face, but she could hear it in his words. They rang with sincerity. Choked with emotion.

She pressed a kiss to his lips. "Then yes, Harlow Telford,

Duke of Dangerfield," she whispered. "I shall risk my heart on you. I will marry you, and be your duchess."

His lips sought hers in a possessive kiss. His taste and touch swept any misgivings from her mind. Her body hummed with longing and she ran her hands all over his arms, chest and through his thick hair. His hand began to gather her skirts but she stopped him.

"I'll marry you on one condition."

"Anything!"

She almost smiled. Two brothers. The same response. "I want you to give Mansfield Manor and the estate to Jeremy, as you promised."

Silence. Then he said, in a hard tone, unlike the gentle one he'd used to her for days, "He does not deserve it. Not after what he did."

She sighed. "We all make mistakes, Harlow. Neither of us is innocent in this debacle. Jeremy is young. He will live with his guilt all his life—and that is the worst punishment I can think of. He will need us to love and forgive him. I *want* him to have Mansfield Manor. After what father did to him and your mother, he deserves it. Besides, he will love and cherish the estate more than anyone I know."

He sighed. "God, how I love you. Your generous spirit and beautiful soul humble me." He kissed her tenderly. "If that is your wish, then it's done. I hope Jeremy realizes what a wonderful sister he has."

Caitlin nuzzled his neck, letting his scent fill her darkness. "Why don't you show me exactly how wonderful I am?"

"How I love a challenge." And Harlow gently laid her down upon the bed and didn't disappoint.

EPILOGUE

In the three months since Caitlin lost her sight she had never felt the loss as greatly as she did today.

It was her wedding day, yet she could not see herself in her dress. Nor, when she walked down the aisle, would she be able to see the expression on Harlow's face as she came toward him.

However, while it might not be the day she'd dreamed of as a girl, she could never have dreamed of a better lover, friend, and husband-to-be. Harlow doted on her. She'd stayed on at Telford Court to learn the layout of the house, and so that Jeremy could take over Mansfield Manor. Harlow said he wanted her at Telford so he could be with her every night.

The nights were spent making wondrous love. Her lack of sight hadn't diminished Harlow's desire for her one bit.

However, losing one of her senses seemed to have strengthened all the others, and their lovemaking was more intense and satisfying every time. Harlow couldn't get enough of her.

She pressed a hand gently to her belly. Thank goodness they were marrying, as she was sure she was with child. She'd missed her monthly courses. She hadn't told Harlow yet. She would tell him tonight. It would be her wedding present to him.

She hoped it was a boy, and that he would look just like his father; thick black curls, mesmerizing grey eyes, and a smile that could soften the hardest heart. A wave of sadness filtered through her joy. She would never see her child—or any of her children. But she would not let that spoil her happiness in them. Harlow would describe them to her. She would see them through his eyes.

Caitlin's veil was in place and her nerves had been calmed with a shot of brandy. Finally, the dressmaker hired to make Caitlin's dress declared that she was ready and left the room to give her a moment to herself.

Caitlin didn't really need the time alone but she was grateful for the woman's thoughtfulness. She loved Harlow more than life itself, and she was sure he loved her. But she still couldn't help thinking this wasn't fair to him. He had made so many changes to accommodate her blindness. Everyone had. She'd tried hard to learn her way around without any help—and had the bruises to prove it. She used a stick to watch for objects but the staff were fabulous at ensuring everything stayed exactly in its place.

She turned, and started for the door. Then she remembered her mother's pearls. She'd forgotten to ask the dressmaker to put them on for her. Without thinking, she turned back and hurried toward the dresser and her jewelry box. She took three steps before her shin made solid and painful contact with something in a place where it shouldn't have been. She clawed at the air, found nothing to grab hold of, and fell heavily over the thing at her feet. She cried out. There was a sharp pain in her head as she struck something, and then the darkness got darker.

Caitlin came back to consciousness to a rush of worried voices all around her.

A woman was softly crying. "My apologies, duchess. I'm so sorry. I didn't think to move my stool."

"Should I fetch His Grace?" It was the butler.

"No." It was Lydia, the Dowager Duchess. "She's coming round. She's just had a slight bump, that's all."

It took Caitlin a moment to understand the significance of the grey light around her. Her shin throbbed and her temple ached. She blinked, and then opened her eyes wide.

She could see. She tried not to let her shock show in her expression. She didn't want to let them know—to build up hope. What if she was wrong and the blackness returned? But she could make out shapes, and she could see . . . see Lydia's concerned, motherly face peering down at her.

Caitlin struggled to sit up. "I'm fine, everyone. I simply tripped." She looked down her wedding dress and ran her hands over the satin skirt. She lifted it slightly to check and, without thinking, said, "Thank goodness it's not torn."

The chatter stopped as if frozen in time.

She looked at her soon to be mother-in-law, and saw tears well up in those familiar, beautiful grey eyes. Warm hands framed Caitlin's face, and the duchess showered kisses on her. "Oh my God, you can see."

The room erupted into excited chatter and shouts, and all the servants—and the dressmaker—were in tears.

"Please don't tell Harlow," Caitlin begged them. "I want to surprise him."

They helped her stand, straightened her clothing, and Caitlin walked toward the mirror glass. She stood looking at herself in her wedding dress, not quite believing she could see.

"It's a miracle," she whispered.

"I've called for Doctor Spencer," Lydia said, as she moved to stand at her shoulder. "As a precaution. Just in case."

Caitlin smiled and blinked back tears. "I don't care if I lose my sight again, as long as it's not until after my wedding. I want to be able to look into Harlow's face when I say my vows."

"Then let's not keep him waiting, he might be getting nervous and think you've changed your mind."

Caitlin's father, the Earl of Bridgenorth, had been invited to the wedding. Lydia had said it was time to put the past behind them. But her father had declined to come. No one was surprised, certainly not Caitlin. She'd begun to understand—and come to terms with—her father's character. He could not face up to his past behavior. He would never admit he'd done any wrong, and she could never respect him because of it.

The small village church was filled to overflowing. They were getting married there because Caitlin wanted all the villagers to share in her joy. Mrs. Darcy had baked the wedding cake. In her father's absence she was being walked down the aisle by Henry St. Giles.

As she entered on his arm, Caitlin's nerves vanished. She'd never felt surer of the step she was taking. She loved Harlow so much, and when she saw him gazing at her with such pride and love shining from his eyes, she knew he loved her.

Henry handed her into Harlow's keeping and her heart went soft at her almost-husband's warm endearment. "You look beautiful beyond words, my love."

She smiled, and replied with perfect truth, "So do you."

He looked confused. But only for a second. Then the vicar began the service.

It was not a long one. Once they'd exchanged vows and the vicar pronounced them man and wife, Harlow took her arm to lead her out of the church. She let him guide her down the aisle, hugging her surprise to her breast. She simply couldn't wait to share her news with him—but it had to be done the right way.

Harlow couldn't understand the ripple of excitement and

shared joy on the faces around them. Everyone was whispering and pointing.

Yes, Caitlin was beautiful. In fact he could hardly wait to take her home, strip her of her gown, and make love to her until morning. Yes, they were married, but the excited prattle, giggles, and tears flowing from everyone who packed the church were extravagant, even for a wedding. What the hell was going on?

They stepped into the sunlight.

His mother grabbed him and hugged him as though she'd never let him go, her tears flowing freely. Henry and Marcus grinned like two simpletons out of the madhouse. Jeremy was finally smiling, the haunted look of guilt now erased from features that were growing more like Caitlin's every day.

Then he looked at his bride. She stood at his side, her hand raised to shield her eyes from the sun. *From-the-sun-?*

"I always did love you in your red waistcoat," she said, her eyes bright with love and laughter. "Scarlet for wickedness—and I love it when you are wicked . . . with me."

A lump stuck in his throat as he fought the joy from erupting. Caitlin could *see*? He felt as though he'd been kicked in the chest. She could see. His mouth opened, but nothing came out. Caitlin took his hand in hers and squeezed it while nodding her head.

He drew in a deep breath. "How?"

She shrugged. "I don't know. Just before I came to the church I tripped in my room and hit my head on the bedpost. When I woke up, I could see."

Ignoring the now cheering crowd around them he pulled her into his arms and hugged her fiercely. "I'm the luckiest man in the world."

He led her toward the carriage and he helped her climb in. The cheers were deafening as they moved off toward Telford Court.

They all gathered in her bedchamber: Harlow, Lydia, Marcus, Henry, Jeremy, and Doctor Spencer. Harlow had insisted the doctor examine her before they joined the guests at their wedding breakfast.

Doctor Spencer could find nothing wrong with her sight. He didn't know how to answer her questions, especially her main concern; would she lose her sight again?

"I can't say for certain," he said. "But there have been documented cases like this before—when a person who lost their sight from a knock on the head has had their vision restored by another such injury. No one understands why. And their sight remained perfect for the rest of their lives."

"Well, I'm bloody going to make sure you don't have another knock on your head ever again," Harlow declared, vehemently.

Caitlin simply smiled at him. "You can't protect me from my own clumsiness."

She did not care about the future. Right now her life was perfect—she could see him. She couldn't stop staring at him, drinking in every little detail.

He looked more handsome than she remembered, although he'd lost weight. The bones of his face were more pronounced, his features more chiseled. The lashes ringing his grey eyes seemed much longer and darker than they had been. The heat and love pouring from them as they gazed at her took her breath away. His full lips drew her in. She hoped no one could read her thoughts because she was picturing exactly where she'd like those lips to be right this minute.

Her face heated.

It heated even more when he caught her stare. The smile he aimed at her indicated he knew precisely what she was thinking, and that he'd be more than happy to fulfill her fantasy.

Beside her, Lydia cleared her throat. "Yes. Well. We should leave you two alone for a moment before you come down to greet your guests." She shepherded the others from the room, but before she closed the door she turned back. And winked. "Please try to remember you have guests. Half an hour. That's all." And on that parting shot she closed the door behind her.

They were finally alone.

"Caitlin," Harlow said in a voice that was equal parts warning and humor. "If you keep looking at me like that you won't be leaving this room for a week."

Was that meant to make her behave? "I have several months of staring to make up for. Besides, if you weren't so gorgeous I'd have already stopped."

His cheekbone tinged with red.

She laughed. "Harlow. You're blushing."

In answer he scooped her up and carried her to the bed. "We only have half an hour, an hour at most. I want you out of this dress." He laid her on her stomach and began to undo the tiny buttons that ran down the back of her dress. After a lot of fumbling and cursing she heard a tear.

She laughed, and rolled over onto her back. His burning gaze sent heat pooling between her thighs, but she stilled his hurrying hands. "I want to watch you undress. Slowly." She looked up at him through her eyelashes. "Please. I haven't seen you for months."

His gaze softened, the burning desire there dimmed, and he began to remove his clothes. But not particularly slowly. "'Slow' is a word I'll only use when I make love to you."

She lay back in her shift and stockings and devoured him with hungry eyes. When he stood naked beside the bed, she rose onto her hands and knees and crawled to the edge of the bed to press kisses all over his chest. Then she pulled herself up, wound her arms around his neck, and kissed him full on the mouth.

When she'd finished devouring his mouth, she pulled back and said, "I see all of you, Harlow." She felt his manhood pulse against her stomach, and he gave a growl. "I hear you, Your Grace." Her hand slid down to stroke him and his breath hissed from between his clenched teeth. "I feel you, husband." She ran her nose over his skin. "I have always been able to scent you, my love." Then—feeling wicked—she lowered her head. "And I will die if I don't taste you." And she took him into her mouth.

His deep moan filled the room.

She'd loved making love to him when she was blind because, even without sight, it was easy to tell that he was enjoying it. But nothing prepared her for being able to watch him, and pleasure him like this. As she licked, and suckled, taking him deep within her mouth, she watched him, her eyes locked on his face.

His features hardened into a mask of passion. The cords of his neck tightened, and his hands wound into her hair. His mouth opened. His breath became ragged. His hips began to rock, pushing him further, deeper into her mouth. She knew he was about to come when his eyes closed and his head fell back. His hands dug into her scalp and his whole body trembled.

"Christ. Caitlin. Oh God, I'm going to . . ." And then with a series of jerks and a roar, he flooded her mouth with the very essence of him.

She drank him down.

He fell forward tumbling her backwards onto the bed. She savored the heavy feel of him as she licked her lips. He tasted divine. "Now I truly know all of you."

Dangerfield knew he was a man blessed to have such a woman as his wife. He would never have believed he could be this lucky—or this happy. "I love you, my Duchess."

She sighed in his arms, content to cuddle into his side.

"Now," he said. "It's my turn to see,"—he flipped her over and stripped her of her shift—"feel,"—he commenced a leisurely exploration of her body with his hands—"and taste," his tongue probed the soft contours of her mouth as if he was willing to spend all day savoring her like fine cuisine.

She broke off their kiss. "We have to be downstairs soon."

He spread her thighs with his knees, and her hips tilted in unmistakable invitation. "It's our wedding day. We can be as late as we wish."

On the word "wish", he sank into her welcoming heat, determined that no matter how late their arrival downstairs, she'd have a loving she'd never forget.

Like a true partner, her body automatically moved with him, her need building with his. She wrapped her legs around his hips and let him drive deeper into her. Their bodies strove in unison. Locked, heated and slick.

As the flames of desire grew, so did her cries.

"I hear you, my wife," he growled, and with one final stroke they both tumbled into mind-numbing delight, and incandescent sensations of pleasure.

When, at last, they lay spent in each other's arms, and Harlow felt the last of Caitlin's spasms fade, her breathing slow, happiness flooded him.

He took her tiny hand in his. "I've never felt this content. It must be because I'm making love with my wife. I'm truly happy. I don't think I could get any happier."

She rolled onto her side to him. She ran her little finger over his chest. "I will bet you a ride on *Hero* that I could make you happier."

"Christ, woman. I'm not letting you ride *Hero*."

"Chicken?"

"Even your delectable charms couldn't work on me after our second bout of lovemaking. Since the appendage belongs to me, I think I'm pretty safe taking that bet." And he slid his feet off the bed and onto the floor.

"I'm with child."

He froze. Then he looked back over his shoulder and saw the happiness, joy, and pride in his wife's eyes. A slow smile curved his lips.

With a hoot of joy he pulled her to him and kissed her possessively, tumbling her back onto the bed. "You're not riding, *Hero*. Especially now you're with child."

"I don't want to ride your beast." She patted her belly. "I was simply proving a point. You don't get to win all the bets, all of the time."

"Where would be the fun in that?"

It was true. He could live with losing the odd bet. He could live with her, and their children, and be exceedingly happy.

He loved, with a consuming passion, the woman who'd dared the Duke of Dangerfield.

THE END

TO WAGER THE MARQUIS OF WOLVERSTONE

PROLOGUE

London, England, April 1811

As the night air stroked her skin with its soft humid fingers, Sabine Fournier embraced its warmth. It reminded her of her lover's touch. She giggled girlishly at the term *lover*. They were not lovers in the scandalous sense as they had in reality only kissed.

But *what* a kiss he had given her and the past weeks had seen his ardor increase exponentially with each passionate embrace. In return, his lips had set her body on fire. He made her pulse race and her skin craved his touch. All reason fled as his mouth took hers. They both knew he could have taken far more than a few scorching kisses.

But he was a young gentleman. A Lord, in fact, and a man like none other she'd ever known before. By her eighteenth year she'd met very few men, especially one as handsome and as debonair as the Marquis of Wolverstone. Marcus Danvers was a man who completely overpowered all her senses.

Everyone told her he was far above her station, but in fact her father had been a French Comte. Granted he was a penniless one, since her family had fled revolutionary France with little more than the clothes on their backs. But her Father had since made a respectable living teaching French to the children of the aristocracy. And her Father was so delighted for her right now, for he was sure the Marquis of Wolverstone was going to propose to his alluring daughter.

Sabine thought so too. She was sure it would be tonight, for he'd asked to meet her here, in their secret garden—privately. She still had his note tucked into her dress, placed over her heart.

She made herself sit on the small bench by the tinkling fountain, amidst the sweet smelling jasmine. Nerves saw her grip the edge of the seat as if her life depended on it. And in a way it did. For if she did not make a fine match, what then would become of her parents?

That was another reason she was so giddy. She'd found a way to restore her mother and father to their life of ease, to make them safe in their old age, without having to give up her happiness at the same time. Her parents had suffered too much already. Her two brothers had died fighting for England, their adopted country. Now it was up to her to save her elderly parents, the only family she had left.

Finally, she heard footsteps and she rose eagerly to her feet. Her heartbeat thudded to an erratic rhythm in her chest and her nerves sang with a mixture of desire and nervousness. What if he didn't want her for his wife? What if he was simply here to take advantage of her? What would she do if he ruined her reputation? Her beauty and reputation was all she had to make a good match.

No! Her heart rose in her throat. She wanted more than a good match if she could have it. She wanted love. And she was sure the Marquis of Wolverstone loved her—absolutely sure.

He would never discredit her, *never*.

The footsteps drew nearer in the dark and finally he entered the enclosed arbor.

Marcus!

God, *how* she loved him . . .

CHAPTER ONE

London, England 1821—ten years later

They had only just made it to the bottom of the ballroom stairs, when a servant proffered a tray with three large balloon glasses balanced precariously upon it. Marcus hungered for the alluring smoothness of the fine French brandy held temptingly within, but he shook his head. He'd had enough alcohol after the night at Whites. For a change, he wanted to have a clear head in the morning.

He didn't even know why he'd bothered to come to Lady Somerset's ball. Perhaps it was his driving need for her enthusiastic carnal skills. He needed to take his mind off the conversation that would occur with his mother tomorrow morning, and Elizabeth's mouth could do such wicked things to his body; things that would definitely make him forget what his mother was no doubt going to say to him.

Suddenly his companion spoke. "I'd take that drink if I were you. Sabine Fournier is here."

Henry's words sent a slicing chill through Marcus's heart and his hand immediately grabbed a glass from the tray in reaction. He downed the contents in one swallow and took a second glass, determined to become completely sloshed.

Yet the heat from the smooth, rich brandy could not replace the icy coldness invading his veins. It couldn't be true. Was it *really* Sabine, after all these years?

His mind flooded with thoughts of an innocent beauty, quickly followed by the image of a deceptive enchantress. Sabine was the one woman who, ten years ago, had fooled him and played him like a maestro.

He'd not laid eyes on her since.

He turned, knowing exactly where he would find her in the three-hundred strong crowd. It was as if his body sensed the danger. As his eyes drank her image in, she sensed him too, for he saw her stiffen and then turn her head. Their gazes locked and it was exactly like the first time he'd laid eyes on the beautiful French émigré. Desire, lust and then something more erupted within him.

Anger. Betrayal.

He tried to tell himself that he didn't care where she'd been or who she'd been with, but he was deceiving himself. His heart contracted with the pain of remembrance.

She hadn't changed. But that too was a falsehood. For she had indeed changed. She was older and, God damn it to hell, even more beautiful. Her fair hair was stylishly displayed with a long curl winding sinuously over her shoulder to settle within the V of her bountiful bosom, drawing in every red blooded male's eye. She was surrounded by men, of course, all making fools of themselves while vying for her attentions.

"What's she doing here?" he almost spat out the words.

"I can tell you that, darling," and Lady Elizabeth Somerset slid her hand through his arm. She rose up on her toes to whisper in his ear. "She's here for you. She asked specifically to be introduced to Marcus Danvers, the Marquis of Wolverstone.

Silly woman, she clearly has no idea that a man such as you never forgets and never forgives." At his raised eyebrows, Elizabeth added, "I always take the time to learn all about those I share my bed with."

Marcus locked his jaw, distressed at the savage feelings Elizabeth's words awakened in him. Had Sabine really come looking for him? Why?

He had thought his need for Sabine Fournier was long dead. Yet the raging pain running riot within him was witness to the truth—a man never forgets, nor forgives, his first love.

His *only* love.

He was not going to be stupid enough to allow himself to lose his heart ever again.

He'd learned his lesson and learned it very well.

Since Sabine, he'd had many, many women who were just as alluring, and just as beautiful, but none had ever touched his heart in the way Sabine had. He'd wanted her like he'd wanted no other. He'd been willing to sacrifice everything for her—even to deny his family, his peers . . . He'd given her his very soul.

And she'd spat on it from a great height.

Bitter memories saw him slide his arm around Elizabeth and bend to place a scandalous kiss on the widow's eager mouth, all the while holding Sabine's defiant gaze.

Sabine didn't even flinch and for some reason her calm indifference made Marcus's temper soar.

He broke off his kiss and whispered in Elizabeth's ear, "If she wants to talk with me, she'll have to find me first. Come, where's your bedchamber? Your guests can do without you for an hour, but I cannot."

With an eager giggle, Elizabeth began pulling him toward the rear of the ballroom.

Marcus briefly paused at Henry's loud sigh. "I'll see you later then, in the card room?"

He flashed his best friend, Henry St. Giles, the Earl of Cravenswood, an apologetic smile. "Hold me a place. I won't be long." Henry rolled his eyes and strode with determination toward the card room, avoiding the mothers with marriageable daughters. Henry was regarded as a fine catch, while only those mothers desperate enough to approach a scandalous rake bothered about Marcus.

As Elizabeth led him from the overheated ballroom, he swore he could feel Sabine's eyes shooting daggers at his back. He had no idea what she wanted and he didn't care.

He didn't wish to hear anything she said, for her mouth had produced only a litany of lies. Marcus cursed beneath his breath. Sabine had vowed that she loved him and yet she had shattered that declaration with her deceit.

He refused to look back at her. He hoped she regretted her choice now. As for himself, he deeply regretted the day he'd ever met her.

That encounter went better than Sabine had feared; better than she had expected. At least Marcus hadn't turned and left the ball.

Still, her knees shook under her dress. Fortunately, no one seemed attuned to her plight. Most did not even know of her previous relationship with the handsome Marquis. Their relationship, such as it was, had finished over ten years ago. There was more current gossip to keep the braying pack at bay. Most members of the *ton* had even forgotten that she was Sabine Fournier. After all, back then she was nobody, a nonentity who'd tried to enter their world and she'd paid a terrible price for that vanity.

However, she was back. She was now a bona fide member of the *ton*. She was the widowed Contessa Orsini, a rich Italian widow. A widow Society had welcomed with open arms and she would do nothing to taint her position. The revenge she sought, Marcus would obtain for her. And after having glimpsed his demeanor this evening, she was even more certain of this.

Marcus Danvers, the legendary rake, who went through lovers like a dandy went through bright waistcoats. Marcus, the man who'd stolen her heart long before; now she'd fortified it but still her heart felt as if it was buried beneath an avalanche of pain.

She was proud of her ability to maintain her composure when he'd looked her over with such contempt. She refused to let him see how much his opinion still mattered to her. She obviously meant nothing to him. Her father had confessed in his last letter to her that he'd written to the Marquis explaining what had really occurred several years before, but that he'd received no reply.

It was then that she'd realized Marcus hadn't really loved her. If he had, surely, even if he'd no longer wanted her for his wife, he would have forgiven her and perhaps even helped her.

But he was, after all, like every other man. They wanted her for only one thing.

Until Conte Roberto Orsini, that is.

Well, she was no longer the naïve girl who had sat waiting expectantly in the garden. It had taken her years to cleanse the ache of Marcus from her heart. Yet it took only one look at his stunning profile for the old yearning to return.

Her eyes filled with unwelcomed tears as she remembered the last time she had seen Marcus. Hidden in the attic, she watched as his two friends, Harlow Telford and Henry St. Giles had forcibly removed him from her father's house after he'd been given the news of her elopement. Her father had lied to protect her. She'd no choice then but to betray Marcus.

Her heart had been cleaved in two when she registered his shocked desolation at her betrayal. Then she'd seen his anger. He'd gone berserk, smashing up the drawing room. Finally, his friends had managed to drag him outside. As he'd stepped into his carriage he had given the house one final black look and she had registered his chilled contempt. On that day, more than ten years ago, she'd deliberately killed any feelings he may have had for her.

Walking away from him had almost destroyed her. If it were not for her son, Alfredo, she would have shriveled up and died long ago.

There was no point telling Marcus the truth; the past could never be changed. He had moved on with his life and it would only bring him pain.

Besides, her enemy was still too powerful to confront directly. But indirectly, both Marcus and she could seek revenge. However, Marcus's part in the revenge would be unknown to him. He would have no idea the man he was about to ruin was the cause of all their pain, and he never could. She would take that secret with her to the grave.

She inwardly smiled. It was the first genuine smile in a long while. If Marcus thought he could hide from her by engaging in a tryst with this evening's wanton hostess, he was woefully mistaken. With an alluring smile on her lips, she glided through the crowds and slipped into the corridor, making her way toward the ladies' retiring room, looking for Lady Somerset's abigail.

Rose stepped forward to meet her and Sabine followed her without comment as she was led—up the backstairs. She knew her rush to reach Lady Somerset's room had nothing to do with wanting to face Marcus so soon. Rather, it was because she had no wish to walk in on Marcus and his latest lover having sex.

She was strong, but not that strong.

Rose indicated that they'd reached Lady Somerset's door and for a split second Sabine almost lost her nerve. Sweat dribbled between her breasts and her hand shook as she reached out and opened the door. With grim determination, she stepped forward into the brightly lit room.

The lovers were in a passionate embrace. Marcus had the bodice of Elizabeth's dress down at her waist and his lips were pressed to the abundant flesh spilling above her corset. Worse, he too was naked from the waist up. She gave silent thanks that he was still wearing trousers for she had enough trouble thinking clearly with just his powerful chest exposed.

Even so, when he turned at her intrusion, Sabine froze in the doorway, caught in the hypnotizing power of his lust-filled gaze. Even across the short distance, she could feel the searing impact. Her lips parted and she drew a deep breath into her lungs, cursing the faint smile, slow and insolent, curving his mouth.

"Elizabeth, you naughty girl, you didn't tell me Miss Fournier would be joining in our play. Such fun!"

Elizabeth tried to cover her horror with a weak giggle as she pulled up the bodice of her dress.

Collecting herself, Sabine walked further into the room. "It's Contessa Orsini, actually. *Lady* Orsini."

Marcus growled deep in his chest. "I think we both know you're no lady."

Gritting her teeth, Sabine moved further into the room trying to recruit her wits into some semblance of order. "Perhaps you should rejoin your guests, Lady Somerset. Lord Wolverstone and I have private matters to discuss."

His eyes blazed with emotion, burning so fiercely, their anger threatening to scorch what confidence she had left.

"I'm not in this bedchamber for words. If you want to fuck, then by all means stay. If not, then I have no use for you."

CHAPTER TWO

Elizabeth gasped, and being a clever woman, she knew when to retreat. She took one look at Marcus's black countenance and quickly scurried from the room, slamming the door behind her.

Marcus's crudity was meant to shock. He meant to push her away. But Sabine would not be pushed-not anymore.

She moved to the chairs positioned around the blazing fire, averting her eyes from Marcus's finely chiseled chest. "Stop acting like a petulant child. Ten years is a long time to carry a grudge."

His eyes narrowed and he stalked toward her, his anger barely -contained. "Grudge! You have no idea . . ."

He was too close. She stepped back. Her throat closed up and she was unable to utter a reply. His fury swarmed around her like a smothering sand storm—abrasive and deadly. How he'd changed, physically, that is.

His shoulders were broader, his chest harder and his stomach rippled with finely attuned muscles. It was his face that had changed the most, Sabine noted. The fine, aristocratic features were still as striking as they'd been ten years ago. His high cheekbones and noble brow were just as handsome, yet more rugged. But his eyes—his beautiful amber eyes- were cold. Once they'd been warm and soft, full of love and desire. Now they were cold, ice cold, harsh and unforgiving.

She'd always thought him charmingly handsome. Now he was ruthlessly gorgeous. It was all she could do to keep from reaching out to sooth away the frown lines from his forehead.

Sabine eyed him coolly. "Would you please mind putting your shirt back on? You may find some of the ladies swoon at such a blatant display of masculinity, but it has no effect on me."

His mouth twisted slightly. A remnant of his old heart-melting smile, rife with sensual charm, emerged. "Liar!" and he reached out and brought her fingers to his lips, the kiss lingering against her glove. Sabine's heart somersaulted violently in her chest. When he placed her hand on the naked skin of his chest, the heat made her body tighten with a jolt of pure, feminine desire—something she'd not felt in a very long time.

Not since—him, all those years ago . . .

She prayed he'd not noticed her reaction. But when she tore her gaze from where her hand lay and looked up, his wicked smile proved he knew exactly how his nearness had affected her. He was far too experienced to be fooled—especially by her.

Holding his mocking stare, Sabine, with great effort, refrained from withdrawing her hand from his body. Instead, she ran her fingers slowly down over his stomach, watching in satisfaction as the muscles flexed beneath her trailing fingers. He snatched her hand away just as she reached the band of his trousers.

Marcus tightened his grip on her wrist. "No games. What is it you want? We both know it's not my body. You had my heart, body and soul ten years ago and you tossed them aside as casually as a maid emptying a chamber pot."

She did want him. Her response to the simple contact heightened her memories of being held by him. The glorious

149

thrill of having his strong arms around her, her softness crushed against the hardness of his body-she remembered it all. She'd longed for his touch and longed for him for over ten years.

Sabine licked her lips. "I need your help."

He gave a harsh laugh. "By God you've got some nerve. *My help*! After what you did, you want *my help*?"

"Don't keep repeating yourself, I'm not stupid. Yes, your help."

He let lose a string of curses and turning walked to where his discarded clothes lay, he pulled on his shirt, still muttering under his breath.

She felt her shoulders relax a smidgen once the wide expanse of delectable flesh was covered. It had unnerved her enough to be alone with Marcus for the first time since she'd broken his heart, without trying to dampen her physical response to his blatant masculinity as well.

"Please, Marcus. Won't you take a seat? What would it cost you to listen to me?"

Cost? Sabine, the only woman he'd ever proposed to, was asking about cost. The last time he'd listened to her sweet, honeycomb voice and the soft endearments and promises to love him forever, he'd been screwed over.

It had cost him his heart; cost him everything, in fact.

Fury engulfed him.

He advanced toward her composed, luscious figure, displayed to perfection in her strategically draped gown, with slow, determined strides. Standing directly before her he let his eyes roam over every inch of her. Her quick indrawn breath did not escape his notice. She wasn't quite as calm as she appeared.

Good.

He stood regarding her for a moment, letting her unease grow. She licked her lips, while heat pooled in his groin. His gaze then dropped to her slightly opened mouth. The sweetness of her lips drew him and he leaned toward her, lowering his head until his warm breath was close enough to mingle with hers. His injured male pride was alleviated as he saw her sway toward him. She wanted him to kiss her!

Abruptly, he drew back and moved to take one of the empty chairs by the fire. Sitting, he shifted uneasily in his seat and crossed his legs, silently cursing the hot blood that stirred in his loins. For the first time ever, he wished to disown his fierce arousal. He urgently needed to exercise more control.

He'd not been prepared for her response to his nearness and it had almost been his undoing. Being alone with Sabine, in a bedchamber, was having a profound effect on his body. Worse, the blank daze of desire swirling in her beautiful sky blue eyes, in anticipation of his kiss, sent a shock of raw need through his every extremity.

He refused to look at her until she took the chair next to his. He needed the time to compose himself. She too looked as if she was struggling to compose herself. . Her face held a pink flush, as if they'd just made love. Suddenly, he desperately wanted to see Sabine in the throes of passion. He'd never had the privilege of having her beneath him and, by God, he wanted it almost as much as the air he breathed.

She thankfully interrupted his raging carnal thoughts.

"I know you have no reason to help me . . ." she paused briefly and continued "after what I did to you, but I'm hoping you won't hold that against my Father. He greatly admired you, you know."

Marcus tried to concentrate on her words as he sat, utterly fascinated. Sabine was everything he remembered and more. Her hair was still as fair as dried wheat in the heat of summer. The tight coil was softened by a few soft wispy tresses that flowed over her bare shoulders. His gaze wandered to her bosom. Her breasts seemed fuller and more womanly than those of the

151

young girl he remembered. He clenched his fists, fighting the urge to pull her into his lap and bury his face between their plump splendor, to slip his tongue into the valley between her breasts and stroke across her nipples . . .

He shook his head to clear away the tempting images. He'd never known her in that way. A few kisses were all he'd allowed himself. What a fool he'd been. He castigated himself furiously. Why did she still have the power to make him want her so much? Was it simply because he'd been denied the delights of her inviting body?

"Are you listening to me?" A flush crept up her neck as she noted where his gaze was lingering. He refocused his attention with a start.

"Your father was a fine man, as were your brothers. How they must have turned in their graves over the way you treated me."

The flush fled her features and her face became deathly pale. "You're right. I'm sure my brothers would have ensured my life turned out quite differently, but I cannot change the past." Her eyes seemed to blur. "No matter how much I want to." she whispered.

"Humph! Change the past? It seems to have worked out very well for you, *Lady* Orsini."

Her soft voice held a wistful note. "Appearances can be deceptive."

"I know. You taught me that lesson very well."

She stiffened in her seat, upright like an alabaster statue, unable to meet his gaze.

They sat in silence, the only sound the crackle of the fire.

"I'm sorry. I'm truly sorry for hurting you." Her voice shook, and her eyes when they met his were full of unshed tears. "Is that what you want to hear?"

"Only if what you state is true."

She nodded, blinking rapidly to stop the tears from falling.

Marcus exhaled in a rush. "Why? For god's sake, why? You owe me that at least."

She bit her lip so hard he thought she'd make it bleed. Finally she shrugged, as if in defeat. "I was young and stupid and I made a mistake. A mistake life has severely punished me for. You don't need to heap any more upon me."

Need, no. Want, yes. Or did he? Sabine appeared to be genuine in her remorse. But then again, he'd thought her genuine in her feelings for him in the past.

"What is it you want from me? Where you are concerned, I have little to give."

"It's not for me, it's for my father and mother. I want you to enter and win a card game—*the* card game."

Marcus found it difficult to control his surprised reaction. This was the last thing he'd expected. "You need money?"

"No, not at all. What I want of you is to enter and then win the Gentleman's Annual Whist Tournament that begins in three days' time."

Now he was interested. . He did not have a name as the most skilful of players. Did she in fact want to see him lose? He remained silent, his steely gaze fixed unwaveringly on her face. She licked her lips and yet again his balls tightened. God, how could he still want her so badly? His mind pictured all the things those luscious lips could do to pleasure him.

She continued. "You have never entered this tournament before and therefore will be an unknown."

Marcus felt his shoulders bunch and ripple. "You want me to win the tournament? Why?"

"I mean to destroy the man who ruined my father. His actions lead directly to the deaths of my parents. Women cannot enter this tournament. Therefore, I need your assistance. As well, I need you to give me that element of unknown in my quest to trounce my enemy. I wish to entice a certain gentleman into betting against you. I will lure him to bet on the favorite, Lord Prendergast. He's won the tournament for the last five years. When you win, this said gentleman will have lost everything."

"I have always considered you devious after what happened but this . . . I'm truly lost for words. Not very honorable is an understatement but, really, I shouldn't be so surprised."

She took a deep breath. Her eyes glinted with anger and he saw her hands were shaking; her fury was glaringly obvious. They sat staring at each other for what seemed like hours but was, in reality, merely minutes.

As he expected, she gave in. "This man is using my father's money to stake his bets. He is using blood money to try and make a fortune. I *won't* allow it to happen. It is pure and simple revenge. He left my parents to die in abject poverty . . ."

Marcus watched her closely. Her face was deathly pale and it was clear she was not lying.

"Why did your father not ask for help?"

"He thought the law would help him. He also thought he could deal with this man himself. He was sorely mistaken. I don't intend to make that mistake. By using you, by you putting up your stake for the game, this man will have no idea I am behind his impending demise. For who would believe you'd ever help me?"

His conscience then came knocking loud and clear. He remembered her father's letters. Had they been a cry for help? Guilt made him ask, "Who was the man?"

She shook her head. "I don't want you involved. I simply want you to win the game."

His mouth firmed but her chin took on a stubborn tilt. She would not tell him. Well, he would not push at this moment, but he would learn his name.

He let out a harsh laugh. "And what happens when I win?"

"You'll win a very large sum of money, plus I'll give you a bonus of one-hundred thousand pounds. I'm a very wealthy woman and money is no object." she said in a haughty voice.

The bloody nerve of the woman—money! She thought money interested him! He had more money than he knew what to do with. Making sound investments was an innate talent of his and he'd more than prospered over the years. He managed his friends, Harlow's and Henry's, finances, as well as his own.

No. Winning more money did not excite him. He knew exactly what would excite him. He wanted her, in every which way a man could take a woman, until he'd had his fill.

God damn her to hell! He shouldn't want her like this. He blamed her for re-entering his life unbidden, and his anger at how alluring she still was, grew until he felt white-hot fury that she still had the power to make him feel so much.

His eyes drank her in thirstily. Sabine was no longer the innocent girl he'd fallen in love with, if indeed she ever had been innocent. He wanted her with a man's relentless desire. Ten years ago his desire for her was mixed with tenderness. Now, he simply wanted her with a raw, naked hunger. How much he wanted her, frightened him and rendered him vulnerable.

Agreeing to help her would be a mistake. Every honed instinct screamed for him to deny her and stand and leave. But part of him still wanted what had been ripped away from him all those years ago. He craved what she'd dangled before him so temptingly and then so callously cut away.

This time, he would make her fall in love with him and then *he*'d be the one to walk away.

"You're obviously under some misconception that I care about money," he finally proffered.

"Then, if not money, what is it that you do care about?" she queried in a manner that was faintly taunting.

"Pleasure-and then some more," Marcus responded, observing with satisfaction her horrified expression. "Come, don't act so surprised. If you have taken the time to learn about me, then you must have learned of all my favorite pursuits."

Involuntarily, she glanced at her hands and he saw her swallow nervously. "You are one of the most notorious rakehells in all of England. The minute I returned to England I could hardly avoid learning that." She raised her eyes to meet his. "Perhaps I had a lucky escape."

Calling on all his willpower, Marcus reined in his violent irritation at her provocative words. "I used to be exceedingly discriminating about the women I pursued. However, after you . . . after *you* taught me how ridiculous that sentiment was, I didn't much care who I bedded. I simply buried my pain in pleasure."

Her lack of response at his proclamation needled him further.

"Fucking, in another word. Actually, I have become rather good at it. I'm sure, given your lack of particularity about who shares your bed, that you've become quite the expert too."

Some emotion flickered in her eyes in response, something vulnerable and too fleeting for him to identify. Then she lowered her eyelids as if to shield the secrets she hid within.

He leaned forward in his chair. "In fact, you can take the blame for turning me into, as you so succinctly put it, a notorious rakehell."

Finally, a reaction! With her mouth turned down in sharp disapproval and her eyes dark with anger, she ferociously defended herself. "I'm sure you were already well on the path to depravity and wickedness before I met you. You certainly didn't behave like a proper gentleman, especially with me."

He threw back his head and laughed. "You think what *we* did was wicked? Hop on that bed and I'll show you the true definition of wicked!"

"I don't think that will be necessary"

"And why not? Unless, of course, you still enjoy teasing the men in your life. Do you dangle your body temptingly like a piece of heaven before them and then watch them writhe in pain when you deprive them of the physical satisfaction you so falsely promised them?"

CHAPTER THREE

Sabine hissed at him through clenched teeth, trying to protect herself from his cruel taunt. "That, I believe, is none of your concern."

"That's where you are wrong, siren. If you wish me to help you with your distasteful plan, then who you may be bedding is very much my concern. I won't be cuckolded again."

"I don't understand? How can I have ever cuckolded you? We were never lovers, nor are we likely to be." She gasped in sudden comprehension and a shudder ripped through her. "Oh, no! Absolutely not."

He laughed, a rich sound that skittered down her spine, reminding her of a more pleasant time, long ago.

"Haven't you ever thought about us and how it would have been in my bed? I'm considered quite the expert. I must admit"—he ran his eyes insolently over her until she felt as if she were naked under his gaze—"I've often fantasized about what I'd do to you—with you—if you were ever mine."

"I haven't thought of you much at all," she retorted, praying he'd believe the lie. She'd thought about him almost every lonely day over the past ten years.

"Well, my lovely, if you want my help that is all about to change. I want you thinking about me every second of the day and night and me only, if you can manage that?"

Hearing his bitterness, Sabine stared down at the carpet. Tension constricted her throat. Marcus would never forgive her, that much was obvious. Her plan to avenge her father—as well as herself would fall apart without Marcus's support.

Worse, she didn't deserve his derision or his hatred. She'd suffered more than he knew. But if Marcus learned the truth, he'd be more than eager for revenge. That had been why she'd done what she'd had to do, all those years ago. She knew the revenge he'd then insist upon taking and that would put his very life in danger. She couldn't live with the guilt should something happen to him.

"I'm not asking you to do this for me. I'm asking you to help me extract revenge for my father and mother."

His face softened slightly at the mention of her parents. "Tell me what happened."

"My father was a proud man. As he got older, his work began to dry up and he looked around for an investment which would keep them both in their old age. He was introduced to a man who had a sure fire investment."

Marcus interrupted. "Let me guess, Gower suggested investing in Northern Mining."

Blast! She hadn't wished to reveal her target quite so soon. Reluctantly, she confirmed his guess. "Yes, yes." She opened her palms wide, willing the tears not to come. "They lost everything. They died of malnutrition and disease in a poorhouse." She held back a sob at the memory of the letter that had arrived too late in Milan. Her father had written telling her of their plight. By the time she'd returned to England, they were both dead. "I've done some investigating. Northern Mining was a paper company with no assets. Gower knew what he was doing, yet the law won't touch him."

Marcus nodded his head, understanding. "The men behind the investment were clever. It all looks legitimate on paper." He looked grim. "You are proposing your own brand of punishment. You've learned of Gower's weakness—gambling. I've heard he's in dun territory."

"Yes, I've learned a lot about Lord Gower. He is not a very good card player. He doesn't ever enter the Gentleman's Annual Whist Tournament but he wagers on the outcome. I believe he's placed a very large bet on Lord Prendergast with the field. He's positive the bet is a sure thing. The odds are in his favor, Prendergast has won the last five years."

"Gower thinks he'll clear his debts from this one tournament. Everyone at Whites has heard of his exorbitant wager."

She lifted her gaze to Marcus, and as their eyes locked, the painful past was a chasm between them. "Will you help me?"

It was all the pleading she'd do. Pain lashed her at the cold expression on his handsome face. Having met with Marcus, even after ten years, Sabine realized that time had not mitigated the raw hurt of her necessary betrayal. She was mud under his boot.

"If you want my help, I have a wager of my own."

The hairs on her arms rose and her stomach began to churn. What was coming could not be good.

He continued. "If I win, I want more than money. I want flesh and blood. If I help you obtain your revenge, then you must help me gain mine."

She wasn't stupid. There was no point in pretending she didn't know exactly what he was implying. He wanted his revenge against her.

He spoke huskily but firmly. "We shall have our own wager, you and I. If I win the tournament for you, you must become my paramour for as long as I desire." He glanced at her with his glinting amber eyes, the dark lashes shielding his true thoughts. "And I have ferocious desires."

Even though Sabine had known what he was going to demand, the shock made her give a choked cry. "I thought you many things once, but never petty."

"I'm a changed man. *You* changed me when you used me to capture another's affections, hopping from one bed to another . . ."

She couldn't resist her own taunt. "We never shared a bed."

Her words made his mouth snap shut in remembered pain. He tried not to clench his fists. He let his hands lay flat against his thighs. He'd never let on how much her words cut him to the quick. Sabine had taken great pains to keep his passions subdued, nothing more than a few dizzying kisses. He'd behaved like a gentleman, while all along she was playing him false and for a fool.

"Were you sharing his bed while teasing me? Did you laugh at my chasing after you like a whipped puppy?"

Sabine's eyes narrowed on his. "I did not share a bed until I married."

"So, Orsini was the man you eloped with. Your father would not tell me his name."

Sabine looked at the floor. She brushed her brow with delicate gloved fingers and sighed. She slowly raised her head and looked directly at him. "What good does it do to rake over the past? I cannot change it, nor can you." She looked up at him, the blue of her eyes flashing dark as if a storm was approaching. "I can't make up for the hurt I caused you, but I can avenge my father with your help. Will you do it? If you cannot do it for me, then at least for him"

He couldn't look away from the appeal in her eyes. Tension gripped him. For some reason, he knew this decision would be a turning point in his life. He should say no and deny her what she so badly wanted, just as she had denied him all those years ago. But he was a man who wasn't used to denying himself anything. And right now, he desperately wanted her.

Keeping his voice even he said, "I've explained the terms of my wager. Do you think I was joking? If I win the tournament, you must agree to become my lover for as long as I desire it of you."

Before she could bat it away, a rush of excitement flared and skittered through her body. His lover! Something she'd forever longed to become. Her heart thudding, Sabine swallowed the urge to willingly agree to his request. She had others to think of, her son for one. One of the reasons she had sought out Marcus was she'd thought he'd not want anything from her. She had hoped he'd agree to help her because of her father. However, she'd never dreamed he'd want her in his bed as he had no trouble finding willing lovers.

It truly appeared he was a man who did not overlook slights and she'd more than slighted him. She'd cut him to the bone.

"Well?" he asked the menace evident in his tone. It was a challenge of sorts and one that would reveal just how desperate for his help she was.

"I thought you despised me. I cannot believe you want me in your bed?"

He held her stare and his mouth curved into a cruel smile. "I do despise you, but . . ." and he let his eyes roam insolently over her clothing as if stripping her bare, "I'm also a man and as I said, I want what you dangled before me and teased me with all those years ago. I'm sure once I've had you I'll soon forget you. As easily as I forget every other woman I've ever slept with."

She drew a steadying breath at his blatant insult. He'd made it perfectly clear this was about revenge. She was simply another woman to bed before he moved on. She was no one special, merely a woman with whom to slake his urgent desire for retribution and nothing more.

Never again would she see him smile at her with tenderness and devotion. The thought of it sent pain coursing through her.

Over the years she'd learned to shelter her heart from loneliness, with Alfredo giving her only the will to live on. But to give herself to Marcus, the man she loved, knowing it meant nothing to him, that if anything it was his means of revenge, a way to punish her for the past, would be almost too much too bear.

"You must hate me so very much," she offered in a quiet voice.

Marcus shrugged his shoulders. "I hadn't thought of you at all until today. Why so reluctant? You don't have to behave like a chaste virgin. I doubt you were one when we first met and I'm positive, Lady Orsini, you aren't one now. Sharing my bed will bring you pleasure. I've learned a few things since I last knew you, as I'm sure have you. Unlike ten years ago, neither of us will be satisfied with just a few kisses."

She refused to rise to his taunt. She was a virgin when they first met. But none of it mattered now. All that mattered was making Gower pay. She was determined to exact revenge for the lives that were stripped from her, Marcus, and her parents by this one evil man.

She would get her revenge, she vowed silently. She'd sworn it as she lay next to her elderly husband and shriveled up inside each time he had touched her. A man she did not love but to whom she belonged. A man who knew how she felt but still came to her bed. Not only that but a man who had tried to make her love him—and had failed. For that she felt forever guilty. Roberto Orsini had been a good man. He was a man who had deserved more.

"I have a son." She saw him blanch at her words and he moved uncomfortably in his seat. His gaze lowered. She went on, determined to make him understand. "Alfredo, the future Conte Orsini. I don't want any scandal. I have to protect him until I return to Italy."

Marcus's eyes glinted with triumph as he returned her stare. He lent forward in his chair. "I assure you I can be very discreet."

"Like you were tonight, slipping away with the hostess of the ball,' she said sarcastically, claws slipping free of her self-imposed sheath.

He ignored her barb. "So, other than safe-guarding your reputation, you have no objections? You accept my terms then?" His voice held a hint of victorious excitement.

She nodded but her show of bravery faltered. "I accept your wager. After this we will be even. I hope it gives you the peace you seek. My brothers will be turning in their grave at *your* behavior," she said flatly.

His eyes filled with respect. "Touché!" Then in one swift move he was on his feet pulling her into his arms. "Good, then we will seal out wager with a kiss."

She placed her hands on his chest, feeling the heat of his body through the thin linen of his shirt. Panic flared and she pushed at his chest. "No! You have not earned my favors yet."

CHAPTER FOUR

It was too soon. She couldn't . . . her stomach plummeted sickeningly. Sabine swallowed hard. She couldn't let him overwhelm her in case she gave far too much too soon. He had to win the wager first. Besides, she didn't want her first taste of him to be in Lady Somerset's bedchamber, where he'd been about to bed that wanton woman. He could not expect her to simply walk into his arms as if the past had never happened. But then he didn't know her true feelings. He thought she'd tossed him aside as callously as a farmer shoots a cart-horse with a broken leg.

Her legs suddenly felt weak. They wouldn't support her weight and the room swam. Two strong arms gripped her tightly for support.

"I didn't realize my touch held such revulsion for you," he said harshly in her ear.

"It's not that. Whatever you may think of me, I am not a courtesan used to kissing men I don't know on command. It's been ten years, Marcus. You no longer know me and I certainly no longer know who you are."

He didn't release her as she expected, instead he stroked a

finger slowly down her neck.

A seductive smile curved his mouth and he arched an eyebrow at her. "Then by all means let us be reacquainted. If I recall, you loved it when I nibbled your ear," and he bent his head and she felt the soft press of familiar lips against the skin of her neck as he nuzzled closer to her ear lobe. She couldn't stop an inhalation of breath. A familiar sensation streaked across her skin and her heart suddenly seemed too big for her chest. She breathed deeply and his scent flooded her lungs. Dark and spicy, it was intoxicatingly unforgettable.

His words mirrored her thoughts. "You smell just like I remember," he murmured against her skin. "You're trembling. I remember that too. How you pushed against me in your eagerness. We both know that I could have taken you many times in the garden where we used to meet." His hands roamed down her sides and her body quivered in his arms. He cupped her bottom and drew her in tight against him. "I was a fool not to. Then I would not have spent the last ten years dreaming of how you would feel with me buried deep within you." His words were said with such derision she gasped with suppressed pain, awash with regret at what they'd lost all those years ago.

She could feel his erection bulging against her stomach. She'd dreamed of him-of this moment- for many years but in her dreams he'd wanted her because he'd forgiven her, vowing that he still loved her.

She'd never dreamed he'd want to make love to her to satisfy his thirst for revenge, nor that his desire was driven by hate. She knew hate was as strong an emotion as love. She knew hate intimately.

Marcus's lips moved down to the hollow at her throat. She tried not to allow it, but her body sought comfort from his. She pressed closer. He growled against her skin. He seemed to want to punish her. He didn't need to. She'd been punished enough.

She'd wished for his arousing touch almost every day. However, she hadn't expected him to ever want to make love to her, and especially not this evening. Not here. Not now.

Make love, at these words her heart clenched. This was not making love. She felt a tear slip from the corner of her eye. But even so, her body craved the idea.

He drew back suddenly and wiped one of her tears from his face. His eyes opened in astonishment, "If anyone should be crying over the past it should be me." His voice held a wounded tone and she longed to tell him the truth and appease his pride.

Then the image of her gorgeous boy, Alfredo, stopped her.

She'd allowed Marcus to fall in love with her—and then she'd broken his heart.

Could she make him fall in love with her again and this time perhaps they could find their happy ever after? It would be dangerous to think so. The only person who would be devastated by her failure was herself. Could she face that kind of loss yet again?

For a chance of winning everything she desired—maybe she just could.

"I'm not as cold hearted as you believe. I was, for a moment, overcome by memories. It has been a long time since I have wanted a man's touch."

What an actress she would have made. She could have been on the stage with conviction like that. Yet he bit down on the inside of his mouth to stop his tender response to her words. Were they perhaps the truth? He suspected she lied. But then bitter-sweet memories flooded his mind. He'd fallen for her sweet entreats once before. He wasn't sure he could ever believe anything that passed between her lying lips.

But with her standing this close, the light fragrance of lemon filling his nostrils, her skin soft under his hands, he did not have the strength to turn and walk away.

He should have known the effect Sabine would have on him.

Not only was she the most desirous woman he'd ever met, she was the only woman who had ever left him. She was the one who, without hesitation, brought him to his knees, before coldly casting him aside. No other woman had denied him anything before or since.

He gazed into her eyes, their irises big and dark, her desire not faked, it would seem. She reached out and touched his face, the simple gesture a stronger aphrodisiac than if she lay naked before him.

He needed to regain control. This repentant Sabine unnerved him.

In a soft voice, so quiet he almost didn't hear her words, Sabine said, "Do you think that if you take me here and now you'll be able to move on, and help me avenge my father?"

Move on. She thought one quick fuck would erase the years of pain and longing, the years of not understanding why she had crushed him in every respect.

Was she that callous? Was revenge for her father all she valued? Of course it was. He should have known that emotions, true heart-felt emotions, very rarely entered into her plans.

The painful memories were too much for him. He stepped back to put some distance between them. She was the devil disguised as temptation. He left her standing by the fire, a vision of smoldering sensuality. He turned his back on the sight and struggled to gain control of his fluctuating emotions. For one moment he wished he'd not offered such a wager. He wanted to say no to her request, to reject her out of hand in the way she'd rejected him. Why should he care about her father and mother?

Then a delicate, tiny hand touched his arm. "Please, Marcus. Do you want me to beg? Because, trust me, I will do so, if that is your wish. I will do *anything* you require . . . I have only ever willingly slept with my husband. You can believe that or not, but I will let you take me, here and now, if that is what you need in order to help me."

The reminder of what Orsini had taken from him was too much. She should have been his. He should have been her first and only lover.

He swung around and pulled her against him, taking her mouth in a bruising kiss, trying frantically to block the image her words incited, that of Sabine in the arms of another man.

She stood rigidly but then slowly melted against him. This he remembered well. The taste and eagerness of her, it was as if he could smell the fragrant flowers of her parents' garden where they used to meet long ago. His senses flared and his desire bolted as if from a tightly held leash. He couldn't stop now even if he wanted to.

And he didn't want to. He held his dream. He held Sabine.

His Sabine. His—only his.

Passion roared in his veins, and all thoughts vanished but his driving need to sink deep within her.

His hands grasped her arms and he pulled her against his hard body. A small squeak of distress escaped her. She tried to still the rush of desire that flamed deep within but it had been too long.

A strong arm curved around her waist, binding her close.

"I will have you. When I win the tournament you will come to me willingly . . ."

The sudden possession of his mouth took her by surprise. The warmth of soft yet firm lips molding to hers made her raw nerves scatter. The heat rose and it was like being engulfed in fire. As his tongue swept into her mouth she relaxed into the kiss, unable and unwilling to prevent the wild reaction of her passion starved body.

It was different from the kisses she remembered. It was raw hunger coupled with possession and mastery. It was the kiss of a man who knew exactly how to get a response from a woman. Rough fingers trailed down to the base of her neck, where a long finger slid under the edge of her bodice.

A wave of familiar desire swept over her. Her breasts swelled and her nipples hardened, her corset restricting her breath. Sweet heaven! No wonder women fell into his bed at the crook of his finger or the taste of his tongue.

His mouth was like a drug. A drug she'd been without for ten long years.

As he deepened the kiss, it drowned out every aspect of the past. She found herself clinging to him with abandon, while clever, knowing fingers undid several buttons at the back of her dress.

One tapered finger slid its way under her corset, and she gasped as he gently but expertly eased her breast free so that her nipple was exposed. Before she could stop him, he lowered his head and flicked his tongue over the taut bud. Scorching heat flickered over her, and she could not stop the soft cry of delight the moment his teeth lightly clamped on her and suckled at the nipple in a seductive rhythm.

His mouth let her experience long forgotten memories. The taste of him was better than her soul destroying imaginings. How she'd missed him . . .

The pleasure spiraling through her body was indescribable. Moist heat gathered at the apex of her thighs. For a brief moment she pictured his hand cupping her there. His fingers delving . . .

Shocked by the traitorous way her body was behaving, she braced her hands on his chest and tried to break his hold, tried to push away.

His fingers skimmed her exposed breast, palming her sensitive flesh. The touch made her mouth dry and longing gripped her. What would it be like to be Marcus's lover? Immediately her mind careened to a halt. It would be torture. She loved him while he held her in contempt. Bedding her would simply ease a wound he'd longed to heal. Would he celebrate in victory if she revealed how she felt about him?

Sweet heaven, she needed to keep a reign on her true feelings where Marcus was concerned. If she exposed the truth too soon, all could be lost. Marcus could be hurt more than she'd already hurt him.

She needed to close this wager and flee with what little dignity she still possessed.

Wrenching herself out of his arms, she backed away from him.

His voice sounded hoarse. "Perhaps I'll not have to wait until after I win the wager to take you. As always you seem eager for the sport."

The hard edge in his voice raised the hair on the nape of her neck. Yet the icy glint of triumph in his burnt amber eyes held a hint of something else that made her struggle to turn and walk away. Was it regret?

"I can wait to taste your body, for there are plenty of willing women to appease the ache in my cock."

The shocking words made her gasp, but she refused to comment. Hurt beyond belief, she struggled to hide her pain. She adjusted her clothing speedily. She had to leave. She pulled her dress back into place, as though it were a suit of protective armor, being all the while fully aware of his dark eyes watching her.

If only she knew what he was thinking, he'd be much easier to manage. *Manage!* But only in her dreams . . . Never had she expected him to react like this. Once her clothing was firmly back in place and she was feeling more composed, she lifted her head, only to see him smiling at her, the glow of desire still in his eyes.

She could only stare at him with a sinking feeling of horror as he offered her a knowing smile.

"Are you jealous, my love?"

"No. And I am certainly *not* your love."

171

"True. You never were, were you," he added sarcastically.

Her senses somewhat restored by his cutting remark, she glared back at him. "Think what you like of me. All that matters is that I have your agreement to help me."

The desire fled from his gaze and his mouth firmed into a disapproving line. "In three days I'll win the tournament and then I'll collect. You will come to my bed, when and where I desire it." His eyes narrowed and his hands rose to his hips. "You'd better not be thinking of reneging once I've won. I'll come after you and you'll not like my anger."

"If you win, I'll give you your pound of flesh, and I hope it chokes you," she retorted and sweeping around him, she made for the door.

CHAPTER FIVE

Marcus didn't need the forthcoming meeting with his mother to put him in a bad mood. He woke this morning with Sabine's scent and taste still swirling around him. He hoped that soon satisfying his carnal need for her would diminish somewhat the pain of her betrayal. He could look back on the past and shrug his shoulders, as if her deceit in eloping with another man hadn't altered his life or persona at all.

Unfortunately, the pleasure he'd found in Sabine's kiss had not diminished his desire for the vexing French beauty. Rather it had reignited a flame that had refused to die. He'd woken with a rampant erection, desirous of another encounter.

As Parsons, his stoic valet shaved him he made the decision to take Sabine into his bed the night he won the tournament. The sooner he bedded her the sooner he could send her away. He was desperate to extinguish his burning hunger for her. Then, and only then, could he finally move on with his life. *Move on.* He knew his appointment this morning with his mother was about moving on.

A full fifteen minutes before the requested meeting time,

and perfectly groomed, Marcus made his way to his mother's, Collette's, drawing room. He knew what the meeting would be about. She wanted an heir for the Wolverstone name, but more importantly, she wanted grandchildren.

He'd learned very quickly that a woman set on grandchildren was a force to be reckoned with, especially when it was his mother, the reigning Dowager of the *ton*.

Worse, he loved his mother and had terrible trouble denying her anything. He remained a bachelor largely because she had been content to let him sow his wide oats up to now. Dowager Wolverstone had wanted her son to find the right woman. Little did she know that he'd found loads of *right* women. They were right for bedding, which is all he wanted from any female. He did not trust any of them, certainly not enough to give them his heart.

He'd give them his name, perhaps, but not his heart.

However, over the last few months, since his thirtieth birthday, Collette's patience concerning his taking a wife had disappeared like the grains of sand in an egg timer.

As he stood outside his mother's room, he knew the timer had run out of sand.

He knocked and waited for her to bid him entry.

"Come in, dear."

He strode in with a grin on his face. "How did you know it was me," he asked as he kissed his mother's proffered cheek.

"It was the tone of your knock. It sounded annoyed. You hate it when I summon you."

He took the seat across from her. He admired his mother tremendously. Not just her graceful beauty, for she still turned heads at almost a half-century, but for her composure and loyal heart. After his father's death, she could have remarried, should have remarried. Yet, she could not bring herself to dishonor her husband's memory. If only there were more women of his mother's nature, women whose love was true and ever-lasting. His father had chosen well, while he had chosen like a fool . . .

He left his bittersweet memories behind and prepared himself for battle. "It's not so much the summons as the reason behind it."

His mother laughed gaily. "If you know the reason, why haven't you done more to progress my wishes. I've left you alone for the last three months and nothing . . ." Her smile vanished. "And now I hear Sabine Fournier, has returned to London in a new guise, as the Contessa Orsini."

His smile remained plastered on his face with an effort. "Why should that concern me?"

She sighed and shook her head. "When will you learn, my boy. I see and hear *everything*. I heard she purposely attended Lady Somerset's ball to seek a meeting with you."

Marcus uncrossed his legs. "Lady Orsini is of no concern to me. She's in my past and is of no consequence."

"Rubbish," Collette spluttered. "She is the first woman you loved."

"Loved, as in past tense. I have no feelings for Sabine now." *Liar.* You have feelings for her, but none you can discuss with your mother. An image from last night of Sabine's golden tresses spilling over her naked breasts set his mind racing. He hastily recrossed his legs.

She studied him quietly before giving a triumphant smile. "I'm very pleased to hear you say that. Sabine Fournier almost destroyed you once. I'll not sit by and let her do it again."

"Nothing Lady Orsini could do would ever have any impact on me, mother."

"Then you'll not mind paying court to Lady Amy Shipton."

Marcus rubbed his brow, his headache worsening. "Paying court?"

"As you don't seem to care for one particular woman, I thought *I'd* find you a wife. Grandchildren, my boy, I want plenty of them before I'm too old to enjoy them. I've waited long enough. I'd like to see your engagement announced by the end of the season, and an autumn wedding would be super."

His mother was nothing but direct. He admired that about her. She didn't play games. "Does the lady know of this plan?"

"Her mother does. And she approves, regardless of your well deserved reputation. Amy is the most sought after debutante this season. She's beautiful, but best of all she has a brain. I know you'd be bored with a simpleton."

His lips turned up with a hint of a smile. "Your idea of beauty and mine might be quite different," he teased.

"Oh, it's not my idea. I simply chose a woman who looked very much like all your mistresses. I assume that is your preference. A woman with dark hair, dark eyes, and a much fuller figure—voluptuous I believe the look is called."

His face flared with heat and he choked back a snort. How did his mother know of such things?

"Amy is the exact opposite of Sabine Fournier, and considering you've never bedded a fair-haired woman since her, she would be what I assume you would desire."

Now that statement from his mother was too close for comfort and exceedingly embarrassing.

"I have no idea how you came by that piece of information and I don't wish to. But mother, really . . ."

"You've got to get on with your life." Her hands were waving which wasn't a good sign. It meant she was winding up for a passionate explosion. "You've let Sabine Fournier rule your life for almost ten years and I'll not put up with it anymore. You're a wonderful, warm man if only you'd let people close enough to see it. Do not judge all women by one jezebel's actions. I had hoped your parent's marriage would demonstrate how wonderful a family could be." Her voice broke on the last sentence. "I still miss your father terribly."

"I do know how wonderful your marriage with Father was. I've never seen two such devoted people. That's why I have not married. I haven't found that with anyone."

"Don't think to sway me. You haven't exactly been looking. Well, not looking in the right places. You don't marry mistresses." She pulled her pleading, helpless look. "Would you do this for me? Will you at least meet Amy and consider the idea?"

He could never deny his mother when she was like this. Besides, Amy was exceedingly beautiful in that dark, Celtic manner. He'd have no trouble rising to the occasion of begetting an heir and the much wanted grandchildren.

He usually stayed well away from debutantes but he remembered the dark beauty. She'd caught his eye at a ball; he couldn't remember which one. One of the other beauties of the season had spitefully spilt a drink on one of the wall-flowers, and Amy had stepped forward in her defense and proffered a cutting remark to the perpetrator. Then she had escorted the ugly duckling away to be cleaned up. He'd admired her for her compassion and good-heart.

His mother was watching him with a raised eyebrow.

Perhaps letting his mother select a wife wasn't such a bad idea. His disaster with Sabine flashed through his mind. He'd made a complete hash of it the first time on his own. His mother would know the young lady's character better than he ever could. He wanted a woman who would be true to him, who would be an excellent and caring mother and who could step in and fill his mother's shoes within Society. A high expectation he knew. But who else was better qualified to find his mother's replacement than the woman who had previously held the title of Lady Wolverstone?

"You're over-thinking this, Marcus. Why not pay attention to the girl and see what develops. That is all I'm asking."

"May the devil take you, Mother! You know that is not *all*

you're asking. The minute I step out with Lady Amy Shipton, the *ton* will assume I've selected her to become the next Lady Wolverstone. I've never once encouraged a virginal miss."

"Mind your language, please."

Marcus tipped his head back and laughed. "You can discuss my preference in bed partners but I cannot utter the word *virginal*?" He shook his head. "Sometimes Mother, you really are priceless."

He rose and walked to kiss her goodbye. "I'm leaving. I've promised to meet Henry at the club, although of late he's become a pain in my rear. He's almost as bad as you. He's enraptured of Harlow's marriage to Caitlin. He believes true love will make us content." He gave a harsh laugh. "He doesn't realize how rare true love is."

Mother and son shared a special smile. She said, "Well, I do. And I know Amy Shipton is the right woman for you if you'll simply give her a chance."

As he made his way to the door, he made a final comment over his shoulder. "As you knew you it would, your wish prevails. Set your plan in motion in regards to Amy. Simply tell me where I have to turn up and I promise I shall be on my best behavior." He paused before he exited and gave his mother a stern look. "But if I don't like her, I will not be persuaded. Do I make myself clear?"

"Perfectly, my dear."

He closed the door behind him on his mother's triumphant smile. Knowing his mother, his life as a bachelor was now on borrowed time. He should make merry while he still could.

He immediately thought of Sabine, picturing her naked and in his bed.

His pulse quickened and his body hardened.

It was best he got on and enjoyed his freedom while it lasted.

Marcus hurried up the steps of White's set on finding Henry and getting his friend to take his mind of his predicament. He strolled into the cool interior of the club and found Henry reading the paper at their normal table near the back. No sooner had he taken his seat than a glass of brandy appeared on a tray before him. "Keep them coming, George. It's going to be one of those days."

"Yes, my lord," and George, the ever patient and efficient servant discreetly fetched the decanter and left it on their table.

Henry peered over the top of his paper with disapproving eyes. "Why am I not surprised? This requirement to drink yourself senseless has nothing to do with last night, does it?"

"No."

"Funny. I can't remember you joining me in the card room as you said you would."

"I was waylaid."

Henry folded the paper neatly and laid it on the table. "Waylaid? Is that what they call it now? By whom may I ask? Lady Somerset reappeared in the ballroom rather suddenly without you, I may add."

Marcus blushed and he gulped back the alcohol in his glass.

Henry continued with a wry smile. "And who else seemed to be missing from the room? It was none other than Sabine Fournier herself. A coincidence? I think not."

"Damn it, Henry. I'm not in the mood. This morning mother coerced me into agreeing to court Amy Shipton. I don't need another lecture."

Henry sat back in his chair and pursed his lips. "Amy Shipton." His head nodded. "She's a good choice for you, Marcus. She's kind, beautiful and as bright as a button. She could make you happy."

Why did the image of Sabine's beautiful face flash before him whenever he heard the word happy? Sabine would never make him happy. He would never forgive her for her deceit. He couldn't. What if he opened his heart again and she knifed it a second time?

Marcus groaned.

Henry continued. "Then why did you spend last evening with Sabine Fournier? She's trouble. I don't want to see you hurt again. Remember I was there to pick up the mess she left behind her last time."

"If you must know she has had the audacity to beg a favor of me."

Henry's eyebrow rose. "I hope you told her to sod off."

A smile broke over his lips. "Actually, I have agreed to help her. Her father was one of Gower's victims and died in the poorhouse because of it. She wants revenge. She wants my help to ensure she gets it."

"If she has a good plan, then I'm in too. Gower ruined a lot of good people, Millicent included. She lost her life's savings."

"Which I'm sure you will help her replenish."

Millicent was Henry's current mistress. Henry had stayed true to her for over two years and she was the main reason why, although he talked about the joys of marriage, he did not parttake of it. Marcus thought his friend was hoping for a miracle. That somehow Society would condone a marriage to his mistress.

"What's her plan?"

"She wants me to win the Gentleman's Annual Whist Tournament."

"How did she know about your card skills? You rarely play in public."

Marcus shrugged. "That's her strategy. It doesn't actually matter if I win or not; rather, I'm to enter and ensure whoever Gower has backed *doesn't* win."

"And that will ruin him?"

"He'll lose everything. He's desperate and has staked everything he owns on Prendergast being in the final pair. I suspect Lady Orsini is buying up or has bought up all his vowels."

Henry grimaced. "Knowing how cold hearted she is; I doubt she'll show any mercy."

Marcus started. *Cold.* When he'd held her in his arms she'd been anything but cold. She was fiery passion personified. His blood raged hot at the thought of having her beneath him again. He'd take his time. He'd learn every inch of her . . .

For some reason he wanted to defend her. "Her parents died in the poorhouse. Gower's treachery sent them there. She has every reason to want revenge."

Henry frowned. "And it begins all over again. You're defending her after only one meeting." He paused and eyed Marcus sharply. "What happened last night? How did she persuade you?"

He couldn't hold Henry's gaze.

"Shit. You let Sabine, *of all women,* seduce you *again*?"

"No!" Marcus cursed. "If you must know, I offered her a wager. She becomes my lover if I win the tournament. And I intend to win it for her. It is a fair exchange."

Henry sighed. "What are you doing? That woman destroyed you once before and now you let her walk back into your life as if nothing had ever happened? You could have avenged her parents . . . wait!" Henry sat up straight. "This is about *your* revenge, isn't it?" Henry sipped at his drink. "I can't say that I blame you. I know what her betrayal cost you. Just be careful. You could never think straight when it came to Sabine Fournier."

"I'm only fucking her, not marrying her. I'll wash her from my system, marry Amy Shipton and live a happy life ever after."

Henry laughed. "I must admit the idea of destroying Gower warms my heart. I'll help you practice." He looked around. "But not here. We don't want anyone to know how good you are.

How about we adjourn to my townhouse for a few hands? I'll invite Millicent; she has a very lovely friend over from Paris visiting with her."

Before Marcus could reply George approached with a note on his tray. "For you, Lord Wolverstone."

Marcus recognized his mother's aristocratic crest on the stationery and opened the note.

My dearest son,

You are to please attend the Duke of Barforte's ball tonight with me and dance the first waltz with Lady Amy Shipton. I have taken you at your word. We are expected there promptly at ten.

Love, Mother

Henry must have noted his frown. "Not bad news I hope?"

"No. Mother has simply instigated her plan rather more quickly than I'd hoped. I'm to declare my intentions toward Amy Shipton tonight at the Duke of Barforte's ball. The noose is tightening." Marcus cursed and stood to take his leave. "I appreciate the offer of practice. But I'm not in need of female company."

Henry drained his glass and rose with him. "It's started already. I've never known you to turn down female delights before. Sabine's twisting you up inside."

"She is not. I merely need a clear head. Wait for me outside while I enter my name in the tournament."

With that he departed, ignoring Henry's knowing smile and headed towards his fate.

CHAPTER SIX

As Sabine pulled her gloves on with determined tugs, she was still fuming over her reaction to Marcus. Thoughts of him made her heart lurch with an intense pleasure she couldn't control. She'd not slept a wink; dreams of lying in Marcus's arms quickly turned into nightmares. She had given herself to him, and once he'd taken her, he'd cruelly walked away leaving her bereft.

She stepped through her front door, on her way out to visit her friend, Monique Baye. Monique's family had also fled France and she now made a living for herself as a modiste in London. Monique had tried to help Sabine's parents in their time of need, but she did not have enough money and by the time she had earned enough, Sabine's parents were both sick. Monique had seen to it that they had had a proper funeral and were not buried in paupers' graves. The least Sabine could do was support her friend's growing business. Before Sabine left England and returned to Italy for good, she intended to make Monique the most sought after modiste in London.

It was the clatter of horses' hooves and the sight of Marcus and Henry St. Giles on their fine mounts which stopped her from entering her carriage. Their mounts weren't the only things that were fine. The men astride them turned heads everywhere.

"Perfect," she muttered under her breath. She had thought she'd have a respite from his company for a few days. She shivered as she remembered that her planned revenge on her parents' behalf would see her have to submit to the one man who would not be able to value her sacrifice.

She almost stumbled as her heart leapt into her throat. Both men looked so handsome mounted on their impressive stallions. But it was the dark haired Marcus that drew her eye.

Squaring her shoulders, she stepped back onto the pavement. It was obvious that Henry St. Giles, the blond demi-god of London, held her in contempt. His barely civil, "Good day, Madam," was testament to his feelings at her return.

She acknowledged Henry's greeting with a nod of her head. "Gentlemen. To what do I owe the honor of a personal call at this early hour of the morning?" she said as she smiled sweetly at Marcus.

He dismounted with a masculine grace that saw her blush. She couldn't take her eyes off his muscled thighs, remembering how they'd felt as she'd pressed shamelessly against him. Her body hummed at the memory of the power and pleasure his touch had given her.

As he took her extended hand, he placed a lingering kiss on her glove, and a tremble of awareness flashed over her and his amber eyes gleamed with unbridled fire at her response.

So he'd felt this quickening too.

His eyes glanced at the façade of the house behind her. "You've bought Dowager Spencer's house I see. You're Henry's neighbor." He indicated across the street. "Henry will be able to keep an eye on who enters and leaves your house. Remember our wager. You're mine, and only mine, for as long as I desire."

She tried to take back her hand from his warm grasp but he

held tight. "I've leased her house, actually. Once my business here in London is completed, I intend to return to Italy."

"Only when I allow it." His tone was a sharp reminder that he expected her to be at his beck and call.

She gave him an innocent smile. "I still have two days before you *own* me. I was hoping I'd not see you until then. The less we're seen together, the better. I'm attending the Duke of Barforte's ball for his daughter's coming out. I suspect you won't wish to attend." She knew he'd not wish to attend the ball. There were too many mothers, wanting husbands for their daughters, in attendance.

"Actually, I too am attending the Barforte's ball, but I think I can resist you for one night. After all, I've not thought of you for ten years."

She swallowed her surprised exclamation. Marcus attending a debutante's ball? Hardly! He was obviously going to keep a close eye on his prospective prize.

She smiled brightly in farewell. "Until tonight then, gentlemen."

He tightened his hold on her hand and offered a gallant bow. "Two days then. Enjoy your freedom while you can. You'll be otherwise engaged once the tournament is over."

She looked up and down the street, all the while trying discreetly to pull her hand free of his grasp. While maintaining a polite smile that she hoped indicated mere acquaintance rather than intimate friendship. She hissed under her breath, "I know the terms. You don't have to keep reminding me. Remember, you promised you'd be discreet. Don't call on me at my house— *ever again!*"

He let her hand go and stepped back. Sabine turned to enter her carriage.

"Then don't force me to come looking for you. You approached me, Madam. I'm the one helping you. Don't forget that. We agreed on a wager between us and I suggest you honor it . . . But wait, I forget. Perhaps you need reminding of what honor is."

She stumbled and choked back a curse, sending him a look that would send meeker men fleeing.

A neighbor descended the steps next to her. Just what she didn't need, gossip about her relationship with a notorious womanizing scoundrel, just when she was trying to ensure her respectability in this town.

"Are you all right, Lady Orsini?" Marcus called, grim determination in his question.

Through gritted teeth she replied, "Perfectly, thank you, Lord Wolverstone. Thank you for stopping by with the message."

"Until tonight, my lady. I hope I have delivered my message satisfactorily and it is fully understood."

She entered the carriage and slammed the door. "It was most succinctly delivered. I remember it word for word. I shan't forget the meaning," she paused and looked him directly in the eyes, willing him to feel some smidgen of regret at his behavior, "*ever.*"

With that she drew the curtain and banged on the roof, indicating the carriage should move on, quickly. She had to put some distance between them before she did something very unladylike.

Sabine was still full of fury as she took her seat in Monique's sitting room. She smoothed a hand over her hair, trying to compose herself.

Marcus's behavior confirmed her worst fears. He hated her, and was bent on extracting his pound of flesh. His revenge would be to see her humiliated, just as she had humiliated him all those years ago.

Pain rippled across her chest and no amount of rubbing would stop the ache of what could have been and should have been. Worse, try as she might, she couldn't bring herself to hate Marcus.

Being with him stirred something inside her that she had believed long dead. *Hope.* If she could extract her revenge against Gower, and send him fleeing from England, broken and penniless, never to return, then she could perhaps settle here again and earn Marcus's forgiveness. He hadn't married. And she was a widow.

There was hope.

She touched her lips, running her fingers where his mouth had taken hers in delicious assault. She hadn't meant to succumb quite so easily to his touch, but her reserve melted under the strength of his desire for her. Besides, she'd wondered for ten years what it would be like to be taken by such a man.

But she still longed for . . . she longed for something she knew Marcus could not give, at least not to her.

Tenderness, love and his heart.

For she'd held it in her hand once before . . .

"Sabine, it's wonderful to have you back in England. And you're now a Contessa, of all things." Monique bent and kissed her on both cheeks, laughing gaily. "You're still as beautiful as ever."

Sabine smiled. "You mean, for my age. I can't believe it's been ten years since we last spoke."

"You haven't aged a bit. Whereas I," she indicated her body, "I have become even more voluptuous. It's better than saying fat, non?" Her smile crumpled disarmingly and she leaned over and placed her hand on Sabine's where it lay in her lap. "I'm so sorry about your parents. I should have tried harder to . . ." Monique's breath caught at the memory and her eyes filled with tears. "They were always good to me."

Sabine patted her hand reassuringly. "Oh, Monique, it was not your fault. I'm grateful for all that you did for them and that they had someone who cared for them at the end." Monique sat back and dried her eyes with her handkerchief. Sabine added angrily, "No. I know who is to blame and he will pay and pay dearly. He will end up in the same situation he placed my parents, the poorhouse." The silence was deafening. Sabine tried to lighten the moment. "By the way, you're not fat. I've missed you."

"I suspect not as much as you've missed a certain gentleman. Now at last you can be together, non?"

Sabine's smiled died and the pain in her chest returned. She shook her head fighting tears. "It's not that simple."

"Oui, it is. You must tell him the truth."

Pain gripped her. "I'm no longer sure he'd believe me. He's changed. He's not the fun loving man of his youth." Her eyes welled. "I did that to him. I took away his ability to experience joy and love. He no longer has the same happy disposition; instead he's filled with mistrust and hate." A small sob escaped. "He hates me and I don't think I can bear it."

"Hate and love, two sides of the same coin, m'amie. He still has feelings for you. If he didn't, he would not be so hurt. He would not care about the past. It's been ten years. He should have moved on with his life but he hasn't. Your reappearance would mean nothing to him if he did not still have deep and passionate feelings." She looked at Sabine coyly. "I believe he would forgive you, especially when he learns the truth. You *must tell him.*" She took a sip before placing her tea cup on its saucer. "He will no doubt be angry that you didn't tell him ten years ago, but I'm positive he still loves you. He'll welcome you back with open arms."

Sabine chewed on her lip. Would he? She had a son. A son who would forever remind Marcus of the past and the ten years they had lost.

"I'll tell him when my parents have been avenged. The tournament will be over within a few days. Not long to wait, given that I have waited almost ten years."

"Marcus has agreed to help?"

She hesitated. "Yes."

Monique leaned forward. "What are you not telling me?" Silence settled over the room. "Well." Monique prodded.

Sabine placed her cup on the side table with a shaky hand. "He offered a wager. He'll win the tournament for me and when he does, I am to become his paramour until he is finished with me."

Monique's face broke into a sly smile. She clapped her hands. "Parfait! He does still desire you. You will win him back. Once the wager is won, and Gower has been destroyed, you can reveal the truth about the past and then you can live happily ever after."

"You make it sound so simple. Nothing where the Marquis of Wolverstone is concerned is ever that simple."

Monique nodded before pouring the tea. "I did not say it would be easy." She laughed gaily. "But I suspect it will be very pleasurable. If I were you, I'd enjoy the man's bed. He's rumored to be an expert lover. Your wager with him could be to your advantage. Seduce the man, Sabine. Make it so he'll never want to let you go."

A shudder rippled through her at the mere thought of trying to seduce such a renown and experienced rake. What did she know of seduction? Nothing! Being in his presence once more, she understood why so many women had fallen at his feet. Marcus wasn't just handsome. His sinful dark looks made a woman think of sex. More disturbing were those piercing amber eyes that promised heaven. There was an air of command about him that made any woman want to be commanded—preferably in his bed.

She seduce him? It was laughable. He was far more likely to seduce her into doing something stupid—like fall in love with him all over again. That would lead only to pain and disappointment.

"He'll never ask me to marry him. If he decides to keep me as his mistress I'll have no choice. I agreed to be his paramour for as long as he requires it of me. Part of me hopes he beds me and immediately sets me free, while the other side of me wants very badly for him to keep me forever."

"Then to get your heart's desire, you'll have to tell him." Monique raised an eyebrow and sipped her coffee, before saying, "Nothing is gained without risk, ma chere amie. We both have learned that. The question you need to ask is this: what are you prepared to risk to win your happiness back?"

She relaxed back into the chair and stared out the window. It was a good question. She deserved some happiness after the life she had led. "I'd risk anything, except Alfredo's happiness."

Monique seemed satisfied with her answer. "Good. So you've agreed you should tell him?"

She nodded, fear clutching at her insides. "But it doesn't mean he'll believe me."

"Don't be ridiculous. You have proof."

She frowned, her terror rising, and shook her head. "No. Don't ask that of me."

Monique stood and moved to where Sabine sat. She knelt at her feet and took her hands. "If you want a future with Marcus, you must confess everything. You are not a coward, Sabine. If you were cowardly, you would have stayed safely in Italy. For once think of yourself." At Sabine's silence, Monique whispered, "There was a reason you fell in love with Lord Wolverstone. Whatever else he has become, he is still honorable at heart. Have some faith in him."

She leaned forward and hugged her friend. "You're right. I

should have had more faith in both of us. I'm not a helpless girl of eighteen anymore. I can forge my own destiny now. Once Gower has been defeated and fled England, I'll tell Marcus everything."

CHAPTER SEVEN

Sabine couldn't seem to relax and enjoy the Barforte's ball. Her stomach churned at the thought playing continually in her mind of what would happen when Marcus won their wager.

Her head was filled with Monique's words. *Appease his wounded pride. Turn the game on its head and make him fall in love with you, again. Seduce him, again.*

Her nerves were taut. What did she know about seduction? Her husband came to her bed in the dark, nightshirts remained on and the business was all over in a matter of minutes.

"Sabine, are you all right? You appear to be miles away."

She pulled herself together and smiled weakly at her old friend, Lady Judith Harcourt. "Memories . . ."

"I've learned to hide from them, even the good ones. And speaking of good memories . . ."

Judith pointed to the stairs. Sabine looked up and tensed as she noted Marcus's arrival. He was a dashing sight as he walked down the stairs with his mother on his arm. Every female's eyes fell upon him. His seductive dark looks were a warning, yet in equal measure, an enticing invitation to every woman in the ballroom. There was an air about him that stirred the ladies' senses.

His trousers clung provocatively to his well muscled, powerful thighs as he continued his descent. His exquisitely tailored midnight blue coat caressed his fine physique; the color complemented his dark hair which gleamed in the candlelight. *My, God*, she thought. He was so handsome her heart almost stopped.

"Behold the notoriously addictive Wolverstone! Beware of him, he hunts women with a wolf's instincts, with cunning and flair, but in the end, he leaves them pining."

She noted the wistful look upon Judith's face. A stab of jealousy seared through her. "You sound as if you speak from experience."

Judith couldn't seem to tear her eyes away from Marcus as he made his way down the stairs. She sighed. "He's a marvelous lover and fiendishly inventive in bed. The best I've ever had."

Old wounds re-opened and she gagged on her pride. He'd slept with the woman who was the closest thing to a friend she'd had from within the *ton*.

Raw pain beset her. Her heart desperately needed armoring. She should have been prepared. She looked around the crowded room and realized he'd likely slept with half the women there. She doubted any of them had ever regretted doing so.

Judith was the daughter of an Earl. She and Sabine were the same age. Sabine's father had taught Judith's brothers, and the two girls would often play and day-dream together while her father taught, even though their stations in life were very different.

At eighteen, Judith had gone on to marry Viscount Harcourt. It was not a happy marriage by all accounts, but her husband had died only twelve short months later. Judith had no intention of ever marrying again. She enjoyed her new found freedom.

When she heard Sabine had returned from Italy as Contessa Orsini, Judith had welcomed her with open arms. Judith's help within the *ton* had made it far easier for Sabine to enact her plan.

The ladies stood watching the handsome Marquis escort his mother toward the group of powerful dowagers holding court at the far end of the room. Once he had delivered his mother into their midst, he turned and surveyed the crowd as if looking for someone. She caught her breath as she met Marcus's bold hungry gaze as his eyes sought her out from across the room.

Suddenly, the ball proved too much of a crush; the heat almost suffocating.

Judith's wry comment brought her back to her senses. "It would seem Lord Wolverstone has a new conquest in his sights. He looks as if he wishes to devour you. I remember you were his favorite many years ago." With bitterness edging her tone, she added, "Enjoy, but be careful. That wolf has a bite."

Sabine panicked. No one must know about her relationship with Marcus Danvers. "I have no intention of allowing him to bite me."

Judith tipped her head back and laughed gaily. "I'd let him do more than bite. You would enjoy it, but don't lose your heart to him. He doesn't have one."

"He used to," she said under her breath.

A shadow appeared before her, blocking her view of Marcus. The strains of the first waltz could be heard. A man with a familiar voice bowed low over her hand. "Lady Orsini, may I have the honor of this dance?"

Henry St. Giles in all his angelic beauty stood before her. She ignored Judith's teasing look and replied, "Of course." Judith did not realize, St. Giles was not there to pursue a pleasurable liaison with her.

As they moved toward the dance floor, she heard hushed gasps from the crowd; the guests parted as if Moses was parting the Red Sea. There, at the other end of the room was Marcus, with a young debutante on his arm. He was leading her in the waltz. She was a young, beautiful, moonstruck debutante, with dark chestnut hair. Sabine's step momentarily faltered.

"Her name is Amy Shipton; she's the Duke of Cavendish's daughter. This is her first season."

What was Marcus up to? Jealousy engulfed her and she could barely breathe, but then she calmed herself. She looked at his mother who was beaming. As she'd surmised, Marcus was doing a favor for his mother, that was all. "Dowager Wolverstone at least seems pleased."

Henry pulled her toward him as his arm slipped from around her waist. "She should be. She plans to see Marcus wed her at the end of the season."

Sabine knew Marcus would never marry a girl so young. "I hardly think Lord Wolverstone would be interested in a girl almost young enough to be his daughter." She looked across to Judith. "He has no need to marry. There are plenty of women willing to share his bed."

He gave her a victorious smile. "You sound almost jealous. Now, why would that be, given that you once left him? Perhaps you'd like another chance to devastate him? Run out of men to torment in Italy, have you?"

Her hands itched to slap the bitter hatred off Henry's face. Instead, she remained silent, going through the motions of the dance, refusing to look at the couple dancing nearby.

Henry wasn't going to let her off so easily. "Didn't you hear the gasps from the crowd? Marcus has never danced with any debutante before, and certainly not the first waltz."

She felt her hands get clammy within the confines of her gloves. "And your point is?"

"He is seriously contemplating marrying her."

Sabine did stumble this time. Her head swirled and she thought she would faint. Henry cursed under his breath and pulled her toward the doors leading onto the balcony. As he waltzed them outside, he urged. "Take deep breaths."

He waited while she fought to regain her equilibrium. *Marcus married?* She didn't know why she should have been so surprised. She'd been relieved when she'd arrived in London and learned he was still unmarried. Blind hope had then enveloped her. She was not too late.

"Marcus understands that it's time he did his duty and produced an heir. Amy could make him happy. She's kind, intelligent and beautiful."

"It sounds as if you should marry her yourself," she blurted out.

He leaned on the balcony rail next to her. "Why did you seek Marcus out; don't give me that rubbish about avenging your parents. You don't need him for that. I know of many men who would like to earn the amount of money you've promised Marcus. Men who are much better card players." His eyes swept her from head to toe. "You also have other incentives that would make a man do anything for you. Why did you go to him?"

She swallowed, her dry throat closing up at the memories his words evoked. She could hardly tell him that when the tournament was over Marcus would relish his revenge and that this was the safest way to achieve her goal. She wanted Gower to suffer as she and her parents had suffered, but not at the risk of Marcus's life—or her son's.

"My reasons are personal."

He stood taking the measure of her, as if trying to assess her true intentions.

"Leave him be. If you ever truly loved Marcus, then let him finally put you behind him and move on with his life. Don't ruin what his mother has put in train. I believe Amy will make him happy, and so does he. Make him happy. Amy could do something for Marcus that you never could."

The truth of Henry's words cut her to the bone. Now she

knew that in taking her to his bed, Marcus truly wanted only revenge. There had never been any chance that by becoming his lover more would follow. He'd already selected his wife. He was using her and when he'd humiliated her enough, he'd walk away and marry an innocent, a young girl who was more deserving than she. He'd probably forget he had ever known her.

She thought she'd crumble into pieces at Henry's feet. She felt as though she'd fold in on herself until she no longer existed.

At her lack of response Henry grunted and turned away from where she stood gripping the rail with two hands least she fall down.

"As usual you're thinking of no one but yourself. Know this. I'll do everything I can to ensure he marries Amy. I'll not let you destroy him a second time."

The tears began to fall as soon as Henry's last harsh, angry words were spoken. Through the numbing pain, she heard his footsteps fade and soon she was alone in her misery.

A wrenching sob escaped her and she struggled to hold back the sound of her distress. Perhaps Henry was right. You can't go back and undo the past. Perhaps it would be better to simply let Marcus think he had his revenge on her and then walk away. Was she being selfish? The truth would only bring him further pain.

As long as Gower suffered, she should be thankful. She had a home in Italy. And most importantly her son would be safe from the truth and disgrace of the past.

She'd only just finished wiping the tears from her face when she heard a man's heavy footsteps behind her. She swung round and was frozen to the spot with fear. Her heart pounded in her ears, her stomach knotted and bile rose in her throat.

"It's been an awfully long time, Sabine. Rather awkward to see your change in station."

She gazed aghast into the face of the man she hated most in the world. He had changed little. He still looked like a monster wrapped in the guise of an angel. His dark copper hair was immaculately styled over his ears and seemed to surround his head as if it were a halo. But the angelic look was merely at face value. His nose looked a good deal more crooked than she remembered; it gave his face a more rugged look. He'd aged—badly. Although roughly the same age as Marcus and Henry, he looked years older. His green eyes in his lined dissipated face silently mocked her as they swept intimately and indecently over her gown.

"Stay away from me, Gower" she finally forced out. She tried to step back from him but felt the balcony railing between her shoulder blades blocking her.

He laughed intimidatingly and crowded in on her until his chest was flattened against her breasts. "*Lord* Gower, to you, my dear. The past is best left in the past, if you take my meaning." His breath stank of brandy and her skin crawled as a finger traced around her lips. "You may be Lady Orsini now but, trust me, no one will believe any of your tales from years gone by."

She shoved at his chest and tried to squeeze around him. Just when she thought she'd made her escape, his hand grabbed her upper arm in a vice-like grip. "If I find you've told anyone *anything*, I'll make sure you'd wished you'd never been born. I hear you have a son . . ."

Her horrified gaze flew to meet his. He was evil personified.

"I'm sure you'd hate to see anything bad happen to the little lad, wouldn't you?"

"What have you done to him?" She cried.

"Shush, will you! Nothing, yet. But I have men who know how to make little boys disappear." He leaned in close and menacing. "If you say one word to anyone about our former acquaintance . . ."

He didn't need to say more. Her ears were ringing; her frantically beating heart felt as if it would fly from her chest. She'd die before she let this man hurt Alfredo. She tried to tug her arm free and felt her dress tear.

"I think the lady wishes you to take your filthy hands off her." The intervening words were punctuated with steel.

Marcus!

Gower stepped away from Sabine and plastered a sickening smile on his face, raising his hands in the air. "Don't get on your high horse, Wolverstone. I'm just a man a little worse for drink."

Dark amber eyes, filled with anger, flashed in her direction. "Are you all right, Lady Orsini?"

She moved quickly toward where he stood. "Yes. I'm perfectly fine."

She wasn't. Marcus could hear the terror in her voice. "Apologize to the lady, Gower, before I beat you senseless."

Gower, making an exaggerated bow from the waist, almost toppled over. "My apologies, my lady. Please forgive my boorish behavior, too much brandy."

Marcus took a menacing step towards Gower and he beat a hasty retreat. He turned to Sabine and noticed her trembling like a leaf in the breeze. "Not much of an apology, but I expected nothing more from a louse like him. He didn't hurt you, did he? Perhaps the simplest way to rid the world of that odious man would be to challenge him to a duel."

"No!" Sabine cried and gripped his arm. It was the first time she'd voluntarily touched him and it sent a jolt of scorching heat, like the touch of a branding iron, right up his arm. "That is, I prefer to hurt him where he will feel it the most, in his pocket."

There was more in play here he suspected. Sabine was hiding something, something about Gower. She appeared to be unusually petrified for such a feisty woman.

"Did he threaten you?"

She looked into his face and seemed to collect herself. "No. He was simply drunk and overstepped his bounds."

She was lying. For once he could read every nuance on her

beautiful face. Perhaps his years of experience meant she could no longer fool him. He was no longer the green, love-struck calf who would have done anything for a mere smile from her ravishing lips.

She looked at her dress and then back at him. "You'll have to excuse me. I will have to go home. I can't return to the ball; he's torn my dress."

Unbridled rage engulfed him. How *dare* Gower lay a hand on Sabine! He started at these thoughts. They were possessive and intensely territorial, as if Sabine was his to protect. Yet she'd never been his. Except that soon, he would *own* her. After the tournament she would be his and at his bidding only, and he would not have her sleeping with any other man during their arrangement. He had insisted on that. Jealousy raged within him like a wildfire and he couldn't dampen it down.

"He seemed very eager to become better acquainted with you. Was it your plan to seduce him too?"

"Don't be ridiculous. I shudder at the thought of the man touching me." She eyed him with surprise. "You're jealous!"

The dark flare of anger scorching his veins told him that she had sensed the truth; though he was loathe to admit to it. "Not jealous, merely a sense of possessiveness over what I consider to be mine. It's a primitive male instinct, you know, nothing more, nothing less."

She reached out and touched his arm. "There is no need to be jealous and you know it. He's the last man on earth I'd ever willingly allow to touch me."

The venom in her voice appeased his jealousy. So she really did hate the man, and with good reason. What he had done to her parents was heinous.

He looked her over and the simmering tension that lay between them was reignited. God, *how* he wanted her! He prayed that when the tournament ended this rapacious hunger for her would be satiated. He wanted to move on. Henry was right. He needed to look to the future and there was no future with a woman like Sabine. He could not trust her with his heart—or—in fact, with anything. Look at the game she'd instigated with Gower, and the wager she'd accepted with him. She'd sink to any level, it seemed, to get what she wanted.

"Since you cannot return to the ball, I shall escort you home."

He saw the pulse at the base of her delectable collar bone quicken in response to his proposition. She licked her lips and he hardened immediately, longing to put her luscious lips to good use.

She eyed him coolly. "Aren't you worried that you'll disappoint your mother? Or Amy Shipton?"

He gave her a taunting smile. "Now who's jealous?" He'd expected an angry denial but instead she dropped her gaze from his and turned her back to him.

He watched her delicate shoulders shudder as she struggled for composure, and after several minutes, she said, "It would seem that I am more human than you." Her quiet words chipped at the block of ice surrounding his heart. "After what we shared in the past, it's difficult to imagine you married to someone else. You expect me to come to your bed while you are engaged to another." He saw her shoulders slump. "The Marcus Danvers of old would not be so cruel—to me—or to Amy Shipton."

"I can't believe you have the audacity to comment on my behavior. Wasn't it you, who ten years ago swooned so eagerly in my arms, surrendering willingly to my kisses while all the time playing me false? If one man was not enough for you then, why should one woman be enough for me now?"

Sabine whirled around to face him. "Two wrongs do not make a right. Amy Shipton is an innocent. Don't use her as part of your vengeful plan against me."

"I have no intention of hurting Amy. Presently I have no

understanding with her or any other woman for that matter."

She raised an eyebrow.

"But I am in search of a wife. You have your son; I too would like children. Amy Shipton seems an ideal candidate. She's loyal to her friends, has a kind heart and is very beautiful. Once I learned how devious women could be, I set my sights lower. There'll be no grand love for me, it's safer that way. I won't be disappointed a second time."

He heard her draw in a deep breath at his insult. He caught himself just in time and just stopped himself from pulling her into his arms and soothing the hurt he saw register on her face.

Instead, with his characteristic charming, predatory smile, Marcus stepped closer to her. "Speaking of not being disappointed, I am looking forward to my victory. I promise you you'll enjoy our reunion."

She straightened up to her full height which still only saw the top of her head reach his shoulders. "It would be unwise for anyone to see me leave with you. I shall slip through the gardens and meet you at your carriage."

And before he could argue, she had turned and descended the outside stairs and, like a ghost, disappeared into the gathering gloom.

Marcus turned back into the ballroom. He couldn't dampen the growing excitement circulating in his blood. Soon he'd finally be able to take his fill of the woman who'd haunted his dreams for years. Surely then he could wipe her from his memory.

As he made to step back inside, an arm came across the door to prevent him. "Where would you be hurrying off to?" Henry peered over Marcus's shoulder at the empty balcony behind. "Your mother bade me fetch you. She thought Sabine may have cornered you."

"Since when have you been so eager to do my mother's bidding? I don't need a nursemaid. Bugger off!" And he pushed his way past Henry and into the crush of people.

Henry dogged his footsteps. "You aren't leaving, are you?"

Marcus continued his path toward the stairs, eager to leave the crowded room. He watched Henry's perceptive gaze scan the room. "Sabine seems to have left too."

"She had to leave. Gower accosted her outside and ripped the sleeve off her dress. I arrived just in time or there could have been an ugly scene."

Henry cursed. "Sorry. I shouldn't have left her out there alone but I couldn't stomach her apparent act of being so heartbroken."

Marcus threw an accusing look at his friend. "You took her outside? Why? I hope you are not meddling in my business."

Henry shrugged and smiled at a young lady he'd previously danced with standing nearby. "She became overly upset when I mentioned you were considering marrying Amy."

But Marcus refused to countenance what that might imply and as the two men entered the hall. Marcus strode purposefully toward the door. "Leave *me* to deal with Sabine," he hissed under his breath at his friend.

Henry halted half way and called after him, "You've been warned. Don't do anything stupid. She cannot be trusted."

"I'm well aware of that," Marcus growled and walked out into the night, the anticipation of the forthcoming pleasures scorching a path in his veins.

CHAPTER EIGHT

Sabine had not seen Marcus since he'd delivered her home two nights ago after the Barforte's ball. For that she was thankful. She needed the time to compose her battered nerves. Soon, very soon, she hoped her long awaited revenge against Gower would come to fruition. But then the most agonizing aspect of the painful saga would begin. She would have to fulfil her side of the wager she'd been forced to make with Marcus.

She stepped down from her carriage, listening to Judith's chatter, trying to ignore the gut-wrenching fact that her plan hinged on the outcome of today's events.

The Annual Gentleman's Whist tournament was being held at Richmond Park on the outskirts of London. The area was perfect for the masses who would gather for the day's free entertainment. The park allowed for a family atmosphere with picnics and children's games, and of course the placing of wagers.

The beautifully manicured grounds was playing host to countless carriages and hundreds of horses, as the fine weather had drawn in an enormous crowd.

Sabine had talked Judith into accompanying her. However,

Lady Harcourt had needed no coercing when she heard Marcus had entered. She, like all of Society, was surprised. Marcus had never been a man to play cards before.

The second round was well underway when the two ladies arrived and Sabine breathed a sigh of relief upon spying Marcus still at one of the tables inside the large tent. He'd survived the first round.

It promised to be a long day. There were over fifty gamblers partaking which was hardly surprising given the size of the purse—two-hundred thousand pounds, which meant there was one-hundred thousand pounds for each of the two winners.

Sabine could see the bookmakers all around the park still busy taking bets. She scanned the crowd but couldn't see Gower, but she knew he'd be here. He'd be sweating until the very end.

Sabine wore a hat with a large brim to obscure her features. She didn't really have to hide her identity as there was no reason why she shouldn't be there. If Gower came across her, with Judith at her side, he wouldn't be at all suspicious of their attendance. After all, half of the *ton* was here today, all eager to have a wager on the outcome of the tournament.

The ladies settled on a rug under the trees not far from the officials' tent. The two women attracted a lot of attention. Many of Judith's admirers stopped by to share a drink and to discuss who they believed would be the victors.

"I was wondering, Lady Harcourt, since you are well acquainted with Lord Wolverstone, if you knew he'd be entering?" Lord Cornwall asked as he settled on the rug next to her. "I didn't know he was a good card player."

"I didn't either," Judith responded. "However, if I recall, the man is good at everything," and she gave a wicked knowing laugh.

A wave of irritated jealousy skittered down Sabine's spine. "Surely, he stands no chance against these gentlemen. I've heard there are professional card players in the tournament."

The toot of a horn interrupted the conversation. "Well, we'll soon see." Lord Cornwall said as he stood up. "That signals the end of round two." He scanned the tent Marcus's group was in. "Yes, it looks as if he's through to the next round."

When Sabine learned of her enemy's wager she knew Marcus was the man who'd be able to trounce Gower for her. A good memory and head for numbers gave a player a distinct advantage. If there was anyone who understood numbers and whose memory seemed very long, it was Marcus.

At each of the tables, players sat in two fixed partnerships, the partners facing each other. Partners were assigned at random, and were changed after each hand to avoid any coercing or cheating.

Whist is part luck and part skill. Starting with the player on the dealer's left, the rounds are played clockwise. Each player throws down one card. The other players have to match it by throwing down a card of the same suit. The idea is to win each round with the highest card of the suit being played. This is called a 'trick'. There are thirteen tricks in a game and each trick earns a point for the winning pair.

There are also trump cards. The rules of the tournament see the trump suits designated before play begins. For the first deal, it is hearts; second, diamonds; third, spades; and finishing with clubs.

The pair at each table who won the best of three deals would progress to round three. Now there were only eight players left at two tables.

Sabine drew in her breath and took a large gulp of champagne. She wished she could move closer to better view the play but she was scared her intense interest in the game would be noticed.

Luckily, it was Judith who gave Sabine the opportunity to

see the game up close. Judith wanted to cheer Marcus on.

They made their way to the tent and Sabine barely stifled her gasp when she saw who was in Marcus's final pairing. He was playing with Bottomly against Prendergast and a man called Sir Deverell.

Sabine squeezed her eyes shut. She knew what this pairing signified. Marcus had to win. If he did, Gower was finished. It then wouldn't matter if Marcus was the overall victor or was knocked out in the final round.

Gower had wagered Prendergast to win the field. In other words, Gower would win a huge amount of money if Prendergast was in the final victorious pairing with any other player. If Marcus and Bottomly won this round, knocking Prendergast out, Gower's bet was lost.

Gower would forfeit everything.

Marcus suddenly noticed her presence and gave her a slight smile. She noted the strain on Prendergast's face and she began to pray. Could her victory come this quickly? She followed the cards as they were played and noted Marcus and his partner inching ahead.

The next smile Marcus gave her one was filled with triumph and she knew they must be winning.

She could barely keep her breathing stable; her feelings were running amok with the tension. Her eyes began to search for Gower among the crowd in the tent. She wanted to see the look on his face when he realized he was ruined. As if pulled by an invisible force, she looked to the left and there, in the far corner of the tent, was Gower himself. His face was ashen. She could see beads of sweat trickling down the sides of his temples.

She allowed a victorious smile to break over her lips as his eyes met hers. His eyes narrowed in return and his look of despair changed to one of intense fury. His face grew dark red in rage and she could see his fists clenched tightly at his sides.

Sabine didn't care. It took only a few more minutes for a hush to descend on the tent when Prendergast pushed back his chair and shook Marcus's and Bottomly's hands in acknowledgement of defeat.

Marcus's eyes sought her out immediately and she mouthed the words *thank you* before taking Judith's hand and leading them both out of the tent.

"How marvelous, Lord Wolverstone has really caused an upset." With a wink she said to Sabine, "I told you he was good."

Sabine didn't quite know how she felt. She had had her revenge, at last. She'd ruined Gower as she had so ardently desired, but somehow the victory seemed flat. She had not experienced the much anticipated sweetness of success. She began now to understand more clearly that when she had approached Marcus for help, she hadn't been solely hoping to avenge her parent's deaths. She'd hoped for—well, she didn't really know what she'd hoped for.

Marcus. She realized she wanted Marcus to love her again. She almost doubled over in agony. Could this be her new beginning?

Fear invaded her body. If Gower was run out of England due to his inability to pay his debts, she'd have no excuse, no reason not to tell Marcus about the past. How would he react? Would he even care? It was both terrifying and exhilarating that soon she might be able to regain the happiness she'd been so sure of ten years ago.

Overcome by her conflicting emotions, Sabine slipped away to gather her thoughts. She walked toward the lake and peace flowed over her as she noted the King's deer frolicking in the brilliant sunshine from across its shining surface.

She raised her face to the sun and whispered, "I've done it, Papa. You and mother can rest in peace now."

Suddenly life was full of possibilities. A ray of hope burst within her and warmed her cold and tired soul. She didn't fight the happiness that flooded through her, not this time. It was her turn to walk in the sun.

"You look rather pleased with yourself. I wonder why?"

A dark shadow descended over her bright day. She swung around at the sound of her nemesis's voice and took a step back. Gower looked utterly enraged. He was standing far too close. Keeping calm, she replied, "It's a beautiful day. Why would I not be happy?"

His mouth tugged on a cheroot. He blew the smoke insolently into her face before adding, "I think it has something to do with Marcus Danvers knocking Prendergast out of the tournament." His eyes narrowed and his nostrils flared. "I couldn't understand why Marcus would suddenly enter." He moved closer. "It was *you*. You asked him to." He towered over her threateningly but she refused to cower, not to this man, not ever again. Marcus's victory had given her sudden strength.

He spoke through clenched teeth. "Do you know what else I've learned today?" His voice dropped to a menacing hiss, as, flicking the cheroot away, he grabbed her by the shoulders, his fingers biting into her flesh. But Sabine refused to acknowledge the pain. "A certain lady has been buying up all my vowels." She peered over his shoulders. "Marcus won't save you this time. He's still playing."

"Let go of me, you bastard." Anger flared and she gave him a back hander across the face. He didn't see it coming and it was enough to knock him off balance and for Sabine to break free of his hold. "You're right! I did buy up your vowels. I hold your very existence in my hands. How does *that* feel?" He pulled a handkerchief from his pocket to wipe away the trickle of blood where her rings had caught his lip. Emboldened, she pushed on. "If you don't leave England by the end of this week, I shall call in your vowels and let everyone know you're bankrupt." She leaned in closer, overcome by a surge of confidence. "I've always known how morally bankrupt you are. Now you're going to be financially bankrupt too."

He didn't attack her as she'd expected—or perhaps even hoped. Her pistol was in the pocket of her skirt and she was prepared to use it unhesitatingly.

Instead, he snarled, "I don't think so." An evil smile broke over his lips. "You don't want Marcus to know what happened ten years ago. That's why you came up with this silly plan and got Marcus to enter the tournament, isn't it? You get your revenge and no one has to know what a little slut you were back then, especially not Marcus. You don't want him to know under any circumstances because you understand what he would have to do."

An icy uneasiness chilled her warmth. He moved closer once more. "What would you do to keep Marcus from learning the truth?" A finger roamed down her neck heading toward her bosom. His touch made her stomach heave. "You know what he'd do if he ever found out, don't you? You also know that I'm deadly with a sword and if he issues a challenge, I get the choice of weapon." He leaned in and spoke into her ear, his breath making her recoil in revulsion. "You will sign over *all* the vowels to me. And then you will leave England and go back to Italy where you belong. Besides, think of Alfredo. What if something were to happen to the boy . . ." He bit down hard on her ear and she had to bite the inside of her mouth to stop herself from screaming. Horrid memories of the past blazed to life again, paralyzing her with fear.

He stepped forward, viciously squeezing her breast. "And for all the trouble you've put me through, I think I'll give myself a bonus. You are to come to my bed. He laughed at the look of utter horror on her face. "Why should Marcus have all this deliciousness?"

Sabine simply stood mute, all her dreams evaporating like a ghost racing the dawn. She stood shaking her head, unable to believe what was happening. Her brilliant plan lay in tatters at her feet.

He moved away from her as voices floated near them on the breeze. "Friday, it's to be then. You'll bring me the vowels on Friday. I've a house near Holborn which I use for entertaining. We'll make a night of it." He bent and kissed her hard on the lips. "I'll be waiting." With that he turned and left her standing alone in Richmond Park, a quaking mess of jangling anger and fear.

Her one moment of glory had been annihilated in a split second. Her enemy knew her too well. She had three days. She drew in a shuddering breath. Tears welled in her eyes. She would not let Gower win again. But she had to do this on her own. She would not risk Marcus getting hurt. She'd already hurt him enough.

She angrily wiped the tears from her eyes, pulled herself together and calmly walked back to where Judith waited for her with her band of merry followers.

There was only one thing to do. Give the vowels to Gower and then flee England, get her son to safety and protect Marcus from the truth.

Gower would be able to carry on with his life as if nothing was amiss once she left England, as she could never call in the vowels from Italy. He'd simply ignore them. Worse, *far worse*, she would have to give up her tentative hope of a life with Marcus. But then she didn't even know if she stood a realistic chance of any life with him. Henry St. Giles was right. Marcus would be perfectly happy with Amy Shipton.

She didn't know what devastated her the most. Knowing that she'd failed to inflict revenge on Gower or the fact that she'd never see Marcus again. She drew up short to re-consider her position.

She had three days only. It would take a bit of organizing to pack up her house, to cancel the lease and to book a passage back to Italy.

If she knew Marcus, he would call on her to make good on their wager tonight. He would not wait to taste his revenge.

She placed her hand over her heart, trying to control its fluttering. She squeezed her eyes tight. She could have one night at least.

Excitement replaced the pain; the sensation racing its way through her body like a raging river. It made her long to be in his arms and experience the delight she was certain she'd find there. Just for once, she wanted to make love with the man who'd owned her heart and soul for the last ten years.

After everything she'd endured, she deserved it.

They both deserved it and perhaps it would allow Marcus to find peace.

That would be her parting gift to him.

Pleading a headache, Sabine arranged for Lord Cornwall to escort Judith home, her friend's appreciative smile indicating her pleasure with that arrangement, and left. She had much to accomplish before tonight for it was her intention to make her part of the wager a night that would last her a life time.

CHAPTER NINE

It had been a long day and an even longer night. It was close to midnight before Marcus finally won the tournament. The pressure had eased off him once he'd ensured Gower was ruined at the end of round three.

He and his sixth round partner, were victorious—the outright winners. Although he'd won one-hundred thousand pounds, he didn't care about the money. He was satisfied that Sabine had been able to avenge her parent's treatment by Gower.

Yet he felt uneasy and somewhat troubled. He should be feeling elated. He'd won their wager and Sabine would be in his bed very soon. A sharp pang of regret rocked him as he made his way toward his carriage, undoing his cravat as he walked. His victory felt hollow. He'd forced her to her come to him like a whore—bought and paid for.

"Bloody hell," he muttered.

A sharp pang of regret sliced through him. What he wanted was for her to come to him of her own accord. To tell him she'd made a mistake all those years ago and that he was the only man she'd ever loved. Then he wanted to start to learn how to believe in her and trust her again.

He laughed at himself. He wanted a fantasy.

He wearily climbed into his carriage, uncertain of his next move, when a movement flickered in the darkness and caught his eye. "Who's there?"

A vision of beauty suddenly leaned forward, visible in the moonlight spilling in from the open carriage door.

It was Sabine.

"I thought I'd save you the bother of hunting for me. Don't say I never pay my debts. Thank you, Marcus. Thank you for today."

He didn't say a word. His decision was made the instant he locked eyes with Sabine. He closed the door and banged on the roof. The hatch opened. "A change of plans, Jeeves; take me to Roberson House."

"Aye, Sir."

Marcus leaned back against the squab, cursing the rapid beating in his chest. He was almost giddy from desire. The woman who'd haunted his every waking moment and pleasured him in his dreams was his to take.

When he entered and found Sabine seated inside, the impact of all he'd won hit him like a rampaging bull.

She was finally his.

He wished she'd stop licking her lips, it was driving him insane.

Giving into his need he said, "Come here," and a thrill raced down his spine as she readily obeyed. He pulled her onto his lap. "I can't wait." He kissed her passionately. He hadn't meant to admit his craving for her, or to succumb to his body's driving need. "I've thought of nothing but undressing you since I saw you that first night at Lady Somerset's ball."

"Marcus . . ." She shivered at the desperate desire that swept over her body when his mouth settled on the swell of her bosom.

214

"I promised myself that when I entered your body it would not be a rushed coupling. I'd savor you until I'd had my fill. But God help me, you are driving me to the brink . . ."

With a curse, he rose and placed her on the seat opposite and went down on his knees before her.

He slid his hands up her limbs, pushing her skirts up as he went. His lips found the inside of her thigh and he seared her skin with his searching kisses. She could barely sit still. Her breath came in small rapid pants.

The sensuous path he made up the inside of her leg spoke of pleasure beyond imagining. She'd heard whispers about a man's intimate kiss, but she had never experienced it. Sabine had no idea that it would feel so exciting, and yet so wicked, all at the same time.

"We don't have enough time for what I'd really love to do to you, with you, but I can't wait to taste you." His voice was intoxicatingly sensuous. "I swear I'll have you screaming my name before we reach Roberson House."

Desire played over her skin in ascending ripples of response. When she looked into his eyes, their color dark like molten honey, her legs parted of their own accord, allowing him greater access. His groan only inflamed her passion.

He used his hands to part her even further, until she felt open and exposed. He kissed higher up the inside of her leg, his lips setting her on fire. A soft moan escaped and she didn't care.

"Marcus, oh, God . . ." she gasped into the confines of the carriage.

"Don't hold back. I want to hear your cries."

She could feel how wet he was making her and he hadn't even touched her yet. When the touch of his fingers finally came, the beguiling strokes raised a throbbing need inside her that built and grew until she could barely sit still.

His tongue traced a molten path closer to the apex between

her thighs, leaving a cool trail behind; elsewhere her skin was hot with a feverish need. His unhurried movements fed her impatience. She let out another enraptured moan as his tongue swept closer to the part of her that desperately wanted his attention.

Just as she felt his warm breath at her core, he suddenly drew back. She looked down. Her skirts were around her waist, laying her feminine flesh naked to his possessive gaze. He reached out and ran a finger over her glistening womanhood and then raised his wet finger to his mouth. She could see it covered in her juices. He sucked it and licked his lips.

"Ten years. I've waited ten years for this. You're worth it." He didn't hide the hint of smug male satisfaction in his voice.

She should have felt ashamed but she didn't. She'd never responded sexually to any man before; yet, he only had to look at her and she grew wet, but wet for him alone.

She spread her legs wider, biting her lip to stop herself from begging him to continue kissing her.

Finally, after one more lingering look, he leaned forward and touched her with his tongue, just lightly caressing her. Her body recognized the sensation and she pushed her hips forward begging for more.

His hands encircled her buttocks, pulling her down and then upwards to give his mouth better access. Marcus knew exactly where and how to touch her to prolong her pleasure. She'd never ever felt anything like it and she was sure she was about to faint from the heightened sensations sweeping over her.

Her breathing grew ragged. She no longer cared whether Jeeves or anyone else heard her cries. She wriggled closer, urging him on. His tongue stabbed deep within her, making her shudder. Her head dropped back to rest on the seat. Her flesh seemed to burn; a heat was consuming her from the inside.

It was almost too much to endure, yet she prayed he'd never stop. Her eyes widened in anticipation of what was yet to come;

then she closed them up tightly as her climax ripped through her. His tongue lapped at her, making it last, drawing out each shuddering sensation until she sagged limply against the seat, so satiated that she couldn't move.

Before she could gather herself together, he stood over her and took her mouth in a deep searching kiss. His tongue swept in so she could taste herself on his lips. Her arms crept around his neck and he pulled her in close to him.

"God, you're addictive. I want you more than I've ever wanted any other woman. The taste of you drives me wild. I wonder if I'll ever have enough of you."

She stiffened in his arms recalling that this was not real. This was not about a man who owned her heart or one who loved her. She was with a man she no longer knew and it killed a little to know this meant nothing except vengeance. She'd never experienced this sort of pleasure before. He'd probably done this with hundreds of women. She was simply one more.

She pushed at his chest and put a little distance between them. "That was incredible. Thank you."

He pressed another kiss to her lips. "The night is only just beginning. Take that as an appetizer to the main course. By the time I'm finished with you, neither of us will have the energy to talk."

Without thinking, she looked at the bulge in his breaches and asked, "Can a woman kiss you in the same manner that you kissed me?"

He hesitated and slowly turned to face her squarely. Her cheeks were burning with shame. "I'm sorry, I don't know what made me think the idea was possible . . ." She hung her head. "I've never done . . ."

He eyed her with a look of disbelief. "Did your husband never make love to you with his mouth?"

She shook her head.

"Has any man?"

"No," she said curtly.

"Are you telling me this is the first time you've experienced oral sex, my love?"

She blanched at the endearment he used, but nodded.

"Christ, he must have been an idiot." His look turned to one of anger. "Did he ever give you pleasure?"

Tears welled suddenly. How could she tell him that no man but him had ever given her pleasure? "My husband was quite old. We were always clothed and I simply lay beneath him . . ." Her words petered out under his stare of disbelief.

He leaned back and ran a hand through his hair. Quietly, he spoke. "Why did you marry him? Your father swore he had not forced you to choose him. Then why did you enter into this marriage? It didn't and still doesn't make sense. Why would you choose him over me?" He beat his chest as if trying to stamp out the built up pain within.

She took his large hand in hers and drew it to her mouth to kiss. She took a deep breath. "I did choose him, I suppose, but I did not really have a choice. I know that won't make sense but that's all I can tell you. I did not mean to hurt you. If I could have, I would have stayed with you. But sometimes we cannot always get what we want, no matter how much we wish for it."

"What are you not telling me, Sabine? What happened ten years ago to make you leave me?"

Her tears fell again. She could feel them sliding down her cheeks. "Please don't ask me. I can't tell you. The past cannot be relived but—but perhaps the future can."

He reached out and tenderly wiped a tear away. "Tell me one thing. Did you have feelings for me? Did you love me?" His voice cracked with emotion on the last question.

She cupped his cheek in her palm and looked him in the eye. "Yes, I loved you. I have *always* loved you. I've never loved another."

He crushed her to him and kissed her like there would be no tomorrow. He hugged her against his beating heart, holding her close as if he'd never allow her out of his arms again.

She responded by pouring all the sadness of the last ten years into the kiss, willing him to understand and simply leave the past buried.

Both of them were panting by the time the carriage began to slow to a stop. He broke off the kiss. "Sabine, what am I to do with you? I should hate you for the misery you put me through, but I can't." He gathered her into his arms, and kicking open the carriage door, he carried her into Roberson House.

Marcus surprised her when he didn't take her straight up to the bedroom, but rather into a drawing room. The fire had been lit and the room was warm and inviting. The table was laid with food and a bottle of wine stood open next to two empty glasses. The room was elegantly furnished, not disreputable looking at all. A day-bed had been placed before the fireplace. She'd somehow built Roberson House up as the epitome of wickedness where all manner of debauchery occurred. Instead it reminded her of a family home.

"I thought we could have a late super and, as you requested, reacquaint ourselves."

Her mouth opened in surprise. "Thank you. That is very thoughtful."

She took a seat in the chair by the fire as Marcus poured them some wine. She watched him as he moved gracefully toward her. His trousers still bulged tellingly. "Are you sure that you can wait," she pointed at his rampant erection. "Are you not in pain?"

He handed her a glass. "Where you are concerned, Madam, I'm used to pain." When she flinched, he added, "Sorry. A reflex reaction; I'll manage." With a wicked smile he added, "At least hopefully until after we eat."

He sank his large frame into the chair opposite and eyed her warily. "So, Sabine, tell me about your life over the past ten years. Were you happy?"

His breath caught as he watched the happiness currently blazing from within her eyes, dim.

Her chin lifted slightly and in a shaky voice she uttered, "I survived." She took a gulp of wine.

Marcus didn't know what to say. Whenever his mood darkened and he thought of her, he always hoped she was miserable. Now seeing the pain clearly written on her face, it wrenched at his heart.

"You have a son. What's his name?"

Her smile returned. "Alfredo. He's my life." In a quieter tone, "He's all I have now."

"Is he a bright boy? How old is he?"

She hesitated before answering. She couldn't look at him. "He's almost ten."

Possessive jealousy ran rampant through him. "Ten! You must have got with child very quickly after you married. Yet, you've had no other children since."

She started to say something, but instead she simply sighed and shook her head. "No. I was never blessed with another child."

Silence hung heavily between them.

"You don't have to do this, Sabine. I—I thought I wanted to see you humiliated, to treat you as I had once been treated, callously and cruelly. But you are correct. Two wrongs will never make this right. I'm tired of hating." He stared into her mesmerizing eyes. "If you want to leave, I won't stop you. I release you from our wager." With that, he stood and walked to the window keeping his back to her.

He desperately wanted her to stay. He'd love her to stay of her own accord, and be with him because she had freely chosen it.

"Thank you. You don't know how much those words mean to me." Her husky voice made him tense then his shoulders slumped with disappointment and regret. She didn't want him.

"I'd love to share a meal with you, if you agree not to rake over the past. Also, we agree that tonight is just about tonight, the here and the now. That we are two—friends becoming reacquainted." Her voice came from right behind him. He hadn't heard her approach. He turned around slowly and she stood quietly smiling up at him. She reached up and offered him his glass of wine.

He sent her a smoldering look. "It's agreed, although I cannot ever think of you as just a friend." At the flicker of hurt on her face, he added softly, "I do not wish to be just friends with you, Sabine."

"Then do you want me to leave?" Her bottom lip trembled slightly.

"No. I very much want you to stay." Her mouth opened in surprise. The warm look in his eyes clearly indicated his need. "I want you. I've always wanted you," he felt his heart lighten as he finally admitted the truth.

She stepped forward and laid her petite hand over his heart which was beating as if that rampaging bull was chasing him.

She smiled at him. "Then tonight you shall have what you desire. I'm yours, as I've always longed to be, yours to command and yours to take."

"As you should have been in the first place," he finally whispered, looking into her eyes with renewed steamy intent. He reached out and put his glass on the windowsill and gripped her around her tiny waist, pulling her tight against him.

They studied each other in long, searching stares, the past forgotten, the immediate future theirs to write.

"Sabine," he breathed.

His fingers tightened on her hips. She could feel the hard

221

length of him pressing urgently against her stomach. She thrilled at the sensation.

One hand continued to grip her as if she would suddenly try to flee, while the other roamed upward, tracing her curves, molding to fit perfectly over her breast. He gently squeezed it and hot need flared from deep within her. She pressed even closer.

"God, I want you. I've always wanted you." He kissed her deeply, his hands roaming wildly over her back, breasts, and bottom. She responded with a soft, eager moan, reaching up to slip her arms around his neck.

When they both finally came up for air, Sabine stepped out of his hold. She let her desire show on her face. "You won our wager. I'm your prize, but a prize freely given. You want me; you shall have me."

Marcus's mouth dried in tension. She slowly and seductively removed her gloves. Her movements were simple yet erotic. Like ripples on a pond, his desire spread and deepened, building to greater intensity as more of her pale skin came into view. Hell, he wanted to tumble her on to the floor this second. No seduction, no foreplay, just give in to the raw passion driving them both.

He couldn't recall any woman ever igniting his need quite like Sabine was doing. This urgent want inside him he couldn't label simply as lust. His heart expanded in his chest and in the back of his mind, he'd already admitted that he still loved Sabine. This time, he would not let her go. She would be his—forever.

A small smile titled the corners of her mouth, while just a hint of hesitation filled her eyes. She reached up and pulled his already untied cravat from around his neck and tossed it aside. Her hands slid up his chest and pushed his jacket from his shoulders. It fell to the floor in a crumpled heap. Her fingers worked diligently at undoing his waistcoat and it quickly followed the way of his jacket.

He breathed deeply. Beneath the white linen of his shirt, his muscles rippled in expectation. Her fingers trembled as she tugged at his waistband and his impatience got the better of him. He quickly pulled his shirt up and over his head. Her gasp when his chest was revealed heightened his excitement. One small finger reached out and tentatively touched him.

"Soft but so strong; hard as steel but so warm."

He closed his eyes to keep a rein over his burgeoning emotions. Her voice hummed seductively as she explored his body in wonder and awe.

He was beautiful and she'd not yet seen him completely naked. Her heart beat frantically, her attraction to him overwhelming her. The thought of one day maybe lying with this man every night, was intoxicating. Shoving that dream aside, Sabine reminded herself that he was hers only for tonight.

Tonight she would freely give herself to the man she loved and she would then savor the memory for eternity. She'd enjoy Marcus's touch and she'd give everything of herself to ensure he was satisfied.

"You're beautiful, Marcus. I've always remembered you as beautiful," she added wistfully. "At last, I have my dream within my reach."

"You've been my dream for so long, Sabine. I'm not sure how much longer I can wait." The deliberate plea in his voice saw her reach for the placket of his trousers. Her fingers fumbled and she heard him issue a curse before he swept her hands aside and freed his rigid erection into her waiting hands.

Her hand firmed around the thick length and at her first stroke Marcus sighed and tilted his head back. She explored him and realized her touch pleased him.

Finally he let out a groan and he pulled her even closer to him. They stood pressed together, each relishing the feel of the other. "You have far too many clothes on," he huskily murmured. "Turn your back."

When she complied, he began to undo the hooks of her dress. The dress drifted from her shoulders and fell in a pool of silk at her feet. Without speaking, they both removed the rest of their attire until they stood naked, facing one another.

"You're even more beautiful than I had ever imagined." Marcus brushed a strand of hair behind her ear. "You're worth waiting for, but I've waited far too long. And I'm hungry for you."

She placed a hand on his chest. His heart raced beneath her touch. "Tonight I'm yours. I'm not going anywhere."

He took her hand and dragged it down over every ridge and muscle of his torso to his groin. She was startled by the warmth pooling in her stomach at feel of him, hard and hot beneath her palm.

"See what you do to me, sweeting. I don't know if I'll ever get enough of you, but I won't be satisfied until I'm buried deep inside you."

The earthy rawness of his words sent a shudder down her spine. Her loins contracted hotly as he encouraged her hand to explore more of him.

He cupped her chin and the suddenness of his kiss started a fire raging in her belly, and she gave herself up to pleasure as his hands explored her naked flesh.

He kissed her. It was a demanding kiss, possessive and controlling. Hot and needy, his tongue swept into her mouth. The taste of maleness on it tantalized her taste buds as it swirled around hers until her knees almost gave way. A strong hand ran over every inch of her goose-bumped skin, igniting the heat of passion within her. He deepened the kiss. It tugged at her, demanding a response and she gave it willingly.

The feel of his soft chest hair upon her sensitive nipples shot tiny frissons of sensation across her skin. He felt so large, so big and so overwhelming as she stood in the protective shadow of his massive frame.

The skilful touch had her melting. His dark, spicy scent was like an aphrodisiac, inciting her on. She pushed even closer, exploring further.

Cool air brushed her mouth as his lips danced across her cheek in search of first her ear lobe, and then her neck.

"You were always so responsive to my kisses. It used to drive me crazy. Now, that I am holding you naked in my arms, I think I shall lose my mind."

An instant later, a large hand intimately cupped her, while his thumb brushed across her nipple. She shuddered in his embrace and with a low moan of pleasure, her head fell backward, allowing, and encouraging his lips to glide down her throat. His teeth gently nipped her as he moved his mouth ever closer to where his thumb continued to circle around the stiff peak of her breast. She was soon craving his mouth upon her nipple.

It was heaven, it was hell, it was everything she'd fantasized about and then more . . . Heaven to allow herself to succumb to his tantalizing touch; hell to have so much hunger.

The second his mouth gave her relief and he captured and sucked firmly on her sensitive nipple, another moan poured out of her. The wet heat of his mouth reignited another wild need and she demanded satisfaction. Her fingers sought the hard, length of him and circled around his thickness.

Her touch drew a moan of delight from him, and he moved his body so that his member thrust in and out of her grasp. The thought of him, the size of him, sliding deep within her, made her shiver with a mixture of trepidation and excitement.

A sigh of bliss slid past her lips as he massaged her other breast as his mouth continued to devour her engorged nipple. Never in her wildest imaginings had she experienced such deliciously sinful sensations. He aroused her completely. Fire flooded wildly through her veins, and the moment his teeth bit down, her insides grew slick with her desire.

Not once had her body responded in such a manner to her husband. Only Marcus could make her feel this way. With her heart pounding in her breast, she resisted the deep pang of regret and the horrid memories of the past, from encroaching on this one perfect night.

The palm of his hand caressed her throat before moving down to her belly. A tremor rocked her to her core.

"Are you hot and wet for me, Sabine? You're my beautifully responsive girl, my dream come true."

His lungs burned as if on fire as he sent his fingers seeking the warmth and heat between her legs. She did not disappoint. As she released a soft sound of excitement, possessiveness surged through him and he kissed her again and again, lusting after the fresh sugary taste of her tongue against his.

With an eagerness that pleased him, Sabine pressed herself upon his hand, her damp curls enticing his throbbing cock. Christ, her abandoned passion made his gut lurch with desire yet again. He wanted her like nothing he'd ever experienced before. No woman had affected him like Sabine had. Perhaps that was because he'd never wanted any woman like he wanted her.

Her fingernails lightly scored the skin on his back as she murmured his name in an aching plea. He'd never heard anything so sweet in all his life.

Eager to bury himself deep within her wet heat, Marcus swept her into his arms and lowered her onto the daybed. With great gentleness, he laid her upon her back; she truly was a feast for his long denied eyes. Aroused, she stared back at him from the depths of her deep ocean blue eyes. It took his breath away; his erection pulsed.

"God, the sight of you almost unmans me," he whispered as he struggled for control.

She smiled seductively and let her legs drop open. The strong scent of her arousal assailed him and coupled with the image of her womanhood glistening in the firelight, it saw his control flee completely.

Surprise swept over her face as he grabbed a cushion and situated it beneath her bottom.

He couldn't wait any longer so he used his thighs to part hers wider and pressed his aching cock into her, savoring her tightness as he inch by inch he slowly entered her until he had filled her to the hilt.

Her eyes rolled back and she let out a deeply satisfied sigh. "I never knew it could feel like this."

Gratified by her response, his body rejoiced at the hotly aroused sight of her beneath him. He held himself still above her, his arms shaking. He wanted to pound into her but knew if he did so he would not last.

When he refused to move, she opened her eyes, "We have all night, Marcus. Take me! Take me how you've always longed to take me. I am your prize."

She was a prize all right. God almighty, she was tight and fiery around his cock. She punctuated her words by arching her body, forcing him to withdraw and then sink back into her, penetrating her deeper. As she moved he looked down and the sight of his erection coated with her juices increased his own craving until he could not deny her more. At this rate, she would make him come faster than an inexperienced youth.

He used his hands to steady her hips so he could thrust in more deeply. He pushed her legs up higher, opening her fully and at last his control evaporated. As if on the edge of insanity, he pounded into her hot depths. She tilted her hips, matching him thrust for thrust, her bountiful breasts jiggling enticingly as he slammed into her. He could feel his sacs become tight and full as they brushed against her. He could not last . . .

A sharp cry broke from her lips, as her fingernails dug deep into his buttocks, and her tight sheath contracted around him with spasms of pleasure, her breath coming in loud gasps

As she continued to contract around him, the tightness drew out his own release. With roar, he thrust one final time and spilled his seed deep inside her. He collapsed on top of her, completely spent, unable to hold himself up any longer. His body throbbed with a pleasure he'd never experienced before. It was as if every woman that had come before Sabine had been a mere scrap, while she was the feast. She had just succeeded in wiping the memory of all others from his mind.

He drank in big gulps of air, enjoying the feel of the slowly ebbing waves of their climax. If it was always like this, tonight might just finish him off, but at least he'd die a very satisfied man.

A shiver of trepidation crept its way down his back. If he wasn't careful, Sabine would once more become an obsession. His plan looked to be a noose around his own neck. Instead of diminishing his desire for her, it appeared to be feeding his hunger to have her with him always. But the very thought scared him witless. One thing he definitely knew was, that he would never understand where he stood with this woman. He was petrified of trusting her.

As luminous, sky blue eyes fluttered open to look up at him, he swallowed hard. Like a stupid fool, he'd let her burrow back into his heart. He didn't hold out much hope he'd survive any better from the experience than he had the first time.

CHAPTER TEN

He finally pushed himself off her, and rose from the day-bed on shaky legs. He walked to fetch them sustenance because he needed a minute to process his feelings. He hadn't expected to be so moved by the connection he'd just had with Sabine. What they had just shared was unlike anything he'd ever experienced with any other woman before.

He collected their wine glasses and then selected a plate of meats for them.

"Do you think we'll ever make it to a bed?" she asked teasingly.

He paused to stare at Sabine. Lying naked on the plush silk of the day-bed, her skin flushed with arousal, she looked like a goddess. His body stirred once more.

"Not if you continue to stare at me like that," he answered honestly. "Let's eat. I'm starving. I've been playing cards all day, remember?" He let his gaze wander longingly over her breasts. "Besides, I think I'm going to need sustenance in order to not disappoint you for the rest of the night."

She blushed at his bold stare and remark. But then she turned saucy and began to study him with appreciation. "Oh,

I'm hungry too," she purred, "but not for food."

Naked desire flared again and sped through has veins. It was close to two in the morning, and they'd just made-love, yet his body craved hers once more as an addict craved opium.

"Tonight has already exceeded my wildest fantasizes. To have you wanton and eager in my arms is a dream, but what about to-morrow, Sabine?" He ran a hand through his hair. "This time, *no* secrets so no one gets hurt. What is it you want from me?"

The smile fled from her eyes. "Earlier this evening you re-leased me from our wager. I gave myself to you of my own free will." She looked away and uttering softly, "One night, Marcus. It can only be one night and you know it. Too much has happened in our past to think we could make more of this. I have a son to think about. And you need to marry. Your mother thinks Amy Shipton would be a good choice." She swallowed hard. "And she is. She would do the Wolverstone name proud." She turned back to him and looked directly at his face. "This is something my name could never do. Besides, your mother would never accept me."

He fought the urge to drop to his knees and vehemently de-ny her statement. Surely, they could make a life together, couldn't they? But only if he could truly trust her.

Unless she confessed what had happened all those years ago, he would never be able to fully give her his heart. Eventually, if she couldn't confide in him or trust him to understand, the not knowing would turn him bitter and resentful. He'd always be suspicious of her.

The way her sad eyes interlocked with his, he knew she un-derstood what he was thinking, but her lips remained closed.

"You're not going to tell me, are you?"

Her eyes brimmed with tears. "Don't ruin such a perfect night, Marcus, with these painful, stupid memories."

"If that's all they are, painful, stupid, then tell me what hap-pened, and end my suffering. Let us clear away what happened in the past and then perhaps we can make a life together. I'd trust you enough to do that if you confessed the cause of your treatment of me. For pity sakes, just this once prove to me I'm the most important thing in your life and you'd do anything to be with me."

She stretched out her hand to him in appeal, yet he would not budge. He would never trust her with his heart without first understanding what had happened.

Her hand fell back to the couch. "Do you want me to leave?" she asked quietly.

His heart closed up tighter than the clutch of a child frightened by a nightmare. Sabine would never love him like he craved her to. He'd been a fool to dream otherwise. The woman he'd fallen in love with in the gardens long ago was a figment of his deluded mind.

Henry had been right. He should find someone more worthy. Amy Shipton's innocent and beautiful face appeared in his mind's eye.

He opened his eyes and looked at the beauty lying provocatively on his daybed. His body wanted to sink again deep between those lovely pale thighs. His physical need was ferocious, but his mind refused to allow him to contemplate the act.

He'd set out to bed her, to slake his revenge, only to discover she still possessed his heart as she had done for the last ten years. In fact, as she had possessed it ever since he'd first laid eyes upon her all those years ago. Couldn't he simply keep her as his mistress?

No! He would be strong. He would walk away before he was unable to do so. Before, he would accept her in his life on any terms. That would only led to more heartache and bitterness and he was sick of being unhappy and of only living half a life; a life of empty pleasures.

He wanted and deserved more.

He put the plate and glasses down. "I can't do this. I can't make love to you again knowing you're only in it for the pleasure."

At her look of shocked surprise, he went on. "I know of my reputation as a rake better than anyone, but having you back in my life has taught me I want more than that. I *do* want a home and family. But I want one filled with love and trust like my parents had." He walked over to his discarded clothes and began to dress. "I know I can never have that with you. You hold too many secrets. You have deliberately kept me out of the essential aspects of your life."

Tell him! Her brain and heart urged in her head. Tell him and make him understand. Then, cold fear clawed at her body. If she told him, she knew what he'd do and if, as a result, he was hurt, or even worse, killed . . . Or Gower came after Alfredo . . . She shuddered at the very idea.

She had no other choice but to let him go.

She too rose and began to dress, the agony of her predicament almost ripping her in two. For a brief instant, she wondered how she was ever going to walk away from this pleasure— from him–without dying. Then she thought of her son, Alfredo, and all she risked by staying.

When they were both fully dressed, they stood looking at each other, sorrow shrouding both their faces.

She reached up and cupped his cheek. "Be happy, Marcus. You deserve much happiness."

She watched the man she loved, would love until her dying breath left her body, briefly close his eyes and breathe in deeply. She prayed for some sort of miracle. Foolishly, she prayed he'd pull her into his arms and say the past didn't matter; that only she mattered.

"Thank you for a memorable night. I'll treasure it always." The raw emotion behind his words almost saw her buckle at the knees and throw herself into his arms to confess all.

"It is *I* who should thank you. You helped me when you had no reason to."

"I'd always help you, Sabine. You know that. You will always be someone special in my life."

Tears that she thought she'd managed to keep at bay, slipped silently down her cheeks.

"Come, I'll see you home."

Sabine wiped the tears from her cheeks. She stared at him drinking in one last, yearning look, a look which would need to last her a life time. His warm amber eyes were pools of unshed tears, his chest quickly rose and fell and the harsh planes of his face were drawn tight. She remembered the lean hardness of his body when it pressed on top of hers. He was so incredibly handsome it pained her just to look at him.

This was a memory she would cherish forever.

Pain wrapped an icy hand around her heart. Now that the moment had come, she hadn't realized how difficult it would be to simply walk away from him and from all that she had ever wanted in life.

Swallowing the anguish welling in her throat, she nodded, and let him guide her out into the cold and empty dawn.

CHAPTER ELEVEN

"You are leaving England?" Monique's startled question must have been heard in her modiste's salon, because it suddenly went quiet in the room on the other side of the curtain. "But your life—your heart—is here," she added in a subdued tone.

Sabine shook her head. "No. I was mistaken."

Today was Friday. Tonight she would go to Gower and give him what he desired. Then she would leave England, never to return. Marcus and Alfredo would be safe.

Just as in her youth, she'd arrogantly thought she could take on the powerful and win. And, once again, she was to pay a very heavy price for this.

"Excuse me, Madam Baye, Lady Shipton is here. Apparently, she needs a new dress urgently for tonight."

"For tonight? She has a dress, the blue silk, to wear to the Earl of Skye's ball."

"She states she now needs a far grander dress. Her engagement to Lord Wolverstone will be announced tonight."

Sabine gasped and smothered her mouth with her hand, feeling suddenly nauseous. Two days, he'd waited *only* two days before moving on-without her.

Monique said, "I'll be there shortly. Show her ladyship the deep burgundy damask. It will suit her complexion."

Sabine rose unsteadily to her feet. "I should go. You're busy."

Monique's hand gripped her arm. "Is he the reason why you are leaving? He rebuked you, didn't he? The cad . . ."

"*No!*"

Monique sank into the chair she'd recently vacated. "Oh my God, you didn't tell him." She looked up at Sabine. "*Why not?* You've dealt with Gower. You hold all his vowels. He'll have no choice but to leave England . . ."

Sabine's mouth dried up. What could she say? "I under-estimated Gower, yet again. He's threatened everyone I love. I can't risk it." She turned away from her friend's searching gaze as bitterness clogged her throat.

She heard the rustle of Monique's dress as she rose and moved behind her. Two warm arms came around her waist from behind. "What have you agreed to? What does that pig of a man want from you now that would see you flee back to Italy?"

She sank back against her friend soaking in the warmth of her sympathy. "He wants me to hand back his vowels tonight. At his house," she added in a shaky voice.

Monique's arms tightened around her. "And? What else? If you go to his house, you know what will happen."

A wave of nausea washed over her again and she swayed. She would have fallen without Monique's support.

"What else can I do?" she cried. "I won't risk Alfredo or Marcus's lives. He's threatened them both. He can make little boys disappear, he said . . ." She started sobbing despairingly.

"Gower's such a bastard. I'd like to kill him with my own hands. You must go to the magistrate if he's threatened Alfredo, or at the very least allow Lord Wolverstone to help you."

The curtain between Monique's showroom and her private parlor rustled and a young woman stepped into the room.

"Excuse me, but I couldn't help overhearing. Is Lord Wolverstone in danger?"

Amy Shipton stood in the doorway, her innocent face a dark shadow of concern. She stepped further into the room.

"I've heard that you're a good friend of Marcus's—that is, Lord Wolverstone. You seem very upset, Lady Orsini. I'm sure he would help you, or at least wish me to offer help if I'm able." Her voice was low and gentle and conveyed nothing but understanding and kindness.

Mortified embarrassment flooded Sabine's face. She could barely look Lady Shipton in the eye. This was the woman who would marry Marcus, share his home and bed, and bear his children. She'd thought herself numb to the pain, but the sharp ache in her chest told her otherwise.

Amy was beautiful. With a serene beauty and blessed with alluringly good looks, a person might be forgiven for thinking he was gazing upon perfection.

Amy stood full of sympathy, looking between the two women. The pale rose tint of her gown enhanced her faultless ivory complexion, while setting off the dark gleam of her hair. Her dramatic coloring was the complete opposite of Sabine's own pale and blonde features. She felt insignificant against the unusually tall and slender beauty.

In spite of her height, Amy looked as if a strong wind would break her.

Worse, Amy seemed to know who she was. Had Marcus discussed her with Amy? How mortifying that thought was!

"Truly, there is no need to bother Lord Wolverstone with my silly problem." She shot Monique a warning look.

Amy kept looking between the two women. "It doesn't seem to be a small problem." She stepped forward. "Oh, you've been crying. Please, let me help."

Sabine gathered herself together, feeling inadequate in the face of Lady Shipton's generous spirit. Perhaps the young girl was too naive to understand or know the real details of her relationship with Marcus. She would not hurt her by allowing the nature of her connection with Amy's betrothed to raise its unseemly head.

"Thank you for your concern, Lady Shipton, but I should be leaving." She gave the girl a big smile. "I'm excited to be heading back to Italy tomorrow and I'm simply sad to be leaving such dear friends behind."

Amy looked dubious. "Well, if you are sure that is all it is . . ."

"I'm sure." She turned and collected her cloak from the chair behind her. "I'll leave you to sort out Lady Shipton's dress." She smiled warmly at the young girl, letting excitement enter her tone, when she in reality she was choking with grief inside. "I hear there is to be a big announcement tonight. As I shall not be present, may I offer you and Lord Wolverstone my warmest congratulations? He's a lucky man indeed."

Amy's face broke into a smile and she grew even more beautiful. Sabine could understand why Marcus was captivated by her. Their children would be stunningly beautiful.

Amy actually giggled. "I'm not supposed to tell anyone, but since you won't be attending the ball . . ." She looked excitedly over her shoulder. "He proposed to me this morning. Marcus, that is Lord Wolverstone, got down on one knee and rather stoically told me that he wished me to be his wife and . . ." she laughed again, a delightful tinkling sound, "asked me to make him happy. *Happy*." She sighed. "Not quite a declaration of love, but I mean to do everything in my power to see to his and my own happiness."

Sabine swallowed back the tears. "Good for you. He's a fine man. I'm sure you'll make him exceedingly happy. Now if you'll excuse me, I must leave," and she hurriedly pushed out into the store and out onto the street. Monique was close behind.

"I'm sorry, Sabine. I did not know she was coming today."

She hugged her friend tightly. "Hush, Monique. At least I leave knowing Marcus is in good hands. She's a lovely girl. She'll make him a fine wife." She turned and stepped into her carriage.

Monique pushed the carriage door closed after her and leaned in the window. "He doesn't love her, so how happy can he really be?" She gripped Sabine's arm when she refused to answer. "Don't go to Gower's house tonight. Have the vowels delivered."

"That won't be enough. I've made a fool of him. He'll demand retribution . . ." She leaned and kissed her friend goodbye. "I'll survive. I always have," she whispered under her breath.

As the carriage rolled on its way she didn't look back. She'd learned that there was no point ever in looking back. The memories were too painful.

Amy stood hesitantly on the steps leading up to Lord Wolverstone's, Marcus's, front door. She could hardly believe she was betrothed to the notorious rake in England yet, having met him, she knew he was not as his reputation signified. The heady rush of happiness made her legs shake.

She knew she shouldn't be here, but the scene in the modiste's this morning made her stomach churn with worry. Something about Lady Orsini gnawed at her conscience.

Marcus had asked her for her hand, and requested that she make him happy. He'd not asked her to love him. He had not professed love for her either. Why would he, they hardly knew each other, and she understood few men of privilege did—love— that is. But she felt uneasy about marrying a man who might love another. That was something altogether different.

She moved up a step.

She'd heard rumors at Lady Somerset's ball, that there may be something between the gorgeous, fair-haired French émigréé, who'd made a successful marriage to an Italian Conte, and Lord Wolverstone. There were rumors abounding that they had been lovers.

She understood that a man kept a mistress. That she could tolerate, if, and only if, the transaction stayed financial. But she could not bear to marry a man whose heart lay elsewhere. That would condemn her to a life of misery. For who wanted to be the cause of another's pain?

Her foot took her another step closer to the door.

Did she really wish to hold such an awkward conversation? Would she like the answer if she did so?

She bit her lip, unsure of what to do next. Perhaps she should talk with her older sister, Clarissa, before doing something so foolish. Clarissa had recently married and had always been a source of sound advice to her younger sister.

Why did she suddenly fear this marriage? After all, what woman would not want to become Lady Wolverstone? The position alone would overcome any woman's hesitation in marrying such a rogue, and the idea of sharing a man of such experience's bed—delicious! He was handsome beyond compare. So why did she hesitate?

Too late! The front door opened and Marcus stood staring down at her. Upon seeing her, concern immediately flooded his features.

"Amy, is everything all right?"

Her heart began to race, almost propelling her up the stairs toward him. He looked as devastatingly attractive as ever, even with a frown on his handsome face. His thick, black hair was immaculately groomed and when he smiled at her, she flushed a little. While his high cheekbones gave his face an arrogant cast, his straight nose and nicely chiseled jaw made him every woman's dream. Then why did she get the feeling he would never really be hers?

"If you have a moment, I'd like to talk with you." Her words came out in a breathless rush as he walked down to greet her. She faltered. "Unless of course you're busy . . ." She made to turn, "Of course you're busy, silly of me"

"Stop. Slow down. I'm never too busy for you." He took her hand and placed it on his arm. "Come, let us have some tea; then you can talk with Mother and tell her all about your dress for this evening. She's dying to know the color so she can ensure I wear a matching waistcoat."

They were soon settled in the drawing room. The door remained open for propriety's sake. His servants had brought tea and scones, but her stomached churned so much she knew she couldn't eat a bite.

They sat in awkward silence. She could tell Marcus was getting impatient with her. Before she lost her courage altogether, she blurted out, "What is Lady Orsini to you? Is she your mistress?"

Christ! Amy's question was spoken quietly but with determination. Marcus shifted uneasily in his seat. "She is an acquaintance I knew long ago."

Amy's eyebrow rose. "So, she is not your mistress?"

"No."

He saw that Amy was not fooled. His mother had told him she was smart. "But she was?" There was no condemnation in her tone.

Marcus felt his face redden. Yet, as he would soon be taking this young girl to his bed, surely they could have a grown up conversation now.

"The relationship I had with Lady Orsini was in the past. I promise you that when we marry, I will not have a mistress. I'm sure we will both be content with each other."

"How recently in the past?" she persisted.

Marcus ran a hand through his hair. "I'm not sure this is any of your business, Amy," he said as kindly as he could. "I have reassured you about my lack of a mistress."

She waved a hand. "I don't care about a mistress, Marcus. I know most men of the *ton* have them. What I wish to ascertain is whether or not you are in love with another woman. If so, that would not be fair on either of us."

He looked blindly to the door, hoping for the first time ever that his mother would enter and save him from this hell.

"Do you love her?" she prodded on mercilessly.

Marcus drew in a deep breath. "I beg your pardon," he spoke in steel-clipped tones, "but I don't believe that is any of your concern."

Her eyes became round saucers of puzzled blue. "Not my concern?"

"I did not ask for your love and I did not offer you mine. I merely suggested that we try and make each other happy."

She carefully placed her cup on its saucer. "Happy?" She looked him directly in the eye. "How can you be happy when you are not with the one person you love above all others? What about me? Will I always be compared to another and found wanting? Is that fair on you or on me? Tell me that, Marcus."

He remained silent, searching for an answer he himself did not know. She then made a totally unexpected comment. "I think Lady Orsini is in trouble."

Marcus's head jerked up from where it had been lowered to avoid her knowing gaze.

She gave a wan smile. "I saw her crying at my modiste's this morning. She is great friends with Monique Baye. They were discussing Lord Gower"

"*What's that about Gower?*" he snapped harshly.

Marcus knew who Monique was. Most of his former mistresses frequented her establishment.

"You sound jealous." Amy smiled at Marcus and gave a small sigh. "You *do* love her . . ."

Marcus couldn't seem to voice his denial. He did God, help him, *he did*. He loved Sabine and deep in his heart he knew he always would.

Amy pinched the bridge of her nose in confusion. "I don't understand. If you love her, why are you not marrying her? She is a respectable widow."

Pain carved through his heart. To have to speak of his humiliation was too much. "Because . . . because she will not have me."

"Rubbish! Then you have not tried hard enough. If there is ever a woman in love with you, it is Lady Orsini. You should have seen how pale her face got when I told her of our engagement. Her friend had to support her."

Marcus leaned forward in his chair. *Could this be true?*

"That is why I must know your heart. I couldn't bear to be the cause of two people, who are so obviously in love with each other, not being together. I saw her pain and desolation . . ."

Marcus pondered Amy's words. Did Sabine really love him? Then, if so, why did she keep him at a distance? He looked across at Amy. He would not find his answers here. But he knew *who* could tell him all he needed to know. He should have thought of Monique before.

"I would speak with her if I were you. Lady Orsini has to deliver something to Lord Gower tonight, and Monique is scared for her. I could hear it in her voice. I have never liked that man. He paws at the young girls whenever he thinks no one is watching."

Before he could respond, he heard his mother's footsteps in the hall. He saw his opportunity to leave. He was on his feet before his mother entered the room.

"Mother, Amy has arrived to discuss her dress for tonight." He looked at the clock on the mantle and then back at Amy, flashing a grateful smile at her. "I shall take on board all that you have told me, Lady Shipton."

"Then you will give me your answer tonight?" she challenged him.

He bowed low over her hand, placing a kiss on her knuckles, "I will. Thank you."

"Secrets, I do love secrets." He heard his mother say to Amy as he gathered his gloves and hat from the entrance table and departed the house in a desperate search for some long awaited answers.

The hushed silence that greeted his entrance at the fashionable modiste's owned by Monique Baye was hardly surprising. He did not have a lady on his arm this time.

The ladies Arbuckle and Rutherford were looking through dress patterns and their mouths dropped open in amazement as he took off his hat and bid them good afternoon.

Before they could gather their wits, Monique herself came through the curtain at the back, and being the experienced modiste that she was, immediately broke into a smile. "Lord Wolverstone, you must be here to collect your mother's dress. If you'd please step this way, I have some instructions regarding how it should be worn."

Once they'd moved into her private sitting room, Monique rounded on him. "I trust you are here because you've *finally* come to your senses. You've got to stop her."

He advanced toward her. "I want answers first. God damn it, I deserve answers. Tell me what happened ten years ago."

Something sad and chilling flashed in Monique's eyes. Suddenly his skin felt cold and clammy. He knew he would not like what he was about to hear. He stumbled for a chair.

Monique looked at him with pity shining in her eyes. "You do love her, I can see it. Then trust me when I tell you that you must talk to her. *Force* her to tell you the truth."

"Why can't *you* tell me? I've tried asking her. What is so terrible, that she cannot tell me?"

"I cannot betray Sabine's trust." She straightened and gave him a sly smile. "Have you met her son, Alfredo?"

"No." He wasn't sure he wanted to see the evidence of her marriage.

Monique pulled him out of the chair and began shoving him toward the store's exit. "Go to her house now. Meet Alfredo, then ask her for the truth."

Before he knew it he was back out on the street. Marcus knew something terrible had happened to Sabine; he knew it in his bones. He would go to her house and demand answers. And this time, he would *not* leave until he had them.

CHAPTER TWELVE

Marcus was shown into the drawing room. Apparently, Sabine was not at home and none of the servants knew where she'd gone. Nevertheless, they invited him in to wait.

He looked grimly around the room and wondered how Sabine could abide living here. He instinctively knew that the leased house was not to her taste at all. The drawing room was shabby and in need of redecoration. She obviously had not lied when she'd indicated she was in London temporarily. So, her plan had just been to secure his help, get her revenge and leave. It had never been about *them*.

A wave of sadness and longing washed over him for what life could have been. A home, he truly wanted a home. However, the thought of sharing his home and his life, as well as his bed, with Amy Shipton held little appeal.

The minutes ticked slowly by; he was going mad with the waiting. Why had Sabine left so precipitously ten years ago? Monique's cryptic words indicated that there was far more to this story than he'd originally thought.

When he finally heard rapid footsteps in the hall, he

marched to the drawing room door and threw it open. The high pitched squeal of a young boy directed his attention to the bottom of the stairs.

A boy of about ten, Alfredo presumably, had slid down the stairs and landed on his bottom with a thump at the base of one of the intricately carved banisters.

He giggled in glee. "I'm not supposed to slide down the banisters. Mama says it's dangerous."

The boy picked himself up and moved toward Marcus, his face alight with mischief and curiosity. He looked up at Marcus and smiled, "Buon giorno, Sir."

Alfredo. A cold, cold chill slid through Marcus's veins, engulfing his chest. He stood looking down at a face he'd seen before. The hands of betrayal gripped and squeezed his newly blossoming heart, the tentacles of its barbed vines smothering his new hope.

But somehow this new found hope in his heart fought back; a gong clanged in his brain that said *no, this is not right.* But yet the proof was standing here before him. Ten years ago Sabine must have taken Gower as a lover, for there was no doubt that the child before him was of Gower's bloodline. The resemblance was uncanny.

Alfredo's smile slipped away and he took a step back in alarm at Marcus's thunderous expression.

"Alfredo, come here at once." A woman about the same age as Sabine hurried to Alfredo's side and took his hand. Her mouth firmed when she noted Marcus standing there, transfixed at the sight of the boy. "Go up to your room, there's a good boy. It's bath time. I'll be up shortly."

Alfredo took one look at Marcus's face and fled.

This prim and proper servant sparked yet another memory from deep within Marcus. "I remember you. You were in the Fournier household."

Her expression remained grave. "Yes, my Lord. I was one of their maids."

"You went with Sabine when she married?"

"Yes, I'm Claudette, her lady in waiting. I also serve as nanny to Alfredo."

At the mention of the boy's name, Marcus's eyes momentarily closed.

"You will not tell the world who her son's father truly is." It was a command, not a question, and it was issued with contempt. Her antipathy was clear in her stance and from the flash within her dark eyes.

"I have no wish to tattle about Lady Orsini's affairs."

A heavy silence ensued.

Then Claudette's eyes widened in comprehension. "You think she *willingly* lay with that despicable man, don't you?" Her voice was incredulous. "Men! You are, par"- she spat and prodded him with her finger, overcome with anger. "How *can* you think she would do that when you were her world?"

A sound like an animal in pain escaped his mouth. *Oh, God.* Horror gripped him and almost forced him to his knees. He used his hand to brace himself against the hallway wall. He looked into Claudette's face and saw the truth as plain as the new day. Bitter bile rose in his mouth. As understanding dawned over him he hastily covered his mouth; the urge to vomit was strong.

With sudden brutal clarity, he remembered Sabine's words from the first night in Lady Somerset's bedchamber. *I have only ever willingly slept with my husband.* He'd not understood the nuance behind her words until now.

He raised his anguished eyes to Claudette. "Why? Why, in God's name, was I not told?"

"It was to protect you, of course, My Lord. She knew what you would do. Back then Gower was a champion swordsman. You, you . . . were not so good."

Brutal fury engulfed him. It pressed outward until he thought he'd explode. "She *should* have told me." The wrenching grief in him threatened to suffocate him. Ten years; they'd wasted *ten precious years*. For ten long years he'd hated her and loved her equally. Back then, he should have tried harder to see her. He had known, deep down inside, that his Sabine could not have played him false, but he had let his overweening male pride get in the way.

He felt a tear slide silently down his cheek.

Claudette cupped his chin and appealed to him. "She has gone again, to deal with that devil, because of her love for you and her child. Will you help her this time?"

"What . . . what are you talking about? Gower is ruined. She holds his vowels . . ."

He watched her raise an eyebrow.

A stark foreboding gripped him. "*He's threatened her, hasn't he?*"

Claudette nodded. "Gower threatened to tell you the truth if she didn't sign the vowels over to him. He also threatened to make Alfredo disappear."

He squeezed his eyes shut. She was trying to protect him again and he'd . . . he'd simply let her walk away.

"How long ago did she leave the house?"

"Too long, my Lord."

That was all Marcus needed to hear. He ran for the front door. Luckily, Henry's house was across the road. He'd need Henry's help to get into Gower's residence.

He had to get to her. He would save her this time. And when he got his hands on Gower . . . A black fury hazed his vision at the thought. His hands would not leave Gower's body until he was dead.

Sabine took a hackney to Gower's residence in Holborn. She could guess what he used this house for, and the type of women he brought here as it was in the seedier part of London.

She made the driver take her around the block for almost an hour before she summoned up the courage to face Gower. She listened to the horses clip clopping along the cobblestones, willing herself to find another way out of this mess. If not for her time with Marcus and her revenge for her parents deaths, she'd wish she'd never set foot on English soil again.

Realizing she'd run out of time, she signaled for the driver to stop. She alighted at the corner, five houses down from where her enemy lay curled up like a snake, ready to strike and fill her with his poison. Already she could feel fear clouding her brain and she needed to pause and think. Somehow she had to prevent Gower from touching her. She wasn't sure she'd be strong enough to survive him a second time.

As she forced her sluggish brain to think past the horrors of what Gower would be likely to do to her, she patted the small pistol that lay comfortingly in her pocket. In addition, it had been Claudette's idea to wear trousers under her skirt. She would not make it easy for Gower this time. This time she'd fight back. She wasn't a scared naive girl of eighteen anymore.

Gower had seen to that.

Perhaps if she fought back hard enough, she would find an opportunity to escape. She and Alfredo were booked on the schooner heading for Rome, first thing tomorrow morning. Surely she could avoid Gower's retribution until then. He would have the vowels and they were all he really wanted.

Sabine stood at the bottom of the steps leading to Gower's bright red front door and knew her time was up. Taking a deep breath she began slowly and resignedly walking to meet her fate.

Gower must have been watching for her, because she had only just raised her hand to the door knock, when it swung open and he pulled her inside slamming the door ominously behind her.

Needles of panic drove deep into Marcus's chest as he stood waiting for Henry to get his pistols and sword. The thought of Gower's hands on Sabine filled him with wild fear.

Henry arrived back in the entrance hall grim faced. "I'm ashamed to face her after how I have behaved when she sacrificed herself for you. She was so young, only eighteen and that bastard . . . I'll kill him; after you've finished with him, of course."

He clapped Henry on the back. "*You* owe her an apology? What do you think I owe her?" The fear that tore through Marcus was entangled with fury and fierce self-recrimination.

Their carriage raced across town. Thank God Claudette knew where Sabine had gone. However both men knew of Gower's second residence in Holborn anyway. The thought of Sabine in that house made his insides recoil.

They too parked the carriage at the entrance of the street and in the dimming light, made their way toward the rear of the property.

Marcus asked, "Do you think he'll have the house guarded."

"I doubt it." Henry added dryly. "He knows Sabine would never risk her son's life by doing anything foolish, or your life for that matter." Under his breath, but still loud enough for Marcus to hear, his friend said, "What an amazing woman."

Marcus growled. "Infuriating woman, she should have come to me." Inside his heart swelled with an all consuming love, coupled with pride. She was indeed a very special woman. "Let's use the servants' entrance. He won't want any witnesses and has likely sent them away for the evening."

Gower pushed Sabine ahead of him up the stairs to a room that could only be described as part drawing room, part bedchamber.

Shadows flickered eerily across the walls from the small

number of lighted candles. The fire had burned low. There was a bottle of wine and two glasses sitting on a small table along with a plate of breads and meats.

It almost looked like a scene set for seduction. However, Sabine knew from past experience that Gower didn't seduce—he took.

He raped.

Her mouth grew dry as she stepped into the room with Gower at her back. She quickly crossed the room to stand by the fire, only to be disappointed that the poker iron was not sitting in its cradle.

Gower noticed and laughed. "You didn't think I'd leave a handy weapon around for your use did you?" He closed the door softly behind him. "Come, sit. I promise I won't pounce on you." His smile widened to a grotesque grin. "After all, you are here to do my bidding." The smile died and the face of the devil was revealed. "You don't want me to have to hurt those you love do you? Alfredo. Such a handsome boy, so like his father."

"You are a monster. You'd hurt your own son"

"Be careful, my fiery French beauty. What would happen to the Orsini riches if that fact became known? There'd be forfeit to the church. Under Italian law, the Pope has claim on any noble wealth when there are no heirs. Hence we know why Roberto Orsini was so desperate to marry a lady already with child. He wanted to ensure the church got nothing from him.

As soon as you arrived back in London, I spotted the boy by chance in the park. I'm surprised his nanny didn't tell you. I found it rather amusing. She too understood who I was as soon as she saw me. She looked as if she'd like to knife me through the heart. I discovered that if the Pope learns of your deception, you and the boy would be in the poorhouse just like your parents."

Sabine swallowed her rage. She needed a calm head in order to deal to her enemy.

He walked slowly toward her. "You need me to keep quiet and for me to ignore my own son. Well, given how terrible it is for me to be unable to acknowledge him, you'll have to pay a price for that." He paused for added effect, "And you will continue to pay until I am satisfied. Why should a father not profit from his son's good fortune?"

"You're no father. You're not even a man. The only way a woman comes to your bed is by force or because of money."

His hand shot out and gripped her tightly by the throat. "Tut. I was going to be nice." His face moved closer, his lips in a cruel snarl. "I was going to let you have a few drinks to warm that frigid body of yours, but perhaps I'll simply take you like I did ten years ago. Hmmm . . . would you like that?" He kissed her hard on the mouth and she bit his lip so hard it drew blood.

The hand choking her throat disappeared and he stepped back in order to put more force into his backhanded slap. She saw stars and felt the blood trickle from the corner of her mouth. "Bitch." Then he gave a smile that would freeze hell. "I do love it when my women play rough. But before I rip that God awful spinsterish gown from your delectable body, give me the vowels."

Sabine was angry with herself for not being able to keep her hands from shaking as she fumbled for the papers. This was going to be far worse than that night long ago when Gower raped her in her parents' garden. At least it had been dark and she couldn't see him as he had rutted her from behind.

She clenched her fists and told herself to bide her time. Gower would pay. She knew it was wrong, and God help her for it, but she desperately wanted him dead.

She carefully drew the papers out of her pocket, the touch of her small pistol giving her strength. He grabbed for the bundle and tore the ribbon off them. His eyes began to scan through all the documents.

"They are all there, as I'm sure you knew they would be. I

would have one favor from *you*." At her words, his gaze flew back to her. "Tell me, how did you know I'd be in the garden that night?"

Before answering, he walked over to the fire and began to throw each individual piece of paper into the flames and watch them burn.

"It was easy. I saw you one day walking in the park with Judith, the now widowed Lady Harcourt. The two of you, beautiful young ladies, made quite the picture. What a vision you were with your fair hair and rosy cheeks. Imagine my surprise when I saw Lord Wolverstone stop to say hello. But it wasn't Judith's hand he lingered over, it was yours."

"He visited your parent's garden often. I assumed he was grooming you to be his mistress. It was inconceivable that you could become the wife of a Marquis." He shrugged his shoulders. "Imagine my surprise when I found you to be a virgin."

She gritted her teeth. "How did you know to send me the note?"

"I followed Marcus. Over the course of a few weeks, I followed him and spied on you both when you met in your parents' garden. So eager you were in his arms. And I didn't send you the note, he did."

Sabine's blood ran cold. Marcus was in on this. She shook her head; *no,* it couldn't be.

The last of the vowels disappeared into the flames and he turned his cold eyes on her. "I waited for a note to be sent, and I ensured that Marcus would be unable to make the rendezvous. I then came in his place. You should have seen your face when you realized I wasn't Marcus."

He walked toward her and ran a finger down her face. "I never forgot your choked screams as my hand covered your mouth. Nor your tight, virginal body."

His hand cupped her breast and squeezed it hard. Sabine

253

froze with revulsion. She couldn't, she *couldn't* go through this again. She closed her eyes.

"It was so obliging of you not to tell Marcus. He would have had my balls, or my life, for touching you. I considered cornering you again for another bout, but you never met in the garden again after that night."

Sabine closed her eyes. She'd not been able to walk back into that garden ever again after Gower's rape of her. The horror and humiliation were too great.

"He started to openly court you. I knew if you wanted to become the Marquis of Wolverstone's wife, you'd have to keep our 'liaison' quiet; for who wants a man's seconds as his wife?"

Sabine's hand fumbled in her pocket and found her pistol.

"Every time I drank with Marcus and his friends, I silently gloated, knowing I'd been there first. I thought for sure you'd finally told him, when a month later you suddenly disappeared. Seeing Alfredo, now I understand why."

"Well, I bloody well don't understand why, perhaps you'd like to tell me." Marcus advanced into the room, white hot fury rampant in his eyes, his voice edged with steel. "And take your hands off her, you prick of a man."

Faster than you'd expect a man the size of Gower to move, he'd grabbed Sabine round the throat and swung her in front of him using her as a shield against Marcus's pistol.

Her fingernails clawed at the fat fingers squeezing the life-giving air from her lungs.

Her breath rasped through her teeth, her eyes widened, and her hope soared as Marcus moved from out of the shadows. She could see the molten rage flaming within his eyes. His nostrils flared and his lips were taut with anger.

She looked up into Gower's eyes which were now filled with alarm. A sneer spread, turning his face into a monstrous mask of ugliness. His hand tightened at her neck.

"Such a pretty neck; it's so slender and graceful, and so easily snapped."

Marcus stopped in the centre of the room, breathing hard as he took in the scene before him. His amber eyes pierced the dim room with outraged intensity. He looked like Mars, the god of war, a dark, vengeful, exotic beauty.

Sabine lowered her hands from the steely arm encircling her throat. She fixed her stare and all her faith on Marcus.

"Stand aside, Wolverstone," Gower warned, "Come any closer and I'll snap her neck."

"Like I stood aside ten years ago and did nothing? I'll not be so dishonorable a second time," and to her horror, he crouched and relinquished his weapon to the floor. She turned and looked at Gower's triumphant smile. It wasn't until she'd turned back to look in stunned disbelief at Marcus, that she saw Henry St. Giles step into the firelight.

"This time we settle it, man to man, coward. No weapons, just our fists." Marcus's tone was coolly scornful, his stance was relaxed, but suppressed violence simmered and rippled under his impeccable attire, and he moved with predatory panther-like grace.

Sabine stared, mesmerized by the guilt she saw in Marcus's eyes. "It was not your fault, Marcus," she said softly.

"Shut up, bitch." Gower stepped back. "You call this honorable. If it's honor you want, then call me out. If you kill me here and now, how will you explain it to the magistrate? As soon as Society claps eyes on dear Alfredo, they'll think you killed a rival."

"He's right, Marcus. Let him walk out of here. He won't hurt me. He's got what he wanted. The vowels I held have been destroyed." Her desperate plea fell on deaf ears.

Marcus's cold fury cut through the fraught atmosphere. "I know him. He'll just want more and more. He'll continue to use

Alfredo to get what he wants."

Gower tightened his grip. "Marcus understands me only too well. What will Society say when they learn the demure Lady Orsini spread open her legs for me"

"Bastard," and Marcus took a step closer.

Gower lifted her off the floor with his hands. Darkness beckoned as her throat was crushed and she fought valiantly to breathe.

"Tut, tut, careful."

Marcus stepped back, filling the already overheated room with cusses and Gower let her feet touch the floor once more.

Gower turned and peered out of the window to the street below. "Where's your carriage? You must have one."

Marcus looked at Henry and nodded. Henry withdrew and she heard his footsteps on the stairs.

"Good man. Now if you'd simply move toward the fire, Sabine and I shall be leaving and taking your carriage."

"Society be damned. I'm not letting you leave here with Sabine."

Sabine closed her eyes and prayed. She knew what Marcus would say next.

"I formally challenge you to a duel. Choose your weapon."

To her surprise Gower moved closer to the door. "I don't think so. For to challenge me, you'll have to reveal Sabine's sordid past. How she willingly came to my bed, hoping to trap me into marriage with her pregnancy. Easy, easy, my sweet treat," he added at Sabine's vehement cry of protest.

"I was never willing. Your touch makes my skin crawl."

Marcus held her gaze and she nodded. She was not ashamed of the past. She had no reason to be ashamed. Alfredo would have to learn the truth if they were to stay in England, for the gossip would be cruel, but it would be better to be prepared than for him not to understand.

Marcus sneered. "The truth should come out so that all of Society knows the kind of man you really are; a bully and an abuser of women."

"You can't be that naive. It's her word against mine. Wait until I tell them how she was begging me for it; how her enthusiasm for the sport knew no bounds"-

-"You're wrong. It's my word and her word against yours. I'll stand by her. I'll protect her like I should have done ten years ago. Who do you think Society will believe?" A smile filled with utter hatred spread over Marcus's sensuous lips. Lips that she remembered had been hot and tender on hers. "Pick your weapon, scum."

"No." She cleared her throat. "No. I won't allow it."

Marcus's incredulous gaze swung her way. Then his lips firmed into a disapproving line and he hung his head.

She ignored the large hand at her throat. "I won't be used as an excuse for any more violence. Please, just let him go. Killing him, and in the process ruining yourself, won't change the past. I'm sick and tired of looking back. I want this to be over. Revenge is not the answer. I thought it was, but it is hollow. Getting on with my life and living a full and happy life is the answer."

Marcus gave an anguished cry. "Gower took my happy life away from me. He took *you!*"

This time she beat her chest, willing him to understand. *"Marcus, can't you see. I'm still here."*

Chapter Thirteen

She felt Gower moving restlessly against her back. He was uncertain and getting agitated. The silence sharpened to a razor's edge as the two men stared at each other with venom in their gazes.

"Once in the carriage, he will release me. Won't you? The vowels have been destroyed." Sabine wasn't sure who she was addressing her last comment to.

At her plea, Marcus's fiery eyes flicked to meet hers. Behind the fury was sorrow and remorse. The fleeting look vanished as his lips tightened.

Henry arrived back in the room. "The carriage is at the door. I've instructed my driver to take you wherever you wish to go."

Marcus's voice lowered to a terrifying hiss. "If you touch one hair on her head, I'll hunt you down like the rabid dog you are and kill you—slowly, painfully, remorselessly."

"As will I," Henry added.

"Yes, yes. Clear a path to the door. You too, St. Giles."

"No. Your word as a gentleman first," Marcus sneered as he pronounced the word *gentleman*. "Give your word that you'll leave her on the front steps. In exchange, I promise not to come after you. And my word, at least, you can trust."

The fingers at her throat squeezed even tighter and Sabine saw dark spots. Her hands rose and she clawed once again at the hand at her throat.

Marcus said, "Go. I don't need to kill you. Society will shun you forever for your cowardly behavior. I'll enjoy your disgrace."

"Not as much as I enjoyed being Sabine's first lover. It must kill you to know I was there before anyone else. I took her virginal blood, and if you don't step back, I'll take her life as well."

Sabine could sense that a volcanic force of molten rage about to explode from Marcus. "It's alright, Marcus. They're only words and words can't hurt me."

Her two rescuers moved in unison over toward the fireplace, leaving a clear path to the stairs.

Gower pushed her quickly before him, all the while keeping the men in his sight. "Walk to the window. Keep looking down. If I see either of you start to move before I'm safely on my way, she's dead."

In a blur, they made it to the carriage. Gower entered first, still holding her neck in his vice-like grip. He began to drag her inside. She looked up and saw Marcus pounding on the window before she was pulled inside. The carriage, on Gower's urgent command, took off at sped. Her last glimpse was of Marcus and Henry dashing down the street after her.

"What have you done?" she cried.

"I need money. You have it. I'll risk Marcus's wrath. He won't hurt me with you still in my grasp."

"We will drive to Calais. One in France, you, my sweet, will organize funds for me, so that I may disappear. I hear America is the land of opportunity. If you behave and are—how I shall put it, *agreeable*," his lecherous look made her stomach heave. "Then I may set you free." He pulled her roughly onto his lap. "Or, once we become reacquainted, you might like to come with me."

Sabine feared she'd vomit. "You stupid man. Now Marcus will come after us. If you touch me, there will be nowhere on earth you can hide."

"But he can't do much when I hold what is most precious to him—you, my dear." He looked down at where her gown gaped from where it had been ripped in the struggle. Sabine tried to cover herself but he stopped her. A sinister look had flooded his eyes and she froze with fear at the sight of it.

"It's a very long drive to Calais. A man has to have some entertainment . . ." and as fast as a cobra striking its prey, he flipped her beneath him on the seat. She felt his hand rummaging around the edges of her skirts. He started laughing. The manic sound reminded her of a madman. "What have you got under there? Trousers! As if they would stop me!"

He briefly let go of her hands and flipped her skirts up over her head, trapping her under her clothes. Sabine felt the panic rise in the darkness as his hands tore at the protective breeches she wore under her skirts. Her breath came in terrified gasps. A picture of Marcus and Alfredo swam into her head. She took deep breaths, fighting desperately to get her fear under control.

Slowly her hand reached to where her pocket now lay within easy reach. She inched her hand into it, until she felt the cold steel of her pistol. Her fingers gripped it and she immediately felt a rush of courage. She'd rather die than let Gower rape her a second time.

She closed her eyes and drew the pistol from her pocket. Gower was so busy ripping her clothes from her body that he'd not noticed how still and quiet she'd gone. She gave a silent prayer for her son and drew her arm free of the tangle of her skirts and touched the barrel of the pistol to Gower's temple.

"Not this time," she said softly as Gower went motionless, suddenly still in stunned silence. "Get off me and move across to the other seat."

He reluctantly did as she had asked, his face a mass of startled disbelief.

"Now tell the driver to turn the carriage round."

Gower's disbelief turned into calculation. "That little pistol won't kill me."

She lowered her aim to his groin. "Maybe not, but I'll make sure you can't rape again."

He paled and crossed his legs.

"Order the coach to turn round."

He hesitated. "If I do that, I'm dead."

"For a man like you, better dead than a eunuch I suspect," she said harshly. "Quite frankly, I don't care. Either way, I'm happy to oblige."

His lips tensed and an apprehensive silence invaded the carriage. They sat facing each other for several minutes, until slowly color began to seep back into his face. "I think you're bluffing. You don't have the bottle to shoot me."

Sabine tried not to let her hand shake. She did wonder if she had the ability to coldly shoot an unarmed man, but if he tried to hurt her again . . .

"Try it and see. If you're not going to tell the driver to turn round and go back to London, I will." With that she stood slightly to bang on the hatch. That's when he moved.

Before she could even knock on the roof, Gower was upon her, trying to wrestle the gun from her grasp.

"There they are," Marcus yelled across to Henry as they galloped toward the carriage. Less than ten lengths behind, Marcus and Henry had been frantically chasing the carriage as it thundered its way on the road to Calais.

He dug his heels into his stallion's flanks thankful he'd invested a lot of money in his horses. They'd made up the lapse in time perfectly.

Marcus had realized Gower would aim for Calais. Sabine was French and Gower would use her and her money to help him flee. He should never have let him leave the house. He cursed his own foolhardiness. If Sabine got hurt, it was his fault for a second time. Worse, if she died . . . the pain in his chest at this thought almost knocked him from his horse. He couldn't lose her again. He *wouldn't* lose her again.

Not only would Gower *not* escape, he was a marked man. He couldn't bear thinking about her alone with that depraved pervert.

"How close do you think we should get? If he realizes we're here, he might act out of desperation." Marcus knew Henry was right.

He narrowed his eyes against the swirling, gritty wind and indicated that they should split and ride down each side of the carriage.

To their surprise the carriage then began to slow. It wasn't until they drew closer, that Marcus clearly heard Sabine's terrified screams.

Then as if time had stopped, the wind dropped, the screams died and the sound of a pistol firing filled the air.

He heard Henry curse and advance on the carriage which had rolled to a halt. Marcus leaped off his galloping horse and threw open the carriage door with his heart in his throat. Gower was on top of Sabine but neither of them was moving. He reached in and grabbed Gower, dragging him out of the carriage on to the ground. There was blood everywhere; it was all over Sabine's dress and the floor of the carriage.

With his heart beating hard, he clambered into the carriage and tentatively reached out his hand to feel for Sabine's pulse. Her eyes were closed, her skin was warm, and then, miraculously, he saw the tiny flutter of a pulse at the base of her neck. Sabine was alive but was she injured? He began patting her clothes as she turned her head.

"Marcus." She let out a half cry, half sob and flung herself into his arms. "I've kill—killed him. He was trying to kill me . . ."

He picked her up in his arms, and held her tightly, cupping her head against his chest. She sobbed inconsolably and held him as if he might disappear. "Sshh," he whispered, "Are you hurt?"

She shook her head. He gave thanks to God. He kissed the top of her head, then took her face between his hands and said, simply. "Let's go home."

She reached up to kiss him and he savored the taste and feel of her. She was alive, safe and unhurt.

He slipped out of his coat and helped her into it. Her dress was soaked with blood and she shivered when she looked down. "Don't look at it." Then he helped her out of the carriage into Henry's care while he fetched his horse.

Thankfully, Henry had covered Gower with his coat. It seemed that Sabine's shot had torn a hole in his neck and he'd bled to death very quickly; too quickly, in Marcus's opinion.

Once Marcus had mounted, Henry handed Sabine up into his arms.

"I'll take care of everything here, just get her home," his friend said.

The terror he had felt when he'd heard that shot would haunt him for the rest of his days. He'd almost failed her again but, by the grace of God, she'd survived. This time, he would *never* let her go. He knew that both she and Alfredo belonged to him now. The long painful wait to claim her was over.

She was back where she belonged. In his life, his arms and soon, as his wife, in his home.

CHAPTER FOURTEEN

Sabine was sound asleep by the time they arrived back at her home. Marcus carried her up the stairs to her room and handed her into Claudette's care. The French woman kept thanking him as if he was some kind of hero. He wasn't.

As he rode home, weariness invaded his limbs and his heart was heavy in his chest.

Ten years ago he'd been unable to protect her. Looking back he could pinpoint precisely when she had been attacked. It was the day she no longer wanted to walk in her parents' garden. He'd thought it odd at the time, and from that day on, she'd slowly withdrawn from him. She was no longer the carefree and happy young girl he'd given his heart to. When he'd heard she'd eloped he thought she'd backed away because she didn't love him and had given her heart instead to another.

But she hadn't. He still didn't understand why she hadn't come to him for help. Did she think so little of him? Was she afraid he'd scorn her for something that wasn't her fault?

Arriving home close to four in the morning, Marcus assured his butler that he wasn't hurt. The blood on his clothes was not his. He was told his mother had been asking for him. Damn, he'd forgotten about the ball.

He was also handed a perfumed note. He knew who it was from, Amy. Christ. No wonder his mother wanted to see him.

He opened Amy's missive and read—

My Lord,

Since you did not appear at the ball tonight, I have taken it that your decision regarding Lady Orsini is made. This is good. Love is hard to find, but once found, lasts a lifetime. Your love is to be envied.

I release you and wish you much happiness.

With my blessing and understanding.

Lady Amy Shipton

He smiled inside. Amy was a quite a woman. She deserved someone special too. Perhaps Henry should consider her . . . Hmmm, a plan was forming in his head as he walked down the corridor to his bedroom. He'd think on that some more, once his own situation was resolved.

He needed to bathe. His clothes were covered in blood.

Tomorrow he'd have to face his mother and declare to her his intention to marry Sabine. He was sure that once his mother learned the truth, she'd welcome Sabine with open arms.

But first he had to learn the complete story, and once he was bathed and dressed in clean clothes he set off again, back to Sabine's townhouse, this time determined to get all the answers he needed.

Sabine lay in her bath. She'd been unable to sleep well, with the picture of Gower's face tormenting her as he lay dying on top of her. She'd killed a man. Yet, she somehow couldn't bring herself to feel any remorse. He would have killed her, she was sure of it. She touched the bruises at her neck.

She kept scrubbing at her skin till it was raw in an effort to cleanse herself of the taint of Gower, just as she'd done ten years ago. Gower, even in death, still had the power to make her feel dirty.

Now, at least, the two men she loved most, Alfredo and Marcus, were safe. Claudette had told her Marcus had carried her home and then left. No doubt he'd raced off to make his apologies to Amy. They were supposed to have become engaged last night.

How ironic, she was finally free to reveal her secrets but now he was bound to another. She knew Marcus, and realized that he would not be dishonorable enough to go back on his word. She admired him greatly for that.

She heard the door open behind her. She rose from the tub and called over her shoulder, "Claudette, can you hand me the towel please. I'm as clean as I'm ever going to get."

It was his scent that alerted her to his presence first, just before two strong arms enveloped her in the big towel, picking her up and walking through to the bedroom where he seated her on his lap as he sat at the end of her bed. He held her tightly against his chest as she rested quietly listening to his heartbeat beneath her ear.

Before she could speak, he bent his head down and kissed her. The kiss was soft, gentle and possessive all in one. He took command of her mouth, sweeping his tongue inside, sending her senses reeling. She kissed him back, her arms slipping around his neck, dragging him closer and closer to her.

Finally, he broke away from the kiss. "So you do have some feelings for me then, or is this simply gratitude? No more lies between us."

She stroked a lock of hair away from his face. "I've never lied to you."

"Ten years ago you lied about your being in love with another man." He looked closely at her. "Why? Did you have so little faith in my love for you?"

Tears welled at the memory and she cupped his cheek. "No! It was *because* I loved you that I needed to leave."

"I don't understand."

Her wedding day had been the saddest day of her life. She'd wept tears of agonizing grief. Tears for the friend and lover she'd lost in Marcus, tears for the man who would make her his wife, whom she knew she would never love, and tears for the unborn child she was carrying whom she would always see protected, regardless of the violence behind his making.

When Alfredo was born, she knew she'd been right to sacrifice everything for her son. She had never regretted her decision, yet there had been times during the last ten years when living hurt so badly, if it had not been for Alfredo, she'd have quite happily curled up and died.

Why should the innocent suffer? It was so unfair.

"I asked my father to find me a husband and he found Orsini. And you're right, I never loved him."

Marcus's eyes narrowed. "This doesn't make sense. Your father told me it had been your choice. Yet now you say he arranged it."

"I asked him to."

He demanded, "*Why?* I would have helped you. We could have been together—happy." The pain in his voice made her tremble in misery. It appeared that she wasn't the only one who'd suffered during the last ten years.

She owed him the truth.

So quietly that she wasn't sure he'd hear her, she whispered her painful secret. "When Gower raped me, I knew there was a chance I could get with child."

Anger and fury and regret washed over Marcus in equal measure. He felt the inside of his stomach recoil and the bile rose in him. "You can't have thought I would turn you away and desert you if you were."

She wiped a tear from his cheek. "I know you would not have turned me away. That is the reason I had to leave."

He buried his head in her shoulder. "Did you think I would challenge him to a duel and that I might die? I would have—I bloody should have!"

"That was my initial reason for keeping my shameful secret a secret."

"There is no shame."

"Well, it was the reason for not telling you at the time. But it soon became evident that whatever future we might have had could no longer be. I realized I was pregnant."

He pulled back from her to look in her eyes. "Alfredo . . ."

Her tears began to fall. "My innocent son, he doesn't deserve to suffer. I had to give my child a name. I couldn't allow him to be born a bastard."

Anguished tears fell on their joined hands. He tried to blink back the pain. "I would have proudly given him my name."

"No. You were already the Marquis of Wolverstone. If we had married, and my child was a boy, he would have become your legitimate heir. I couldn't allow you to make that sacrifice. It would not have been right. And as it turned out, I did have a son."

He drew in a breath sharply. "Not right. Not right. What is not right is what you have endured." He placed her hand on his heart. "What *we* have endured. I missed you every day. I longed for you every day. If I closed my eyes tightly enough, I pictured you here beside me and I swore I could still smell your scent."

"My dreams of you kept me going. You were never out of my heart. Never, ever."

"And I never will be again." He picked her up and sat her on the edge of the bed and then got down on the floor on his knees. "Lady Sabine Orsini, will you do me the honor of being my wife? Will you and your—our-son, Alfredo, fill my life with love and happiness and make me whole again?"

Her smile died. "But aren't you engaged to Amy?" she asked quietly. "I won't let you sacrifice your honor for me."

He softly cupped her cheek in his hand. "You have sacrificed much more for me. I'm not engaged to Amy anymore. She turned me down when she knew I was in love with you."

The smile he loved so much returned instantly. "Really? You're free to marry?"

He pulled her up into his arms and kissed her passionately. "I've *never* been free of you. I've loved you for so long, I was never able to love another. Will you? Will you please put me out of my misery and become my wife?"

"Of course I will," she cried as she drew closer to him. "I can't believe this is truly happening to us. I love you so much." She flung her arms around his neck and pulled him down to kiss her.

She pushed herself out of his hold and he groaned. Then his smile turned wicked as Sabine allowed the towel to fall to the floor as she walked to the door and locked it.

"Alfredo might wake soon and I'd rather like some private time with you." Her husky voice and the sight of her glorious body sent waves of heat to his groin.

He stared at the vision before him, feeling his empty soul filling to the brim with love as she padded softly toward him, naked except for her beautiful smile.

Her beauty left him bereft of breath and he became eager to worship every delectable inch of her.

He loved that not only was she strong, but that she still had such capacity to love, after all she'd been through. He intended to spend the rest of his life making her happy.

He lowered his face to her, mute with adoration, as she stood before him. She slid hands up his chest. She took his hand and pulled him toward the bed, then pushed him down to sit on the edge of it, nudging her hand in between his thighs.

"It's my turn now to love you in the way I've always dreamed." She began to undo the buttons of his placard. She freed him to her gaze and pushed his falls further down off his hips.

He gave a wicked smile. "I hope I live up to expectations."

She looked down and curled her hand around his jutting erection and he groaned. "I'm very hopeful," she giggled. Then her face took on a serious look. "I want to do something I've never done with any other man." With that, she lowered herself to her knees, her gaze riveted on his straining erection.

He knew her intention. He remembered her question in the carriage the day she'd come to him and offered herself to him in order to honor their wager. *"Can a woman kiss a man down there?"*

"Sabine, you don't have to do this. Making love with you will always feel like the first time because I love you. Nothing else matters."

The cheeky young girl he remembered smiled back. "Thank you, darling, but I want to do this, it's for me."

Cupping her nape, Marcus leaned down and kissed her softly. "I'm not complaining. And it definitely won't be only for you."

She giggled again and it was the sweetest sound he'd heard in a long, long time. It made his heart soar and fill with love.

She curled her hand around him and tentatively licked the length of him. He surged beneath her touch and she heard his indrawn breath.

She dipped her tongue into the tiny slit where drops appeared and she experienced her first taste of him. Her hand explored him further and cupped his heavy sacs which seemed to tighten and fill her hand as she stroked him with her tongue.

Finally, she grew bolder and took him into her mouth. He pulsed and his hips lifted slightly, pushing him further into her mouth. She could feel tremors running through his thighs as they squeezed tightly around her waist.

She loved the feeling of control. She could make him moan with desire with just a simple suck and groan with need when she removed her mouth from him.

She had no idea if she was doing this properly but when he moaned, "Sabine, you're my love," and his hands entangled themselves in her hair, she thought she must be doing something right.

She grew bolder, taking him deeply into her mouth, nearly into her throat, stroking him with both hands and suckling him faster and harder.

She could feel her own body grow wet with desire. She redoubled her efforts, feeling his grip tighten ruthlessly in her hair, his hips moving in time with her mouth. "Oh, God, Sabine, I'm going to come."

She suckled even harder. That's what she wanted. She wanted all of him. She was shaking as much as Marcus, whose body was taut with tension. He tried to withdraw at the last second, but she held him fast, clasping his hips possessively. With a roar of pleasure, he convulsed and spilled his seed down her throat, pressing desperately into her mouth. She drank every last drop; it was the taste of Marcus, the taste of love. She'd never tasted any other man like that before. He was panting heavily, pulsating in her mouth again and again and again.

He released his fingers from her hair and fell backward on the bed. She relinquished his member with slow licks. "You taste divine," she murmured huskily.

"Come here, my love," he panted. "That was amazing."

She rose on shaky legs and climbed up on to the bed to lie beside him. He smiled and its warmth soaked into her heart. He looked ravished—hair tousled, cheeks flushed but, most of all, he looked happy. He hadn't been happy for a long, long time. She'd done that for him, given him back his happiness.

She gazed tenderly at him for a long moment. "This will be a perfect memory."

"We will make many more perfect memories, I promise. In fact, if you give me a minute, I'll start making more." He rolled onto his side and kissed her.

Just then there was a light knock at the door. "Mama, why is your door locked?"

"Mama's getting dressed, she'll be out shortly. Please go and tell Cook I'm especially hungry this morning. I'll have two eggs."

They heard Alfredo's footsteps disappear down the hall.

"Unfortunately, privacy is scarce when you have a child. That's my son . . ."

"*Our* son," he corrected.

Doubt crept over her features. "Are you sure? He looks so like . . ."

"I'm sure. He's a part of you. How could I not love him?" Marcus sat up and began to button his trousers while Sabine reached for her robe. Marcus took her hand and pressed a gentle kiss to her palm. "We will be a family. A family filled with love. And soon, perhaps we will have a child of our own."

She kissed his cheek. "I'd like that. In fact, I suggest we start on that tonight. I couldn't think of a better wedding gift than conceiving your child."

"Those are the sweetest words I've ever heard. I intend to take you up on that invitation. Now, let's go and introduce me to Alfredo."

"Don't be nervous. He'll love you."

"Are you sure?"

"Absolutely sure, because he'll see that you make me very, very happy. He'll love you simply for that."

EPILOGUE

Some four weeks later, they were married by special license in the chapel at Marcus's country estate, Lanreath. The couple kept the ceremony a private affair with only close friends and family in attendance.

Collette, Marcus's mother, treated Sabine like the daughter she'd never had. The pair of them got along famously, sometimes too famously for Marcus's comfort. At times he felt he'd definitely lost control of his home but it was a feeling he greatly enjoyed.

He looked across the room at where Alfredo was playing happily with his five year old spaniel, Tudor. His glance continued to sweep around the room, and as he gazed lovingly at his wife and child, he felt a wave of contentment engulf him. He walked over to Alfredo and kissed his forehead. "Tudor likes you. Would you like him to be your dog?"

Alfredo looked up at Marcus with awe shinning in his eyes. "You'd like to give him to me?"

He tousled the boy's hair, and in a voice choked with love said, "You're my son. I'll give you anything your heart desires."

Alfredo threw his arms around Marcus's waist. "Thank you, Papa. I'll take special care of him."

Papa. What a sweet word! "I know you will, my son."

Sabine joined them and whispered, "Thank you," tears of love shining in her eyes for both the boy and the man.

Marcus slipped his arms around her shoulders and pressed her close to his side, while taking Alfredo's small hand in his.

The boy looked up at him in awe. Marcus was his hero. Life was good.

Harlow and Caitlin had made the journey for the marriage and celebration and the duke was delighted to see his friend content at last. Henry and Harlow couldn't apologize enough for their mistaken maligning of Sabine and proposed to spend the rest of their lives in service and fealty to her, as if they were her personal white knights.

Caitlin, although younger then Sabine, instantly became her new best friend. Caitlin had news of her own. She let slip that she was with child, and soon everyone at the reception was celebrating the new generation to come.

However, all the friends noticed how quiet and withdrawn Henry had become.

Marcus said, "It's your turn next, Henry. I'm sure love is getting ready to turn your world upside down too."

Henry looked pointedly at the ladies present. "It's not love that I'm lacking." As the ladies drifted off, the men were left to their discussion.

"I love Millicent."

"She's your mistress. Loyalty is not love, Henry," Harlow argued. "Don't confuse the two."

"Leave him, Harlow. I know what it's like to love a woman you think you can't have. It's hell on earth." Marcus smiled understandingly at his friend. "You'll see; you'll find a way. It will turn out alright in the end."

"I hope so."

"I *know* so."

The men raised their glasses "To love," said Henry.

"To love and, my friends, look at me if you ever need confirmation of the power and potential of love." Marcus smiled sweetly across the room at his wife and son, and his chest puffed out with justifiable pride. "I'm truly the luckiest man in the world. I'm living proof that love conquers all; that love, with time and forbearance, overcomes all wickedness."

Henry raised his glass. "Yes. Let's drink to the power of love."

THE END

TO CHALLENGE THE EARL OF CRAVENSWOOD

CHAPTER ONE

London, May 1822

Henry sucked on his cheroot and blew a perfect smoke ring. About the only thing that *was* perfect this night.

"I no longer have to hide while at these events, and that's fine with me. One of the many advantages to married life." Marcus Danvers, the Marquis of Wolverstone, sipped his French brandy, snuck a look at his cards, and chuckled before turning to Henry. "Had enough of hiding yet?"

"I'm not hiding."

Henry *was* hiding, but not for the reason Marcus suspected.

He'd come to Lady Skye's ball praying no young buck, who had no intention of marrying, would be seen dead at the most sought-after marriage hunt held this season.

He was hiding from his twenty-year-old cousin Charles.

He refuted Marcus. "There is no need for me to hide. The young ladies who are determinedly husband hunting, their evil consorts, and their mamas leave me alone."

"Not true. You're an eligible bachelor . . ." Marcus turned to look directly at him, shaking his head while anger scored his mouth. "Christ, you're not going to fall on your sword, are you? I thought Harlow talked you out of that ridiculous and unnecessary sacrifice. Richard's dead and won't care one way or the other."

Harlow, the Duke of Dangerfield, was their good friend who was currently at home enjoying his new family. Caitlin, his beautiful wife, had gifted him with a son, Cameron, six months ago.

Henry felt his face heat at Marcus's disdain, laden with scorn in the way he spoke Henry's brother's name. "Some of us understand about honor and family commitments."

"There is little honor in marrying a woman you do not love. Believe me. I almost made that mistake last year."

Henry wisely kept his mouth shut. Marcus almost became engaged to Lady Amy, the Duke of Shipton's daughter, when he thought his true love Sabine had betrayed him. The topic still turned Marcus into a scowling ball of fury. Marcus couldn't seem to forgive himself for the way he'd previously treated Sabine, who was now his beautiful wife, and the woman he loved to distraction.

Marcus threw his cards on the table, motioning that he was out, and added, "What would marrying Hilda Lulworth accomplish, other than making the rest of your life miserable?"

When his elder brother Richard died, most believed that the new Earl of Cravenswood would honor his dead brother's choice of wife and marry her instead, because it had been an arrangement that suited both families.

It didn't seem to matter that the poor girl was not at all enamoured of Henry. Nor that he would gladly choose to sail to the other side of the world and fall off of it, rather than marry Hilda Lulworth.

Hilda. The name said it all.

The lady had no personality. Staid as dish water, and her face closely resembled that of her dog: a tired and wrinkly basset hound. That was not her fault, of course, but considering she was only five and twenty, that did not bode well for what she'd look like in the years to come. Nor about how they would spend the long, dreary days of married life together.

"Who in your family is putting pressure on you to marry the woman? You have no immediate family, your parents are dead, and your two sisters are already safely married. Who benefits from this arrangement?"

"Hilda." He said the words with gusto. He had to keep thinking of the girl. Richard, had never thought of anyone but himself, hence why he was dead. Why a wealthy first son would try swimming the Thames for a drunken dare was beyond him. Richard had responsibilities. One of those was Hilda. Now they were his. It was the only decent thing to do.

Richard and Hilda had been betrothed in their teens. Hilda's father was a baron who had saved Richard's life as a youngster. Their father had pledged Richard's hand in order to return the favor. Richard did not seem to mind the match. Like most first born son's he realized he had to marry and produce an heir. Love didn't come into the arrangement. That was what mistresses were for.

Now that Richard was dead, Hilda's family would suffer financially without a good match. Considering her personality and looks, she'd be left on the shelf without him and that was hardly fair. If Richard weren't already dead, Henry would throttle him.

"Indeed." Marcus smiled wryly before taking a large gulp of brandy. "Saint Henry rides to the rescue again."

"Don't call me that."

Marcus ignored him. "Well, Henry St. Giles, when is the announcement to be made?"

Henry swallowed the fiery liquid in his glass, warding off the chill of Marcus's challenge. "When I'm bloody ready."

"If I had to marry Hilda Lulworth, I wouldn't be ready until I was in my grave," Marcus muttered. "I'd let your horrid cousin inherit. Or better yet, pay him to marry her."

"That's the first sensible thing you've said all night."

"Glad I could be of service. Now play your hand and let's rejoin the ladies in the ballroom. I've learned it does not pay to leave a beautiful woman alone for too long."

Henry tried to concentrate on the cards, but Marcus's comment about his cousin Charles stuck in his head. He'd been looking for a way to avoid marrying Hilda, an honorable way, and although Hilda would no longer be a countess, she would be married and her family saved from poverty. Was it honorable to foist Hilda onto another?

No formal engagement had yet been announced, although most believed he offer for her. He always did the right thing. He decided to concentrate on the cards for now. He was winning which was the only success of the night.

However, it wasn't long before Henry's night turned to bloody disaster. His cousin, Charles St. Giles, the man who'd doggedly shadowed his every step for the past week, the man Henry was avoiding, found him.

Henry tried to ignore the young man but when he bent and whispered in his ear, the news propelled the words from his mouth before he could stop them.

"How much?" Henry bit the inside of his cheek to stop from letting a series of ungentlemanly curses from issuing forth.

"Two thousand pounds, cousin."

Henry rose from the card table. He couldn't concentrate on cards with his whinny second cousin badgering him for money. "This is the second time in three months, Charles. You gave me your word never again. I'm disinclined to acquiesce to your request."

However, Charles was not alone. He'd brought support in the form of his father, Henry's uncle. He stepped forward to beg his son's cause.

"Think of the family."

"I am thinking of the family. Money cannot be conjured from thin air. It would seem Charles needs to learn that lesson, and quickly."

"You can't mean to deny him, Cravenswood."

Now he was Cravenswood, not plain Henry. Thomas had never given him the time of day until Richard died. The use of his title was supposed to make him understand his duty to the family.

Henry wanted to rant at the world. He shouldn't have been in this position. Richard should have been there to deal with Hilda and Charles.

"If you'll excuse me, gentlemen, I've promised a lady a dance. This can wait until tomorrow. The ball is not the time or the place to discuss such matters."

"When is the right time? You don't appear to be at home of late," his uncle snapped.

Henry pondered Marcus's earlier words regarding Hilda and his cousin. Perhaps there was a way out of both of these messes. But it would cost him a lot of money. Thank goodness Marcus's latest investment had made him an extremely rich man.

He stood and signalled Marcus, who had moved to the entrance of the ballroom. He tipped the dealer and began to follow his friend. "Call on me at ten in the morning."

"Ten!"

"Yes, ten," Henry stated firmly. "The earliness of the hour might stop you losing any more money this night."

Before he lost his temper completely, he stalked off. As he reached Marcus's side Marcus nodded his head in Charles direct. "He deserves Hilda for what he's putting you through."

"Quite. But does Hilda deserve Charles?" That's what he had to decide, and soon. Was he simply forgoing her welfare for his own happiness?

"I'm going to dance with Sabine. Join me and rescue Amy. Chesterton looks as if he's being a nuisance. Sabine's just given me the signal."

At the mention of Chesterton, Henry's mouth firmed and anger filled his soul. Millicent. Millie, his ex-mistress, now belonged to Chesterton. If he could ruin Chesterton's night, then the evening would not be a total disaster.

"I wish that horrid man would go away," Countess Wolverstone whispered in Amy's ear.

"You wish! It's not you he keeps fawning over."

Amy Shipton blamed her father. The duke was encouraging Lord Chesterton's suit, yet she'd already informed her father that she'd rather become a bride of Christ than marry Chesterton.

"Well, he's like an elephant bull staking his territory. Trumpeting and stamping when others get close. No eligible bachelor will approach you. I will not have my plans ruined. We have to get rid of him."

"Just tell me how, besides shooting him, which I'm sorely tempted to do."

Sabine chuckled and kept inching them further along the wall, away from the overbearing Viscount Chesterton. The music hid their footsteps. Luckily, Chesterton was deep in conversation with a man Amy didn't recognize.

"Where is Marcus?" Sabine wondered, looking annoyed that her dashing husband had deserted her for so long.

Sabine didn't realize how lucky she was. At least she *had* a husband to rescue her. Amy had an elder brother who couldn't care less what happened to her, and her father . . . Amy shuddered. Her father would love to see her compromised, for then he could force her to marry. She wondered if Lord Chesterton, or as she secretly referred to him, Lord Creeperton, understood her father's wishes. He'd been trying to lure her into the garden all evening. Where was *her* hero?

On that thought she heard Sabine whisper under her breath, "At last."

Amy followed Sabine's gaze and saw Lord Wolverstone, his brooding presence making the guests part like the Red Sea before Moses, making quick work of the distance between them. He was an extremely handsome man, and not for the first time Amy questioned her decision to decline Marcus's proposal all those months ago.

"Ah, my handsome knight hath come!" Sabine gushed.

She looked at the love shining within Sabine's gaze and knew absolutely she'd done the right thing. Marcus would never have looked at her the way he did when staring at his lovely wife. Like a hungry wolf ready to consume her.

Amy felt a small stab of envy for her friend. Sabine forced her gaze away from her advancing husband to smile and state, "And he is not alone."

Amy spotted Lord Cravenswood behind Wolverstone, and her heart suddenly began thumping faster in her chest. She tried to swallow her excitement. She'd not known his lordship was attending this evening.

Henry St. Giles, the Earl of Cravenswood, was her neighbor. And more. She'd secretly worshipped Henry for aeons. At fifteen, she had fallen from her horse in Hyde Park and broken her arm. Henry had seen her fall, heard her cry of pain, and had raced over to help. He'd dismounted and gently checked her for injuries, not chastising her tears of pain as her brother had. Then he carefully carried her home upon his white charger. He'd even called on her the next day to ensure she was well.

She watched him move across the room, his fair hair tousled as if he'd just run his hand through it. His fringe flopped over one eye, hiding one half of his most stunning feature—his emerald eyes. They sparkled like the gemstones they matched and almost blinded the beauty of his face.

The day he'd rescued her, Amy imagined God had made Henry into a likeness of an angel. His face was exquisitely proportioned. Flawless. His nose straight, his cheek-bones defined and his mouth . . . Gosh, she'd had wicked fantasies about his mouth.

Fantasies that had moved on to involve other body parts, when a few months later, she'd accidentally spied him stripped to his britches and dunking his head in the trough behind his stables. His chest was honed muscle, with an expansive set of shoulders that tapered to a stomach rippled with definition, and his wet breeches molded well-muscled thighs that disappeared into large hessians.

He was most definitely a rake. Who wouldn't be with the looks of a Greek god? He was also the most honorable and kind man she'd had the privilege to meet.

From that day forth she'd judged all men against him and found all sadly lacking.

Unfortunately, as the years passed, Henry had failed to notice that she'd grown up. When he saw her he was polite and teasing, as if she was still a young girl. Couldn't he see she was a woman?

A hot blooded woman that many fawned over. Why was it she could attract Creeperton, but not a man like St. Giles?

Marcus arrived at his wife's side and swept her into his arms. "My dance." It was a possessive command which made Sabine sigh in delight as he led her onto the floor for the waltz.

Creeperton, having seen the men approach, moved determinedly toward Amy. She froze, dreading the thought of having to dance with the man and have his hands . . .

"Lady Shipton, my dance I believe." Henry's words were sweet to her ears.

"I don't think so, Cravenswood. The lady will dance with

me." Chesterton moved closer and his slimy smile disappeared. For once his true personality showed. Poisonous reptile.

Amy's hopes dashed. Henry would be the perfect gentleman and step aside. But to her amazement, Henry's placid features hardened and he moved in front of Amy, blocking Chesterton.

"Are you calling Lady Shipton a liar, Chesterton? She said this dance was mine, is that not so?" He quirked a brow at her.

"Indeed," Amy answered quickly, her earnestness clear. She expected such scandalous behavior from Chesterton but she'd never seen this side of Lord Cravenswood. Normally he was the epitome of politeness. He never caused a scene, but already heads were straining.

To defuse the situation, Amy put her hand on Chesterton's arm. "The night is still young. There will be other dances." Not if she could help it.

With a triumphant smile, Henry put her hand on his arm and escorted her onto the floor. Lord Cravenswood cocked an eyebrow, his mouth curving with male amusement. "You looked as if you needed rescuing."

"A woman could get use to being rescued by you." At his astonished frown she added, "I remember you rescuing me when I came off my horse in Hyde Park. I'm not surprised you can't remember. I've grown up a tad since then." Maybe she could make him realize she was no longer a silly young girl but a woman with desires . . . desires that made her nights restless. Her dreams usually involved various scenarios of her and Henry dancing in each other's arms until dawn.

For a moment he seemed startled. His eyes skimmed over her front, lingering momentarily on her breasts, and back up to her face. *Now you notice.* With a scandalous smile on her lips she stepped into Henry's arms, moving a bit closer than was truly respectable.

Henry hid his shock well. He merely placed her hand in his, slid his other hand to her waist and moved her slightly backward before sweeping her into the dance.

"I had forgotten that incident. It was a few years ago now. I assume the arm healed properly."

"All my limbs are in working order, my lord."

"I'm very pleased to hear that, given Marcus tells me Sabine is playing the matchmaker. You're husband hunting? It pays to have a full set of limbs when courting."

She nodded. "I value Lady Wolverstone's input. Rather her than my father's choice." Her smile died. "My father wishes to see me wed and is more concerned with haste than the fiancé. I'd rather the choice was mine."

"Yet you don't appear to be enjoying yourself tonight. Has Lord Chesterton anything to do with that?"

"He is rather persistent, regardless of my feelings."

"Would you like me to tell him to bugger off?"

"Henry!" She couldn't help the shocked cry. She gathered herself together and tried to remain composed. "I'm perfectly capable of handling Creeperton"-

Henry burst into laughter and every head in the room turned their way. "Never have I heard a more apt name."

Heat flooded Amy's face. She hadn't meant to say the name out loud. "My apologies. That was inexcusable."

"No need. The name fits the man perfectly. In fact, I may well steal the name for my own use."

Amy watched the earl roll the name over his tongue and his face lit with general amusement at her faux pas. It was humiliating. Here she was trying to get him to see her as a sophisticated woman, and she was behaving like a gauche school girl.

"Are you making fun of me?"

"That would not be very gentlemanly."

Amy noted that was not an answer, merely an observation. She saw Henry's gaze fixated on Creeperton. "You don't like the Viscount?"

Henry looked into her eyes but he remained tight-lipped. Finally he said, "Let's just say he took something from me, and I'm concerned at how he is treating his new possession."

"I hope it's nothing too valuable."

He did not answer her, merely twirled her around the floor, a look of consternation flashing across his face. "It is of no concern. Let's not talk about Creeperton, but instead enjoy the dance."

"You dance very well, my lord. Who taught you?"

"My sisters. They needed someone to practice with. I was more than happy to oblige as it got me out of Latin."

"My brother would not be seen dead dancing with me."

"He's older than you. I was younger than them and had little choice in the matter."

"But at least once you grew up you had choices. I seem to have fewer choices as I grow older," she muttered more to herself.

Something over her shoulder had garnered his attention and he did not reply. So much for demonstrating her maturity and womanhood. He even found her conversation lacking. Anger sizzled and she couldn't help herself. "At least Chesterton gives me his undivided attention."

"I do beg your pardon. I was watching Chesterton take his leave. He won't bother you again this evening," he said, slowing as the music floated to a halt.

"Oh," Amy replied, reluctantly retrieving her hand from his. She was pleased to note that his other hand lingered on her waist. "Thank you for the dance, my lord."

Henry released her and escorted her back to Sabine. Marcus smiled at the pair as if husband and wife had just exchanged a private secret.

Henry bowed over her hand and said, "If you excuse me, ladies. Cards beckon. Wolverstone."

Before anyone could reply, Henry pivoted and made his way back across the crowded ballroom. It took him longer to reach the card room because, without Marcus by his side, every mama with a marriageable daughter stopped him and tried to draw him into conversation.

Amy's only consolation was that he didn't appear to be enamored of any woman here. He seemed desperate to seek the safety of the card room.

Sabine tapped her arm, "Amy, Lord Henley was asking after your father."

She forced her eyes away from Henry's departing figure, fine figure, and resolved that soon, very soon, she would make him see what was before his eyes—her.

And only her.

CHAPTER TWO

Henry was completely sloshed. Drunk to be precise. An inebriated state he sought far too often of late. He should have gone directly home after Lady Skye's ball, but watching his best friend Marcus leave with his beautiful wife on his arm made him long for company. He did not wish to go home to an empty house and a lonely bed.

He blinked, trying to focus on the activities going on around him. The room at Mrs. Whites was stifling. He bloody well shouldn't have let George Ashford talk him into accompanying him to the high-class brothel, and he definitely shouldn't have drunk half a bottle of brandy on top of the alcohol he'd already consumed this evening.

He gripped the arms of his chair, rested his head on the back, and closed his eyes, fighting the rising nausea. He didn't miss the irony that bile was the only thing rising. Not even the brief sight of voluptuous beauties cavorting naked on the stage in front of him could make his flaccid member twitch.

He didn't understand this sexual lethargy. Up until eighteen months ago, just before Millicent left, he'd had a ferocious appetite.

Yet it seemed losing Millicent had destroyed his enjoyment for sins of the flesh as surely as she'd bruised his heart and his ego. His father had warned him that men should never fall in love with their mistresses. It never ended well.

His *arrangement* with Millie ended very well. For her. She simply left him a note telling him she'd found someone else.

Henry St. Giles clenched his stomach to hold off the rollicking nausea. He should be over her by now. He was an earl, for goodness sake, and Millie a mere courtesan. If anyone did the leaving, it should have been him.

Anger at himself burned bright, making him struggle to sit up. He should leave the establishment now. He had to admire Mrs. White's cleverness, for her pleasure house was a mockery of the oldest gentlemen's club in England. Now men didn't have to lie to their wives when they left for a night of sin; they simply said they were going to White's.

Therein lay the problem. He didn't have a wife, or family, or a proper home. If he did, he'd certainly not leave them for this establishment.

True, he owned houses, but an empty house was not a home. He'd not had a home growing up. He'd had a house full of people he was related to, yet even with siblings and parents and servants, he'd still felt alone.

Bloody hell, he was in a sorry state. His chest clenched in what he knew was dark-green and vicious envy. Harlow and Marcus. He wondered if he'd ever find the joy, happiness, and love they had found with their soul mates.

If he were honest with himself, Millie was not his soul mate. She had left him for another and it had hurt at first, but looking back it was merely his pride that had been wounded. It was not Millie he craved, but rather the thought of love, the idea of finding his soul mate drove him.

What he felt for Millie was gratitude. She'd been there for

him when his brother died, and he was thrown into the role as head of the Cravenswood family. A role he had never expected or wanted.

He was grateful for her support. He'd needed someone and she had stayed long enough to help ease him into the earldom.

Now he had no one. No close family, siblings or wife. Loneliness seeped into his bones like a smothering cold fog. Loneliness which would not be appeased by marrying his brother's fiancé. Hilda was most definitely not his soul mate.

Tonight he'd hoped the ball, and then the brothel would banish his troubles with mindless, meaningless pleasure. But even that had been denied him. So he'd drunk himself into oblivion. Again.

A body, warm, soft, and virtually naked, slid onto his lap. A feminine hand trailed down his chest, caressing its way to his groin, while the other lifted his hand and placed it on her naked breast.

"Perhaps a private show of our own would keep you awake, my lord?"

Her hand found his member and with expert fingers she coaxed a response. Finally, a twitch of life.

She slid off him to her knees and he felt her unbutton the placket of his trousers. Henry closed his mind to everything but what the woman was doing to him. He let his lids close and in the darkness he pictured Millicent, her dark curls cascading over her creamy bare shoulders, her hands caressing up his thighs, her tongue running up the length of him before her hot, talented mouth enveloped his straining member . . .

His body tensed as forgotten, yet glorious sensations grew within him, then he made the mistake of opening his eyes and he glimpsed the blonde head bobbing between his thighs.

His erection withered and died. The blonde's head rose. He looked into her face and she met his eyes, confusion scored her pretty features.

"Too much drink, my love. Perhaps another night." He buttoned his trousers.

This wasn't Millie.

Millie was now under the protection of Jeremy Montague, Viscount Chesterton. Nausea threatened once more. He'd had a slight victory tonight. He'd annoyed Chesterton. He'd interrupted his pursuit of Amy Shipton.

The memory of soft curves under his hand. Of eager eyes as warm as honey. They spoke of sweetness. Yet deep within burned sparks of passion as yet unrealized. Amy had tried to flirt with him.

Amy Shipton—she'd grown up.

He frowned and tried to remember the feel of her in his arms. She felt . . . comfortable in his embrace. He shook his head. He was drunker than he'd imagined. She was his neighbor, that's why she felt comfortable. He'd known her since she could leave the nursery. He should not be having salacious thoughts about a debutante. Not unless marriage was involved. Now that was a thought . . .

She reminded him of Millie. That was it. She had dark hair and a creamy complexion that begged for a man's lips to taste, just like Millicent.

Hell, she was nothing like Millicent. She wasn't a courtesan for one thing. She was a young debutante whose father was a duke. Best he remember that.

His body sharpened with anger. Millie belonged to another. God damn the devil to hell, he'd heard rumors about how Chesterton treated his women. He'd tried to see Millie, to ascertain that she was well, but she refused to see him.

He briefly closed his eyes and made himself a promise. Tomorrow he would make a decision about Hilda, and his cousin Charles. Perhaps Hilda would be happier with Charles? Or was he clutching at straws, trying to find any excuse not to do the honorable thing.

Only once the situation with Hilda was settled would he start looking for a suitable wife. He was a man in his prime, an earl, and extremely rich. How hard could it be to find his soul mate? If both Harlow and Marcus, two of England's most prolific rakes, could find their better halves, surely he could too.

He gave himself a proverbial kick in the arse.

Definitely time to leave.

He rose on unsteady legs and staggered out into the humid night. He refused the doorman's suggestion of a hackney. It was too hot. Besides, he wanted to clear his head on the walk home.

The moon was out, lighting the pavement, the stars above sparkling like dancing lights. Around him London lay sleeping. As he passed each house on his way through Mayfair, he pictured the types of families that lived behind the closed doors. Were they happy? Or was their marriage a cold, calculating business arrangement, as his parents' marriage had been? At thirty-two he should already be married. He'd known for the past twenty years that he would not let his children, or himself, endure such a marriage. He would only marry for love. A possibility for a second son.

Grinning to himself he laughed out loud thinking of Harlow and Marcus's foolish battle against love. Why did men of his ilk fear it so? Yet, ironically, they'd found love before him.

No doubt Harlow and Marcus were right now enjoying themselves at their homes, soaking up the benefits accruing to happily married men. Six months ago Caitlin had gifted Harlow his heir. A healthy baby boy they'd named Cameron. He'd never seen his friend so happy and content. The way Sabine had been glowing recently, he was sure Marcus too would soon make an announcement.

He reached Hanover Square and stood looking up at his Townhouse. The dark, empty house did not entice him. Besides, it was too hot to sleep.

Instead, he turned and made his way through the gate opposite, and into the square's private garden. He would often sit in the garden staring at the stars. He felt closer to Richard. They had played in this garden as children.

Lately he'd taken to visiting the garden. He would sit and tell Richard all about the estate and his plans. It helped him make decisions, and he felt less alone.

Henry found the bench near the Aphrodite fountain and took out his hip flask. Not that he really needed any more brandy.

He sat looking at Cravenswood Court across the road. The imposing building held no appeal. It offered him no happy memories. He shrugged. He had no unpleasant memories either. Just weary indifference.

Tonight Henry felt the weight of duty. It was his role to protect and raise the Cravenswood name to prominence. His duty to marry and produce his heirs—with Hilda. Life didn't always allow you the opportunity to live your dreams.

He tipped the flask to his mouth, but it was empty. "Perfect. Bloody perfect." He closed his eyes and breathed deeply. "Suck it up, man. Most men would sell their souls to become the Earl of Cravenswood"-

The squeak of the gate behind him stopped his tirade. Someone was entering his garden. He stood up to see who had invaded his private space at this hour of the morning, but in his drunken condition he tripped over the leg of the bench, and pitched headfirst against the base of the statue. His last thought before the blackness struck was that Aphrodite had an exquisite bottom.

The squeak from the closing gate didn't muffle the sound of flesh hitting something solid and unforgiving. The silence that followed the distinct sound of a body falling to the ground saw Amy hurrying towards her favorite fountain. Her heart leapt into her throat. She knew the only other person likely to be here this late, or early in the morning as the case may be, was Henry.

During her own unhappy wonderings late at night when sleep eluded her, she'd ascertained that Henry often came to converse with his dead brother, hence her detour into his garden after Lady Skye's ball, rather than going to her own bed.

The only pleasure in her life at present seemed to be offering silent, distant, unknown and unwanted comfort to a man who didn't know she existed.

Amy dropped to her knees next to Henry's prone body. The sounds of his groans of pain were sweet music; it meant he was at least alive.

She smelled the brandy fumes and noted his hip flask lying discarded nearby. Henry had often seemed worse for drink on his late night ramblings, but when she lift his head to cradle it on her knees she saw the ugly gash on his head. He must have hit the side of the fountain.

She dipped her handkerchief in the water and bathed the gash, wiping the small specks of gravel out of the wound. "Henry," she scolded softly, tenderly wiping a stray golden lock away from his wound. "What am I to do with you? You can't let your brother's death destroy you with sorrow and guilt. Richard would have wanted better for you."

She gazed spellbound at the beauty of the man she tended. His long lashes were dark crescents smudged over his pale cheeks. His brows, the planes of his face, looked oddly relaxed; his lips, full and beckoning, were gently curved in a child like smile. Her heart expended under an emotion she didn't wish to face.

She pressed the cloth to his head until the wound stopped bleeding, all the while gently singing to him.

Amy didn't know how long they'd sat there, but now that the blood no longer flowed, she decided to move and find help.

She tried to lever him off of her but Henry groaned deeply and snuggled deeper into her lap, wrapping his arms around her hips, anchoring her to him.

Despite her precarious situation, Amy's lips lifted at the corner. He was so atrociously handsome, the silky locks of his gold-kissed hair feathered his chiselled cheeks, his long-fingered hands gripped her hips as if he didn't ever wish to let her go, his long body lay boneless across her lap. She resisted the urge to kiss his wound-just.

What now? Amy looked toward Cravenswood Court. She'd have to summon help to move him. She couldn't leave him out here with a head injury. She bit her lip and considered the trouble she was in. How would she explain being alone with Henry in his garden—Henry had no idea she often kept him company. All right, she growled under her breath, he had no idea she spied on him. Besides, her reputation would be tarnished and her father might insist on Henry doing the honorable thing. A shudder of delight raced along her nerve endings. That didn't sound too terrible a fate.

Her smile died as a very large hand suddenly molded her breast and a thumb and finger tweaked her nipple through her clothing. She gasped. Fire danced low in her belly. She should stop him. She closed her eyes and let his hand roam her breasts. His touch was like fire—hot and dangerous. Better than she'd dreamed.

No, it would not be terrible to become his wife.

She heard him mumble and she bent lower to hear his words. His face lifted from her lap and his lips brushed her mouth. He moaned again, the sound was not of a man in pain, more in pleasure. His hand cupped the back of her neck and pulled her closer. His lips teased hers and encouraged her to allow him access. She didn't even hesitate, but opened for him. He swept into her mouth as if he'd been there before. He tasted of brandy and cheroots, a masculine combination that saw her surrender to the passion his clever tongue provoked.

So caught up in the magic of the kiss, she did not notice his hand expertly freeing one breast from the bodice of her gown until the cooling morning air brushed across her heated skin. She broke from his kiss and sat back on a gasp. He levered himself up and on a deep groan, crawled up her body, gently pushing her down onto the path.

She'd never experienced the weight of a man on top of her. It was thrilling and scary all at the same time. Before she could decide what to do, his mouth found her bare, taut nipple and the hot moistness of his mouth stifled any protest. This time the moan came from her.

She heard a rustle and felt his hand glide seductively under her dress and up her trembling thigh. He stroked her leg while devouring her breast with his mouth and wicked tongue. She let the magic of his love-making consume her. She knew she should protest. She knew Henry would be mortified at what he was doing. He wasn't in his right mind.

His fingers danced up the inside of her thigh and she tried to close her legs. His lips found hers once more and he let his tongue seduce her. Her clenched thighs relaxed under his soft touch and his fingers swept upwards to find the damp core of her. He groaned deep into her mouth as his fingers slid through her wetness.

His breath was ragged, and she could not miss the hard length of him against her stomach. He slipped a finger inside her, and she only just stifled a cry before arching beneath him. Her mind screamed at her to stop him. This was getting beyond the point of no return—it was scandalous. But her body wouldn't acquiesce, craving his attentions.

His mouth left hers and trailed a molten path toward her ear. His hand sunk deep into her hair, holding her head at an angle while he nipped at her ear lobe, all the while his finger stroked deep within her. She could feel her body tightening. She struggled for air, panting, urgently seeking some kind of release from the slow building torture of pleasure.

"How I love your responsiveness to my touch, Millicent. Come for me, I've missed you so much . . ."

Amy froze. Pain lanced her chest. How stupid could she have been? Of course he thought she was someone else. Henry never noticed her—not in this way. Why, only last year he'd been more than instrumental in arranging her 'almost' engagement to his friend, Marcus Danvers, the Marquis of Wolverstone.

"What's wrong my love?" He noticed her lack of response because he stilled, his hand leaving her.

Amy was thankful it was dark, but with such a starry night he might not be so drunk that he couldn't recognise her. Panic took hold. She put her hands on his chest and pushed him sideways with all her might. He rolled off her with a grunt of surprise. Too mortified for words, she pushed clear and jumped to her feet. As she righted her clothing, covering her naked breasts, she barely glanced over her shoulder to ensure Henry would be all right before she raced for the safety of the darkness and her home.

"What the hell . . ." Henry shook his head and rose to his knees. His groin throbbed, something he'd not experienced in a while, and his head thumped like a blacksmith's hammer was pounding inside it. He'd awoken from a very pleasant dream to the blazing nightmare of a terrible reality.

There had been a woman in his arms. A stranger.

He spied something bright and dazzling on the path next to him. He picked up the object and brought it closer to his face so he could examine it. An earring.

"Christ, it wasn't a drunken dream." The earring was exquisite. A cluster of emeralds surrounded by brilliantly cut diamonds. It was heavy in his hand. Expensive. This, along with her silk clothing, led him to the conclusion that the woman was no light-skirt. He'd dallied with a woman of prominence.

Whoever she was, she was every hot-blooded man's fantasy. Warm, silky skin, her scent like freshly cut flowers. She was so responsive to his touch. He could still smell her arousal on his hand and he hungered for more.

He staggered to his feet and groaned, holding his head in his hands while he swayed. He touched the gash on his head and grimaced.

When the dizziness and nausea waned he looked around the square. It had to be someone local. No woman of quality would stray far from home this late. But hadn't there been a musical soiree at Lady Answell's townhouse on the corner tonight? Blast, that didn't help. It could have been a guest taking the air.

He closed his eyes and remembered her response. She was young, he was sure of it. Her responses were untutored, hesitant, innocent . . . *Christ.*

Someone young, local, someone who had been out that evening.

Innocent. What if he'd nearly debauched a virgin in his garden? A smile broke over his lips. But he didn't feel shame or guilt. He stood up straighter, invigorated for the first time in months.

He weighed the earring in his hand before slowly closing his fist over it. He would find the owner of this earring. Her response told him very clearly that she was not immune to him.

For the first time in ages he looked forward to his bed. He needed to get some sleep. Soon he would start his very own fairy tale. He had a Cinderella hunt to begin in a few hours.

With lightness in his step, Henry trotted up his front walk.

For a change, his footman was most surprised to hear a whistling and chirpy master enter the house, especially as he had nasty gash on his forehead. But then all of the nobility were a bit crazy.

CHAPTER THREE

Amy tossed and turned in her bed, unable to sleep. Her body still hummed deliciously. Henry St. Giles. She'd kissed him, and more. Her face and skin heated.

The year he'd finished at Oxford, she'd fallen completely in love with the twenty-one year old second son of the earl. She'd stand at her window each day merely to catch a glimpse of him. Any dreams of a marriage were simply that—dreams. Her father would never allow her to marry a mere second son.

But two years ago, after his brother's death . . . He was now the Earl. Her father could hardly object to a match. Unfortunately, Henry obviously had no desire to wife hunt. Or maybe it was simply no desire for her.

One night she'd been hiding from her father in Henry's private garden. She'd overheard him talking to his dead brother. Henry had just become the earl and seemed lost in grief and responsibility. How she'd longed to offer him comfort. She'd meant to leave him to his privacy. She'd been mortified that she hadn't turned tail and fled as soon as he started unburdening his heart. A proper young lady did not eavesdrop. She didn't mean to stay and listen to his personal conversation, but something in his lonely chat with his recently departed brother penetrated her heart.

She'd learned something about Henry St Giles that day. She learned they had quite a bit in common. They both wanted more out of life. Not materials things. They were both looking for something personal, something deeper, a connection with another human being.

Last night they'd connected all right. She plumped her pillow and tried to relax. The morning sun was well up in the sky. She should get up. But she dreaded the morning now. What if Henry realized who he'd kissed in his garden? He'd thought her someone else. His heart might belong to Millicent. If Henry realized what he'd done, he'd try to offer for her. She could not have that. Not if he loved another.

Worse, she had to go back to the garden. She'd lost one of her emerald earrings. They were a gift from Lord and Lady Wolverstone. They'd had them especially designed as a thank you for saving Sabine from a sadistic rapist. It was the first time she'd worn them.

The earring likely came off when Henry's hand sunk into her hair. If anyone found it in the garden and showed it to Marcus, her identity would be revealed.

She knew what would happen then. The duke would see her betrothed to Henry in a snap of his ducal fingers.

Her father had lost his temper with her at Lady Skye's ball last night. He'd wanted to announce her engagement to Jeremy Montague, Marquis of Chesterton. Her threat of causing a scene the only reason her father angrily relented.

Yesterday she had made her own list of possible candidates. She'd gone to the ball to begin her planned assault, determined to thwart her father's list of husbands with one of her own choosing. Sabine had promised to help. Only Amy couldn't confess to her friend that there was only one name on her list. Henry St. Giles, the Earl of Cravenswood.

She had not seen him bestow his favors on any of the young debutants. She'd also investigated him as much as she could without raising eyebrows. According to her friend Latisha's brother, he did not appear to have a mistress. He didn't appear to have anyone. He looked lonely and sometimes a tad sad. His brother's death had changed him.

She'd been delighted to learn that Henry wasn't in love with anyone. But she'd been wrong to hope. It appeared he did have someone special. He'd called a woman's name last night. Millicent sounded more than a casual acquaintance. When he spoke her name, it sounded as if he loved this woman. His voice choked and it held such longing.

So who was Millicent?

With an exasperated sigh she threw back the covers. She wouldn't find out who Henry's mysterious lady by lying in bed moping. She moved to the bell pull to summon her maid. She knew exactly where she would go today. A quick trip to explore the garden and then on to Telford House. She had information to gather.

When she next saw Henry she'd have to pretend indifference. It would be difficult given her body remembered very well what his clever fingers could do. She swallowed her longing. She prayed he would not be visiting with Harlow when she called on Caitlin.

This morning she would visit with the two ladies who knew the most about Henry St. Giles. Or at least would know how to find the answers she sought-who was Millicent and what is she to Henry? Lady Dangerfield and Lady Wolverstone. Caitlin and Sabine would help her she was sure, especially since she'd been instrumental in ensuring Sabine married her one true love, Marcus. If they didn't have her answers, she'd ask them to discreetly extract the information from their husbands, Henry's best friends.

*   *   *

The next morning, Henry was up early. For once in his miserable life, Charles was on time. Just when Henry felt like death had come knocking, his cousin looked fresh and alert. He felt like the world's biggest hypocrite.

His bad temper made the meeting short and functional. He laid out his plan.

"Charles, you will offer for Hilda Lulworth and I will guarantee you an annual income of six-thousand pounds." He held up his hand stilling Charles's cry of protest. "In addition, I refuse to pay any of your gambling debts except this current note, and if you should end up in the poorhouse, I'll move Hilda into the Dowager house on my estate. I'll ensure Hilda's security, but not yours." He turned a ferocious gaze on his useless cousin and added, "Do I make myself perfectly clear?"

Charles made to stand his mouth spluttering curses but his father put a hand on his shoulder, stilling him. "That sounds more than generous. However, one small point. Hilda is expecting a match with you. What if she should refuse?"

"Then Charles will woo her and ensure she doesn't refuse."

"I bloody won't marry that mouse of a woman."

Henry raised an eyebrow, and spoke slowly and carefully, ignoring the pain thumping through his head. "Then I won't cover your notes and you can rot in the poorhouse for all I care. The choice is yours."

Thomas cleared his throat. "I believe Henry is being more than generous, Charles." He stood, indicating to Charles to do likewise. "We shall not take up any more of your time. Be assured I shall ensure your wishes are adhered to."

They reached the door before Henry spoke. "By the end of the season this marriage is to take place. Only then will I pay off your debts. Plus, Hilda will at all times be treated with respect and kindness or I shall cut you off without a penny."

Charles's back stiffened but he remained silent. His only form of rebellion was the slamming of the door upon his exit.

Henry dropped his head in his hands, praying he'd done the right thing for all concerned. He'd have to talk with Hilda. He didn't look forward to that conversation.

Henry wrote a quick note and summoned a footman with directions to deliver it to Lulworth house. He would settle the matter this afternoon.

His stomach heaved—from guilt or his hangover he wasn't sure. But even with a hangover from hell, he couldn't stop from wanting to begin his search for the owner of the earring nestled safely in his jacket pocket.

He rose, moved to the window, and looked out over the garden. If not for the earring he'd have thought last night a perfect dream.

He'd start the search in his garden. He couldn't get the feel or response of the woman from last night out of his mind. She'd felt perfect in his arms. Perhaps she'd thought so too. Maybe she'd return to the garden . . .

He strode from the room, determined to find the answer he sought. As he descended his front steps, his hopes rose when he spied a splash of lavender and white through the foliage. Someone was there. The dress indicated it was a woman. He entered quietly. She could be searching for her earring.

He crept closer, sticking to the grass rather than walking on the gravel path.

As he rounded the bushes, and the fountain came into view, the sight that greeted him saw his senses sharply focus.

Two round globes greeted him. A woman was on her knees,

under the bench. The fabric of her white linen dress pulled taut across her plump behind. His arms moved as if to mold his hands to the beckoning sight, and he had to check himself. Hadn't he molested enough women recently?

She was moving right and left, searching for something. This was his mystery woman. He was sure of it.

He caught a flash of pale skin, raven-black hair, and the scent of citrus. He closed his eyes and breathed deep. Blast. He couldn't swear it was the same scent as last night. He wished his head didn't hurt so much, and that he'd not been so drunk. He opened his eyes and cleared his throat.

At the sound, her head rose sharply and smacked the underside of the bench. "Owe!"

The deliciously plump bottom began wiggling as she backed out from under the seat, and Henry's body reacted immediately. Heat licked at his groin and blood raced south.

She muttered under her breath, twisting to look over her shoulder. Her appalled gaze reached Henry and she froze, eyes widening with shock.

Henry's shock matched hers, but he hid it under what he hoped was a friendly yet non-threatening manner, in the sense *of I'm not about to attack you again* kind of way. It *was* Amy. His neighbor. *Please, dear God, don't let me have molested Amy.*

"Have you lost something, Lady Shipton?"

Warm honey coloured eyes quickly masked her shock and she seemed fixated on his bandage. "Oh, you've hurt yourself." She gave a little giggle. "Who on earth dressed your wound? It looks as if a child has played doctor with your head."

"Quite. Thank you for your concern. I had a small accident."

He watched to see if guilty recognition entered her face, but it remained blank, except for amusement. Irritation stirred. He became more direct.

"In this very garden. Last night, actually."

Amy looked around anxiously. "You were attacked in your own garden?" She took a step back.

He blanched. Perhaps it wasn't Amy. He hadn't meant to frighten her. "Good lord, no. I tripped and fell."

Of course it couldn't have been Amy. Surely Amy would have stopped him immediately. A young woman of quality, an innocent young woman would never have allowed such behavior. Her screams would have brought her servants running. Besides, he'd never been attracted to Amy Shipton.

Idiot. How had he not noticed that she was, in fact, very attractive? Perhaps because, as a second son of an Earl, he allowed himself to harbour hopes for a wife who would love him, but he never looked above his station. Never would he have expected to be able to marry the daughter of a Duke. But now . . . There was nothing to stop him. Why had he never noticed how appealing his young neighbor was?

He ran a critical eye over the young woman before him. *Christ.* His mouth watered. She'd grown up.

Her face was pretty enough. Wide forehead, high cheek bones, and warm, honey-brown eyes. But it was the cupid bow lips that drew a man's gaze. The lips pouted and made a man think wicked thoughts. What he'd love to teach her to do with those lips . . .

He swept his eyes down and then back up her dainty frame. Her breasts were the right size, enough to fill his hands. She curved in all the right places, in exactly the right proportions. Plenty of flesh to cushion his body. Enough for a man to hold on to. She looked like a woman built for pleasure. His pleasure. *Get a grip, man.*

She was however, respectably dressed. In fact, the dress more than adequately covered every inch of her, buttoned up to the neck. Yet, every inch of *his* body reacted to the sight of her. *Unusual.*

His suspicions were back in play. The last few months his body had been reluctant to feel desire, yet here he was reacting like a stallion scenting a mare, to a properly clothed, respectable, young woman. Why? Did it recognize what he could not?

He repeated his question. "You were looking for something. What have you lost?"

She gathered herself reasonably quickly, yet she wrung her hands. "I apologize for being in your garden, my lord. I don't want to get into trouble."

Oh, my God. It was Amy. He fought down his horror at the thought he'd basically molested a virgin. No wonder she didn't want to discuss what occurred last night. Yet, his mind screamed he'd found her.

"You're not in trouble, Amy." First names were appropriate given she would soon be his wife. "Please let me take care of everything."

She looked at him wide eyed. "You can find Tinkles then?"

His mouth opened and nothing came out. At his look of confusion Amy promptly burst into tears. "I've lost Tinkles."

"Tinkles?"

"My guinea pig." She dropped to her knees again under the nearest bush. "I let him out in our garden next door and he fled through the gate into your property before I could stop him. I thought I saw him in the daffodils behind the bench. Could you help me look for him?"

Henry could barely form a coherent thought with her bottom now firmly pointing upward once again. His hands inched forward and he pulled them back, anchoring them at his side. What was wrong with him? He'd not been this randy since he'd lost his virginity with the local barmaid at fifteen. Not even Millicent made his blood quicken as much as one glimpse at this respectably covered bottom.

It couldn't be Amy. He'd watched her grow up and he'd never once wanted to throw her down in the grass and lick her from head to toe, stopping midway for her pleasure.

But here she was. Bottom up, in his garden the night after he'd found a very expensive earring. An earring she could well afford. Guinea pig? Could this be a coincident? The Duke of Shipton's garden did back onto his. The story was plausible.

He had to tread carefully. He couldn't very well discuss a scandalous rendezvous with an innocent debutante. She would hardly be innocent afterwards. The duke would shoot him or worse, expect him to marry Amy. He didn't want to marry Amy. He wanted to know who his mysterious lady was. Then he'd decide who and when he married.

"Shall I summon your servants to help?" If she was lying she'd hardly wish him to involve her servants.

She lifted her head and smiled over her shoulder at him. "Would you? How kind. Ask Clements to ensure Patches stays indoor."

"Patches?"

"My cat." Her eyes welled once more. "She'll eat anything mouse-like."

That clinched it. Amy was far too upset to be lying.

"What color is Tinkles?"

Her bottom lip quivered. "He's about this big," she indicated a small rat, "and he's a light brown-gold color."

"Like your eyes," he said without thinking.

Her face flushed with colour and she started crawling among the bushes once more.

He stood staring at her cute behind, then with an inward curse he dropped down across from her, and on hand and knees began hunting with her. He began searching the bushes on the right side of the fountain.

He could hear her quiet little sobs as she searched more frantically.

He'd once had a puppy that had slipped out of the house

and got lost. He too had cried until it was found, so he could understand her disposition. However, intense feelings for a guinea pig were beyond his imagining. "Have you had Tinkles long?"

A muffled "Not long," came from the other side of the bushes.

"You appear rather attached to him?"

"Tinkles was a gift. I hate losing gifts."

A bloody thorn from the rose bush scratched his hand. He pushed it aside only to have it swing back and dig deep into the flesh of his cheek. He let out a string of curses.

Amy's head popped up. "Did you say something?'

"Nothing for your ears," he mumbled while wiping the blood from his cheek. What was he doing here? Why didn't he just leave? His head hurt, his hand and face were now bloodied . . . "A gift? From someone special." Was this why she was so upset? Tinkles was a gift from a suitor? He rolled his shoulders. He didn't care for that thought. "Tinkles is an unusual gift."

"I suppose."

He kept rummaging and whistling—did you whistle for a guinea pig? "Here Tinkles. Tinkle, tinkle little guinea pig. I wonder where you are?"

Amy actually giggled.

"Will the gift giver be terribly upset if you lose Tinkles?"

She hesitated in her answer. "Arh, no. I don't think so."

Still she didn't say who gave her Tinkles. Curiosity got the better of him. "Who gifted you Tinkles if you don't mind me asking?"

More hesitation. She really didn't wish him to know. "Lord Chesterton," was spoken softly from the other side of the fountain.

He rose to his knees and looked over at her in disbelief. He'd ruined his trousers, his head pounded from looking down, and he'd wasted half the morning on a rodent given to her by Chesterton. His morning couldn't possibly get any worse.

"I see." He didn't see. "You're not afraid of how angry he may be when he learns of Tinkles' loss? You needn't be. I can attest to your earnest hunting. I'll even replace Tinkles for you. I believe Chesterton wouldn't notice. I know how angry he can get, but I doubt he'd hurt you."

"Hurt me?" she scoffed. "Why would he hurt me over an unfortunate mishap?"

Chesterton was a bully with a vicious temper. He was known to fly off the handle at the tiniest slight. "I suppose he wouldn't." What else could he say?

They searched on for another half an hour and covered over half the garden before his thumping head finally got the better of him.

Amy seemed determined to keep looking. He stood and wiped his hands together to remove the dirt and said, "I'm sorry, Amy, but I have to go. I've an appointment."

She sat back on her haunches. "Oh, I don't wish to hold you up, my lord. You've done more than enough. Thank you for trying to help me find Tinkles. I'm stupidly fond of the little thing."

He nodded. "Send me a note and let me know if you find him. You have my permission to keep looking for as long as it takes. I'll send over a couple of footman to help."

She nodded and tears fell once more. Embarrassed, she immediately turned back to her hunting. With one last long full gaze at the most delicious bottom he'd seen in a while, Henry left her to it.

Good lord, the man *was* a saint. He'd helped her search! For an hour he'd crawled around on all fours, grass staining his beautiful trousers, whistling and calling for Tinkles when his head must have been thumping as if a steam train was running through it.

An imaginary guinea pig.

Amy Shipton you deserve to be whipped. How could she do that to him in his condition? Obviously hung over and his head swathed in a bandage.

She shuddered. If he'd called her bluff and gone for help . . . But he hadn't. The waterworks to the rescue. Men hated tears.

She felt dreadful at her deception, but really! What was a girl to do when caught looking for an earring she'd lost when she'd let a man take liberties with her person? A man who hadn't cared who she was, or worse, thought she was someone else.

She'd thought the idea that Chesterton had given her Tinkles would see him abruptly leave. But he hadn't.

Why should *her* reputation be ruined for one small oversight? Her mother expected her to do her duty—to marry to ensure one's position within the *ton*. Why should she? What of her own happiness? She admired Henry, was already a little in love with the man, but that made the situation unspeakable. To marry a man you worshipped and then have to watch him give his heart to another. She'd rather be ruined!

How long would it take Henry to discover who the earring belonged to? She had to get Sabine's help. Marcus couldn't reveal her identity. As soon as Henry showed him her earring the game would be up. It would ruin her life and Henry's. He loved another.

She'd been stupid to search his garden. He was immediately suspicious when he found her here. If Marcus said anything . . . Henry would know. What would she say if he openly confronted her?

She could see Henry's doubt clearly in his eyes.

She'd thought, after the condition he'd been in last night, he'd never be awake this early.

The only thing she could think of to get rid of him was to tell him an even bigger whopper. Lord Chesterton. She'd worked out from his demeanor last night that Henry had no love for Creeperton. Still he'd offered to intervene on her behalf. Why did he have to be so gallant? She was feeling little better than a slimy snail for making him search for a non-existent rodent.

Drat the man. But how could she stay angry at a man who'd got down on his knees for her? She shook her head. Saintly St. Giles.

Even more reason why he could not discover her identity. She would force such an honorable man to wed a woman he didn't love. Especially if he loved another! It would be the situation with Marcus all over again.

To be stuck with a husband who left her each night to spend time with the woman he loved would be torture. She'd not watch quietly while he spent his life with his other family. She couldn't bear it. To wither away inside like her mother . . .

She quickly rose. Time was not on her side. Then she looked at her dress and groaned. Blast. She'd have to change before she met with Caitlin and Sabine.

She refused to contemplate what she would tell her friends. She wasn't at all sure they wouldn't push her to marry Henry. They thought he was a wonderful man too.

She just wished she didn't think him so wonderful as well. She didn't know if she'd be able to say no to a proposal from Henry St. Giles.

CHAPTER FOUR

"Christ, what happened to you?" Harlow's words echoed Marcus's concerned curse as his two friends sank into chairs across from him at White's-the-club not the brothel.

Henry folded the newspaper he'd been reading and touched his head. The gash had still been weeping a bit when he awoke at the ungodly hour of eight this morning, and Smitters, his butler, had fashioned a small bandage. He knew he looked ridiculous.

"A drunken stumble on my way home." There was no way he was confessing his sins to these two. Instead, he laid the paper on the table beside him and took another sip of his brandy. He felt the warmth slide down his throat.

With a flick of his fingers Marcus summoned a footman and ordered himself and Harlow a drink. He raised an eyebrow. "How many brandies have you had today?"

Henry frowned. "I beg your pardon?"

"How many?" Marcus asked without a trace of humor. "I feel you are drinking too much of late my friend, which is unlike you. You weren't drunk when I left you at Lady Skye's ball, so what happened on your way home?"

Henry gave a curt reply. "I went to Mrs. White's fine establishment, if you must know."

Harlow tugged at his sleeve and laughed. "Not solely to drink I hope. I can think of more . . ." Harlow's smile disappeared when he saw the fleeting flash of guilt on Henry's face. "Oh, my God, you did just drink." He shook his head. "Christ, Henry. You're a bachelor. Buck up man. This dry spell is getting ridiculous."

Henry didn't try to hide his annoyance. "What if you lost Caitlin? Or you lost Sabine? What would you do? I suspect there would not be enough brandy in the world for either of you." He picked up the paper again and opened it blocking his view of his soon to be ex-friends if they carried on like this.

Marcus bashed the paper aside. "That's bloody different and you know it. Sabine's my soul mate."

"And for almost ten years, you moped and drank, and used mindless sex to forget her. So don't preach at me. Either of you."

Henry stilled the rush of anger by leaning back in his chair, downing the rest of his drink, and calling for another just to spite them, the bloody self-satisfied . . . Bugger them.

He eyed them both warily. "What are you doing here at this hour, anyway? Normally I have to drag you away from your wives—and son," he said, staring pointedly at Harlow.

The two men looked at each other. *This can't be good.* Henry squirmed in his chair, wishing he had another engagement to go to so he could leave without stating a lie.

Harlow grinned at him. "Actually we've come to meddle, and before you object, just remember how you meddled in our relationships."

Henry's mouth dropped open. "I did not meddle, much. I certainly didn't help. In fact, I almost drove Sabine away."

Harlow ignored him. "We both feel it's high time you found a wife." He paused. "A suitable wife. Let me be perfectly clear. One that is not Hilda."

"Oh, how the mighty have changed their spots," he drawled sarcastically. "You once told me wedlock was to be avoided at all costs."

"Wedlock to Hilda, yes. Marrying Hilda would be a slow and painful death," Marcus added.

"I agree."

Both men's glasses halted at their lips when they heard Henry's agreement.

Henry shrugged. "I realize that I should not have to suffer my brother's mistakes. He would not have wanted that for me," he added softly.

Both of his friends nodded. "Richard seemed to have an affinity with Hilda. You do not."

Marcus rubbed his hands together. "This makes our conversation much easier." He leaned forward in his chair. "I have a challenge for you."

Harlow interrupted. "We have a challenge for you. A challenge we feel will lead to great joy."

Henry merely stared at the two of them. His wariness grew. They looked far too pleased with themselves.

Marcus carried on. "We challenge you to find a wife by the end of season."

"That's only six weeks away," Henry felt the weight of the earring in his pocket. *Hmmm.* One of the reasons he'd hoped to meet these two scoundrels today, was to see if they recognized it.

Marcus feigned shocked surprise. "I know you're out of practice but surely a rake like you can woo a woman in six weeks. Besides, you haven't even heard the forfeit."

"I can hardly wait," the sarcasm made his mouth turn down. He lifted his glass, "Well, what is the forfeit? Something dastardly I'll wager."

Marcus gave a sly smile and Harlow tried to look angelic with little success.

"If you don't find a wife of your own choosing by the end of the season, you will offer for and marry Lady Amy Shipton."

Henry's drink sprayed the room as he choked on the liquid. A coughing fit ensued. "Amy Shipton!"

"Last year you thought her perfect for me," Marcus insisted. "She'd make you an excellent wife. She's beautiful, kind, generous, and her father's a duke."

If he'd been having this conversation a few days ago he'd disagree. But since this morning he'd come to realize Amy was beautiful. She had the same dark, sultry beauty as Millicent. Maybe that was why he'd never considered her. It was too soon after Millie.

He feigned disinterest to ensure his friends did not scent victory. "One slight flaw in the challenge gentlemen. What if Amy says no?"

"Then you'll ensure she can't say no." Harlow had always been the ruthless one of the three; it came with the privilege of the dukedom.

Henry steeled his voice. "Are you suggesting I compromise a lady?" With a guilty start he guessed he'd sort of accomplished that last night. Only he had no idea who.

Marcus tried to balance Harlow's ruthlessness. "Then perhaps you best ensure it doesn't come to that."

Henry thumped his glass on the table. His head ached, he'd had little sleep, he spent the morning crawling among the plants, and he had no humor for these two mischief makers. "Absolutely not. I may have decided not to honor Richard's betrothal and marry Hilda, but I'm a gentleman. A gentleman does not compromise a lady. That is not the way to start a marriage." Especially if he wanted a love match.

Marcus and Harlow sighed and shared a look before Marcus said, "Then you leave us no choice. Find a woman you do wish to marry and convince her to accept you or . . ."

"You do have a choice. You can stay out of my personal affairs."

A shiver of unease snaked down his spine, which he straightened. He was in the right. Nothing they could do would make him accept this challenge.

"If you had *personal affairs,* we would. But you've been behaving like a eunuch for far too long."

Henry felt his face heat at Harlow's sneer.

Marcus sat back, his elbows on his knees, his fingers touching in a tripod. "Unless you accept our challenge, I'm going to Dowager Spencer and I'll tell her you're desperate to marry by the end of the season. In fact, we shall offer to help her arrange a fine match."

"Christ, you bloody . . ." He gripped the arms of his chair so as not to punch the smug look off Marcus's face.

Spears of icy fear tore at his stomach. If Lady Dowager Spencer, his great aunt and the authority within the *ton,* heard he was seriously looking for a wife, his life would be turned upside down. He wouldn't be left alone for five minutes. She'd make it her mission to parade every available debutante in front of him. She'd descend on Cravenswood Court and not leave until he was leg-shackled. She wouldn't care to whom. His life would be a living hell.

"Bastards." His so called friends didn't even look at him with pity. They merely kept drinking with smirks on their faces.

Defeat slipped through him like a ghost. "So, let me get this right. I may choose a bride by the end of the Season, or you two reprobates, or Dowager Spencer, thrust one upon me."

"Or you marry Amy Shipton."

"Why are you so set on pushing me at Lady Shipton? She's my annoying neighbour."

Marcus's gaze softened. "I know you both." He slapped his chest above his heart like a warrior. "I know you'd be perfect for each other. You're kind, generous, and honorable. That's why I know that if you accept this challenge you'll not renege." He sat back and threw his arms up. "For God's sake, why not try courting her? What have you to lose?"

The earring moved in his pocket. He did wish to marry. But marry the right woman. A woman he could come to love. A woman who had fire in her soul and hot blood in her veins. A woman like the siren in his garden. Christ he was lusting after a woman he knew nothing about. He didn't even know what she looked like.

As much as he hated to, he'd have to tell them. He cleared his throat and tried to sound as if he'd not been cornered by a rampaging bull. "As it so happens, I may have found a lady that I'm interested in."

"Thank Christ," he heard Harlow mutter.

"What is her name?" Marcus asked, immediately suspicious.

"I'm not exactly sure."

Marcus's eyes narrowed. Henry rushed on. "She did not give me her name."

Harlow's grin widened. "There is a story here. I bet it involves that," he waved a hand at Henry's wound.

"He's blushing," Marcus laughed and Harlow joined in.

"When you're done laughing at my expense, I shall tell you." He proceeded to inform them what had occurred the previous night to much ripping and amusement. "So you see, I have no idea who she is, but she must be someone who lives in the square."

"Then it can't be too difficult to find her." Harlow stated.

He shook his head. "There are five young ladies, two spinsters, and three widows in my street. Plus there was a musical soiree there last evening. My only clue is this earring," and he pulled it out of his pocket. He thought he glimpsed something close to recognition in Marcus's eye, but when he looked again there was only curiosity.

Harlow took the earring and examined it. "It's a very expensive piece. She must be a lady of quality."

Henry nodded. "My thoughts exactly."

Marcus said, "So what is the problem? Simply advertise that you've found an earring and she'll likely come forward to claim it. There is no need to state where or how you came by it."

"But the lady herself will know. What if she is married already and is too ashamed to come forward, or worse, she is an innocent and is frightened due to my atrocious behaviour last night? She probably thinks I'm a drunken pervert who attacks young ladies in the dark."

"Henry's right, Marcus. We have to take a subtle approach."

Marcus shrugged his large shoulders. "Then what are you going to do?"

"I thought we could engage the services of your lovely wives. They could perhaps make discreet inquiries. When they learn the lady's identity, I can decide if I wish to enter into a courtship with her."

"You want to see what she looks like." Harlow gave a low throaty chuckle and raised his hands in defence. "Not that I blame you. Making love is much more fun with the candles, or sun, blazing."

"That's why I think you should consider Amy. She's beautiful. If I couldn't have Sabine, I'd have been more than content with her as my wife."

Henry opened his mouth to retort and found he couldn't. Amy was beautiful; why had he never really noticed before?

"I'd start with the jewellers." Harlow's idea had merit. "Any jeweller commissioned to make this piece would know who the earring belonged to."

Henry sat back in his chair and folded the paper and put it aside. "That's the first sensible suggestion either one of you have given me today."

Marcus raised his eyebrow and said, "So, it's agreed. You are engaged by the end of the season or you marry Lady Amy Shipton."

"I think Amy's pointless. It would appear Henry is set on finding his mystery woman."

"Nevertheless, Harlow, it would be wise to have a back up. Henry must agree Amy Shipton is an appropriate candidate."

"What is it with you, Marcus? Why are you determined to push Amy on me? Is it because I pushed her on you? This is your revenge?"

Marcus frowned. "Good Lord, marrying Amy Shipton is hardly a punishment."

Henry had to concede that point. He could do far worse.

"We want to see you happy. We both thought you needed a bit of a push; you've been procrastinating too long. You're the Earl of Cravenswood and as such you need an heir. You need to marry."

Marcus was correct. He did have an obligation. If anything happened to him the title and estate reverted to his Uncle, and with a son like Charles, the estate would be bankrupt within a year.

Why was he fussing? Hadn't he risen this morning with just this plan in mind? He wanted a wife and a lover and a friend. He just didn't appreciate his friends bullying him into it. But they were his friends, and at the heart of their challenge lay his best interests. God preserve him from reformed rakes.

"All right, I accept your challenge. One way or another I will find myself a bride by the end of the season."

*   *   *

Marcus stood on the top step, having just left Harlow and Henry still inside the club. His grin grew as he tugged on his gloves with a satisfied smile. He couldn't wait to get home and explain to Sabine the plan Harlow and he had hatched. Especially now he'd seen the earring and heard Henry's wish to locate the owner.

He directed his groom to turn the phaeton around. He had to stop at the jewellers before he returned home. Marcus wasn't about to let this be easy for Henry. In his experience, love needed to be worked at. The reward in the end was immeasurable. It would not do for Henry to learn too soon the identity of the owner of the earring.

CHAPTER FIVE

Lanreath, Berkshire, a week later

It must be here somewhere. Her maid Lorraine had pried the information from her beau, Henry's valet Smitters. Henry had found the earring and now carried it about with him. He was trying to identify the owner.

She couldn't let him find the owner—couldn't let him find her.

So here she was, at Lanreath, Lord Wolverstone's country estate, for a week long house party with almost thirty others.

When she'd called on Sabine the day after her encounter with Henry, asking questions about Henry's heart, Sabine immediately organized a week long house party. The excuse was to escape the humidity of London for a short period.

And of course she'd invited Henry.

And Amy.

Sabine was definitely matchmaking and Amy wouldn't discount the fact she was likely working with her husband. Traitor. Sabine understood Amy's stance on marriage best of all. Last year, Amy had turned Marcus down because he loved Sabine. She'd explained to Sabine about her father's behavior and his 'other' family. How much it hurt knowing he'd rather spend time with his illegitimate children than with her. She'd never put her children through that.

Now, no thanks to Sabine, Amy was no closer to finding her earring or who Millicent was, or what she meant to Henry. Sabine appeared to know nothing.

It was their second day at the beautiful estate and the men were out riding. Amy sank to her knees, heedless of how it would crumple her gown, and lifted the lid of Lord Cravenswood travelling trunk. It was the only place left to look. But it was empty. His belongings unpacked by Smitters.

Blast. Why was he carrying it around? She wasn't sorry she'd let Henry St. Giles, the man known as the saintly rake, take far too many liberties with her person in his garden, but she wasn't about to let the episode see her father insist on a marriage.

Ever since her mother's death three years ago, her father couldn't wait to see Amy married off. It was of no importance who her future husband was, as long as he was titled and rich. The duke thought it would be relatively easy to see her married; after all she was his daughter, and she had a large dowry. Men were lining up to offer for her hand.

Her father did not wish to see her married out of any fatherly concern. No, he simply wanted to be rid of her.

If she married, he'd be able to live in the country with his other family, his mistress and their children. The woman he had loved his whole married life. Amy's half brothers and sisters— who she'd never formally met—were party to her father's affections, while none was ever given to his legitimate progeny.

Think damn it. The men had all gone for a ride this afternoon. She needed to find her earring before her absence was noted. She mustn't be caught in Henry's room. She did not need her brother, who was also here, asking awkward questions and reporting back to their father.

Like most of the nobility, her parents had not married for any reason except alliance and money. Her father had been in love with another, a woman who could never become the Duchess. So instead, he'd made a cold-blooded marriage contract, and then continued to live separate lives.

Now that her mother was dead, and her older brother married and settled in the London townhouse, her father wanted to retire to his estate and move his mistress and their children into his home. He couldn't do that with an unmarried daughter. Society may turn a blind eye to a man as powerful as her father indulging himself in his later years, but they would not condone his actions with an unmarried daughter within the same household.

Well, her father could go to Hades. There was no way Amy Shipton would be forced to marry any man. The image of Henry's handsome face flashed before her eyes.

The night in his garden had been magical. She would never forget the passions Henry's touched ignited. His kisses were incredible. The ravishing hunger of his lips. Even now she remembered the hard press of his body as he gently pushed her down. The burning heat of his embrace, his devouring mouth, his clever fingers . . .

His tender savagery had kindled a response in her that was basic, primitive, wholly feminine, and exciting. Her body's fierce yearning to surrender to his touch, to open and accept everything he had to give her was most unexpected. She'd never dreamed a man's touch could be so arousing. No other man had elicited even a spark.

If he hadn't spoken Millicent's name and ruined the moment, she wondered if she'd still be a virgin.

What would she have done then?

She stood up and brushed out her dress, checking the creases in the Cheval mirror.

327

Her bitter family experience meant she had only one rule where marriage was concerned. She would not marry any man who was in love with someone else. It was unfair to all parties.

But recently she had written a second rule.

Having seen Marcus and Sabine together, and having met their friends Harlow Telford, Duke of Dangerfield, and Caitlin his duchess, she, Amy Shipton, the daughter of a duke, had made a curious discovery about herself.

Like Henry, she wanted more. She wanted a husband who would love her back.

She wanted love full stop.

She was turning her back on everything her mother and grandmother had drilled into her since the nursery. *A lady did her duty and married for social position and wealth—nothing more.*

She puzzled over why Henry insisted on hunting for the owner of the earring? Amy's heart thrummed as she banged the lid shut with a muttered curse. What good could come of it? He probably thought his midnight rendezvous woman was eager for seductive games. He was a rake.

She stood and gazed around the masculine room. The earring hadn't been in the pockets of any of his coats in the dressing room. Perhaps he kept it on his person.

Heat flooded her veins. How would she retrieve it then?

She'd already searched his armoire, trying not to disturb his neatly folded shirts, collars, and cravats of rich silks.

She turned her attention to his dressing table. Perhaps his valet had emptied Henry's pockets and put the earring with his cuff links or watches.

As she advanced toward the imposing dresser, she prayed it was there. Not that such a thing would solve her dilemma, for if it went missing, Henry would want to know where it had gone. She'd have to leave the Wolverstone estate immediately. She bit her lip and halted mid stride. But then Henry would logically deduct she'd taken the earring, and then he'd know exactly who he'd had in his arms. Knowing Henry, he'd offer to do the honorable thing.

Blow honorable men. She tried to gather her wits. What a pickle she found herself in.

Sanity fled when she heard heavy footsteps and voices approaching along the corridor, heading towards the door of this very room. She froze, holding her breath. The men should all be out riding.

The footsteps stopped outside the door. An icy sweat broke over her skin. If she were found in his room, it would certainly ensure she ended up wed to Henry St. Giles.

Hide, you fool. The dressing room? No, she'd never reach it in time; already the door handled turned. *Under the bed!* She dived just as the door began to open and scrambled beneath the large oak frame, her heart pounding in her chest.

From under the bed she saw Henry's booted feet, and to her horror, a woman's slippered feet entered the doorway as well.

Please, please don't let it be a liaison.

Amy tried to ignore the sudden pain in the region of her heart. Why should she care that Henry forgo riding to have some afternoon delight with . . .

"Darling, I know why you cried off joining the other gentlemen for an afternoon ride. You'd much prefer to be riding me."

At the woman's seductive purr Amy stifled a gasp. Her ears burned. Oh, my God, it was Lydia, her brother's wife. *Please, please don't let her discover me under Henry's bed.* She inched herself toward the other side of the bed. To her horror Amy had a clear view of the couple in the cheval mirror.

She watched in mortification as Lydia pushed Henry into the room and began to close the door behind her. Henry immediately shoved his booted foot in the way so that the door could not fully close.

"Now, Lydia, run back to the ladies, there's a good girl. I simply came up here to get my gloves."

Henry's voice held a hint of annoyance. *Good for you.* Amy knew her brother's marriage was like her parents, a merger of family wealth and an alignment of assets, but Lydia had yet to give her brother his heir.

"Don't be shy, Henry. All the ladies know you've struck a bit of a drought. Some of us are wondering if your *weapon* still works."

Amy bit her lip to stop from defending Henry. His *weapon* seemed to be in working order in his garden the other night.

"It doesn't work with married women. I don't let it."

Amy gritted her teeth as she watched Lydia reach out and stroke Henry's *weapon*. Henry didn't stop her. *Men!*

After a lengthy silence, Lydia murmured, "My, my, it does work. Why don't you close the door and I'll help end your famine. The ladies of the *ton* will be pleased to hear you're back in working order."

"How much do you win for *cocking my weapon*?"

Lydia laughed gaily and dropped to her knees, her hands fumbling with the placket of his trousers. "Not as much as I'll gain in pleasure, I assure you."

Amy slunk further under the bed, she couldn't watch this. Lydia on her knees fumbling with Henry's trousers was not a sight she wished to see, although why Lydia had to be on her knees to undo his trousers was a mystery.

But Henry swiped her hands away. "I'm sorry but this is one wager you'll lose," and he lifted Lydia back onto her feet and pushed her none too gently out into the corridor and shut the door on her indignant face.

"Not what I bloody needed this week. A bitch in heat."

Amy stifled her giggle. At least Henry had good taste in his women. Her smile faded as she noted Henry didn't walk to his armoire to collect his gloves. Instead, he sank down on the end of his bed, his booted feet almost within touching distance of where she lay.

Amy heard him sigh and with racing heart she watched in the mirror as he lay back on the bedspread, and began to fumble with the his trousers.

Her heart almost stopped. She watched in fascination as he reach inside and draw out his 'in prime working order' manhood. He spit in his hand. She clamped her hand over her mouth to mute her gasp. She shouldn't look. She knew what he was about to do. You didn't grow up with a brother and not at some stage stumble upon him pleasuring himself.

This was an intimate moment and she had no right to intrude.

She held her breath least she disturb the silence settling over the room. Her mind screamed at her to reveal herself before he went any further, but embarrassment and fear of the consequences kept her silent. She lay quietly and turned her head away from the mirror so she could not peek.

Amy offered up a silent prayer, hoping he would finish quickly. She lay as tense as a woman waiting for the guillotine to fall.

Then the most erotic sounds flooded her hearing, arousing groans, soft sighs and the sound of skin intimately touching skin. *Don't you dare turn your head!* But the urge defeated her. She moved and let her eyes stray to the mirror.

Heat flooded every inch of her skin as she breathlessly watched Henry St. Giles take his earthy pleasure.

Liquid oozed from the tip of his rather large shaft, making the dark-plum head glisten. He palm slid faster and faster over his straining rod, only to slow down and almost stop, before speeding up once again.

His breathing became irregular. He began to move on the

bed. She could see where the imprint of his body was twisting, and he thrust his hips forcing his erection through his white-knuckled fist.

His heavy breathing turned to grunts, growing in volume and intensity, and the headboard began to knock gently against the wall. His eyes were closed, his neck corded with tension. His shirt rose up and she glimpsed his flat, and rippled with muscles, stomach. A dusting of brown hair arrowed a path to his groin, where his phallus arose wrapped in his hand. She had never seen anything so magnificent.

Amy's face felt like it was hanging over burning coals. The image of a naked Henry flashed in her brain. It was nothing like the sight in the mirror.

She closed her eyes, and covered her ears, trying to block the sight and sounds from above. His movements became more boisterous and his groans grew in volume.

She tried not to look and listen but part of her wanted to hear him. Definitely wanted to see him. Her breath came in quick little gasps, her breasts felt tight and uncomfortable within her bodice and a warm pulse beat between her thighs. She'd never seen or heard anything so erotic.

The image of Henry pleasuring himself . . . sent feminine heat crawling over her skin. The primal urge to enjoy the masculine beauty of the act made her curl up into a ball.

His frantic grunts, almost snarling in his passion, only made the scene more erotic. She watched Henry, exposed on the bed, his fist wrapped around his phallus, his hips lifting, his body thrusting through his fist . . . She knew he was big, she'd felt how large when he lay atop her in the garden, but he looked enormous.

She remembered his kisses and how his fingers felt when they'd delved deep within her. She'd wanted to touch him that night but she'd been too overwhelmed by the feelings he evoked in her. Too much a coward.

What would he feel like if she were the one fondling him? What would he think if she crawled out from under the bed and offered to help? Scandalous! The desire to do so, to touch him . . . she almost let out a moan herself.

She pulsed all over. His sounds grew louder, the bed creaked and groaned under his movements, the headboard banging in a steadily increasing rhythm, until finally he let out a roar and cursed like a blue-blood pirate. She felt him flop onto the bed above her on a drawn out sigh, and she watched Henry shudder and relax, slowly working his manhood until it went soft. His breath still coming in rasps.

Yet Amy didn't feel relaxed at all. Her nerves strung tight. Her body primed like a pistol about to fire. Good God, she wished she could touch herself in the same way.

In the ensuing silence Amy wondered what he had been thinking as he stroked himself. He'd more than likely dreamed about the lady whose name he'd uttered as he lay atop her in the garden on that titillating night.

Her arousal vanished, and her salacious thoughts halted altogether when an object hit the floor. It appeared to have bounced off the bed. It must have been lose on the bedclothes. It glittered in the sunlight spilling into the room.

Her earring.

He'd been holding her earring.

She watched him clean himself up with his handkerchief. "Pathetic, one fumble in a darkened garden and you can't get the woman out of your mind."

Amy shoved her fist in her mouth.

Without thought her fingers inched out from under the bed, reaching for the gem, only to snatch them back when Henry sat up.

The heady joy dissipated when she remembered he didn't know who she was. He'd simply taken his pleasure to a nameless, faceless woman.

She slid further under the bed when Henry bent and retrieved the earring. He stood, straightening his clothes, and placed the earring in his pocket. He buttoned up the placket of his trousers.

He briefly glanced at himself in the mirror, tidying his hair before pivoting, collecting his gloves and leaving the room. Amy breathed a sigh of relief but waited a good ten minutes after she heard Henry's booted feet descend the stairs. Then she crept out from under the bed, noted her flushed countenance and knew she had to seek fresh air.

*   *   *

Henry needed some fresh air. His mouth worked to swallow past his disbelief.

Amy Shipton was his mystery lady, he was sure of it. Little Amy. His neighbor.

Tinkles! He bet there never was a Tinkles. *The bloody conniving . . .* an hour he'd been crawling in the dirt looking for a guinea pig.

He'd like to put her over his knee and spank her till her bottom turned red. *That's not all you'd like to do.*

He'd like nothing more than to turn around, march back up the stairs, and pull Amy Shipton out from under his bed and lay her firmly atop it, then do all the things he'd just dreamed of doing.

She *was* his mystery lady.

Why else would Amy Shipton be in his room and under his bed? He'd obviously caught her hunting for her earring.

At least Henry now knew who the earring belonged too. He hadn't quite known what to think when he'd glimpsed a pale, delicate hand in the cheval mirror, inching out from under the bed toward the piece of jewellery that had rolled onto the floor. He'd been holding it while he'd dreamed of lush curves and satin skin.

Then he'd taken a longer look in the mirror, letting his eyes drift up the gloved arm and follow it to its owner, and he'd seen Amy cowering under the bed.

What had she felt as she watched him? Had her stormy eyes widened in shock, or had she grown aroused, her body heating, her heart racing, seeing his hand gripping his erection . . .

Images and memories of the lush feminine body, Amy's body, as he lay atop her in his garden, had aroused him to an explosive finish. Christ, if merely thinking about her could bring him such ecstasy, what would actually making love to her be like?

If he'd known she was watching, he wouldn't have been able to last more than a minute. Already the thought of her seeing his primitive male display made his groin ache, and he felt himself begin to harden again.

He'd known instinctively not to confront her. She'd have been mortified, and he had yet to work out why she was keeping her identity a secret.

She obviously felt at least desire for him, as she'd not run screaming from the garden. He could still hear her moans of pleasure in his head.

The puzzle deepened.

Most likely she was worried about her reputation. A lady's reputation was all she had to ensure a good match. She was the daughter of a duke after all.

He'd once recommended Amy as a suitable candidate to become Marcus's wife. Why had he never considered that she'd be perfect for him? Millie—she looked too much like Millicent.

He briefly wondered why Amy wasn't already betrothed. He stopped in his tracks and frowned. Hell, she wasn't, was she? Betrothed? Is that why she was so desperate to retrieve her property? It was scandalous what had occurred in his garden. It might ruin a match for her.

He continued on his way to the stable, his temperament somewhat dismayed.

He hoped he wasn't too late and that she did not already belong to another. What a silly sod he'd been to have a woman of Amy's ilk in his street and not have noticed.

When mounted, he set his horse to a gallop and quickly caught up with the rest of the men. He eyed them all in a new light. Was there anyone here who could be a rival for Amy's hand?

Comte Le Page, the enigmatic Frenchman who owned estates in France and England, was rumored to be wife hunting. He'd been one of the men flocking around Amy at Lady Skye's ball. Henry hoped Amy hadn't fallen for the dark, swarthy type, or he was in trouble.

Then there was the Earl of Roehampton. Bertie was nothing to look at, true, but he was one of the wealthiest men in the Kingdom and Amy's father would look favorably on a match.

"Is something the matter?"

Marcus's question interrupted his analysis of his competition. He'd not even heard him riding up.

"Who drafted the guest list for this gathering, you or Sabine?"

Marcus looked over the men riding in front of them. "Strange mix isn't it. Sabine. And I believe Caitlin helped make up the list."

For some reason Henry hesitated revealing he had learned the identity of the lady whose earring burned in his pocket. Something was going on here. Marcus had been pushing Amy's cause vigorously.

Marcus continued. "I think they've taken it upon themselves to find Amy a husband. Sabine wants to repay Amy for her kindness. Sabine feels she owes her since Amy helped save her life."

"I'm sure Amy doesn't need any help finding a husband."

Marcus nodded. "True. However, Sabine says Amy's father is determined to see her married by the end of the season and is pushing a match with Chesterton."

Henry's heart clenched. Chesterton wasn't good enough for Millicent or Amy.

"I feel the need for speed." With that Henry gathered his stallion and took off at a gallop.

The power of the horse beneath him focused his mood. The air raced passed his face and the rush of speed dimed the irrational anger at the thought of Chesterton married to Lady Amy Shipton.

The image of her hiding under his bed would not diminish, and made him desperate to have her on his bed and *under* him. He knew what that meant. The only way that would happen was through marriage.

The power of the ride sent a surge of release through him.

Yet, he didn't really know her. He knew she was kind, generous and beautiful, but he did not know her heart. What did she want out of life? Did someone already own her heart?

The idea that she loved another made his anger grow. He felt that rush and roar of primitive jealousy pouring into his body.

If you want her go and get her. Woo her you damned fool.

How did one woo a woman? He'd never seriously needed to know. Perhaps desire was the answer. She'd not been immune to his—he couldn't call their night in his garden a seduction . . .

He might not be a rake of Marcus's experience but he knew enough about women to know he could seduce her. She'd been more than eager in his arms. If she surrendered to him, then she was obviously interested in marriage. For any surrender led directly to them becoming wedlocked.

He decided there and then that nothing would please him more.

CHAPTER SIX

The following afternoon bloomed into a glorious sunny day, and yet even though the sun shone, Henry had no idea how he was going to woo Amy. However, God must have listened to his prayers because Henry found himself partnered with Amy for Sabine's torturous treasure hunt. They had ten items to collect, with some of the clues more like a foreign language than Queen's English. Still, he was determined to make the most of the opportunity that Sabine had gifted him. An afternoon in Amy's company.

Unfortunately, Amy didn't look so happy about the situation. For the life of him he couldn't fathom why she bristled every time he came near. It seemed logical to deduce her heart favoured another. It must be Le Comte. Bloody damn Frenchman.

The guests, in their pairs, were sent out in different directions. The two of them had been sent toward the formal gardens near the back of the property. The manicured grounds overflowed with rose bushes, citrus trees and Sabine's favourite flowers. The centre piece of the large expansive hedged-row gardens was a bubbling fountain, very similar to the smaller version of his fountain in his garden in London, and in the distance was the summer house.

"The first clue says, *'Look in the green where water meets the Gods'*. Whatever can Sabine mean?" Amy stood at the top of the garden stairs and surveyed the acreage before her.

He put his hand up to his brow to shade the sun. "The fountain looks very familiar." Amy's face flushed a pretty pink colour. She could hardly admit she recognised the fountain's design or she'd be admitting to him that she'd been in his garden. "The fountain in my garden is similar, although much smaller, but I do believe the focal point is Aphrodite."

Amy clapped her hands. "Oh, yes. *Water meets the Gods* must be the fountain, and the *look in the green* is," she spread her arms wide, "the garden."

Clever girl. He offered her his arm. "Shall we?"

She slipped her hand over his arm and smiled, her joy in puzzling out the clues touched him. If she was determined to win, he'd help her.

"What is the prize if we win," he asked her.

"Apparently the winner gets to choose whatever prize they wish."

"As a gentleman, I insist that if we win you may choose. If we win, what will you choose?"

She smiled at him and said, "That's easy. I'd like to name Orsini Rose's foal."

His heart thudded in his chest at such a simple request. Orsini Rose was Marcus's prime breeding mare and his wedding gift to Sabine.

At his silence she said, "You think my prize strange."

"No. Not at all." He cleared his throat. "I hope the birth goes well. Foaling sometimes ends in tragedy, especially if it's the mare's first foal. Are you aware of that?"

She plucked a rose and twirled it under her nose. "Death is part of life isn't it? Life is not all roses, there are also thorns."

"True. Sometimes you don't appreciate the rose because of the thorns." He added wistfully, "I didn't really appreciate all my brother did for me, and our family, until he was gone."

"I'm sorry, that was a stupid thing to say. To make light of life and death . . ."

He plucked the rose from between her fingers and tapped her nose with it. "The day is too beautiful to be morbid. We have a prize to win."

She laughed gaily and the mood lifted. "Come on, we should hurry. Games are played to win, Lord Cravenswood. It might be the only time I ever get to name a thorough-bred."

He couldn't agree more with her sentiments. Games were played to win and he meant to win their private game. More pointedly he meant to win her heart.

They reached the fountain and both had to shield their eyes from the water's glare. They stood staring around them trying to ascertain where the next clue could be found.

"I see it," Amy cried. She pointed at the statue in the middle of the fountain, "there's a piece of paper tied around Aphrodite."

She looked at Henry expectantly and he gallantly offered, "I'll retrieve the clue, shall I?"

"That would be super, thank you."

With a sigh he sat on the edge of the fountain. "You're going to have to help me remove my boots." She chewed her bottom lip, looking adorable. "I'm not ruining my best boots for a silly treasure hunt."

She nodded in agreement. "I'll do it instead." She sat beside him and said, "Look away." She shooed him with her hand. "Hurry, we don't have time to get those boots off. I'll get the clue." Amy stared pointedly until he turned his head away. He heard her slippers plop to the ground and the rustle of skirts as she removed her stockings. Then a squeal as her feet hit the cool water.

Unable to help himself, Henry turned at the excited sound. The sight of creamy skin greeted him and made his throat dry and his groin heat.

Amy waded determinedly toward Aphrodite her skirts hiked up and her long, slender limbs on display. The sun gave her white skin a sparkling glow. She looked like a pagan goddess. His own flesh and blood Aphrodite. She was exquisite.

She glanced back at him over her shoulder. "Are you peaking? Stop it."

He could no more stop drinking in the arousing sight of her than he could stop breathing. "Amy," he said, his voice raw with need. "Do you know what a stirring sight you are? You're a water nymph."

He couldn't look away. She grabbed the clue from the statue and turned to wade back.

She would not look at him. It was scandalous the amount of flesh she was displaying but she liked to win and it was not only a test of brain-power but of speed. They had to beat the other teams. When she reached the edge of the fountain she risked at quick glance at him.

His hand was extended to help her from the water but that would mean letting her skirts get wet. He saw her predicament and swept her into his arms, lifting her clear of the water.

Amy should shout, protest, tell him to put her down but the words died on her lips. She could only watch dazed as he carried her to the grass and gently slid her down his body until her bare feet touch the fresh earth. All thoughts of winning the treasure hunt vanished like a ghost racing the dawn.

Her breath came in short, rasps.

She couldn't look away from the blatant desire etched on Henry's handsome features. They stood looking at each other, heat and need rising with each blink of their eyelashes.

Henry's eyes darkened as he cupped her face. "So, beautiful," he whispered.

The look in his eyes was one she would never forget. Such longing. More and more she wished she knew his heart.

Reluctantly she stepped away. "I want to win, Lord Cravenswood. We must hurry. Turn your back and read the second clue while I redress," and she handed him the scrap of paper.

On a sigh Henry obeyed her command and began to read the words out loud. "*Toward the setting sun you go, to the porch of the house that is not a home.*"

Amy scoffed. "That's easy. The summer house."

Once again Henry offered her his arm and she happily accepted it. "Have you thought of a name for the foal?" he asked.

"Of course. Athena if it's a girl and Hermes if it's a boy."

"Greek names?"

"My brother's tutor would let me listen to the stories he told of the Greek Gods. Athena is the Goddess of wisdom, warfare and strategy. She's very clever. Athena will need that to win races. Especially against the stallions."

Henry laughed at her logic. "She may be kept for breeding and never race."

"In that case she will need strength to breed a champion. Hermes is the messenger of the Gods and has to be flight of foot. He'll be a champion racer."

"You've had an interesting education."

She couldn't help her temper flaring at his words. "For a woman, you mean. I think a woman needs to be clever to survive in this, a man's world."

"Survive? You're one of the lucky women who live a life of privilege. You have a father, brother and soon hopefully a husband to ensure your survival."

"Why are men always so literal? I don't necessarily mean survival in the physical sense. There is more to surviving than physical comforts bring appeased. What about a woman's emotional needs? She must find a way to live in a world where she has very few rights. Men hold all the power."

Henry halted and turned her to face him. "I know what you are saying and why. I realise that like my parents, your mother and father did not marry for love. But you cannot let their relationship cloud your judgement. Look at Lord and Lady Wolverstone and Dangerfield. I don't believe Sabine or Caitlin believes they are merely surviving."

"They are the exception I'll give you that."

"No. Not the exception. I, for one, will only marry a woman I love. Relationships are not about power. Marriage should be a partnership of equal standing."

Her heart flipped in her chest. Why couldn't a man like this love her? This is what she longed for. He was what she longed for. He spoke of love. This was her chance. *Ask him*. Ask him if his heart belongs to someone.

But before she could force the words from her mouth, a piercing scream filled the air.

The both turned in the direction of the summer house, bumping heads on the way. A woman was crawling up the steps of the summer house. Henry looked at her and she said one word, "Go."

He took off at a sprint and Amy tried to catch up. He'd already lifted the distressed woman into his arms, and had forced open the doors to the summer house by the time she arrived completely out of breath.

The woman was still moaning and it didn't take long for Amy to realise why, she was heavy with child. Henry was placing her gently on top of the day bed and Amy rushed to her side.

"I'm so sorry, my lady, I thought I'd make it home . . . but the babes coming." Another choking scream began. The sound like a wounded animal.

"Shush, it's going to be all right," she whispered as she stroked the woman's head. Beads of perspiration dotted the young woman's brow. "What's your name, dear?"

"Johann . . ., my lady," the last words yelled into the still and overheated room. "My husband, Timothy, is a groom at the house."

"Is this your first child?"

"Nooooooo." She was breathing heavily. "This be my second. I think it might be coming soon. I hope it's a girl . . . *I already have a boy*," she screamed.

She turned to Henry. "You'll have to go for help."

Henry was trying to make the woman comfortable. Arranging her clothing and placing pillows under her head. He drew Amy a short distance away. "Have you been at a birth before?" Amy shook her head. Henry noted her clenched hands, the grip making her knuckles white. "Would you prefer me to stay and you go up to the house for help? It's not something a young lady should see."

"I don't see why not. I'm liable to have a baby of my own one day." The woman's cries made it difficult to think. "You'll be faster than me." She pushed him toward the door. "Go." With more confidence than she felt she gave him a steady smile. "We'll manage."

Henry took another look at Johann, took off his jacket and handed it to her. "You'll need something to wrap the babe in." At her dismayed look he added, "Just in case," and took off at a run. Amy looked at the jacket hanging over her arm. She could smell his masculine scent on it and she prayed he'd get back with help in time.

She took a deep breath and turned with what she hoped was a confident smile. "Now then, Johann, let's see what this wee babe is up to . . ."

Henry ran as fast as he could, directly to the house. He sent one of the lads off to the village to notify the midwife, he collected Honeyton, the cook, who'd proclaimed she'd had several children, and then on the way back made sure to stop at the stables and bring along Johann's worried, but ecstatic husband, Timothy.

Henry and Timothy made it back to the summer house before the women, only to be greeted by wailing from a very healthy sounding pair of lungs.

Timothy entered first and raced to his wife's side where she cuddled a baby hidden in Henry's ruined jacket. But Henry's eyes were drawn to Amy.

She sat on the floor at Johann's feet. Her clothes were covered in blood and they clung to her with sweat, yet she was the most beautiful woman he'd ever seen. A wondrous expression plastered her face.

Henry crossed to her and crouched down. "You did it, Amy."

"Johann did all the work. I just caught the baby at the end. Isn't she the most beautiful thing you've ever seen?"

"She?"

"It's a girl."

Honeyton finally arrived and Henry scooped an exhausted Amy up into his arms heedless of the mess. "Let's get you back to the house, you look tired and you definitely could do with a bath," Henry laughed.

She tugged on his sleeve. "Take me over to Johann. I want to say goodbye."

The two women smiled at each other with tears in their eyes. "Thank you, Lady Amy. I don't think I could have done it without you."

"Nonsense. You were very brave. It was humbling to watch a new life enter this world. Thank you."

"Timothy and I have picked a name for." She smiled shyly up at them. "Amy Henrietta Gordon. After you both."

A tear slipped out of Amy's eye and she clung to Henry. "Thank you. That means so much to me. I'll come and visit Amy tomorrow, once you've rested."

They said their goodbyes and left Honeyton and the other women to help the lass home. Henry carried her back toward the house his heart light.

He tenderly wiped a stray wisp of damp hair from her face and tucked it behind her ear. "You lost the treasure hunt. You won't be able to name the foal."

She beamed up at him dreamily. "A little girl was named after me. A baby I helped bring into this world. Nothing could be more perfect."

He was so proud of this woman. Many a debutante would have fainted away at the thought of helping Johann but Amy stood her ground not phased at all. Not only that, she was moved by the glory of new life. She never hesitated in giving where needed. What a wonderful woman. What a wonderful wife and partner she'd make him.

"Named after both of us. Amy Henrietta Gordon. She shares both our names."

He wanted to share his name with Amy and make her his wife. She was perfect for him. He was even more certain Amy was his soul mate.

Today he'd hoped to start his wooing but it hadn't turned out exactly as he'd hoped. It was even better. They had shared something profound and he could now feel a special bond between them.

The distance and remoteness Amy used to hold him at bay over the last few days was gone. Now he could finally begin to make progress and he was determined to take advantage of her euphoria. Tonight he'd start his campaign in earnest.

*   *   *

"Do you ride, Lady Amy?"

Turning to look up at Henry, Any froze as she met his intense gaze. He stood looking at her in a manner he'd never used before. Like a starving man at a feast. Just like Marcus sometimes looked at Sabine. Her heart stuttered as did her mouth.

Today had altered the balance between them. They'd shared something special. Witnessed something personal and unique, and she was having difficulty keeping her feelings for him in check. She had to move their relationship back to formality in order to keep her distance. It was that she didn't trust Henry, she didn't trust herself.

"P-Pardon?"

"Ride . . ."

He looked utterly gorgeous. Speaking of starving . . . He looked good enough to eat. She put her hand on her chest and felt her heart begin to race wildly.

His tawny fringe was pushed to the side highlighting long sweeping lashes, which lowered slowly as his gaze swept down her figure, then lifted again so that his stare captured hers. One perfect eyebrow lifted.

Amy licked her lips in order to pry them open. Her mouth suddenly dry. "Yes, my lord. I do ride."

"Then perhaps you'd like to accompany me on a ride in the morning. The Roman city ruins near Silchester are said to be worth investigating, and it's only a half-hour's ride from here."

Breathe. "I'd like that, thank you."

Amy found his continued perusal disconcerting. He'd never paid her this much attention before. From a distance he'd been enchanting, but up close he hummed with vibrancy, heat radiating from his body in waves.

"I haven't had the occasion to formally thank you for helping

Sabine. You've made my good friend, Lord Wolverstone, very happy."

Her face began to heat. "It was nothing that anyone else would not have done. Marcus was the hero. He got to Sabine in time to save her."

His smile momentarily slipped, why she was not sure.

"I'm not sure many young ladies would have helped as you did. Not when they could become Countess Wolverstone by remaining silent."

There seemed to be some hidden meaning behind his words. His face was alert, searching for . . . what?

"Marcus did not love me."

Henry laughed. "That has not stopped women before. The ranks of nobility are full of marriages void of any love or real affection."

Amy promptly scolded herself. Of course he would laugh at her notion. Yet it hurt. After listening to his late night discussions with his dead brother, she thought Henry wanted what she did—love.

Perhaps not. He was looking for the owner of the earring even when he'd whispered another's name. Men. They were all alike. Love was convenient when required to gain what they most desired. Trouble was love lasted only as long as the pleasure.

She rolled the stem of her empty glass between her fingers and wished Sabine would call them all into super.

She risked a glance at him. She wished she could think of something clever to say. Instead she burbled forth quite forcefully, "I will only ever marry for love."

"Very wise," he replied.

Was he teasing? She was saved from further conversation by a servant. Henry stepped aside to let the man refill her glass. As soon as he'd left, Henry took the seat beside her on the settee.

She gulped back a moan. She should have invited him to sit, but his presence was throwing her off-kilter.

A gleam entered his eyes. He leaned close, his thigh touching her leg through the silk. "Did you have anyone in mind?"

Amy glanced at him uncertainly, wondering if he were making fun of her, but his countenance screamed seriousness. "I beg your pardon?"

"Are you in love? Come, it's a simple enough question."

Amy looked quickly around the room, was he serious? As if she would tell him such personal information. She looked across to Marcus and caught his eye, pleading for help. He simply lifted his glass and smiled back at her.

"Marcus is considered to be an extremely handsome man. He has broken many hearts in his time. Not intentionally, of course."

She tried to repress her flush of embarrassment. "I'm sure you're right, but I think of Marcus as purely a friend." She had not meant to have her words come out so sharp but really! "Why are the secrets of my heart so important to you, Lord Cravenswood? Perhaps you'd like to share who your heart belongs to?"

There, that will put him in his place. Who is Millicent? But to her horror he picked up her hand and brought it to his lips. They scorched her skin even through her glove. Suddenly he gave her a slow, charming, devilish grin that seared all her nerve endings. "There are many secrets I'd like to share with you, my sweet."

She opened her mouth to reply, then shut it again, deciding it wiser to halt this conversation before she got herself into real trouble.

At her muteness, the gleam in Henry's eyes intensified. "For instance, did you know men find the thrill of the hunt very exciting?"

Hunt? Amy's eyes flared and she stifled a gasp. Was he indicating his hunt for the owner of her earring? Did he know it was hers or was he simply ferreting for information?

At her confusion he leaned further toward her and whispered, "However, it's what we do once we've caught our pray that is pleasurable."

Scandalous. His words were scandalous.

His eyes held hers with remnants of a challenge swirling in their depths. There was something intimate, almost possessive about Henry's scrutiny, and Amy once more found herself remembering what it felt like to kiss him, remembering the heat and hardness of him . . .

She gave a light shrug of her shoulders. "I was of the opinion that unmarried earls with considerable fortunes were the hunted. You have plans for letting yourself be caught perhaps?"

"Indeed. Capture is not so terrible when caught by the right woman."

Amy's stomach flipped. "Oh? You have someone in mind."

"Perhaps. How's Tinkles?"

At his question Amy completely forgot the glass of sherry in her hand, and it tipped when her hand flew to her mouth, depositing the contents of her glass straight into his lap.

"Oh, no!" she exclaimed, looking utterly dismayed as she brought her hands to her mortified cheeks. "I am so very sorry, my lord. How dreadfully clumsy of me."

She pulled out her handkerchief and bent over Henry and began urgently wiping the staining liquid from his breeches. She was not about to let this opportunity pass. If she could reach his pocket . . .

The fabric was already thoroughly soaked, she noted to her chagrin. No matter how much she dabbed, her efforts were not helping stop the spreading stain.

Then she moved the handkerchief higher, padding near to his pocket, toward the juncture of his thighs, and Henry sucked in a sharp breath. With a jerky movement, he caught her hand, holding it away from his lap. "You best leave that to me, or I'll reveal certain personal secrets, my sweet." His eyes had gone very dark, full of fire and his voice held a strange huskiness. Just as it had in the dark a few nights ago. What did she expect? She'd been fondling his *loins*, for mercy sakes.

Amy dropped her soaking handkerchief as if it were on fire and jumped to her feet. "Please forgive me. I . . ."

"No harm done. I don't think I've ever enjoyed a soaking as much. Or the clean up."

It wasn't so much his words, as the way he said them, full of devilish wickedness.

Swallowing hard, Amy made a valiant effort to compose herself. "I'll of course pay for the trousers. The stain is unlikely to come out."

"Don't be ridiculous. It's not as if you did it on purpose."

Amy's pink face felt as if it turned an even brighter red. "Of course I didn't do it on purpose. Why on earth would I . . ."

The earring. Did he think she'd done it in order to grope his pockets? Blast. She *had* tried to take advantage of the opportunity.

"If you'll excuse me, I must change before supper is called." He made a polite bow and left her pondering just how much Lord Cravenswood new about the owner of the earring. If he knew, why was he playing games with her? She stood looking after his retreating back her mind a whirl.

Marcus made his way to her side. "Have you frightened Cravenswood off?"

"An accident of the liquid kind, I'm afraid."

He smiled down at her like a mischievous school boy. "I haven't seen you wearing the earrings I gifted you. You did say you loved them."

Amy had made Sabine and Caitlin promise not to share any details with their husbands, fearful it would get back to Henry, but Marcus's look was too knowing.

"I do love them, but they don't go with this dress."

Caitlin came to her rescue and soon Marcus drifted off to talk with Harlow.

"Nice work with the drink. I saw you getting intimate with Henry. Was the earring in his pocket?"

Caitlin's pronouncement made her face heat once more. "I . . . I couldn't tell."

Caitlin laughed. "But you found his family jewels, so to speak. Excellent start."

Amy's face turned scarlet at Caitlin's ripping and she wished this night would end.

*　　*　　*

Climbing the stairs, Henry gritted his teeth as he waited for his overheated pulse to cool. Since the night in his garden, the mystery lady, whom he now knew was Amy, figured prominently in his erotic dreams. His dreams consumed him, largely because he'd been unsexed, so to speak, for so long. His hiatus was well and truly over. He was rock hard and fit to burst from her simple touch.

To have Amy's slim fingers pressing against his cock, stroking him just as he'd imagined . . . Christ, it almost unmanned him.

There was no doubt Amy Shipton was a very desirable young woman. If her heart already belonged to another, he'd kick himself. All this time she'd lived just across the road. Harlow was right; since his brother's death and Millicent leaving, he'd become a eunuch.

Her enchanting smile, full of innocence, quick and bright as the sun, had brought a sharp hunger leaping forth in his body. He took great delight in teasing her. The moment she'd smiled up at him, his heart had suddenly started beating as if after a long sleep.

He had to get this yearning under control. He still didn't know her heart. Her beauty appealed to him. She looked very much like Millicent, except younger, more innocent and that worried him.

Was his physical attraction because of her similarity to Millie? While he never loved Millie, he certainly desired her greatly. Were his eyes fooling his heart into believing there was more to this girl? He really knew nothing about her.

Amy had luscious thick, black as a stormy night, tresses. Millicent's hair was very similar. It was far too easy to visualize exactly how it would look spread out over his white pillows. He knew how it would feel sliding over his bare skin—like silk.

Henry bounded up the stairs to his room, eager to change and get back to the intimate gathering.

*　　*　　*

Henry's dinner had not been to his liking. Oh, the food was excellent, but the company left a lot to be desired. He would definitely have a quiet word with Sabine. She'd seated him at the opposite end of the table from Amy. Worse, she'd seated Comte Le Page on Amy's right.

His frustration was still simmering by the time the men moved to rejoin the ladies after a few ports and cheroots. It shot to boiling when he noted Amy was not present.

He wanted to spend more time with her. He knew he affected her, for he watched the tiny pulse at the base of her neck jump when he was near. Of course, it could be her pulse jumped in fright. She might be expecting him to launch himself on her again, as he had in the garden.

What must she think of him? No wonder she was avoiding him.

"I believe Amy is in the conservatory, escaping from Comte

Le Page. Why don't you go and rescue her?"

He swung round at Caitlin's words.

He noted the Frenchman wasn't in the room. "Perhaps she'd be disappointed if I rescued her." He watched Caitlin's face carefully.

"Would that bother you?" she asked.

His jaw tightened and he clenched his fists.

"She'll be pleased to see you, I'll give you that," and she moved to join the other guests.

Pleased. What the hell did that mean? Amy had been avoiding him for the last few days. He'd never understand women.

He tried to stroll towards Marcus's conservatory but his body hummed with nervous energy and it was almost a run.

The door to the conservatory was ajar and heat and the smell of plants hit him when he entered. The perfume from some of the roses and colorful flowers was overpowering. Marcus's mother was a keen gardener and the large rectangle conservatory housed many exotic plants commissioned from all over the world. It was a mini jungle, and he swore as a leafy twig snapped back and hit him in the eye.

He could hear murmurs from deeper in the room. The moon was almost full and he needed no lighted candle to find his way.

He stepped around a large palm and stopped dead. There on the other side of the glass room was Amy. He couldn't see her face clearly in the dim light, but she was gesturing wildly and appeared to be in some distress. He was about to rush forward, thinking the damn Frenchman was accosting her, when the man with her suddenly pulled her into his arms and placed a tender kiss on her head. She didn't seem to struggle. In fact, she appeared to melt into his embrace.

Was this a clandestine affair?

*   *   *

"Why can't you get the earring?" Amy pleaded.

Lord Wolverstone faced Amy under the palms. Amy had met him on Sabine's badgering, hoping to talk him into snatching her earring back.

"I can hardly take it without him knowing. If I did he'd tear the house to pieces looking for it. He might even accuse one of my guests of stealing it."

Amy's eyes widened in alarm. "I can't have that. What if the story of how I lost it was to come out? I'd be ruined."

Lord Wolverstone didn't appear to understand the gravity of the situation.

"Not ruined. Cravenswood would offer for you of course. He'd never stand aside and see you ruined."

"That cannot happen."

Marcus's chuckle grated like boots on broken gravel. "I promise you'll enjoy being married to Henry."

Amy waved a hand in front of her face as she paced back and forward. This couldn't be happening. She couldn't be having this conversation with Marcus of all people.

He leaned closer and whispered, "I know what occurred in Henry's garden. So, I'm a little confused as to why you have not pressed your advantage. If Henry knew what he had done, you'd be betrothed by now."

"Exactly. Please listen to me. That cannot happen."

"Why on earth not? What's wrong with Cravenswood? Your father can hardly object now that he's the Earl."

Amy grabbed his arm when he made to turn away. She couldn't tell Marcus why she could not marry him. He was a lord who did not understand what it would be like married to a man who did not love her. Her father loved another, and her mother lived a lonely and pitied life, dying of a broken heart. That would not be her fate.

"I have my reasons and I expect you to adhere to my wishes.

He is not to know who the earring belongs to."

Marcus frowned. "That puts me in a very awkward situation."

Tears welled. "Please! Please don't tell him. You must help me get the earring back. You must!"

Strong arms muffled her anguished cries as he pulled her into his embrace.

"Shush, Amy. I'm sorry. I didn't realize you felt so strongly. I'll talk with Sabine. We will find a way to put this right."

*   *   *

Henry stepped back into the shadows and stifled a curse. The man who held Amy so intimately was Marcus. But why?

Questions flooded his mind. What the hell was going on? Why was Amy meeting with Marcus? He'd had enough of this tomfoolery.

He stayed hidden as Amy walked quickly past him, her scent teasing his nostrils and stroking his senses into painful awareness. Images of her lying beneath him in the lush garden flooded his brain. It took all his willpower not to grab for her as she glided past.

She stopped at the door looked tentatively up and down the corridor before slipping out. He waited for Marcus to follow. But the bugger left by the outside door, slipping out into the darkness like a ghost running from the dawn.

"You're not going to escape me that easily. You've got some questions to answer, my friend," Henry muttered into the darkness.

CHAPTER SEVEN

The race was exhilarating. The wind ripped her bonnet from her head and her hair now tumbled around her shoulders like a wanton. She'd never felt so free.

At breakfast, when Henry had challenged her to a race across the fields to the Roman City ruins, she'd eagerly agreed. She loved to ride.

She'd chosen to ride one of Marcus's prize geldings and he was big and strong. Toby was a tall chestnut with a big heart. He was sturdy and fast. Yet, she had expected Toby to be no competition for Henry's gray stallion, Hercules.

Amy looked over her shoulder, back at Henry. She sensed Henry was holding his mount back, purposely letting her win.

Her heart warmed. He looked handsome. His hair was also messy from the wind. The golden curls, rumpled and wind-blown, made him look—a thought flashed through her mind—as if he'd just rolled out of bed.

Banishing that thought, she found it hard to swallow, and it wasn't from the warm wind rushing into her mouth. He was beside her now and she soaked in his powerful thighs gripping his stead as he urged Hercules on. Her gaze continued travelling over him, across his shoulders and chest, down powerful arms to elegant hands gripping the reins. Magic hands.

"What prize to the winner?" he shouted.

She laughed into the wind. "I win, I chose. You win, you chose."

His wicked grin was instant. He gathered his stallion, kicked his heels, and bending low over his horse's head, he took off. That's why he'd been holding back. He'd been keeping his stallion fresh.

Her smile deepened. He would win, and with a thrill tingling her insides, she wondered what he'd ask for as his prize.

The huge Roman wall was no more than a few yards away and already Hercules had passed through the gap into the overgrown plain that contained the ruins. Henry swung his horse around to greet her with a triumphant smile.

She drew Toby up beside him. "That's not fair. You're horse is faster and stronger."

"You're not going to be a sore loser, are you?" He jumped from his mount and walked to help her dismount. "You didn't have to accept my challenge."

"True." She couldn't hold his gaze. She looked around nervously. They were alone. Unchaperoned. The towering ancient walls blocking them from the rest of the world.

He tethered their horses to the wall and then offered her his arm. "Do you know anything about the history of this place?"

She shook her head, struggling to concentrate on their surroundings. All she could smell and see was Henry.

"These walls supposedly used to enclose a Roman city." He pointed to the right. "An amphitheatre is just over there. Shall we explore?"

"It's strange to imagine people living here in a city hundreds of years ago. I wonder what will remain of our houses and lives in a thousand years from now."

At her words, Henry stopped and looked around him. "I hadn't really considered that much. I'm hoping my descendents don't let my estate run to wrack and disrepair like these ruins."

She moved into the centre of the tumbled stones. "It's funny to think that in the future, someone else could stand on this very spot and think about us as the past. As history." She paused and looked over the ruins. "Makes you want to ensure you live a happy life."

He frowned down at her. She hadn't notice how close he'd come. "Is your life not happy?"

She shrugged. "I'm not *unhappy*."

He brushed a strand of hair off her face. "You deserve a life full of happiness."

"You don't believe in duty, then. My mother told me a life was not about one's happiness. A life of privilege comes at a cost—duty."

He nodded. "I have only recently learned the real meaning of the word duty." He looked to the sky and back to her. "When Richard died."

She reached and put her hand on his arm. "I'm sorry. That was thoughtless of me. Of course you understand duty."

"Perfectly all right. I never expected to become the earl. Life was easier, more enjoyable, when everyone didn't look to me. Now I understand why Richard did crazy things to let off steam."

Amy remembered how Richard died, drowned swimming the Thames on a dare. "I hope you're never that stupid."

He simply smiled. "So what duties are you expected to perform?"

"Look pretty, smile at everyone, and marry to strengthen the bloodlines and coffers."

"That doesn't sound too onerous."

She nodded. "That is what everyone thinks, but sometimes I

feel like jumping into the Thames like your brother. If I have to smile and be pleasant to one more man whose only interest in me is my family connections and dowry . . ."

"I see."

She rounded on him and crossly said. "I very much doubt it. You have choices."

"Choices? What choices."

Her face heated and she sat down on a pile of stones deflated. She debated whether to tell him but he appeared genuinely interested. "Who and when you marry."

"Sometimes I'm not sure I do," he said softly.

That made her mouth fall open. Was he being pressured to marry? She thought of Richard's fiancée. Rumor was Henry would honor the engagement. So, was Millicent the woman he wished to marry and couldn't? She longed to ask him who his mystery woman was, but then he'd know it was her in the garden.

"Lord Wolverstone—Marcus, tells me your father is pushing you to accept Chesterton."

She nodded her head miserably. "I can't stand the man. His touch makes my skin crawl."

"Then the solution is simple. You'll have to find someone else. Surely there is some man who doesn't make your skin crawl," he asked with eyebrow raised.

Caution. "Perhaps." She craned her neck to gauge his expression but the sun shaded his face.

"What are you looking for in a husband?"

"I'm not sure this is a proper subject—"

He sat down beside her. "Even for friends? We are friends, are we not? You've lived next door to me all your life. Sabine did not raise any objections to an outing unescorted. She knows she can trust me."

But could she trust herself. She couldn't seem to breathe

when he looked at her with his green eyes sparkling in the sunlight. His lips beckoned. She wanted a taste as much as a young street urchin wanted sweetmeats.

In a husky voice she answered him. "I don't want much. I simply want a man who loves me." When he remained silent she said, "I know I'm supposed to think of family alliances, fortunes, and bloodlines, but I won't be left to live the rest of my life alone, unloved, while my husband finds joy with his other family." A tear slipped from her eye and Henry gently brushed it aside with his thumb.

Now he understood a little more about her. Henry knew of her father's second family, as did most of the *ton*. His heart softened realizing what it must be like to be the family the duke saw only as a means to do his duty.

"Is that why you released Marcus? You saw how he loved Sabine."

She nodded. "He would have been a good choice. Handsome, rich, and kind. A better choice than Creeperton."

At her wistful sigh, Henry's fist clenched as jealousy stabbed its way into his heart. Was she in love with his best friend?

"I too will only marry for love. Or at least a woman I believe I can grow to love. My parents had an arranged marriage too." He took her hand in his and ran his thumb over her palm, satisfaction flooding his limbs at her tremor. "I grew up in a large house but it definitely wasn't a home. I was not abused in any way but there was little love in my home. I don't want my children growing up in a cold, emotionless family."

Tears welled in her eyes at his words. He wanted to lighten her day, take away her pain.

He moved closer. "I'm going to claim my prize now."

For one tense moment, he held her gaze, and then he raised his hands to cup her face, as he tipped it up and brought his lips down on hers.

It was a gentle kiss.

A kiss that he hoped told her he wasn't about to pounce on her like the first time. A kiss meant to worship.

But Amy leaned into him, and with just one taste all his good intentions fled.

He took her lips, then her mouth, and before long he kissed her with the raging need he'd kept pent up for so long.

Ragged, desperate, aching need welled and poured through him, and into the kiss. He didn't stop to think. One step beyond control, edged with wildness he'd never felt before. Her lips were as ripe and luscious as he remembered. The soft cavern of her mouth made a delicious feast.

One he fully intended to gorge on.

To take his fill until his famine was quenched.

Without restraint.

And his body surged with triumph because she let him.

His lips moved on hers, steely and firm, so different than the night in his garden. Now, they were masterfully commanding, demanding in a way that sent hot thrills down Amy's spine.

His arm snaked around her, pulling her further into his embrace and she didn't fight it. His hand anchored her head so she was his to devour.

She should stop him, push him away, but her body wanted more. All she cared about was experiencing more, tasting more, feeling the same hot thrills she'd experienced in his garden.

Her lips parted, letting him fill her mouth, letting his tongue lay claim as he had once before. No other man had kissed her like this. He mastered her in a manner she found exciting, thrilling, and sensually stimulating.

The overwhelming physical sensations wreathed her mind and hazed her wits. She wanted more, all . . . For the second time in her existence desire stirred and roared to life.

She wanted . . . to kiss him back, to make him sweep her up

in a dizzying passion. She wanted him in whatever way would appease the hungry need inside.

Her hands had come to rest against his chest, and she had enough wits to slide them upwards to his shoulders, broad and hard, then farther into his nape, and the honey-colored curls. She let her fingers sink into the silky softness.

She played.

A thrill shot to her core. Her touch affected him, because he slanted his head and deepened the kiss, his tongue stroking hers in heated persuasion.

Unlike their previous fumbling in the dark, Amy grew emboldened. She hesitantly kissed him back—tentative, unsure of anything except of her need for more.

His response momentarily frightened her. A storm of passionate desire raced through him and into her, almost as if he were pouring his soul into their kiss.

The power, the hunger—the raw need she sensed behind it—should have shocked her, but instead she embraced it. Clinging to him with abandon.

Her tongue tangled with his, exploring, tempting her further into sin.

Through the kiss, through the hard pressed lips, and the warm hands that held her tight against his unyielding body, she sensed a primitive male satisfaction. He was pleased with her acquiescence. Pleased she had responded to his touch.

She was falling and soon would not be able to stop. She detected heat, welling pleasure, and the addictive power of his touch. He called to her at some feminine level she'd never broached before. And for a moment she was scared she'd lose herself in him. *That mustn't happen!*

She broke the kiss on a soft cry. Stared, stunned into his passion filled eyes. The green so dark it was almost black. Desire stared back. His desire.

She wrenched out of his arms and tried to stand but her legs were weak. She gripped his shoulders for support.

He whispered, "I'd race every day in order to receive that prize."

She quickly looked away from his knowing gaze. Flustered. "Perhaps I should talk to Sabine about how trustworthy you are."

He laughed out loud, merriment and something akin to male pride dancing in his eyes.

He left her to compose herself while he fetched their horses.

His hands lingered slightly too long as he helped her mount. "Care for another race tomorrow?"

She edged Toby clear and gathered the reins. Before she galloped off she gave one parting shot. "Perhaps I'll ask the Comte to race me tomorrow."

The smile immediately disappeared from Henry's face and with a very feminine chuckle she urged Toby forward. That will teach him for being smug.

She tried not to think about the kiss on the long ride home. What she did think upon was the fact that her earring wasn't in Henry's pockets today. While he'd ravished her mouth, her nimble fingers had checked.

She'd talk to Marcus tonight. Time was running out. He had to obtain the earring for her.

If Henry was interested in courting her, she'd let him but with the risk of being completely compromised still hanging over her head, she'd not relax until the earring in was her possession. Or she knew Henry's heart.

He kissed her as if he couldn't live without her, but he was a rake. Didn't they all kiss like that? She wished she had more experience. Perhaps she should kiss the Comte to test her theory.

Frustration at her circumstances dimmed. Surely if Henry could kiss her like that, perhaps his heart didn't belong to another.

Tonight she would not let Marcus slip away until he confessed all. If Henry had a mistress she damn well wanted to know. Marcus would have to overcome his sensibilities and tell her the truth. She would not let the fact a young unmarried woman was not supposed to know about such things stop her investigation. If anyone knew Henry's heart, it would be his best friend. What did Marcus not wish her to know?

*   *   *

Marcus's weary body simply wanted its bed. He'd been busy all evening avoiding both Amy and Henry. This match making business was exhausting.

He desperately wanted to join Sabine in their cozy bed, especially since he imagined the erotic welcome he'd find there. Ever since she'd learned she was increasing, she'd not been able to keep her hands off him.

His heart swelled in his chest and he couldn't believe how happy he was. Life was extremely good and he wanted Henry to have the same.

Sabine was with child. He didn't even care if it was a boy or a girl. As long as wife and child were healthy, that's all that mattered. He'd tried to wrap Sabine up in cotton wool when she gave him the news. If anything happened to her, or the baby . . . His body chilled as it always did. The thought of losing her again—permanently. His life would be over.

So he bit back an impolite, devilish curse, when one of his servants handed him a missive. If it was from Henry or Amy he'd throw it in the fire. He'd tell Sabine she was right and bloody well steal the earring and expose the two of them himself.

But it wasn't from either of them. It was from his head groom, Johnson. A problem with Orsini Rose, his prize breeding mare. He briefly glanced with longing at the stairs. Sabine would have to wait a few more minutes. He smiled to himself as he exited the house and made for the stables. It would make for a very demanding welcome on his return.

But when he entered the stable it wasn't Johnson waiting for him. Just as well, or he'd have torn the groom's head off for allowing himself to be used in this set up. Amy sat waiting on a straw bale in her nightdress and robe, a very determined look upon her face.

*   *   *

An hour after the company had retired for the night, Henry halted at the bottom of the central stairs. Where in Hades was Marcus? Marcus said they'd talk when his guests retired. So where was he?

Henry had searched all the public rooms of the house, checking every last reception room, inadvertently trapping himself for a few moments with Lydia. She'd once more tried seduction, overconfident, very aware of her charms. Charms she'd clearly intended to use to seduce him.

Dragging in a breath—shackling his temper, suppressing his emotions so he could think—he finally thought to look outside. He remembered Orsini rose, Marcus's wedding gift to Sabine, was in foal and it was near her due date. Perhaps Marcus was at the stables.

Marcus knew he wanted to talk with him. He wanted his friend's advice. Marcus seemed to have Amy's trust. Did Marcus or Sabine know if Amy was in love? And if so, with whom?

He heaved a resigned sigh, and headed straight out of the house.

Descending the front steps, he turned and made his way across the cobblestones. As he neared the stables, voices drifted out to him on the breeze. He stopped dead in his tracks. One was Amy's. The other masculine voice was Marcus's.

He immediately flattened against the stable wall, inching his way toward the doors, desperately straining to hear what they were saying.

He couldn't make out the sentences but he heard snippets of words—"Please . . ." "Mistress . . ." Marcus cursing. The next thing the stable door flew back and Amy, dressed in her night clothes ran passed him, close enough for Henry to smell her unique scent.

Before he could even gather his wits, a voice came out of the shadows from the corner of the yard. "Well, well. Who would have thought it of young *Lady* Amy? Marcus, I can perfectly understand. Quite pleased I didn't offer for the chit. Marcus, lucky bastard. Up to his old tricks again. Didn't take him long. He never was satisfied with only one woman."

The essence of the vile words spewing like deadly sulphur from Chesterton's mouth finally penetrated Henry's brain. A basic, primitive, rage engulfed him.

"You will apologies for that slanderous statement or by God I'll shove my fist so far down your throat, you'll be talking out of your arse."

Chesterton sneered and blew the smoke from his cheroot in Henry's face. "It's hardly slanderous when it's true. You saw. She was in her night clothes. Plus, I heard him offering to make Amy his mistress."

Henry grabbed Chesterton by the lapels. "You lie. Marcus would never"-

"Never what? Goodness, Henry what on earth are you doing?"

He released Chesterton and sent him a warning look that said *say one word and I'll kill you*. He spun towards the woman who'd arrived unnoticed to stand behind them—Sabine.

He gave Sabine one of his saintly smiles. "Marcus would never endanger his horses just to win a race."

Chesterton added under his breath. "Marcus would ride anything."

Henry dug his elbow viciously into Chesterton's ribs.

"I concur. If any of his horses, were even remotely favoring a leg, he'd pull them from a race."

Sabine frowned. "I didn't think any races were coming up."

Chesterton stepped into the light. "I'm thinking of challenging his stallion Zeus to a race to Silchester and back. I'm positive my horse can win."

Sabine shook her head as she moved toward the entrance to the stables. "I doubt it. Not unless you have an advantage I know nothing about. No horse can beat Zeus." And she bade them goodnight and disappeared inside the large open doors.

"I have an advantage all right," Chesterton muttered under his breath. "I'll tell his wife who he's been riding if he doesn't let me win."

Henry swung round. "One word of what you witnessed tonight and I'll call you out."

Chesterton's smile deepened. "So, I'm only one of many enchanted by Amy's charms." With an evil chuckle Chesterton sauntered towards the house. "I hope your intentions are more honorable than your friend's, although I wouldn't take seconds if I were you."

Henry stood in the dark breathing heavily. Sick to his stomach. It must be a mistake. Marcus would not ruin an innocent. Never. He glanced toward the stable where Sabine had recently entered and realized he'd have to wait until morning to discuss the situation with Marcus. Now more than ever he'd have to offer for Amy. Chesterton had seen her with Marcus. She was ruined even if it was all a misunderstanding.

A little niggle at the back of his brain voiced what he feared to consider—it was just a misunderstanding, wasn't it?

CHAPTER EIGHT

Henry stood outside Garrard's debating whether to go in. Marcus had lied to his face about being in the stable with Amy last night, and Henry couldn't help the terrible thoughts swirling in his head.

He hadn't revealed to Marcus that Chesterton had seen them together too. There were just too many questions unanswered.

Instead, Marcus had suggested he take Amy for a drive. Marcus kept pushing the two of them together, why? Marcus knew he was searching for his mystery lady. Marcus didn't know that Henry knew who that lady was.

Did Marcus know it was Amy? If so, why play these games? Marcus had sworn he didn't recognize the earring.

Marcus's fixation on the virtues of Lady Amy Shipton bordered on obsessive. Could a man be in love with two women at the same time? Marcus was hiding something and Henry didn't like the implications of what that could be. He'd slipped back to London in the early hours of the morning on the excuse of an important estate matter.

When he'd first shown Harlow and Marcus the earring, Harlow said the earring looked like Garrard's work, his suspicions resurfaced. He wanted an answer, but at the same time dreaded it.

Marcus only ever bought jewellery from Garrard's, who were renowned for quality gems. So here he was on Garrard's doorstep far too early in the morning. His gut told him to enter and prove his disloyal thoughts false. More shame on him. He'd welcome the shame. Wanted to be proved wrong.

For if he was right, there could be only one reason Marcus did not want Henry to know the earrings were a gift from him.

He'd already asked in Garrard's once before, but they'd denied the earring was their work. He surmised that Marcus was such a good customer they could have protected his privacy if he'd demanded it of them.

His heart felt heavy in his chest. He could be doing his best friend a huge disservice by seeking the truth. But *his* future happiness was at stake.

With grim determination Henry entered the exclusive store. He presented his card and was soon being fawned over. However, as luck would have it, it was not the same man who he'd question previously.

"I'm looking for a pair of earrings for my mistress. Something that screams money. I'm not in her good books at present." *Best not to ask about emerald earrings immediately.*

"Certainly, my lord. Do you have a stone in mind? Diamonds, sapphires . . ." the jeweller asked eyes speculating the amount he'd make today.

"Something large and expensive looking is the requirement."

"Quite. Perhaps a pair of oval cushion sapphires with diamonds set in white gold."

Here was his opening. "They are beautiful. Her eyes are

green. Would emeralds be preferable?"

"Very observant, your lordship. We can make whatever design you wish."

"I have no idea what she'd like."

Here it comes . . .

"If you don't mind me asking, sir, has she admired any other woman's jewels of late?"

He pretended to think. "I don't really pay that much attention." He paused and stroked his chin. "However, I did hear her and some of her friends gushing over a pair of earrings Lady Shipton was wearing at the opera the other night. I couldn't even begin to describe them though."

The man beamed. "No need. I know the exact pair. I designed them especially for the young lady."

"A present for her come out no doubt. From her father."

The man leaned in conspiratorially. "Oh no. They were commissioned by the Marquis of Wolverstone."

"No doubt before he married. There was a rumor the Marquis was thinking of offering for the young lady."

The man was busy sketching a picture of the very earring burning hot as hell in Henry's pocket. "No. I was commissioned to design them recently."

A cold fury engulfed him. Why would Marcus give Amy Shipton a pair of earrings and not want him or anyone to know? Not just anyone, him, Henry St. Giles, his best friend. He'd showed Marcus the earring and yet his friend denied knowing the identity. Why? What game was Marcus playing?

For surely it was a game. He could not possibly be unfaithful to the wife he adored and worshiped. Nor would Marcus risk Amy's reputation.

Would he?

Prior to Sabine's return, Marcus was known to be cold and ruthless when it came to women. Sabine ripped his heart to shreds and he'd gone a little crazy when she'd left. He fortified his heart and proceeded to never get romantically involved. He loved and left and broken many a woman's heart in the process with little care.

The image of Amy in Marcus's arms stirred in his gut. At first he was prepared to give Marcus the doubt. Obviously Amy had been upset about something, but Marcus blatantly lied to his face. Told him he'd not seen Amy that evening.

And he'd lied about the earring.

His heart heavy with painful doubts about the honor and integrity of his friend, he walked out of the store.

He owed it to his friend to give him the benefit of doubt. He ordered his coach back to Cravenswood Court. He needed to get back to the house party in Berkshire and speak with Marcus.

*   *   *

His chat with Marcus was delayed when, upon his return, he learned the hosts and their guests had driven to Reading for a day of shopping and museums.

It was nearing dusk and Henry was impatient for Marcus's return. He lurked near the stables and was feeding Hercules a carrot when he heard feminine voices over the tall hedge at the side of the stables.

He sauntered nearer, boredom driving his ill-mannered eavesdropping. He couldn't see into the garden as the hedge was well above his head, but to his surprise and good fortune, he recognized one of the voices—Amy. Although what he heard made his blood run cold.

"Lorraine, I can't . . . I can't risk it."

"But he's so incredibly handsome. I'd risk anything for a night in his arms. *Any*-thing!"

"That's because you're my ladies maid and as such you don't

have Society's expectations on your shoulders. The consequences should I be caught would be very high. You know what will happen to my reputation. I couldn't bear that." Henry could almost feel her shudder from where he was hiding behind the hedge.

"But don't you wish you could have one perfect night with the man you loved before you buckle under and do your duty? One night to cherish forever, before you sell yourself for duty and elevated social position."

He heard Amy give a small sob. "I don't think I can do my duty. The thought of a loveless life is too horrific to contemplate." The silence spoke volumes, her distress palpable.

"Then why not go to him?"

"Because I can't marry him," Amy cried. "He loves another."

"Then I'd stop drawing these indecent sketches. If anyone finds them they'll think the worst anyway. He's naked. *Completely naked.*"

Amy sighed. "That's simply my imagination. I've only ever seen him with his shirt off."

"Oh la la, you have a very vivid imagination. If anyone else sees these," he heard paper rustle, "they won't believe it's your imagination, my girl."

More shuffling of paper and the rustle of items being collected. He heard them as they began to move away toward the house.

"Then they shall remain hidden in my room, away from prying eyes. You can forget . . ."

Blast, he couldn't hear more. Henry stumbled back, the hard stones of the stable wall merging with his body to form a fortress around his heart. Amy was in love—with Marcus. It could only be Marcus. *'I can't marry him.'* True Marcus was already married. *'He's in love with another.'* There was no doubt Marcus loved Sabine. Or did he? From what he'd seen last night Marcus wasn't exactly discouraging Amy.

If he recalled, last year it was Amy who rejected Marcus.

Perhaps Marcus would have preferred to marry Amy, given she was the duke's daughter. He could have kept Sabine as his mistress and enjoyed both women.

Anger flickered and erupted deep in his soul. He didn't blame Amy. Very few women could resist Marcus's charm. He'd watched him in action hundreds of times.

Right now he wished he had something to hit. Marcus's face would do nicely. He clenched his fists tight. Their chat was long overdue . . . If not for Sabine he'd call Marcus out.

There was only one thing he could do. Marry Amy and ensure Sabine never learned of her husband's betrayal. She'd been through enough already.

His heart felt heavy in his chest and his soul frozen with disappointment. Dreams of being happily married dissolved. But by Jove once they married he'd forbid Amy to ever see Marcus or Sabine again.

But first he had to destroy the evidence. Those sketches could never see the light of day. It would devastate Sabine, and after everything she'd been through she deserved better.

*   *   *

Henry took a deep breath before entering the drawing room and joining the guests before dinner. His eye immediately found Amy deep in conversation with Caitlin. He scanned the room and found Marcus on his own at the sideboard pouring himself a brandy. He crossed to his side.

"A word with you if I may."

"Only one? How unlike you, Henry. What have I done now? You're wearing your saintly frown."

Henry bit back his annoyance at Marcus's comment. Right now he felt anything but saintly. He wanted to smash his curled fist into Marcus's smug face.

"What the hell are you up to?" he said through clenched teeth.

"I'm pouring myself a brandy. Shall I pour one for you? You sound as though you need one. Was the estate business worse than predicted?"

He looked around the room. No one appeared to be paying them any attention. "I know what you're up to. I saw you."

Marcus handed him a glass of brandy and frowned, "I don't follow, old chap."

"You were in the stable the other night. With Amy."

A slow, smirk of a smile shaped Marcus's lips. "How do you know that?"

Henry took a step back. He'd walked right into that. "I was looking for *you*."

He chortled. "You didn't find me."

Henry clenched his fist around his glass. *Don't let him make you lose your temper.* "I know that. Odd time of night to be meeting a young lady in your stables. In her nightdress . . ."

"Oh, that. She'd had a missive from her father that she begged my help with. You know my father and hers were close."

"And she had to discuss it with *you*? Alone? In the stable? So late at night?"

"I've been advising her."

I bet you have, bastard. "About what?"

"I'm not sure I can share her confidences."

"I wonder what Sabine would think about you sharing—*confidences*—with Amy."

Marcus's countenance abruptly changed. The glass banged down on the side board. "What the bloody hell does that mean? It better not mean what I think you're implying or I'll knock your teeth down your saintly throat."

"Why so defensive? Do you have something to hide? I saw her in your arms a few nights ago too."

Marcus looked over his shoulder. "I was comforting her. Her father is forcing a match with Chesterton, whom she hates. I suggested she work on the Comte." He nodded his head in a direction over his shoulder. Amy was smiling gaily at the Frenchman. Henry wanted to knock *his* teeth down *his* throat too.

"Whatever is wrong with you? How could you imply . . ."

"Don't make light of this. I know you gave her the earrings."

Marcus's gaze turned to cold fury. "As a gift for helping aid Sabine."

That held the ring of truth. Doubt crept in again. Then he steeled himself. "I heard her talking this afternoon. Amy's seen you with your shirt off. Explain how an innocent young lady of quality has seen you in a state of undress," Henry hissed through clenched teeth.

Before Marcus could respond, Sabine arrived at his side. "What are you two scoundrels up to? Marcus, have you been teasing Henry again? He looks as if he'd like to snap you in half."

Marcus flashed a warning glance at him. "Henry was being a bore. It would appear he's let the green-eyed monster ruin his evening."

The fact that Sabine automatically looked at Amy silenced Henry. What had Marcus told her? "Stop pouting, Henry." She slipped her arm through his and led him across the room to where Amy sat engrossed in her Comte. "Amy is going to play for us tonight. Would you like to turn the music for her?"

Henry couldn't face her. He couldn't sit and converse with a woman who was playing her supposed friend false. Worse, Sabine didn't deserve this. From either of them. If she learned of their betrayal, after everything she'd been through and survived, it would destroy her.

Henry thought about the sketches. "I'd be honored, but I'm feeling a bit under the weather tonight. My ride to London has left me with a terrible head. Would you think it rude if I retired for the evening?"

Annoyingly, Amy looked relieved. "If you're unwell, of course you're excused."

Sabine concurred and quickly arranged for the Comte to help Amy with her music. Henry was quickly forgotten as Sabine organized Amy's recital, and with purposeful intent he quietly exited the drawing room and made his way upstairs.

Now all he had to do was find Amy's room and confiscate the drawings before they fell into the wrong hands. Then he'd show Marcus his evidence and make him see sense. She could already be with child.

He did know what he'd have to do. He'd offer for her. He would not let Sabine's or Amy's plight become public. It would hurt too many people.

It didn't take him long to reach Amy's room. Sabine, or was it Caitlin, made sure he knew where Amy's room was the minute he'd arrived for the house party.

With a fervative look up and down the corridor, Henry placed an ear to her door, checking the room was empty before letting himself in. Upon entry he stilled, assailed with emotions. He was immediately arrested by the feminine sights and smells. Luckily Amy's maid had left one candle burning. It was enough light to allow him to search with ease.

To the left stood the bed, a large four-poster that required small steps to ascend. The sheer curtains were untied, ready for their mistress to slink into the bed and slumber.

He breathed deep. Under the window was her writing desk, and next to that stood a low dresser with an oval mirror. A vase of white lilies, their scent perfuming the air, reminded him of her. Her skin carried the same perfume.

Desire clenched his gut. Memories of the way Amy's body molded to his, how he'd breathed her in, set his body on edge.

Even knowing the way she'd behaved with his friend, and that she loved another, he still reacted to her allure. *No wonder Marcus could not resist her.*

Cursing himself, he quickly closed the door behind him, crushing his response under a wave of righteous anger. He didn't have much time to find the drawings. If anyone found him in Amy's room—quite frankly the problem would be solved. He'd be forced to marry her and this mess could be put to bed.

However, while his body wanted her more than any other woman he'd ever known, his heart balked at marrying a woman in love with another. A woman who could behave so dishonorably.

CHAPTER NINE

God damn it to hell. It should be simple enough to find drawings. He'd searched her writing table. While it contained paper it certainly didn't contain any drawings, especially not of an intimate nature.

He searched her luggage but the cases were empty. He'd even entered her dressing room and rummage through her under garments and other clothes.

Stifling a sigh he calmed his impatience. He still had time. *Think!* Where would a young lady hide incriminating evidence of an affair?

He stood in the middle of her bedchamber and drunk in the essence of Amy. The room was as neat as one of Prince Regent's hedge rows. Nothing was out of place. He recognized this trait in Amy. Her appearance was immaculate. The picture of the perfect duke's daughter.

How she had them all fooled.

He cocked his head to one side and considered the only piece of furniture he'd not yet searched. Her bed.

He picked up the lighted candle from the dresser and moved

closer. He put it on the side table next to the bed. Something caught his eye. A piece of bed linen hanging down. The rest of the linen was tucked under the mattress with almost military procession. Why was this piece loose?

Pushing the curtain aside he sat on the edge of the bed and lay back, propped on her pillows. His arm hung down the side of the mattress. It hung in exactly the same location as the stray linen. With certainty his hand slipped under the mattress and his fingers gripped paper.

Success.

With trepidation he pulled Amy's private etchings into the light. His muscles tightened, he had to force himself to look. Almost with one eye closed he drew the first image closer.

"Bloody hell." He caught his breath—every muscle he possessed froze. His mouth dried as he realized what, or more importantly, who, he was staring at. He sat up. His wits had brutally focused.

They were images of a naked man.

The man was very clearly him.

He began to leaf through her work. His body hummed with shock and then amusement and then with blinding desire.

Amy had talent. The images were intricately drawn. The lines and shading making the images come alive.

The drawings were very erotic. The erotica of an innocent. He could see the naivety in the hesitant charcoal lines. His manhood was drawn sometimes flaccid and sometimes erect, not quite anatomically correct and somewhat blurred, the outlines smudged as if she were embarrassed.

He flushed with heat as he gazed upon himself through her eyes. She'd made him look like a Greek God. The knowledge shook him.

He marvelled at what he looked like through her eyes. Pure unbridled masculinity. Pure beauty. Pure sex.

He lay back and closed his eyes on a groan. Marcus knew. Marcus knew Amy's heart. He'd been playing a game all along. He could throttle his friend for what he'd put him through these past few days.

Henry almost laughed out loud. The bloody bastard had known all along. Marcus and his challenge. A bloody dangerous game as it turned out because, not only had Henry thought the worst of his friend, but Chesterton also misunderstood what he witnessed last night. Amy's reputation was in tatters.

Anger quickly replaced his humor. How could Marcus have been so stupid as to risk Amy's reputation? It may be a game to Marcus, but this was his future wife.

His breath caught. Wife. This week, he was quickly noticing her sense of adventure and her keen mind. And now he knew categorically that she was as loyal a friend as he'd initially believed, more than ever he wanted Amy as his countess. Yet, for some reason Amy didn't appear to be seeking the match. Why didn't she come to him for help? Why was she keeping the fact he'd almost made love to her in his garden a secret?

He looked down at her sketches.

Why?

These clearly were drawn in admiration, even perhaps lust. She'd even drawn a picture of him pleasuring himself. But the drawings gradually changed. As he continued to leaf through a woman joined him in the pictures. The couple were always entwined. The man always on top of her. He smiled. He would love teaching her many varied and pleasurable positions. The woman in the drawings looked very much like Amy.

Henry hoped she didn't think his intentions were dishonorable. He wondered what she did hope for.

Deep in thought, his first warning of approaching danger was the door opening. He'd been engrossed in his own vanity for too long. He lay as still as a statue, hoping she did not see him through the diaphanous curtains hanging around the bed.

Her maid entered behind Amy.

"Help me off with my gown will you, Lorraine, and then you can find Smitters. I can manage the rest myself."

Henry frowned. Smitters was his valet.

"If you want me to, I'll withhold my favors until Smitters tells us where the earring is." Lorraine's voice was full of teasing.

"Don't bring Smitters into this. He'll get into trouble. That wouldn't be fair." Amy began to take her hair down. Long sable tresses fell about her shoulders like a shawl of black silk.

Without conscious direction he raised his arm reaching across the bed, almost pushing the curtain aside, wanting to touch the silky softness. He quickly pulled back.

Lorraine worked steadily, and soon Amy stood before the looking glass in nothing but her transparent shift. Henry had been rock hard the minute she stepped out of her dress, her milky skin, beautiful in the dim light.

His heart thundered in his ears. It was a wonder neither woman heard it.

Lorraine departed, leaving Amy sitting at her dresser, brushing her hair, lost in thought.

He lay there on her bed, soaking in the beauty of the woman before him. She would become his wife. Her life would meld with his just as surely as her body would tonight. For once he claimed her there would be no turning back. She would be his.

And only his.

The knowledge shook him. The profound truth that he loved her soaked into his blood like a virulent fever.

Amy slowly lowered the brush to the dresser and stood. She glanced over her shoulder to the bed. Her night gown lay at the end of the bed, half concealed, as he was, by the curtains.

Facing the mirror once more, she slowly slipped the strap of her shift off one shoulder.

Henry stilled, barely breathing in case she sensed him and stopped. He was desperate to feast on the secrets of her body.

She slipped the second strap from her other shoulder and the shift fell to her waist. In the mirror, he saw her firm breasts, pert and plump. His mouth watered. He closed his eyes on a silent groan when Amy stared at herself in the mirror and then cupped her breasts, running her thumbs over her dusty rose nipples until they tightened into hardened buds.

Heat consumed him. The delights of her body were succulently displayed. His eyes flew open, scared he'd miss any inch of her.

When she ran her hands down her sides to where the shift was caught on her lower curves, he prayed she would not stop. He wasn't disappointed. Amy pushed the material down over her curvaceous hips until it slid silently to pool on the floor around her feet.

Her derriere, plump and firm, could drive a man wild. Her long legs evoked dreams of the pleasure he would find when they wrapped around him.

He clenched his jaw to stifle his gasp. Amy was a real-life fantasy. Her hand moved to span her flat stomach before erotically sliding lower to rest in the silky black curls between her thighs.

Excitement sped through him like a drug at the thought of watching her take her pleasure, but on a sigh she turned away from the mirror and reached for her night-rail.

A primitive need saw his hand grab the night-rail first. Amy tugged, but he would not release it. Instead he scooted to the end of the bed, parted the curtain and said, "Leave it."

Amy's eyes widened in shock. She stood naked before the man who owned her heart. His eyes, dark, burning, focused totally on her, his hunger and need for her clearly visible.

Warmth infused every inch of her as she realized Henry was looking at her exactly how Marcus, in unguarded moments, looked at Sabine. With a ferocious hunger.

She didn't even bother to question why he was here. She simply didn't care.

She dropped the night-rail and straightened. Her skin tingled with excitement and a hint of apprehension. He leapt from the bed like a prowling lion, his hair a burned gold in the candlelight.

He reached for her; palm curving about her jaw, he tipped up her face, drew her close. He studied her eyes—as if searching for a truth. She didn't even contemplate hiding herself from him.

"You know you're mine. Since that night in the garden you've belonged to me."

Her gaze focused on his lips. She watched, mesmerized, as he drew in another breath. Opened his lips to speak again—

She stretched up, drew his head down, brought her lips close to his—murmured, "I've always been yours."

He covered her lips with his, kissing her voraciously, all consuming. Hands splaying, sliding over her bare skin like a whispered caress. Reverent. Worshipping. Claiming . . .

He closed his arms about her, pulling her close, molding her to him. Any chance of stopping him died the instant she'd set eyes upon his face, on all he said in just one hot, burning gaze.

Naked in his arms, she clung, and returned his kisses greedily, avidly—flagrantly encouraged him to seize, take, and claim.

Halting, he asked, his voice a husky promise, "The drawings . . . Who is it you fantasize over? Is it me?"

She nodded mutely.

On a groan, he lifted her and turned with her in his arms to face the bed. He let her down, sliding her body down his, his hands cupping her bottom, pressing her to him, molding her softness against his erection while his tongue plundered her mouth, leaving her a mass of aching need. Heat bloomed and fire took hold—she wanted more.

This time, she wanted it all.

She reluctantly eased back from his kiss. "I want to see you. See if you're all I imagined," she added breathlessly.

With eager hands she pushed his coat wide, trapping his arms. With a curse, he let her go, stepped back, wrenched off his coat, and flung it aside.

Her eyes widened at the violence behind the movement. He stilled. "I'd never hurt you. You do know that?"

In answer she stepped back into his embrace, her lips brazenly seeking his, her hand covering his heart. She knew the man he was. Gentle, giving, kind—loving. Loving was why she found him so attractive, why he and only he would do for her.

That revelation was simply there, its truth resonant and clear. She loved Henry to the depth of her soul. He loved her back. His actions here tonight proved it, for he would never do anything dishonourable. He would never knowingly ruin her. He knew that by kissing her, by claiming her, he was locking his life to hers.

The astonishment of that fact almost overwhelmed her. She forgot all about the mysterious Millicent, about the fact he might want another. All she saw, felt, and heard was that he wanted her—now!

And she wanted him—now!

Amy acted on it, yanking the halves of his waistcoat apart, stretching to slip it from his board shoulders. Impatiently he pulled his shirt over his head, and finally she had her hands on hot, rough, skin. She ran her fingers over his chest and stomach, the muscles beneath rigid and locked. His chest was a wonder of rough hairs the color of a lion's mane. She leaned into him and licked. He tasted divine, addictive.

He once more plundered her mouth, his hands closing

about, and then provocatively kneading the globes of her bottom. The long muscles framing his back flexed like steel beneath her wandering hands. She ran her fingers down his back, counting the ribs as she traced the muscles leading her down his sides and back to his waist, to caress the rippling bands across his abdomen. They flickered at each touch.

Gaining courage, her fingers quested lower. He sucked in a breath and held it as she lightly traced the prominent line of his erection. He stilled, his lips on hers, his tongue in her mouth, when she reached for the buttons at the waistband of his breeches. As she undid the first button, he groaned into her mouth. Thrilled at her newfound power, Amy hurriedly undid the rest and slid one hand inside the opened flap, and found the rigid length of him. Hot with skin so very soft and smooth . . .

He was under her spell, entirely focused on her hand and what she was doing. Her fingers explored freely, and learned the size and shape of him. He was solid, larger than she imagined. He more than filled her hand. Growing bolder, she closed her fingers around him, circling him, and this time his groan was accompanied by a shudder.

She knew she was playing with fire, but she took her time, fondling his sac, wonder blooming as it tightened in her hand. She could feel the surge of heated passion rising through him, provoked by her play, and it rose in her body in kind. She throbbed and grew damp between her thighs.

His mouth finally left hers, but he didn't stop her games. He truly was a saint because he let her play. She could see the tension in his neck, the cords tight as a bow.

Henry clenched his jaw and endured her touch, when all he wanted was to throw her on the bed and sink into the heaven he knew he'd find there. He wanted to bury himself so deep and let her wrap those gazelle-like legs around him.

Though she was innocent, her touch was pure heaven, her

instincts sound. He watched the wonderment in her smile and another surge of heat, of pure unadulterated desire rose, hardening and lengthening the part of his anatomy that was currently the determined focus of her being. He didn't know how much longer he could hold himself in check.

Not long, as it turned out. He made the mistake of looking down as she sent her thumb stroking over the aching head of his shaft and found a latent drop. She looked deep into his eyes, brought her thumb to her lips, and tasted, murmuring approval.

Control slipped. He caught his breath, nudged her face up and found her lips again, drew her into a drugging kiss, and ruthlessly, deliberately, took over. He didn't hold back. He seized and devoured, claiming her mouth, her lips, with a promise of what else he'd claim this night.

He would dictate the pace. He impatiently drew her hand away and efficiently divested himself of the rest of his clothes.

He looked magnificent. A Greek God come to life. She took in the sight, drank in the glory.

He drew her close, then closer until there was not even air between them. Silken skin caressing his chest, her arms, his erection, cradled in her softness, while he plundered her mouth, holding her and her senses captive.

Amy tried to move closer. She wanted him more than she'd wanted anything in her life. Far from resisting, she sank into his arms, gave herself up to his commanding kiss, surrendered and waited, nerves tight with anticipation, for him to make her his.

Without breaking their kiss, he lifted her and climbed onto the bed. The sheer curtains closed behind him, enveloping them in their own world.

They were on their knees facing each other and Amy let out a cry of disappointment when his lips left hers, only to moan in relief as his mouth found one tight, furled nipple.

His hot mouth suckled and savoured. Her head fell back; her

gasp shivered through the room. He feasted like a starving man. He laved her breasts, suckled, nipped—sending arrows of heat to her core. His hot mouth gave such pleasure she prayed he never stopped. Her hands closed on his skull, holding him to her; she was never letting go. His mouth was heaven on her flesh.

She rode the waves of delight he evoked. His hands roamed her curves while his mouth devoured her breasts. A wild wantonness erupted within and she reached for him. She gloried in the feel of his hard body, the evidence of his desire never more real. Amy gave stroked his cock once, and he growled deep in his chest. He urged her back on the bed and she went willingly. Her skin was flaming, her body melting, all her senses heightened and in scattered disarray. He followed her down, one knee rising and pushing between hers, parting her thighs, exposing the musky scent of her arousal to the room.

Amy was momentarily embarrassed when his muscled thigh, raspy with masculine hair, rode against her dampness, but his groan of admiration saw her glory in wanton incitement. He deliberately shifted, pressing against the most sensitive spot, knowingly winding her tight . . . Her breath tangled in her throat.

She traced the rock-hard muscles in his arms as he braced himself over her, his other knee joining the first, pushing her legs apart, spreading her thighs so he could settle between them.

Their eyes locked and silently communicated. He looked down her bare torso to where their bodies would join and the set of his face told her all she needed to know. The angles and planes of his handsome face were sharp with desire. There was an elemental rawness of conquering male, and it thrilled her. She cupped his face and nodded. She was putting herself into hands, into his body, into his heart.

He lowered his head to place a gentle kiss on her lips as he shifted between her thighs. The hardness she'd been caressing probed her slick entranced and she tried to relax, tried to memorize her first taste of his broad, blunt head and its inherent strength and heat as he inched slowly within her.

"Relax, my darling. Breathe slowly. I promise I'll try and make it as painless as I can."

He flexed his hips and pressed further in. She felt every inch of his hardness, stretching and filling her. He reversed direction and she let out the breath she'd been holding.

"I know it will hurt the first time. Why not just get it over with?" she said through gritted teeth.

He pressed back in, a little way further this time. "It doesn't have to hurt. Patience."

He repeated the process several times, each entry just that little bit further. Each short stroke enough to tantalize, to drive her insane. She moaned his name.

He covered her lips, took her mouth, adding to her screaming senses. She was combusting from the inside. Soon she was lifting her hips, writhing on the bed, urging him for more, her body aching, wanting . . .

He continued teasing her, only just entering her and then withdrawing, until she was wet and open and almost delirious with desire. Moving in a rhythm that was as ancient as time.

She lifted her head and found his lips. He took her mouth, his tongue mimicking his delicious torture below. He slid deeper, and his tongue plundered, ruthlessly. He settled more heavily between her legs, and she felt the power and strength of him.

Then he thrust powerfully.

She cried out in surprise, his mouth capturing her strangled gasp.

He stilled above her, raining kisses all over her face. "The pain will dull in a few moments. Are you all right?" The concern was very evident in his voice and the worried green of his eyes. He tenderly stroked down her side and molded his hand to her hip.

The sharp pain lessened to a dull ache and she could feel

him throbbing within her. She could not help but move. At the slight lift of her hips, he drew back, and gripping her hip, he pressed in again. There was no pain this time. He didn't stop but drove on, all the way in, steadily pushing deep, stretching her, impaling her. She tried to remember to breathe as the sensation of him, hard and strong, embedded deep within her, filing her fuller than she'd imagined.

He rose up on his forearms and his eyes, emeralds under his lashes, glinted down at her, the weight of his lower body holding her immobile as he looked down and watched as he withdrew and slowly, even more powerfully, entered her.

She followed his gaze and watched as he claimed her. She felt every inch as he filled her, felt her body tighten until she arched beneath him.

"God, you feel so good." She struggled to catch her breath, "My body's on fire. I don't know if I can take—"

"You can. You will." It was a growled command. "Close your eyes and let it happen."

He continued to move above her and her body wound itself as tight as a drawn bow. She closed her eyes and gave herself over to passion's power. The intimacy of the moment sharpened as he slid deep and she felt the first stirrings of overwhelming passion.

She sent her hands sliding over his shoulders, running them over his back until she found his buttocks. She held on as they flexed. He began to move more forcibly than before, her hips lifted to match his rhythm the friction of their bodies sending spiralling pleasure to her very core.

"Oh. My. God—"

The restless flames of desire erupted within her.

Erupted into a firestorm.

At her first scream, he took her mouth. Their lips melded, tongues tangled, hands gripping, their bodies merging in a frantic and driving need.

He thrust harder, faster, and ever more powerfully. She gave herself over to him, sinking her nails into his buttocks, pulling him close, urging him deeper-wild to provoke him further.

They were desperate for each. Neither trying to dominate, both wanting to take this journey together. Sharing, loving, being one. Their senses held, locked, overwhelmed by the slickness, the heat, the gasping urgency of their loving.

He drove her on, ensuring the road to her release was expertly travelled. He thrust deeper yet and her body gathered him close, holding him, tightening around him and suddenly she was floating, riding a wave of joyous and consuming pleasure. Her body imploded in heat and glory and satisfaction. Sensations rioted down every nerve to suffuse her every inch of her being with satiation. The waves continued, no longer gigantic, but ripples of contentment. She clung to him, felt him thrust deep and roar against her mouth, the sound flowing into her, as did his seed. They lay still, panting, soaking in the glory of their union as the waves slowly ebbed.

Henry fought to regain his senses. Eyes closed tight as he felt the last spasm faded. A tsunami of feelings rioted within his chest. She was his. He'd bound her to him—forever.

He rolled off her. He slumped exhausted wrung out beside her, pulling her hard against him into the cradle of his arms. Protecting her automatically as he would for the rest of his life.

Peace flowed over him and through him. He'd never felt anything like it in his life and he just wanted to lie here and reveal in the joy of it.

The joy of her.

They lay wrapped together, too drained to stir, and very content.

Henry couldn't stop touching her. He stroked her silky skin and tried to think.

Tried to understand the past week. Why did Amy hide from

him? The thought focused his mind on where they were, what they had done, what was to come.

"Why, Amy? Why did you hide from me?"

He sensed her stiffen beside him. He turned to look in her eyes, the depth hidden by the now nearly extinguished candle.

He felt rather than saw her withdrawal.

Like a queen she asked, voice steady, "Who is Millicent?"

He stilled. Her question hit him hard. "Where did you hear that name?"

"Does it matter?"

"Did Marcus say something to you about Millicent?"

She shook her head.

"Sabine or Caitlin?"

"No. I heard her name from you."

CHAPTER TEN

Lips compressing, he narrowed his eyes, and wondered what game she was playing. "I very much doubt that."

She rolled away from him onto her back and stared up at the ceiling. "I guess I've been a little in love with you since I was fifteen. Do you remember when I came off my horse?"

"Yes. You were very lucky. I saw you fall, it was nasty."

She sighed. "I heard *you* fall that night in your garden. I often used to-let's just say spy-on you talking to your brother."

He swallowed a terse curse, affronted by her behavior. She hurried on. "I was attending to your wound that night when you kissed me, and I let myself be carried away. I wanted something beautiful to hold on to should I find myself betrothed to a man like Chesterton."

He rolled onto his side, propped on his elbow. "That will never happen now. Over my dead body." She sighed in exasperation and he said, "Go on."

"I let myself be caught up in the moment. I knew you had no idea what you were doing or who you were with, but I couldn't bring myself to make you stop." She turned her head to look at him. "I'd never experienced anything so wonderfully exciting . . . Then you spoke her name. You called me Millicent." She choked on the name. "I was mortified. I thought you loved another."

He ran a finger down her cheek. "She is a woman in my past, Amy. I haven't seen or spoken to Millicent in almost two years."

"Did you love her?"

Henry hesitated before answering trying to understand what he did feel. "At the time I thought I did. Now I'm not sure. I do know I cared for her deeply." He knew it would hurt her but he wanted to be honest. "I still do care for her. She was a good friend."

Amy turned to stare at the ceiling again.

He took her chin in his hand and turned her face toward him. "But I never wanted to marry her. I do want to marry you, Amy. You belong to me. With me. I know it in my bones."

Her eyes filled with tears. "You know what I swore."

He nodded. "And I swear to you my heart does not belong to another. Once I marry I will never keep a mistress. If you did spy on me talking to Richard, then you know what I want. What I need."

He bent and placed a gentle kiss on her lips.

"I want a woman who I can come to love and who could love me. I want a true matching of souls. I want a warm and happy home filled with children who are wanted."

She burrowed closer. "I want that too. I want it so much it scares me."

"We will be happy together, Amy. We *will* have a good life. Together. I promise."

Never had she experienced such abiding joy. It filled her completely. She curled into his side.

"So, will you do me the very great honor of becoming my wife?"

"If you truly are not in love with anyone else, then it would be a dream come true. Yes, I would be thrilled to become Countess Cravenswood." She looked at him shyly. "I love you."

He drew her closer, a warm, silken bundle beside him, her head cradled on his chest. Henry let the force that drove him to propose rise and consume him. Unmitigated contentment flooded his body and he squeezed her tightly. Everything would be perfect. She was perfect.

She was exactly what he wanted and needed. Yet he didn't want just her body, he wanted her heart. His heart sang in the knowledge that she loved him.

Her body gave him pleasure, and even if they made love over a million times it wouldn't be enough to satisfy his intense longing. Only her heart calmed his restless spirit.

"I shall leave on the morrow to meet with your father. With his approval, I'll arrange a special license. We can be married in a few days."

She giggled. "I realize when we go back to London that it is unlikely we can be together—like this, but why the rush? I'm perfectly content where I am right now."

He kissed the top of head. "I will admit that I'm impatient to have you in my bed, my home, my life but, umm, we might have a bit of a problem—"

"It pleases me that you don't want to wait. I don't care if I have a large wedding. Plus, my father can't wait to see me wed. He'll be ecstatic to have it over with swiftly."

He told her. "Chesterton saw you coming out of the stables last night. He thinks you were having an illicit rendezvous with Marcus."

She sat up, heedless of the impact on him. His eyes fixed on her pert bosoms. Her glossy hair fell in disarray around her shoulders and down her back. She looked as tempting as sin.

Her eyes narrowed and he could see her brain begin to

awake from its sensuous slumber. He loved her intelligence but right now he wished she wasn't so astute.

"Why were you in my room tonight?"

He knew he should tread carefully here. "I knew you were the owner of the earring."

She covered her mouth with her hand. Then lowered it and said, "How? And since when? Did Marcus tell you?"

His eyes locked on her. "I saw you reach for your earring when you hid under my bed."

The flush raced over her skin like the rising sun over the darkened ground. "You saw me," she managed to squeak.

He leaned forward and kissed her soundly before whispering, "Did you enjoy watching me?"

She kept her voice low and siren like; desire flamed anew. "I thought it was the most beautiful thing I'd ever watched. But now . . ." Her eyes ran down his body. "What we just shared . . . Just looking at you takes my breath away."

Henry reached for her, eagerly locking his lips with hers. She kissed him with unfeigned, innocent hunger, openly encouraging. But then she stiffened and pulled back. "Don't distract me. You didn't explain about Chesterton."

Damn. She would not be denied answers. "He saw you coming out of the stables after meeting with Marcus." He tweaked her nose. "In your nightdress."

She frowned and shrugged. "So?"

"With a man of Marcus's reputation, Chesterton immediately thought the worst."

She was still frowning. "I don't . . ." She gasped her hands flying to her breasts. "No. As if I'd do that. As if Marcus would do that to Sabine. As if *I'd* do that to Sabine."

Henry looked away.

"Oh, my, God. Henry St. Giles look at me. You believed him!"

He looked into the warmth of her eyes and berated himself for thinking the worst. "In my defense, evidence suggested otherwise."

Amy scrambled off the bed heedless of her nakedness.

He rose too. "I heard you and your maid talking in the gardens. Talking about the man you couldn't have because he loved another. I assumed that was Marcus, since you didn't reveal yourself as the owner of the earring. I thought you had something to hide. Perhaps your heart was engaged elsewhere. Plus, Marcus lied to me about the earring, saying he didn't recognize it, yet when I went to Garrard's to check."

"You went to Garrard's to check?"

Her skin was flushed and she was breathing heavily. Her beautiful breasts rising and falling rapidly. He tried to concentrate so he could make her understand.

"*Why* were you in this *room*?" her stuttered words were filled with anger.

He rubbed his hand over his face and prayed his confession did not ruin everything.

"I wanted to find the drawings of Marcus. If Chesterton revealed what he knew, I wanted Sabine protected by ensuring there was no evidence." He hesitated. "Then I was going to insist that you marry me to prove Chesterton made a mistake, it was me not Marcus. Everyone would be protected."

She stood there with her mouth hanging open. He waited for the explosion and accusations to come. Instead she closed her mouth and walked toward him. She placed her hand on his chest, over his heart.

"Everyone would have been happy but you. You'd marry a woman who'd cheat on her best friend, who fell into bed with a married rake, just to protect those you loved." She pressed a chaste kiss to his lips. "You truly are a saint, Henry St. Giles, Earl of Cravenswood."

He was out of his depth. His soul consumed with relief; she hadn't rejected him. "Deep in my heart, I knew there had to be a mistake. I didn't believe it of Marcus and more importantly I couldn't believe it of you."

"Thank you."

He pulled her into his arms and they stood there, skin to skin. They fitted together so perfectly.

They stood like that for several moments until the movement of her small hand down his chest drew his attention. She leaned forward and licked his nipple. His body, which he'd been struggling to keep under control, could be denied no more.

He closed his eyes and willed his body to obey his command. She'd been a virgin and would not doubt be sore. Swallowing a groan, he opened his eyes and caught her wrist.

Amy's look of embarrassing uncertainty tugged at his heart. "God, don't look at me like that. It's too soon, sweetheart. You'll be too sore."

Her other hand drifted from his chest, down over his torso . . . "Perhaps not. You don't want to stop. Your body tells me otherwise."

He cursed, meeting her gaze: rich, warm brown eyes that promised so much, her lips swollen from his kisses. "I don't want you to regret anything about this night."

"I'll regret it more if you leave my bed before morning. Who knows how long it will be before we can make love again?"

He couldn't dispute her words, didn't want to, and her questing hands easily convinced him that taking her back to bed would be the smartest thing he'd ever done.

He scooped her into his arms and fell with her onto the bed.

And as he listened to her moans, and little cries of delight, he congratulated himself on being right.

*   *   *

He left before dawn broke. He hesitated, looking down at her, then bent his head, trailed a kiss to her ear, and whispered, "Next time I have you, you'll be my wife. Then I plan on taking you to my bed and not letting you leave for a week."

Utterly exhausted from their night of lovemaking, Amy had fallen back asleep before he'd even left the room.

Henry was almost to his bedchamber when Marcus peeled away from the shadows, an angry hiss escaping his mouth. He was barefooted, wearing nothing but black trousers and a hastily donned white ruffled evening shirt. "I think I'll thrash you until you can barely walk."

"I thought you'd be pleased. Wasn't it your plan that said if all else fails, I was to compromise the lady? It looks as if I've fallen to your level. Sorry if it disappoints."

Marcus chuckled quietly. "Not that. You bedding Amy is marvelous because *I* know you'd never compromise a lady. You have feelings for her." When Henry didn't respond, he added, "I feel vindicated. I knew you were perfect for each other. God knows why it took you both so long to see it."

Henry walked until he was almost in Marcus's face. "Because my so called friend lied to me about an earring," he uttered in a fierce whisper.

Marcus smiled angelically. "Nothing that comes too easily is treasured. I wanted you to have to work a bit for your happy ever after." His smile died away replaced by a furrowed brow. He poked Henry in the chest repeatedly. "Which brings me back to our unfinished business. You were accusing me of having an affair. My honor has been questioned."

Henry's shoulders slumped and he stepped back from his friend. "I feel like a . . ."

"Yes, go on. Like a . . ."

"I unreservedly apologize." He rubbed his hand over his eyes. "I don't know what came over me."

"I do. A case of man's most hated disease—jealousy." He grabbed Henry's head in a playful headlock. "You're bloody lucky Sabine never got wind of your ridiculous suspicions. She would beat you black and blue."

Marcus released him and Henry cleared his throat. "We may still have a problem."

Marcus's eyebrows rose. "We better not have a problem."

"Chesterton saw Amy leave the stables in her night attire. He knows she was there with you."

"So?"

"Don't be so naive. He thinks you're up to your old tricks. I warned him to keep his mouth shut but I doubt he will. I'm off directly to London to Amy's father. I'm hoping an announcement of an engagement between us might make everyone assume Chesterton's got the wrong man."

Curses issued forth. "I'm upset because it will hurt Sabine. She won't believe the rumors of course, but she'll still be upset for me, for Amy . . . And in her condition . . ."

Henry couldn't help his whoop of glee. "I knew it. Sabine has the same glow Caitlin had when she was with child. Congratulations, old boy. A father! You're going to be a father." He slapped Marcus on the back. "I never thought our lives could be so perfect."

"What are you men doing out in the corridor making such a ruckus? Both of you underdressed, too. What *have* you been up to, Lord Cravenswood? Something naughty, I hope." Sabine glided to Marcus side and he immediately wrapped a protective arm around her waist.

"I caught him coming out of Lady Amy's room."

She immediately became animated. "I see our matchmaking has achieved a result. Fabulous. It took you longer than I suspected it would." She pressed a kiss to Henry's cheek. "I'm so happy for you. When can we make an announcement?"

He smiled at Sabine, warmth filling his heart at the joy his friends took in his happiness. "Not until you go back to London. I'm off to formally ask for Amy's hand at first light."

She looked between the two men. "The duke won't be a problem, so why are you both looking so grim?"

It wasn't Henry's place to tell her. Marcus hugged her tightly against his chest. "It appears our well intentioned machinations have inadvertently caused a slight scandal."

"Not that slight, actually." Henry glanced at the floor, searching for the delicate way to phrase the situation.

Marcus jumped in before he could speak. He stroked Sabine's face and looked her in the eye. "It appears Chesterton thinks I'm back to my wicked ways. He saw Amy and I talking in the stables the other night."

Sabine reached up and cupped his cheek with his hand. "He doesn't know you like I do."

That was all that was said. Henry was humbled watching the look of love and longing the couple before him shared. The absolute trust and faith they had in each other moved him more than he would have thought. He hoped that he would grow to share this unspoken bond with Amy. The way she'd taken his word about Millicent led him to believe they were on the right path. The honesty between them bode well for their future.

He cleared his throat and spoke to Marcus. "Can you protect Amy until I've spoken with the duke?"

"But Chesterton left this evening for London," Sabine told them.

"Damn. Chesterton's angry. I don't doubt he's off to do damage." He looked bleakly at Marcus. "I must leave immediately. Can you take care of Amy and see her safely back to London?"

Sabine nodded. "We'll leave at once. The house party was due to finish tomorrow, but it will just have to end a tad early.

Perhaps Marcus has urgent business in town?"

He kissed Sabine's forehead and shook Marcus's hand. "Once this mess is sorted, then I'll thank you properly for showing me the happiness that was under my very nose."

Sabine smiled. "No need. We love you."

He pulled her close and kissed her forehead. "Thank you."

As he hurried toward his room to change and gather his belongings, it was interesting to come to terms with just how happy he actually was. And it was down to one woman. Amy.

His hopes and dreams hinged on making Amy his wife, and no one or nothing would keep that from happening. Not even the duke himself.

CHAPTER ELEVEN

The Duke of Shipton agreed to see him, even though Henry called unannounced, and at the unsociable hour of eleven in the morning.

The duke seemed perplexed at his arrival and genuinely had no idea why he would call. Henry didn't blame him. The St. Giles's were his neighbors, and had been for at least two generations, yet they rarely called on each other. He certainly had not been interested in courting his daughter.

The duke motioned to a chair with a wave of his hand.

This was perhaps the most important moment in his life and he didn't know how to approach the subject. The duke would no doubt want to understand how his affection had developed toward his daughter and he could hardly explain that he'd drunkenly groped her in his garden.

He moved restlessly in his chair. What if her father refused? The conversation would be most interesting if he did. For the duke was no longer in any position to refuse his suit. Amy was his.

"My lord," he said formally.

"Cravenswood. What brings you to my door this early in the day?"

"I'm here because I wish to ask for your daughter's hand in marriage."

The duke regarded him from under heavy brows. "Amy? We are discussing my daughter Amy?"

"I was under the impression you had only one daughter." The minute the words were out he cursed under his breath as he watched the duke's face redden. He had three illegitimate daughters.

"I want to marry Amy." He paused and then went on. "This is a formal offer and we can involve our solicitors in, say,"—he looked up at the clock on the mantle—"an hour's time?"

"That soon?"

"I want a special license." Chesterton wasn't the only reason for the swift haste. He wanted to make Amy his more than he wanted to take his next breath. The idea of sharing his life with her, his home, sharing his bed . . . He couldn't stop thinking about holding her in his arms and making love to her until he grew heartily sick of hearing her cry his name. That would no doubt take a lifetime. She filled the emptiness in his soul.

"Excellent, my boy. The sooner the better." The duke rubbed his hands in glee.

Henry took in a breath and let it out slowly. Amy was his, but he frowned at her father's lack of concern. "Aren't you curious as to why I want a special license?"

"I assume it's because you need one." Lord Shipton rose from his chair to pour them both a drink.

"And that doesn't concern you? You haven't even asked if Amy is agreeable to the match."

The duke sat down again. "Is she?"

"Of course. I would not wish to marry her if she were not."

"Then what is the problem, my boy? I've given my blessing. The sooner you take her off my hands, the better, as far as I'm concerned."

Too angry to stay seated, Henry stood. He leaned both hands

on the desk. "You really don't care what happens to Amy. You were quite prepared to marry her off to a man like Chesterton."

"She's a woman. She is supposed to marry to strengthen family bonds. What's wrong with Chesterton?"

Henry clenched his teeth so tight he thought his jaw would break. "If you'd bother to assess her suitors rather than trying to wed her off in indecent haste to the first man who proposed, you'd know Chesterton has a vicious reputation with women. Is that the kind of life you'd have for Amy?"

The duke sat back in his chair. "I didn't know," he uttered almost to himself.

Henry sat back down and ran a hand through his hair. "Although I've requested a special license, I do wish to make *her* my wife." He added quietly, "I love your daughter."

The duke raised his glass. "Here's to a happy life then. I wished I'd been sensible enough to marry for love."

"You will do one more thing for me." The duke raised an eyebrow at Henry's steely tone. "You will make a fuss of the fact you have reluctantly agreed to the special license. You will ask Amy if she wants this marriage and indicate that she is under no obligation to accept me. You will make it seem that you are not pushing her into this marriage and that you want what is best for her."

"I see she has told you quite a bit about our family," the duke said wryly. He sat looking at Henry for a few moments. "You really do love her."

"What is there not to love? She's beautiful, accomplished, kind and intelligent."

"Plus, there is her very large dowry."

Henry's temper sizzled once more. "I've no need of your money, but if you'd like to give the dowry directly to Amy, please feel free to so. Or better yet, put it in trust for your grandchildren."

The duke humbly nodded. "Apologies. One of my good friends is a bishop, and I am sure he can expedite proceedings.

When did you wish to marry?"

"As soon as I've formally proposed and Amy has accepted my offer. I want her to have a proper proposal since she will not be having a grand wedding."

"Shall we say a week from tomorrow then?"

Henry rose and shook his soon-to-be father-in-law's hand. "Thank you, sir. If you don't start taking an interest in your daughter I shall make it my mission over the coming years to wreck financial havoc upon you."

The duke slammed his glass of brandy so hard on the table the liquid sloshed over the side. "Are you threatening me? *Me!* I won't stand for it."

Henry leaned menacingly over the desk. "As you seem to have no heart where Amy is concerned, taking your money might make you realize what you've done to your daughter. How you've cheated her."

The duke's face reddened and his eyes bulged. "You impertinent pup. Don't tell me about my heart." He rose to his feet. "My heart's desire has been denied me for years and now I deserve to spend my remaining years being happy."

"At the expense of your daughter's happiness. What kind of man are you? What life does Amy deserve?"

The duke slowly sank into his chair and dropped his head in his hands. "Oh, god. What have I done?"

"There is still time to put things right. Talk to her. See her for who she really is. *Your* daughter."

Henry made to leave when a whispered voice said, "Thank you, Cravenswood. You've saved me from making a terrible mistake with Chesterton. I've been selfish in wanting Amy married quickly. My only excuse is that I have lived the last twenty-eight years longing for a different life. I've not considered others have suffered as I have."

"That would make you a selfish bastard wouldn't it? Perhaps, for once, you can do the right thing by your daughter." Henry moved to the door. "Knowing how a marriage can be, you should have wanted more for Amy. You're a disgrace." With that, he took his leave and went to make the necessary announcements.

*   *   *

Amy was the center of attention. The gossip spread by Chesterton, Lord Cravenswood's unexpected proposal, and the unseemly haste to their wedding saw to that.

The engagement celebration was something to see en fete.

Scanning the floor below, her confidence faltered when she spied Chesterton in the mix. She was already feeling like a fish in a glass bowl, and she hoped Chesterton's presence wouldn't crack the glass.

Henry squeezed her elbow in support, and her father, for the first time she could remember, accompanied them as well. Unbelievable though it was, the duke was taking an interest. She found it somewhat ironic that now, once she had been gloriously compromised, he let her choose whether to marry Lord Cravenswood. Gone was the rush to see her indecently rushed to the altar.

They descended the stairs together, and she did her best to smile and brazen out the ton's opinion.

Lords and Ladies Wolverstone and Dangerfield were at the bottom to greet them. The ladies tucked her arm in theirs and escorted her through the crowd. Both ladies were no strangers to gossip.

The evening from there was a complete blur. She fielded many congratulations, some sincere, others followed with plenty of cynicism.

Henry claimed his two dances, both waltzes, and the feel of his arms around her made her wish the wedding would take place sooner. Still, her wedding day was only three days away.

She took a sip of her champagne and stood watching him from across the room. He looked so incredibly handsome. His fair hair glinted golden in the candlelight, and his broad shoulders looked massive in his black evening attire. As if a sixth sense kicked in, he turned and caught her staring. The smile that broke over his face . . . Her heart thought it would burst with happiness. Never did she expect to find love, let alone a man who loved her equally in return.

Her life was perfect. Well, almost perfect. Once she became Countess Cravenswood it would be absolutely perfect. Tears of happiness welled, and spying the door to the terrace, she decided to take a moment to gather her composure.

Amy hadn't realized how hot the ballroom was until she stepped into the cool night air and walked to the balustrade. She closed her eyes and listened to the music and chatter behind her. She wondered how long it would take Henry to seek her out. She wanted a moment alone with him. She'd not seen him alone since his proposal. He'd got down on one knee to offer for her and the look of adulation and love in his eyes had her saying yes without having to think.

A brittle voice filled with malice broke into her pleasant memories. "Bedded one friend and marrying the other. Quite a busy week."

Creeperton. Amy sighed out loud and turned to face him. Not even Creeperton could ruin her happiness. "Your dirty mind can think what it likes. I'm marrying Henry St. Giles, the Earl of Cravenswood, on Thursday because I love him."

"What a saint he is. That's what you think, isn't it. St. Giles comes rushing in to save your reputation and that of his friend, Wolverstone."

"There would have been no need to save anyone's reputation if you had not deliberately misconstrued the situation," she said through clenched teeth.

Chesterton merely laughed. "You think Henry honestly loves you. What a fool."

Amy cast him an askance look. "Go away. You know nothing."

Chesterton leaned closer, and trailed a finger down her arm. She moved away. He let out a harsh bark like laugh. "He's marrying you because he couldn't marry Millicent."

Amy tensed and he noted it.

"I see you know of Millie, his mistress of over seven years. He was in love with her and she left him—for me," he said proudly. "Why do you think he set his cap at you? He's been jealous of me ever since, and once I'd made it known I was courting you, along comes Henry."

Her heart began a stuttered beat. It couldn't be true, could it? No. Henry only became interested in her after the night in his garden. The same night he saw off Chesterton at Lady Skye's ball.

"Don't be ridiculous. Are you suggesting he's marrying me simply to spite you?"

Chesterton's smile was pure evil. "No. Not solely to spite me. I believe he's marrying you for the very same reason I wanted you. You look exactly like Millicent. You're a Millicent with the appropriate social standing. After all, there is no way a courtesan brought up on the streets would be accepted in Society." He leaned closer to whisper in her ear. "I wonder if he's imagining her as he rides between your thighs."

Amy felt nausea rise. "What do you mean I look like Millicent?"

Chesterton twirled Amy's lose curl between his fingers. "You are the same height and build, voluptuous, I believe the word is. You curve in the same way she does. Your hair is black and straight, in fact the same length, and your skin probably a more luscious cream. Your lips could drive a man wild with want, just like Millie's. Ask him. Ask him what he wants you to

409

do with those lips. He'll want you to suck his cock just like Millie. I wonder if you're as good."

Amy slapped his face, her anger making her hand whip up like a snake. "You lie."

He rubbed his cheek and grabbed her shoulders in a vice like grip. "Do I? He had a portrait drawn of her. It hangs in his study. Go and view it if you don't believe me."

"Get your hands off my fiancée," Henry's ice cold tone had Chesterton dropping his hands immediately and stepping back. "Touch her again and you're a dead man."

Chesterton held his hands up and backed away. "I have no intention of touching her again." He turned and walked back into the house, leaving them alone, yet it was hardly private, Amy noticed, since most of London proper were staring out of the window. Did they know she looked like his ex-mistress?

She turned away to hide her pain.

"Did Chesterton upset you? If he hurt you, I'll . . ."

Amy remained silent, fighting for composure.

Henry didn't know what was wrong. It was the shimmer of tears in her incredible eyes that tore at his heart.

"Can you take me away from all the prying eyes?"

Henry looked over his shoulder at their audience. "Would you like me to take you home?"

She nodded, then shook her head. "No." She looked up at him imploringly. "No, take me to your house. No one will think to look for me there. I want to be alone with you."

Something was definitely wrong. Her voice was brittle. What had Chesterton said to her? This wasn't the place to find out.

They left quietly, not even saying goodbye to their friends. In the carriage ride on the way to his townhouse, she sat in quiet contemplation. He'd love to know what she was thinking. Chesterton had upset her, but she wouldn't open up to Henry. With a twinge of envy, Henry saw that the natural accord Marcus and Sabine shared was not yet within in their reach.

The one thing he'd not anticipated this night was the blood-curling anger he'd experienced seeing Chesterton with his hands on Amy. Possessive raged welled, and he could quite easily have ripped Chesterton's head from his body. He'd struggled with jealousy all evening at the ball. He wanted to banish every man who danced with her.

He'd never felt this possessive anger over any other woman. Amy was *his*. They belonged together. She was his soul mate. Wasn't she?

The walk into his house was silent. Amy thanked the footman for his help in descending the carriage, not waiting for Henry's assistance.

"Timmons, can you organize some refreshments? Tea, perhaps?" he asked Amy. She nodded.

"Very good, my lord. The fire is still lit in the drawing room. I'll see that it is stoked."

"No need, it's rather warm this evening." Amy's response drew his eye to the fact that rather than being warm, she looked deathly cold, pale as a ghost.

She took a seat on the chaise lounge and stared blankly into the fire. He went to her and crouched at her feet. He took her chilled hands in his, so small his fists swallowed them.

"What's wrong, Amy?"

She couldn't look at him.

"Did something Chesterton say upset you?" He squeezed her tiny hands. "You know you can tell me anything. I'll always be here for you."

She looked at him blankly for a moment before saying. "If you'll excuse me, I need the retiring room."

He rose swiftly. "Of course. Timmons will show you the way."

He watched her leave the room with a sinking feeling in the pit of his stomach. Something was dreadfully wrong. If she had a problem or was upset, Amy should be able to talk to him about it. Didn't couples in love share everything? He thought of Sabine and Marcus. Sabine most definitely let Marcus know when anything was wrong.

Yet, Amy wasn't Sabine. She was younger, less experienced, and wounded by a family that didn't love her. Was this why she was worried? Didn't she know how much he loved her?

He drained the brandy in his glass. He rested his head on the back of the chair and realized he'd been a fool. He might have proposed, but he'd never said the words. He'd assumed she'd know his heart. When she returned he'd spend the rest of the night telling her, and showing her, just how much he loved her and wanted her—forever.

*   *   *

No sooner had Timmons directed her to the retiring room, Amy slipped along the corridor heading straight toward Henry's study. She had a fair idea where it was located given the number of times she'd been in Cravenswood house over the years.

Her throat was dry, her hands clammy. She didn't wish to believe Chesterton, but Henry had never once told her he loved her. Oh, he'd shown it physically, but was that love, or did Henry want her because she looked like Millicent? The idea of Henry thinking of another woman when he was with her, in her . . . Pain lanced her body as expertly as a well-aimed arrow hitting the bulls-eye.

The woman whose name he'd spoken in his garden only a few weeks ago—did Millie hold his heart? Was Amy second best, like her mother had been for her father? She had to know.

Who did he really want in his arms? Who did he hold in his heart?

All her life she'd wanted someone to love her just for her. Not her pedigree, or dowry, or social position. *Her!* Was that too much to ask? She thought Henry was that man. The man who'd pursued her, made love to her, asked her to marry him . . . Was it all a lie?

She tried to keep tears at bay as she neared the study door.

She stood before the closed door and took a deep breath. She ran a hand down the worn oak, caressing all the nicks and knots in the wood. So old. If the door could talk, it could tell a thousand secrets. She wished she knew the secret of Henry's heart, so that what she might find within didn't have the power to destroy her.

With a shaking hand, she reached and lifted the latch. She gently pushed the door inwards, holding her breath. Forcing herself to look, her eyes swept the walls, willing Chesterton's words false.

They reached the far right and halted. She sucked in a depth breath to ward off the pain that struck in precise stabs. A black haired woman was smiling down at her. Her face beautiful in its composition, her eyes warm and understanding, her body clothed in an exotic rich burgundy silk, voluptuous in the extreme.

It wasn't like looking into a mirror, but the similarities were there. They shared the same coloring, the same body shape and damn Chesterton to hell, the same pout of the lips.

The pain grew in intensity and she doubled over, backing out of the room. She stood trying to breathe through the hurt, holding onto the door to stop herself from crumbling into a heap on the floor.

"My lady, are you hurt?" Timmons voice brought her to her senses. She had to get out of here. She didn't want Henry to see her like this. Her pain was too raw to face him.

She pushed past the concerned Timmons and raced for the stairs. Reaching the entrance hall, she ignored the stunned look of the footman and tore open the door. Heedless of the shouts behind her, she ran into the night, through Henry's blasted garden to the safety of her home.

*   *   *

Henry, hearing the commotion, strode out of the drawing room, peered over the railings to the entrance hall below and noted the door wide open. "Timmons, what on earth is all this commotion?"

His butler looked up, concern etched on his face. "It's Lady Amy, my lord. I fear she's taken ill. She ran off."

He reached the entrance in record time. "Amy? Where is she?"

Timmons pointed into the dark. "I assume she went home. I've sent Simon to check."

At his words, a panting Simon came back through the door. "Lady Amy ran back to her house. I saw her go safely inside."

"Thank you, Simon." He turned to his stunned butler. "You mentioned she was ill."

Timmons spluttered. "I assumed so. I saw her bent over, holding onto the open door of your study."

The hand of fear ripped through his skin and clenched his innards in its fist, twisting until he thought his insides would spill from his stomach. "My study? She was in my study?"

"Yes, Lord Cravenswood."

He closed his eyes and drew in a sharp breath. He knew what bloody Chesterton had told her. Fists clenched, he imagined his hands were around Chesterton's neck squeezing the life out of him. He'd never wanted to kill a man more.

He started for the door. He had to see her. He had to explain. He called over his shoulder. "Timmons, remove the painting in my study and store it in the attic." As he strode out the door into the night, he berated himself that his butler didn't even have to ask which one. It was obvious. What a bloody fool he'd been.

*   *   *

Amy raced straight to her room, valiantly holding back tears until she reached the privacy of her bedchamber. Once there she dissolved into tears in Lorraine's arms.

"Whatever has happened? Shush, don't cry. It can't be that bad."

In between sobs, she said, "I look just like her."

"Like who?"

"Millicent."

Lorraine's arms tightened around her and she could hear her utter a few choice words about wishing parts of Henry's anatomy would fall off.

She drew in a shuddering breath and pushed out of Lorraine's arms, flinging herself on her bed face down, too ashamed to face the world. "I'm such a fool. I thought he really loved me. *Me!*"

"So, you look like her. That doesn't mean he's not in love with you."

She threw an accusing look over her shoulder. "He still has her portrait on his wall. In his study."

"Oh."

Amy flopped back on the bed. There was nothing more to say. "How am I going to get out of this marriage? Father will kill me if I rebuke Henry. The wedding's in three days. The scandal will ruin me."

Her sobs grew anew, almost blocking the sharp rap at her door. Lorraine hurried to answer it and soon was back at her bedside. "The earl is below demanding to see you."

She rolled onto her back and wiped her eyes with the back of her hand. "I don't want to see him. I can't face him."

"I'll go."

In abject misery, she watched her lady's maid leave the room. She rolled onto her side and curled into a ball. Sobs began anew. The pain was crippling. She was a fool to think Henry loved her. She had known when she heard him whisper Millicent's name that his heart belonged to another. Why hadn't she listened to her inner voice? *Because you love him so . . .* Fresh tears rolled down her cheeks and she let them, too emotionally exhausted to care.

"She doesn't wish to see you, Lord Cravenswood. I feel it best you leave."

Amy's maid, Lorraine, he remembered her name, looked at him coldly.

"I'm not leaving until I've explained." He pushed past her. "Amy," he yelled from the bottom of the stairs.

Lorraine began pushing him toward the door. "This is doing neither of you any good. Come back in the morning when she's had time to get over her hurt."

His heart thudded painfully in his chest. He'd hurt her. He hated to think of her upstairs, alone, hurting. "I have to go to her."

"And say what? You're sorry you kept a picture of another woman on your wall while professing to love Amy? You're sorry you didn't mention she looks like your last lover?"

Henry bit his cheek to stop from berating the woman defending Amy. "It's not as it seems."

Lorraine sighed and pushed him again toward the door. "It never is. Leave her be for now. I promise you, if you go up those stairs, you'll make it worse. She's too hurt to hear any pretty words you may say."

Perhaps it was best to talk to her in the morning when hopefully she'd have had a chance to calm down. It would have been a shock to see Millie's portrait. He inwardly cursed himself for not removing it sooner, but he'd simply forgotten it existed. He would have to put his faith in Amy. She loved him, and she must realize he'd not marry her if he loved another. They'd talked about their hopes and dreams. She'd heard him confess his dreams in his garden, night after night. She would understand.

He placed his hand on the doorframe, stopping Lorraine from pushing him out into the night. "There is no need for her to be upset. I love her. Will you tell her? *Please.*"

Lorraine stared into his eyes, trying to get the measure of him. He let her see deep into his heart. She hesitated before nodding. "I'll tell her. Now go."

"I'll be here in the morning. No one will stop me from speaking with her then—no one."

With that he turned and made his way back to Cravenswood house, fear gnawing at his insides.

*   *   *

Henry was surprised when Caitlin paid him a visit early next morning—very early. She marched into his drawing room, removing her gloves, obviously upset. "What's this I hear about a painting of Millicent?"

His face heated and he was less than a welcoming host. "How did you hear of the painting?"

"Our household staff knows each other almost as well as we do."

He saw Timmons edging from the room. "I'll fire the lot of them," he yelled after his butler's departing figure. "It's a simple misunderstanding—an oversight on my part."

She raised an eyebrow at him and took a seat. When he

417

didn't move, she said, "Well, aren't you going to ring for tea?"

Feeling his temper rise, he replied politely, "This is a long visit, is it? As you may be aware, I have a fiancée that needs an explanation from me. Although how she can profess to love me while not trusting me is making me see her in an altogether different light."

Timmons arrived with a tea tray without having to be asked, no doubt trying to appease his lordship. Silence reigned as, with a curt nod, Henry waited for her to pour.

"I really don't understand why she's so upset. It's only a painting. A gift from Millicent I received a long time ago. I simply forgot it was there."

"You think this is about the painting?" Caitlin set her cup back on its saucer. "Don't you look at me with that angelic face. Millicent looks very much like Amy. Even I assumed the worst when I realized you were infatuated with Amy. If Harlow hadn't assured me you were completely over Millicent, I'd have told her myself." She threw a look at him that would cause even the boxer Gentleman Jack to duck. "You should have told her. Immediately. What's the poor girl to think?"

"She should have more faith in me. Love is built on trust. How can she profess to love me if she doesn't trust me? Perhaps I've made a mistake."

"Don't be ridiculous. She's absolutely the perfect woman for you."

All sense of propriety fled as his words, filled with pain, tumbled out. "She thinks I could make love to her while thinking of another, that's how little she thinks of me."

Caitlin's faced flush a lovely shade of pink. "I see. And men haven't done precisely that before?" His stance remained ridged and he turned his back not eager for her to see his hurt. She sighed behind him. "A woman's heart is as delicate as a rose. It doesn't take much of a storm to come along and scattered the petals to the wind. You know how fragile Amy's was. She's never felt loved for her own sake. Not from her father, or brother, or anyone in her life. So I'm not surprised she has doubts. But the doubts are engrained deep inside her. It has little to do with her faith in you, and more to do with her faith in herself. Has she selected wisely? She watched her mother pine all her life."

He sank down into the nearest chair. "I'm such a fool. I thought my love would be enough. You overcame Harlow's past and mine's not nearly as—robust–as his."

"It may sound strange to you, but I'd have been more worried if Harlow, like you, had one woman he favored above all others. He simply had nameless, faceless many. You, however, had a mistress for a very long time. And you keep a picture of her on your wall. And she looks very much like your current fiancée."

Fear crept over his skin like an insidious smell. "What are you trying to say? Have I blown my chance at happiness?"

She shook her head. "No. I just think you're expecting too much too soon. To keep the bud of love alive it takes more than a few weeks of courting. It takes a lifetime of patience, understanding, and commitment." When he still did not answer, she said irritably, "Perhaps she's right. You really don't love her if you can give up at the first hurdle."

"I know I should have taken Millicent's portrait down eons ago, but if Amy's my soul mate, why doesn't she know I'd never willingly hurt her?"

"Soul mate? Oh, Henry. I hated Harlow at first sight. He might be my soul mate now, but I didn't know that to begin with. In fact, I thought him an arrogant, conceited buffoon of a man when we first met. Like a well-worn pair of boots, you grow into love. It doesn't happen to everyone the minute you meet. Especially women. We have to be more careful than men. The consequences for us, if we make a mistake, can destroy us, socially, financially, and emotionally. There is no way out."

He raised hopeful eyes to Caitlin. "And because of Amy's upbringing she's even more careful." She nodded. "What do you advise I do?"

Placing her tea on the table in front of her, Caitlin rose and walked to kiss his cheek. She stood looking down at him as she pulled on her gloves. "I wouldn't go to her all, 'oh I love you', she'd be wary of that. I'd go in there as if she's being ridiculous. Jar her out of her despondency. Make her angry enough to fight it out."

Henry's mouth dropped open. She pushed it closed with a gloved finger. "Are you sure?"

"Definitely. If you act as if her portrait is nothing of consequence and you don't understand what she's fussing about, it will take the wind out of her sails."

Seeing her off at the door, Henry said, "I hope you're right. Without Amy, I'm lost."

She kissed his cheek and whispered. "Then go find her."

CHAPTER TWELVE

The next morning Amy refused to hide in her room. She rose earlier than normal, still tired from a sleepless night worrying about what she would say and do when she saw Henry.

When she arrived downstairs, she was surprised to find her father at the breakfast table so early in the morning. She chewed her bottom lip worrying about how her father would react if she wished to withdraw from her engagement.

Not really feeling up to facing food, she collected a scone from the sideboard and made her way to the table.

Her father's voice startled her. "I heard about the ruckus last night. I hope the marriage is still going ahead."

"Why am I not surprised you'd take that stance? You don't even care. He's in love with another woman. Just like you, Father." She choked on her words. "I even look like her. At least you chose a wife who looked the complete opposite of Helen."

"I didn't know you'd met Helen," he said quietly.

She shrugged and poured a cup of tea. "I was on an outing with the Sothebys many years ago and I spied you and your *other* family in the crowd."

"I'm sorry."

She turned to him. "For what?"

"For making a terrible mistake and marrying your mother when I did not love her. Plus for treating you as I have. Take your pick."

Amy looked at her father suspiciously. "You. Apologizing? Are you ill?"

His apology was grudgingly given, like blood seeping out of stone. "It was not fair on her. However, I didn't realize she loved me until after we married. I thought she viewed our arrangement as, well, just that—an arrangement. If I'd known of her feelings I would have married another. But most of all, I'm sorry that my guilt made me neglect you."

Amy still bristled with anger. "Yes, well, I won't make the same mistake. I refuse to marry a man in love with another."

"I don't believe he is."

She gave a brittle laugh. "You're saying that so I'll still marry him. All you want is me off your hands."

Her father looked at her solemnly. "You're right. I did. When he came to ask for your hand, Henry tore a strip off me for it too. He showed me how selfish I was being. That if I wasn't careful I would force you into the cold type of marriage I'd endured." Her father shuddered. "I made the wrong choice many, many years ago and so many people suffered because of it. I won't force you to make the same mistake. If you no longer wish to marry Lord Cravenswood, then I'll ensure you don't. Scandal or no scandal." He gazed at her with sadness. "I'll leave it up to you as to who and when you marry."

Amy gulped back a sob. "You mean it? You'd support my ending the engagement. Did Henry put you up to this?"

"Yes. He threatened to ruin me if I didn't let you have your pick of suitors. But give the man a chance to explain. I know you'll probably think I have ulterior motives but I do want you to be happy. I'm telling you the man's in love with you. The question is—what do you feel for him?" He rose and bent and kissed the top of her head. "I think you're scared. Scared of making a mistake like your mother." At her shocked gasp he smiled. "I don't blame you."

Amy sat sipping her tea and contemplated her father's words. She was scared. She only had two days before she became tied to Henry for the rest of her life. If she wasn't so in love with him, there'd be nothing to be afraid of.

The front door chimed, and this early Amy knew who the visitor would be. She'd barely had enough time to replace her tea cup on its saucer, straighten her gown, and run a hand over her hair before Henry entered the room.

He entered like a whirlwind, sending her senses into a spin. His beautiful face was hard and his eyes glinted like the fine steel of a blade. He didn't appear to be a man about to drop on bended knee and apologize.

"Good morning, Amy. I hope I find you in a more sensible mood than last night." He stood before her, legs splayed and hands on his hips.

She blinked. "I beg your pardon."

"The hysterics of last night. I do apologize for not having had the painting removed earlier. It is now in my attic, but there was no reason to run from my house like a burglar."

She threw down her napkin. "This is not about a painting of Millicent being on your wall, and you know it."

"How am I to know that? You didn't stay around to talk. You simply listened to idle gossip, from a man such as Chesterton, and didn't even have the courtesy to allow me to explain."

She narrowed her eyes. "So you know what Chesterton told me. What he implied."

His hands dropped to his sides but he looked anything but contrite. "So, you look a bit like her."

"A *bit!* Can you honestly stand there and tell me that the fact I look like your past lover didn't cross your mind at least once?"

He ran a hand through his hair and there was the first sign of a stammer, "I might have noted once to Harlow and Marcus that perhaps the reason I never originally considered you was because you reminded me of Millicent."

"You discussed it with Harlow and Marcus. Ooohhh." She stood so quickly the chair fell backwards. "You should have told me."

"Why? It makes no difference to what I feel for you. If you remember, I pursued you before I even knew what you looked like. All I knew was you felt right in my arms."

Amy searched his face. "But this is about more than lust or desire. This is about sharing the rest of our lives together."

He strode toward her. "Do you think I don't know that? I've searched endlessly for a woman who completes me. I thought I'd found her, but now I'm not so sure."

"Not sure . . ." She turned away from him least he see her tears. "As it appears neither of us is sure, maybe this wedding shouldn't take place." If he gave up this easily, perhaps Henry didn't love her as much as he thought. The reflection brought a sudden emptiness to Amy's chest, as if her heart had stopped beating.

The room fell silent. Henry's heavy breathing was the only sound.

God damn it to hell, he'd let his disappointment in Amy's feelings drive her further away. "Is that what you want? To cancel the wedding?" He hoped not. She was everything he'd ever wanted and needed, but what about her? Perhaps he'd been wrong. She might be *his* soul mate, but what if she didn't love him as much as he needed or wanted her. She might be happier living her life without him?

The thought of losing Amy was like a knife in his chest; he wondered how he'd survive walking away but if she did not feel the same he'd rather know now.

As he watched her shoulders slump and heard her soft crying, his heart melted and his anger evaporated. He walked up behind her and enclosed her in his arms, pulling her back hard against him.

"How can I prove my love? I'll do whatever it takes. I'm yours to command ." He dropped to his knees before her. "I'd even sing you a love song in front of the whole ton if that's what it takes."

A small smile creased her lips. "You hate singing, and you can't sing."

"I'm quite prepared to make a fool of myself. For you. If it proves how much you mean to me. I love you, sweetheart. When I look at you, God you're so beautiful, I can barely catch my breath. The idea of being able to share my life with you, each and every moment, is a dream come true. Don't take that chance away from me. From us. *Please.*"

"You'd sing in public? For me?"

"I do anything for you. I'd die for you . . ." He kissed her cheek. "I'd even torture the world with a song if I had to."

He felt her tense within his embrace.

"You love me? Are you sure? Perhaps you love me now, but are you absolutely certain that marriage to me is what you want? Could it be that I'm a replacement for who you truly want? Your life will be utter misery if your feelings for me dissolve shortly after the wedding ceremony. What is worse, I'll have no way out. A divorce for a woman is out of the question."

"I love you, Amy. I won't change my mind."

"But you have known me only a short time, not even a month."

"Sometimes you just *know* if a person is right for you. Millie knew she wasn't right for me long before I did. She did the right thing moving on. I just wish it wasn't Chesterton. That's what

425

I'm upset about, not that she left me. That she left me for him."

Amy turned in his arms. "What's wrong with Chesterton, other than the fact he's revolting?"

How to say this without introducing her to the ugly side of life? "Chesterton likes pain." At her confused frown he said, "Some men, and women too, find more pleasure when pain is involved."

"I still don't understand."

He hugged her tightly. "And you shouldn't. Chesterton and others like him, get physically rough during sex. It excites them. They often hit each other, whip each other, or worse."

Amy looked at him in wide eyed horror. "It can't involve love then, because I'd never want to hurt you."

"It hurts just looking at you and knowing you doubt me." He took her hand and pressed it to his chest, directly over his heart. "I love you. You're right for me. I know it here. I know you'll have to be very brave to place your trust in me given your mother's unhappiness, but you are not your mother and I'm not your father. I'd never hurt you. *Ever,*" he fervently declared. "Stop over-thinking things. Love is not always rational. We want who we want, and I want you. For the rest of my life. No one else, especially not Millicent."

Amy felt her throat tighten with poignant tears. She was here at that point, the point where she could risk everything for her own happiness, because without Henry, a future of unbearable loneliness awaited her. The emptiness that swelled inside her at the thought was proof enough of her feelings.

She couldn't bear the thought of him marrying anyone else. Couldn't bear the thought of him being with any other woman but *her*. He was hers . . . Just as she was his.

She looked up and saw the softness and tenderness of his gaze. She saw love shining brightly in the emerald depths of his eyes. It dazzled her, warmed her and thrilled her.

How could she have been so selfish? She'd been so set on her own self-preservation that she'd never stopped to realize Henry's needs and desires or that he truly loved her.

"Henry," she murmured softly, "I love you with all my heart. I was just too cowardly to expose myself. I'm sorry."

"You . . . love me? Henry echoed.

She nodded. "You soothe the lonely ache—" Amy brought her fingers up to her breastbone to cove her heart "—here. I have loved you since I was fifteen years old. I can't remember a time when I didn't love you. And now I can't imagine my life without you."

Henry's knowing eyes bored into hers, making her feel as if he was digging down into her soul. Those intense, handsome features suddenly appeared vulnerable in their masculine beauty. She'd made him question himself and she regretted it deeply.

Without conscious thought, she moved her hands to cup his face. She swallowed hard as she stared up at him. "It has been frightening for me to contemplate marriage. What if I made a mistake like my mother. You can't *make* someone love you, my parents taught me that. But it's more frightening to think of living without you. I want to be your wife."

He remained silent, looking into her eyes. She tried not to feel how hard her pulse was thudding with her own vulnerability. "If you still want me?" She finally stated.

Henry's face broke into a smile. "I'll want you for the rest of your life." His eyes flared with need. "You're exactly who and what I want. A woman who's sweet, kind, clever, and passionate. The woman who completes me." His voice grew husky, "And you make my soul sing every time I look at you."

His lips covered hers possessively, searing her with warmth, desire and heartfelt emotion. When he finally let her up for air, joy lit his eyes. Amy was in no doubt that Henry loved her. The heated tenderness in his gaze made her ache inside.

"You know you never did give me my earring back."

He smiled. "I kept it as a memento. It's in a dish on my tall-boy."

"In your bedchamber?" she asked innocently.

Her future husband wasn't fooled. "Yes."

"Then I think we should go and get it. Together. I think I've lost something else and it may take me a life time to find it."

"What's that, sweeting?"

"My heart. And I'm going to prove it to you once I'm near your bed."

He took her lips in a fierce, marauding kiss that left no doubt about his desire for her. "If you keep looking at me like that, I won't be able to stop myself from making love to you right here."

She threw her arms around his neck. "I'm not stopping you."

Stepping back, he accepted her challenge, and went to the door and turned the key, locking the world out. He turned and a feverish glow erupted in Henry's eyes as she unhooked the front of her dress and let it slide to the floor. The naked hunger on his face made her heart pound.

She stood before him in her shift, garters, and silk stockings, having worn no corset this morning. With a wave of her hand she said, "Where are my manners, my lord? Please, take a seat."

He walked past her and took the large seat at the head of the table. "Anything to please my lady."

In the bright morning sunlight, he looked angelic, his hair sparkling like gold, his lips as tempting as sin. He'd never looked more handsome, and to her full heart, he was quite simply, breathtakingly male. For when her eyes swept down his body there was no doubt that he was fully aroused.

She dropped to her knees in front of him and eagerly freed him from his tight breeches. He sprung rigid and hard into the welcoming air. She circled him with her hand and gently squeezed. He groaned and his head tilted back, his eyes closed.

Emboldened, Amy moved her hand on him. In response, he jerked in her hand and a glistening drop appeared at his tip. Without thinking she leaned forward and licked it. He sucked in a deep breath and she looked up into eyes burning with fire. Holding his gaze, she once more leaned forward and covered the head of his throbbing member with her mouth. She held his gaze as she slowly took him deep into her throat. She could drown in the desire blazing on his face.

"Oh God, Amy, dear God . . ." His hips lifted, pushing deeper still. She began to suckle and stroke him with her tongue, her own need growing as she experienced his heightening passionate response.

She'd only just found her rhythm when he stood and pulled her to her feet. "I won't last much longer if you do that. I want to be inside you when I come. When I make *you* come."

He quickly drew her shift up and over her head, baring her body to his hungry gaze. He bent her back over his arm and took one peaked nipple deep into his mouth, rasping his tongue over her tender bud while his fingers found the wet heat between her legs.

He kissed and stroked driving her closer to the edge when to her disappointment he lifted his head from her breast. "Turn around and place your hands on the table." She immediately obeyed, a hungry longing making her limbs tremble. "Spread your legs for me." His voice was a husky growl.

His hand came down on her back, bending her forward. He hadn't bothered to undress, such was his need. Her body opened to him in this position. She felt vulnerable and totally exposed.

They stood like that for several seconds. She looked over her shoulder and shivered upon seeing the hungry possessive light in his eyes. He was looking at her. She was intimately exposed to his gaze. He was fully clothed while she was completely naked, apart from her stockings and slippers. He could do anything he liked to her and she would not be able to resist. She didn't want to resist.

Not for one moment was she afraid. She knew, deep in her soul that she trusted this man. With her life, her dignity and her heart. She felt the heat rise and stir in her body. The wetness he must be seeing, her arousal he must be scenting, and she could wait no longer.

She wiggled her hips and bent over the table further in a blatant invitation.

He was in her with one hard thrust. He drew her hips back to meet his as he pounded into her. It was rough, urgent, animalistic, as if he could not get deep enough inside her.

One hand moved around her body to brush her aching breasts and then he cupped her woman's mound, his finger stroked her pleasure center. She couldn't suppress her moans. "Faster," she cried.

As her moans turned to gasping sobs, he plunged more deeply, forcing her body down onto the cold table. The coolness a blessing against the inferno building inside of her.

Amy couldn't help reciprocating . . . Moving her hips back to meet each powerful thrust. On a groan he bent over her, gently biting the back of her neck in a possessive branding. He was marking her as his.

His thrusts grew faster, harder, soon her breasts were rocking each time his body slammed into hers. She thought she'd pass out with the pleasure. "Please," she cried.

"I'm going to come, come with me, together, *now!*" He let out a roar and plunged deep, one last time and she shattered around him, her body tightening around his pulsing cock. She slumped spent on the table his limp body holding her down.

They lay like that until both of them got their breathing under control. He feathered soft kisses over her shoulder blade and then as he rose and kissed down her back.

He pushed up off her. "Amy, are you all right? Christ, I didn't mean to get so carried away . . . I don't know . . . What you do to me . . ."

Utterly sated, Amy looked over her shoulder and summoned a languid, wicked grin. He was straightening his clothes and buttoning his breeches.

"Don't look at me like that or we'll never leave this room today. I'll spend all afternoon making love to you on this table, and no doubt the servants would like to set the room for dinner."

With a cheeky grin, she pushed up off the table and turned to face him, no longer embarrassed by her nakedness. She belonged to him as he belonged to her. Nothing they did together would ever make her feel shame.

"Hmmm. All afternoon." She turned away from him and deliberately bent over to retrieve her shift. She heard his soft groan. Sliding the shift over her head Amy said playfully, "I'd still like to retrieve my earring. Do you think you'll have recovered by the time we walk over to Cravenswood house?" She watched the grin break on his lips. "We could perhaps also stop in the garden along the way. I understand men can become quite amorous in gardens."

Henry helped her into her dress and pulled her close to whisper, "Only when they're with you, my sweet. Only with you."

EPILOGUE

The wedding took place in Henry's garden, where it all began. The late-morning ceremony was attended by close friends and family. Amy's father walked her down the makeshift aisle lined with blooming heart-red rose bushes, and the duke even had a small tear in his eye as he handed her into Henry's care. While she would perhaps never have a true father-daughter relationship, he was at least trying to mend the rift between them and get to know his daughter.

Luckily the warm weather continued, and to protect the guests from the sun, the arbor had been covered in flowing white satin. The scene reminded her of a fairytale picnic. But it was real. Her love for Henry was real, as was his for her.

The day before the wedding, with Chesterton away on a visit to his estate in Yorkshire, she'd urged Henry to visit Millicent to ensure she was well. He got to see her and learned she was tired of the courtesan life, and would be retiring as soon as she had enough money to buy a cottage and have enough savings to live comfortably.

On his return, Henry asked Amy if she would mind if he

discreetly provided enough money for Millie to retire immediately. He explained he owed Millie, his friend, that at least. She whispered that they would discuss it after her wedding.

Now standing before the Bishop, she glanced across at her two-bridesmaids, Caitlin and Sabine. They both had tears in their eyes as Henry spoke out his confident, 'I do', and his groomsmen, Marcus and Harlow, looked a bit choked too, gazing adoringly at their wives positioned across from them.

In no time at all they reached her favorite part of the service. "I now pronounce you man and wife. You may kiss the bride". She turned towards her husband a quivering mass of besotted emotion.

The profound look of happiness shinning upon her husband's gorgeous face stunned her. As he lowered his lips to hers he whispered, "Thank you, my beautiful girl. You've made me the happiest man alive." Then he pressed a simple, devotion-filled kiss to her lips.

Amy never one to be satisfied with simple, threw her arms around her husband's neck and proceeded to cause the congregation to burst out cheering and clapping as she kissed him heartily.

Marcus and Harlow stepped forward to rescue him, pulling him away to clap him on his back hard enough to almost knock him off his feet. Leaving the ladies to twitter over the beautiful ceremony, the men walked over to where little Cameron lay in his bassinette. Harlow couldn't resist picking up his six-month old son, who immediately squealed in delight.

"Who would have ever believed our happiness hinged on such delectable creatures?" Harlow said as he gazed proudly at his wife. "She's my world, you know. Caitlin and Cameron, and our children to come."

Marcus nodded his agreement. "I hope our children become as firm friends as we are. However, if Sabine delivers me a daughter, I'll not be letting young Cameron anywhere near her without a chaperon," glared Marcus at his friend.

Henry laughed. "I look forward to *making* my first child. And if you'll excuse me gentleman, I'd like to start trying immediately." He smiled at his two dear friends. "I have some catching up to do with you two in that department too. It still amazes me that you two rakes are ahead of me."

Their laughter followed him as he made his way to his wife's side. Wife. He'd found her. The woman he'd searched for since the age of twenty. And what a woman she was.

He remembered something Marcus told him two years ago. 'You don't find love, it finds you.'

He'd found it all right, in his very own garden, with a woman who'd been right under his nose all his life. His heart pounded in his chest, contentment coursing through his veins as she walked toward him across the grass. The depth of her beauty could have brought him to his knees, but it was the light of trust in her eyes that stole his soul.

Amy reached out and took his hand in hers. They twined their fingers together just as solidly as their lives were now entwined—his forever. "I want you."

Her eyes told him she wanted him too, and always would.

Slipping away from the guests Henry carried her up the stairs and into his bedchamber, placing her in the middle of his huge bed.

He stood looking at perfection before reaching under the bed. "I have a present for you, my sweet." He pulled a rather large box out from under his bed. "Something I seem to remember you once lost." He gently put the box down in front of her and it moved. She gave a shriek.

"It won't bite, I promise."

She noted the cheeky glint in his eye. "What are you up to?" Gingerly she lifted the lid and her mouth dropped open before she fell back dissolving in a fit of giggles. "You bought me a guinea pig."

"Meet Tinkles."

She couldn't stop laughing. "You should have seen yourself on hands and knees crawling through the garden looking for an imaginary Tinkles."

"Wicked woman. I was upset thinking you'd lost something precious in my garden."

"I did. I lost my heart," she promptly replied.

"And I'm so glad you did. You've made me the happiest man alive."

He put Tinkles back in his cage and pulled her into his arms for a drugging kiss. She broke away from him and scurrying to the other side of the bed on her knees she pulled a scroll tied with a ribbon out from under the pillow.

Shyly she looked at him. "I have a present for you too." She handed him the document.

With avid curiosity he opened the scroll and his eyes widened as he read it.

"I hope you're not angry, but when father signed over my dowry, I wanted to do something special for you and I hoped this would make you happy."

Tears welled in his eyes and for a moment Amy worried she'd done the wrong thing. "I know you'll always care for her, that's the kind of man you are, and why I love you. I wanted you to know I understand, and I wanted to help her too . . ." Her words died as she saw the profound love shining within his eyes.

"Thank you. You humble me. Thank you." And he hugged her tightly. He didn't let her go. She could barely catch her breath.

"Do you think she'll like it, the cottage I mean? I wasn't sure but there is more than enough money if she'd like to live anywhere else."

He couldn't believe it. Amy had signed over a very large

portion of her dowry to Millicent, along with her mother's cottage on the Westerly estate.

Henry couldn't move. His arms simply tightened around his wife. The most precious person in his life. He couldn't speak. His throat too thick, his heart too full. He felt love for her so strong it burned with every breath. A happiness so intense it was almost painful.

"Henry," she asked her voice full of uncertainty.

Working his throat he finally answered. "It was the most wonderful gift you could have given me. I knew you were special when I first meet you but this . . . I'm lost for words." He pressed a kiss to her forehead. "I love you, Amy. More than I can ever say or show or prove."

"I know."

Just two simple words but powerful enough to fill his heart to overflowing.

"Will you come with me to give her the present?"

She nodded. "If you want me there."

"I do." He linked her hand with his. "Tomorrow we shall go and give her the present together. I'm sure she'll be happy to make your acquaintance."

She rose and kissed his lips. "Now, there is one more present I want to unwrap. A present I've longed for all my life. You."

As he tumbled her down on the bed, and unwrapped her soft curves, he knew life couldn't get any better.

Nine months later he had to eat his words when his first son was born.

It could get better. Much better.

THE END

READ on for the first chapter of Bronwen's Award Winning
Regency romance, INVITATION TO RUIN.

INVITATION TO RUIN

CHAPTER ONE

London, 1808

The rogue society dubbed "The Lord of Wicked" lurked in the dimly lit recesses of Lady Sudbury's ballroom. To most people the room was the epitome of warmth, with its blaze of candles and displayed finery, but for Anthony James Craven, the fifth Earl of Wickham, it held absolutely no appeal.

He was here to partake in his favorite pastime—sin and vice. Appetites a notorious rake craved drew him like a malefactor summoned to hell. Thanks to his father, he was full of sin. Sin he could never atone for. Instead, he chose to lose himself in pleasure. Pleasure, at least temporarily, helped him block the memories he would give his very soul to forget.

He kept to the shadows, hiding from the sycophantic throng, while he searched for the one woman who'd enticed him into breaking all his own rules and attending the event of the Season.

His lips curved in anticipation of the night's forthcoming liaison. He raised a glass of burgundy to his mouth in mock salute, letting the alcohol take the sting out of the unenviable position of having to hide from mothers of young unmarried daughters.

In the concealing darkness he felt the primitive stirrings of the hunter. His eyes had begun seeking their prey as soon as searching for the flesh-and-blood goddess he intended to seduce.

Lady Cassandra Sudbury, a curvaceous young widow with a taste for the erotic would be his by the end of the night. Anthony stirred from his position propped against the ballroom wall and observed his quarry's bold approach.

With each dainty step she took towards him, his amusement grew. She worked her way through the masses with an air of innocence reborn, yet if tales were to be believed, Cassandra could corrupt a nunnery.

The blazing draft-buffeted wall candles cast flickers over her burnt-orange silk dress, which indecently hugged her every curve. The gleaming Sudbury diamonds, attracting as much attention as her cleavage, emphasized her pale slender neck. Like an opium pipe to an addict, the exposed skin called out for him to lick, suck, and taste.

Moist pink lips parted in an inviting smile. Cassandra moved behind him using one delicate hand to cup his left buttock, while the other slid under his evening jacket and up his back.

Her soft-form molded itself against him, her person hidden from the crowds in the ballroom by his height and size.

"Lord Wickham, is there a reason you're lurking in the shadows?"

Her husky voice caressed him more than the insistent fingers stroking his backside through his tight, and ever tightening, black breeches. Both tactics achieved their desired outcome. His member instantly stood to attention and Anthony smiled to himself. Lady Cassie, as he preferred to call her, was just out of mourning, and she was playing with fire.

Anthony let his silence hang expectantly before murmuring, "I knew if I ignored the most beautiful woman in the room she'd come to me."

Light laughter mocked his senses as she moved to stand directly in front of him. "You know me so well." She trailed her hand over his hip to rub the most intimate part of him, her body shielding her actions from the pomp and ceremony in front of them. "Something's hard . . ." Her hand moved more purposely. "Speaking of coming . . ."

Anthony soaked in the beauty of the woman bold enough to service him in full view of her guests. Very soon she would be his mistress; this very night, in fact. He'd waited long enough.

He did not move, nor give any sign of the sparks searing through his body at the practiced fingers stroking him. "If you do not still your hand I won't be responsible for my actions."

She gave a throaty laugh. "In view of the guests? I don't think so."

Gritting his teeth, he flashed Lady Cassie a taut smile. "Take a peek over my shoulder, sweetheart." His jaw tightened as he struggled to control his body. "Where do you think that door leads? If you don't behave, I'll pull you into the billiard room, lock the door and ravish you on the table until you can no longer walk." He lifted her free hand and kissed the air above her glove. "Guests or no guests."

At his promise she moaned softly and he felt her fingers tremble with desire. Cassie stood on tiptoes to whisper in his ear, "Come to my bed tonight and we shall see who wears out whom."

If she thought he'd not accept the challenge, she was sorely mistaken. Cassandra thrived on games of flirtation. Anthony thrived on challenge.

He inwardly smiled as she peeped up at him from beneath incredibly long lashes and rubbed her hand longingly one more time, caressing his erection to the point of pain, before she set him free. "Tonight?" she whispered.

Anthony's pulse ratcheted up a notch as Lady Cassie moved

close, pressing her plump white breasts against his waistcoat.

"Do not keep me waiting," she almost pleaded, tapping his chest with her fan before drifting off to converse with her other guests.

He watched her swaying hips. She wouldn't have to wait.

Lady Cassie's beauty had driven Anthony to the point of madness over the past week. He felt like a thoroughbred racehorse that hadn't been run in over a month. Now he'd been given his head, he wanted Lady Cassie—rumored to be the most beautiful woman in all England—with a need verging on desperation.

She had jet black tresses, almost a midnight blue in the candlelight, framing creamy milk skin that made you want to lick from toe to breast and back again. He almost lost himself in her exotically framed feline eyes, their color such a vibrant green they appeared to be made of emeralds. Lady Cassandra Sudbury came packaged in a body so curvaceous, so soft; it would drive a saint to sin.

And Lord knew Anthony was no saint.

Finally Cassandra had let him know she was ripe for plucking and here he stood, a starving man, his eagerness to appease his appetite almost making him grovel.

He shook his head. Anthony James Craven did not grovel. He did not prostrate himself at women's feet, quite the opposite in fact. Women were usually fighting over him, the Earl of Wickham. Referred to as the Lord of Wicked by ladies who counted themselves among the ranks of those he'd seduced, and there were many. His 'Wicked Club' as the ladies penned it, was most likely the largest female-members-only club in all of England, if not the continent.

Women were his biggest vice. Not his worst vice, but pretty close. He loved women. All women, but in particular women whose beauty could start a war, or those he would have to fight tooth and nail for. His childhood had been starved of beauty and as an adult he could not help but gravitate towards it.

"What have we here? The mighty Earl of Wickham hiding behind a potted palm?"

Anthony's shoulders automatically tightened and he turned to scowl at his twin brother. "A man of my standing—a wealthy, titled bachelor—has *an* excuse to hide." He paused and raised an eyebrow, "Who are *you* hiding from?"

Richard John Craven, younger by only thirty minutes, had the grace to blush. "Mother, of course." Richard shrugged. "If you would hurry up and do what the head of the family is required to do, marry and produce an heir, Mother would not be bothering me."

Anthony cursed. "What a difference half-an-hour makes."

Richard slapped him on the shoulder. "Duty, Anthony. With the title come responsibilities. It is time you did yours and saved me from mother's constant attentions. There should be no pressure for the second son to bear fruit. I should be free to enjoy all the world has to offer. Seeing Lady Cassandra across the room, I am reminded that there is a lot to enjoy."

Anthony growled low in his throat. "Can't you find a woman of your own for a change?"

"Tut tut, can't handle the competition, eh? She is obviously immune to your charms. I have already given you three nights' head start, only because you spotted her first. You have not bedded her, nor made her your mistress, so I feel free to step in and claim what you have been unable to procure."

Anthony looked at his twin with a cynical smirk. Richard was correct about one thing; Cassie had made him work harder than any other woman.

Richard looked at him with all the innocence of a man who had just strangled his wife and issued a challenge. "Care to make a game of it, brother?"

Anthony feigned boredom as his gaze swept the dancing

guests. "Game?" His blood raced with the challenge. "What do I get if I win, besides Lady Cassie's delights, of course?" He flicked a spot of lint from the arm of his jacket.

Richard thought on it for a few moments. "I shall agree to allow you the first choice of any women we meet over the course of the next year, and I promise not to seduce them first."

Anthony laughed. "That's not even worth considering. The female sex prefers the bad boy—and you, dear brother, are too angelic-looking by far."

"Isn't that what we are about to put to the test? What are you scared of? Losing?"

"You'll lose. I have it on good authority that Lady Cassie will invite me to her bedchamber tonight." Anthony leaned back on the ballroom wall. "In fact, you just missed her issuing me a personal invitation."

Richard's handsome features, so different to his own, crinkled into a grin. "Well, that still leaves me a few hours. I don't need a bed. If I win, if I tup her before you bed her, I get Dark Knight."

Dark Knight was Anthony's prized stallion, and he would hate to lose him. He shook his head. Lose? Richard might be his twin brother but they were nothing alike. Anthony always won their wagers because, when it came down to it, Richard simply was not ruthless enough.

Richard was the family cherub, full of goodness and light. Fair-haired and blue eyed, he took after their mother in terms of facial features. He stood a few inches shorter than Anthony with a much leaner build, but well muscled. Anthony was the complete opposite, large, dark-haired, with dark eyes and looked like his late father—brutish.

He was the dark-brooding twin, the wicked devil.

Anthony tipped his glass to his mouth and drank with relish; he had earned his reputation.

For the last ten years, the Craven twins had been inseparable. At thirty-three, their lives were spent fighting over women, brawling together, drinking themselves into stupors and they were rumored to have seduced more women than all the rest of the nobility combined. Alarmed mothers of Society warned their daughters of the dangers of the notorious Craven twins.

A cunning plan formed in Anthony's head. He smiled at Richard. "If I win, you will marry within a month and sire a son. The son who will become the next Earl of Wickham."

Richard gasped.

Anthony stared at his brother without blinking, before raising an eyebrow, "What? Is the wager too rich for your blood, brother dear?"

"You are really determined to thwart father. Not that I blame you," Richard added hurriedly. "But you are the right and proper heir and as such it should be your son who inherits, not mine."

"A half hour is all that separates us. It was chance I was born first. Society thinks I am lucky for it, but we both know differently. You know damn well I will never father a legitimate child, nor will I ever marry. I'll ensure Father's plans for me come to nothing. I won't ever let Father win."

Richard thumped the wall. "The only man who will lose is you. Think of your life. If you insist on this plan of self-exile, Father wins. And for what? Father is dead. Let it go. Get on with your life."

Anthony raised his hand and traced the scar that ran down his left cheek. "That man, long may he rot in hell, should never have been born . . ."

"I know he was tough on you . . . but you cannot let our sire continue to dictate your life from the grave."

Anthony turned away from Richard's prying eyes. Tough? His father had regularly beaten him until he was almost unconscious. His father had starved him into submission—all in the

447

name of creating a strong heir-apparent, someone ruthless enough to carry on the Wickham empire. He would never let his father's legacy live on through him.

"I'm sorry. I didn't mean that, Anthony. I know my childhood was a bed of roses compared to yours. I just don't want to see you isolate yourself from all life has to offer."

Anthony gave a harsh laugh. "I would hardly call pursuing my next mistress as isolating myself. My father wanted me cold, devoid of human feelings and totally focused on nothing but making money." He gave a wicked grin. "Tonight, money is furthest from my mind."

Richard took another sip of wine. "You're nothing like Father. So give up this pretense that you are. You've done more to improve the lot of your tenants than Father ever did in his lifetime."

Anthony looked at his brother, suppressing the shudder that racked his body. He was exactly like his father. Richard had no idea the lengths his twin went to in order to ensure his dark inner demons never surfaced. Anthony couldn't let down his guard for one moment. The memory of his father's evil and the part he had played in it had almost destroyed him.

His past was tarnished with evil. They were too much alike, father and son. Dark, deadly and dangerous.

When Anthony was young, it had taken weeks to submerge the malevolence back into his soul. It still screamed to get out. Another slip and he might never recover; the wickedness buried deep within would rise up and take him over.

"If I did not know you better, Richard, I would think you were trying to distract me from our wager." Anthony turned to scan the crowded ballroom for Lady Cassie. There she was, just to his right, at the edge of the dance floor. He started to take a step forward, but his eyes narrowed, that wasn't her—not unless she'd changed dresses.

Richard pointed. "I see you've spotted Miss Melissa Goodly, Lady Cassandra's cousin. Almost a doppelganger for her, is she not? The two women look more alike than you and I."

Miss Goodly had black hair too, but not as glowing. Her eyes were a pretty shade of hazel maybe green in a certain light, but not as dazzling. Her skin was alabaster, but not as alluring, and she curved in all the right places, just not as temptingly.

She was definitely not mistress material. She was too much like wife material—absolutely not what he was looking for.

"Although," Richard added, "if I were you, I would stay away from Miss Goodly. Lady Cassandra does not like the comparison. I've heard the two women cannot abide each other."

As she placed an empty glass of champagne on a tray proffered by a servant, and helped herself to another full one, Anthony could see why. The younger woman was still an arresting sight and those men not fortunate enough to have gained Lady Cassandra's attentions stood with gazes riveted on Miss Goodly.

She wore a gown of sea green, trimmed in gold, worn off her shoulders in the current style. Her hair was artfully twisted, held in place by a pearl encrusted comb. A pair of small pearls dressed her lobes, and a single pearl on a gold pendant rested just above the swell of her pert bosom.

Miss Goodly was rather pretty but lacked the depth of beauty radiating from Lady Cassie. She reminded him of a copy of a Rembrandt, not quite as aesthetically pleasing as the original but still a magnificent work of art. The fact she was young and unmarried likely clouded his judgment.

Then Miss Goodly smiled and the air rush from his lungs. Her smile was breathtaking, and she suddenly appeared to be illuminated.

No. Miss Goodly was forbidden territory. Why risk the parson's noose when Lady Cassie was equally, if not more beautiful —and experienced?

He raised an eyebrow in his brother's direction. "Perhaps there is a way we would both be satisfied. As the eldest I get Lady Cassandra, but I won't stop you from taking the cousin."

Richard choked on his wine. "Miss Goodly? Do you think me stupid? She is one and twenty, an unmarried sister of a Baron. If I dally with her I'd be married before I could yell 'save me', and that would be too convenient for you." Richard shook his head. "No, my original wager stands. If you do not bed Lady Cassandra before me, I get Dark Knight. I have plenty of time." He grinned at Anthony, "I'll wager you don't even know where Lady Cassandra's bedchamber is? You wouldn't want to stumble into the wrong room. Think of the scandal."

Anthony's jaw tightened. Damn. He'd forgotten to ask Cassandra for directions. The house was huge, and it could take all night just to find her room. He would prefer to spend all night on the pleasure, not on the seeking.

His brother quietly chuckled. "I will give you a fighting chance. Her room is in the west wing, the fourth door along the corridor on the right."

"And how would you know that?" Anthony asked suspiciously.

Richard held out his arm and studied his immaculately groomed fingernails. "Where do you think I planned to stay tonight? If I have my way I still will. After all, it's a woman's prerogative to change her mind."

"You will accept my terms, then? You will marry and have a child, if I bed Lady Cassandra before you?"

"Of course. You have my word as a gentleman."

Anthony scoffed and permitted himself a cold smile.

Richard put a hand to his heart. "I am mortally wounded at your lowly opinion of my honor." He grinned. "I won't lose, and I want Dark Knight."

Anthony couldn't still the prickle of distrust making its way up his spine. Richard was agreeing to his terms too readily. Had Richard already planned to meet her earlier in the library? He would have to keep his eye on his prize until the ball was over.

Feigning indifference Anthony pulled his pocket watch out and looked at the time. "I accept the wager. The longer I keep you here the easier it will be for me. In fact, I feel so sure of winning I'm going to stir the pot. I shall ask Miss Goodly to dance. That should have Cassie burning to distract me from her cousin."

With that final gloat, Anthony tugged on his gloves and moved deliberately towards Miss Melissa Goodly, who, he noted, had just finished her glass of champagne. His body surged with adrenalin. The chase was on. If it took his last breath he would never let his brother win. Tonight he would bed his new mistress and move one step closer to ensuring his twin provided the much-required heir.

*   *   *

"May I have the pleasure of this dance, Miss Goodly? That is, if your dance card is not already full."

His deep, rich, voice,-—rough with a bite, yet thoroughly intoxicating--made her giddier than the cheap champagne she was drinking. She swung towards the tower of masculinity encapsulating her in his shadow, sending the bubbles splashing over the side of her glass.

The Lord of Wicked wished to dance with her. With her!

It was hard to remain composed with champagne dripping from her gloved fingers. "I don't believe we have been formally introduced, my lord." She tried to shake the drops off her gloves before she had to give him her hand.

Anthony's wolfish smile made her grip the glass harder. "My brother, mother and I, are Lady Sudbury's houseguests, as you

451

well know. You were here when we arrived this afternoon. She's kindly taken us in while my house is uninhabitable." He raised a dark eyebrow. "You have heard about the fire?"

All she could do was nod. Her tongue felt like dried bread.

"I saw you peering down over the banister when we arrived. No one but ourselves will know we have not been properly introduced." His wicked smile widened. "It shall be our little secret."

Melissa's face heated as she stared at the large hand he held out to her. She gripped the champagne glass, looking around for somewhere to put her drink. She wouldn't miss this dance for the world.

"Shall I take that for you?" Without waiting for a reply he pried the glass from her hand and beckoned a servant. Glass dispensed with, he turned his full attention on her. "Shall we?" and he offered his arm.

The crowd of guests turned to vapor. All Melissa could see, feel, hear and sense was him.

She was blind to the glittering candles and immune to the music filling the ballroom. She simply let him guide her, his arms holding her gently in the waltz. His scent filled her being— sandalwood, whiskey and masculinity. Masculinity. He oozed it from every pore.

They twirled around the floor, unrespectable in their closeness. Melissa didn't care. His lean hardness thrilled her. The cut of his evening coat accentuated his broad shoulders. His breeches fitted like a second skin, leaving nothing to the imagination.

Melissa had a wonderful imagination.

His hulking frame and dark, brooding looks together with his rakish reputation, made most of the young ladies terrified of him . . . But up close, his arresting features held her spellbound.

His black hair fell in thick waves almost to his shoulders, his fringe hanging low on his forehead, like a silk curtain shielding his eyes. In the candlelight, his eyes flickered from silver-gray to dark charcoal, so appropriate for such a renowned devil.

She couldn't pull her gaze away. His eyes were disconcertingly direct and totally hypnotizing. The decidedly aristocratic nose, firm mouth and chin, declared that here was a man used to dominating his world, while the scar that marred the left side of his face contributed to the air of danger surrounding him.

The affect was like a mild stomachache, enough to make her tummy churn, but not enough to make her faint.

She wracked her brain for something intelligent to say but his nearness made her brain turn to mush. "Was your house badly damaged?"

"Um . . . what was that?"

His attention seemed to be on another couple dancing across the floor. Melissa turned her head. Cassandra. Cassandra and Lord Spencer. Disappointment flooded her being. That's why he'd asked her to dance. So he could keep an eye on Cassandra.

Everyone knew Lord Wickham was pursuing Cassandra to be his next mistress.

Irritation sharpened her words. "The fire, my lord. Was there a lot of damage?"

His eyes flashed with amusement at her tone. "Luckily only smoke damage. We should be able to move back to Craven house in a few days time, once the house has been properly aired."

This time he kept his dark gaze on her, the attention making her heart pound. His eyes roamed her features and slid down over her breasts, where they lingered indecently. She felt the flush heating her cheeks. His lips curled in a rakish smile of recognition.

"Will you and your brother be staying with Lady Sudbury long? She is your cousin is she not?"

She tried to concentrate on his words, but he'd pulled her

tight into his embrace in order to avoid another couple. She felt warm and delicate against him, her head barely reaching his chest. *Answer him you fool.* "I am unsure of how long we will be here. Cassandra is sponsoring me for the Season."

"You wish to marry?"

She bit her bottom lip and lowered her gaze from his, too scared in case he saw the truth. "If I found the right man, then of course I want to marry. A home and children, isn't that something everyone wants?"

He stiffened at her words and remained silent. She raised her eyes to his. They appeared even more shielded.

"I assume your brother has someone picked out for you?"

It was her turn to stiffen in his arms. "I do my own choosing, my lord."

He smiled wryly. "Is that so?"

"I'm sure you'd not let anyone else make the most important decision of your life, why should I?"

He inclined his head, somewhat amused at her words. "I don't envy your brother."

How did she tell a peer of the realm, a man who'd likely marry for land, titles, or money that she would not marry except for love?

All her life she'd been treated as an afterthought. She was a very late child, eight years younger than Christopher. Her parents, both dead, never really wanted her. They had their son and heir and that was all that mattered. Of course, their opinion changed when they needed looking after. Until their deaths, she'd dutifully seen to their every need. That was why, at her ripe age of one and twenty, this was her first Season and her first visit to London.

Upon her parents' deaths, she'd vowed she would never again let herself be someone's obligation, a burden to bear, a person of no interest. She would never marry, not unless the man needed her, wanted her, and loved her.

With the dance finished, he escorted her back to the place he'd found her, ensuing another glass of champagne found its way back into her hand, and with a bow excused himself. His eyes already riveted back on Cassandra.

Melissa took a long sip from her glass.

If she were alone, she would close her eyes and twirl, pretend he still held her in his arm. She'd dreamed of him asking her to dance again, and more—a nightly fantasy she dare not fool herself into believing would come true.

Lord Wickham was not called the Lord of Wicked for nothing. As much as she mooned over him, she could never let herself fall in love with such a man, a rake of the first order. When she gave her heart, it would be to a man who wanted her beyond measure, a man who loved with all his heart and soul. A man who would cherish her forever.

Melissa stood on the edge of the ballroom, drinking more champagne. The alcohol kept her senses heightened and gave her courage. Was she brave enough to engage him in further conversation?

Melissa watched him from across the room. He did look a little frightening. Yet, his crisp white shirt and immaculately tied cravat lessened the severity of his attire; to the point that Melissa decided he was, quite simply, the most beautiful man she had ever seen.

Her body still trembled as if she'd just returned from an afternoon fox hunt. Her heart raced with excitement and her legs wobbled like custard. Lord Wickham was a heady mixture, especially coupled with the multiple glasses of champagne she'd drunk . . .

A movement to her left captured her attention. Christopher. She turned, stumbled a bit but managed to catch her balance. How many glasses of champagne had she drunk? Four—five?

Focusing on every step, she aimed for the Library--away from her fast approaching brother.

Lord Christopher Goodly, Baron Norrington, reached her just as her hand clasped the latch. *More like 'barren'. You've spent and lost everything we own*, she murmured under her breath.

"You will not run from me." His brandy fumes assaulted her nose.

Perfect. He was drunk as usual. A small giggle escaped. For once, she too was a little worse for drink. However, she needed the alcohol for courage, not to escape the mess she'd made of her life, as was her brother's crime.

"I was not running. I need some air."

"In the library?" His hand clamped down on her shoulder and swung her to face him. "I don't think so. Lord Wickham danced with you—danced the waltz with you. You are the only unmarried woman at the ball tonight to receive such an honor."

She kept quiet. It would do her no good to explain that the only reason the Earl danced with her was so he could keep an eye on Cassandra. A stab of envy hit her squarely below her left breast.

She removed her brother's hand from her shoulder before his sweaty palms stained her dress. They didn't have enough money to buy another. "That does not signify anything, Christopher. Go back to your drinking and leave me be."

He leaned in close and tried to smile. His face distorted, and he looked like an old man pained from gout instead of a man just under thirty. He poked her shoulder with his finger. "We are nearing the end of the season. You will marry, and marry soon. Either you will accept Lord Carthors, or you will ensure Lord Wickham maintains his interest."

She drew a steadying breath and gripped the dresser beside her. Damn the champagne. "Lord Carthors is close to seventy and would likely die in my arms upon the wedding bed."

"Precisely. Then we'd be rich."

"No. I'd be rich."

Her brother growled. "Don't play with me."

She tried to push past him, to escape the conversation. But his arm rose to cage her in. She was trapped by the door at her back, Christopher's arm and the large dresser on her right. "I will not marry a decrepit old man to save your skin."

He laughed in her face and sneered. "Not just my skin. Yours too. If not for Cassandra's generosity, we would be in the poor-house. Let's see how long your principles last when the men running such establishments start pawing you."

She kept her face blank, refusing to show how his threat affected her, but her stomach churned at the thought of what lay ahead of them, if either she or Christopher did not marry well.

"Miss. Trentworth is here tonight. If you are so worried about our position in society, line your pockets by marrying her. Her father is rich. The textile King they call him. Mr. Trentworth is after a title for his daughter."

He stood up straight. "I'm not going to marry any girl with a face like a horse's arse. It is my duty to see my young sister married first. At one and twenty you'll be left on the shelf if you are not careful." He hesitated and his demeanor altered. "Come now. If Carthors is not to your liking, surely Lord Wickham is. He is handsome, rich, and in his prime."

She stamped her foot. "Don't be ridiculous. Even if I did—admire his lordship—The Earl is legendary in his abhorrence for the state of matrimony. He wants Cassandra as his mistress and I'm sure she's willing to oblige. Why would he be interested in me?"

"You look exactly like Cassandra. He could take her as his mistress and you as his wife. His mother is determined he marry this Season. They need an heir. Wickham's father has been dead ten years. Wickham is in his mid thirties. It's time."

Melissa's hands fisted in the sides of her dress, to stop herself slapping her brother's face. How could he be so indifferent to his own flesh and blood? He wouldn't marry a woman not to his liking, yet he was quite willing to barter her off, giving her away to be used as a brood mare, so long as his debts were paid. Well, she had other ideas.

Seeing the determined look in her brother's bloodshot eyes, she tried another tack. "What would Cassandra say if I tried to woo the Earl? Perhaps she wishes to marry him. If she becomes annoyed, we will be flung into the streets. I can't see the Earl or any other man wanting to marry me then."

His face paled at her words. Distracted by his thoughts, Melissa reached behind her and turned the latch. It released with a loud snap. Before she could escape, her brother grabbed her arm. "Then it will be Carthors. By the end of the season you will become engaged, either to a man of your own choosing or Carthors. Am I clear?"

Melissa fought the tears filling her eyes at his painful hold. "Let me go." She tugged her arm free; the sound of the material ripping startled them both. "Perfect. Now look what you have done," she snapped. Anger propelled her to defy him. "I won't marry Lord Carthors. You'll have to drag me kicking and screaming in front of the vicar to ever get me to marry that old leech."

He simply smiled. "Not if I give you a few drops of laudanum. That would subdue you. You'd be pliant all the way to the altar." Christopher crowded her against the doorframe. "Don't underestimate me, Melissa. Come the end of the Season you will be married. To whom, is your choice. If you don't want Carthors then pick someone else—as long as they are rich."

Melissa stepped into the library and slammed the door in her brother's face.

*　　*　　*

Christopher swayed his way back across the ballroom, failing to notice the man stepping out of the shadows from the other side of the large oak dresser.

Richard had heard every word of the siblings' conversation and it was as he thought. The plan he'd set in motion would be welcomed by all concerned—except his brother. He could live with that. Eventually, he felt sure; Anthony would come to thank him for his deception.